'A striking work of the imaginatic  KU-165-029

'A tapestry of a book: a marvel of storytelling'
The SF Encyclopedia

'The "Measures" of the book are precisely detailed and intensely felt, each a masterpiece in miniature'
David Pringle, *Science Fiction: The 100 Best Novels*

'*Pavane* is a rare and beautiful novel'
Brian Aldiss and David Wingrove, *Trillion Year Spree*

Also by Keith Roberts

NOVELS
The Furies (1966)
The Inner Wheel (1970)
The Boat of Fate (1971)
The Chalk Giants (1974)
Molly Zero (1980)
Kiteworld (1985)
Gráinne (1987)
The Road to Paradise (1988)

SHORT STORY COLLECTIONS
Anita (1970)
Machines and Men (1973)
The Grain Kings (1976)
The Passing of the Dragons (1977)
Ladies from Hell (1979)
Kaeti & Company (1986)
The Lordly Ones (1986)
Winterwood and Other Hauntings (1989)
Kaeti on Tour (1992)

POETRY
A Heron Caught in Weeds (1987)

PAVANE

Keith Roberts

The right of Keith Roberts to be identified as the author
of this work has been asserted by him in accordance with
the Copyright, Designs and Patents Act 1988.

This edition published in Great Britain in 2000 by
Millennium
An imprint of Victor Gollancz
Orion House, 5 Upper St Martin's Lane,
London WC2H 9EA
An Hachette Livre UK company

To receive information on the Millennium list, e-mail us at:
smy@orionbooks.co.uk

6

A CIP catalogue record for this book
is available from the British Library

ISBN 978 1 85798 937 3

Printed in Great Britain by
Clays Ltd, St Ives plc

The Orion Publishing Group's policy is to use papers that
are natural, renewable and recyclable products and
made from wood grown in sustainable forests. The logging
and manufacturing processes are expected to conform to
the environmental regulations of the country of origin.

To Graham Walker Esq.,
who should have had this dedication years ago

This aye night, this aye night,
This aye night and all,
Fire and fleet and candle-light,
And Christ receive thy saule . . .
            The Lyke-Wake Dirge

PROLOGUE

PROLOGUE

On a warm July evening of the year 1588, in the royal palace of Greenwich, London, a woman lay dying, an assassin's bullets lodged in abdomen and chest. Her face was lined, her teeth blackened, and death lent her no dignity; but her last breath started echoes that ran out to shake a hemisphere. For the Faery Queen, Elizabeth the First, paramount ruler of England, was no more . . .

The rage of the English knew no bounds. A word, a whisper was enough; a half-wit youth, torn by the mob, calling on the blessing of the Pope. . . . The English Catholics, bled white by fines, still mourning the Queen of Scots, still remembering the gory Rising of the North, were faced with fresh pogroms. Unwillingly, in self-defence, they took up arms against their countrymen as the flame lit by the Walsingham massacres ran across the land, mingling with the light of warning beacons the sullen glare of the *auto-da-fé*.

The news spread; To Paris, to Rome, to the strange fastness of the Escorial, where Philip II still brooded on his Enterprise of England. The word of a land torn and divided against itself reached the great ships of the Armada, threshing up past the Lizard to link with Parma's army of invasion on the Flemish coast. For a day, while Medina-Sidonia paced the decks of the *San Martin*, the fate of half the world hung in balance. Then his decision was made; and one by one the galleons and carracks, the galleys

and the lumbering *urcas* turned north toward the land.
Toward Hastings and the ancient battleground of Santlache,
where history had been made once centuries before. The
turmoil that ensued saw Philip ensconced as ruler of England; in France the followers of Guise, heartened by the
victories across the Channel, finally deposed the weakened
House of Valois. The War of the Three Henrys ended with
the Holy League triumphant, and the Church restored once
more to her ancient power.

To the victor, the spoils. With the authority of the Catholic
Church assured, the rising nation of Great Britain deployed
her forces in the service of the Popes, smashing the Protes-
tants of the Netherlands, destroying the power of the German city-states in the long-drawn-out Lutheran Wars. The
Newworlders of the North American continent remained
under the rule of Spain; Cook planted in Australasia the
cobalt flag of the Throne of Peter.

In England herself, across a land half ancient and half
modern, split as in primitive times by barriers of language,
class, and race, the castles of mediaevalism still glowered;
mile on mile of unfelled woodland harboured creatures of
another age. To some the years that passed were years of
fulfillment, of the final flowering of God's Design; to others
they were a new Dark Age, haunted by things dead and
others best forgotten; bears and catamounts, dire wolves and
Fairies.

Over all, the long arm of the Popes reached out to
punish and reward; the Church Militant remained supreme.
But by the middle of the twentieth century widespread
mutterings were making themselves heard. Rebellion was
once more in the air . . .

First Measure
THE LADY MARGARET

First Measure

THE LADY MARGARET

Durnovaria, England. 1968.

The appointed morning came, and they buried Eli Strange. The coffin, black and purple drapes twitched aside, eased down into the grave; the white webbings slid through the hands of the bearers in nomine Patris, et Filii, et Spiritus Sancti . . . *The earth took back her own. And miles away* Iron Margaret *cried cold and wreathed with steam, drove her great sea-voice across the hills.*

At three in the afternoon the engine sheds were already gloomy with the coming night. Light, blue and vague, filtered through the long strips of the skylights, showing the roof ties stark like angular metal bones. Beneath, the locomotives waited brooding, hulks twice the height of a man, their canopies brushing the rafters. The light gleamed in dull spindle shapes, here from the strappings of a boiler, there from the starred boss of a flywheel. The massive road wheels stood in pools of shadow.

Through the half-dark a man came walking. He moved steadily, whistling between his teeth, boot studs rasping on the worn brick floor. He wore the jeans and heavy reefer jacket of a haulier; the collar of the jacket was turned up against the cold. On his head was a woollen cap, once red, stained now with dirt and oil. The hair that showed beneath it was thickly black. A lamp swung in his hand, sending cusps of light flicking across the maroon livery of the engines.

He stopped by the last locomotive in line and reached up to hang the lamp from her hornplate. He stood a moment gazing at the big shapes of the engines, chafing his hands unconsciously, sensing the faint ever-present stink of smoke and oil. Then he swung onto the footplate of the loco and opened the firebox doors. He crouched, working methodically. The rake scraped against the fire bars; his breath jetted from him, rising in wisps over his shoulder. He laid the fire carefully, wadding paper, adding a crisscrossing of sticks, shovelling coal from the tender with rhythmic swings of his arms. Not too much fire to begin with, not under a cold boiler. Sudden heat meant sudden expansion and that meant cracking, leaks round the fire tube joints, endless trouble. For all their power the locos had to be cosseted like children, coaxed and persuaded to give of their best.

The haulier laid the shovel aside and reached into the firebox mouth to sprinkle paraffin from a can. Then a soaked rag, a match. . . . The lucifer flared brightly, sputtering. The oil caught with a faint *whoomph*. He closed the doors, opened the damper handles for draught. He straightened up, wiped his hands on cotton waste, then dropped from the footplate and began mechanically rubbing the brightwork of the engine. Over his head, long nameboards carried the style of the firm in swaggering, curlicued letters; *Strange and Sons of Dorset, Hauliers*. Lower, on the side of the great boiler, was the name of the engine herself. The *Lady Margaret*. The hunk of rag paused when it reached the brass plate; then it polished it slowly, with loving care.

The *Margaret* hissed softly to herself, cracks of flame light showing round her ash pan. The shed foreman had filled her boiler and the belly and tender tanks that afternoon; her train was linked up across the yard, waiting by the warehouse loading bays. The haulier added more fuel to the fire, watched the pressure building slowly toward working head; lifted the heavy oak wheel scotches, stowed them in the steamer alongside the packaged water gauge glasses. The barrel of the loco was warming now, giving out a faint heat that radiated toward the cab.

The driver looked above him broodingly at the skylights. Mid-December; and it seemed as always God was stinting the light itself so the days came and vanished like the blinking of a dim grey eye. The frost would come down hard as well, later on. It was freezing already; in the yard the puddles had crashed and tinkled under his boots, the skin of ice from the night before barely thinned. Bad weather for the hauliers, many of them had packed up already. This was the time for the wolves to leave their shelter, what wolves there were left. And the *routiers* . . . this was their season right enough, ideal for quick raids and swoopings, rich hauls from the last road trains of the winter. The man shrugged under his coat. This would be the last run to the coast for a month or so at least, unless that old goat Serjeantson across the way tried a quick dash with his vaunted Fowler triple compound. In that case the *Margaret* would go out again; because Strange and Sons made the last run to the coast. Always had, always would. . . .

Working head, a hundred and fifty pounds to the inch. The driver hooked the hand lamp over the push pole bracket on the front of the smokebox, climbed back to the footplate, checked gear for neutral, opened the cylinder cocks, inched the regulator across. The *Lady Margaret* woke up, pistons thumping, crossheads sliding in their guides, exhaust beating sudden thunder under the low roof. Steam whirled back and smoke, thick and cindery, catching at the throat. The driver grinned faintly and without humour. The starting drill was a part of him, burned on his mind. Gear check, cylinder cocks, regulator. . . . He'd missed out just once, years back when he was a boy, opened up a four horse Roby traction with her cocks shut, let the condensed water in front of the piston knock the end out of the bore. His heart had broken with the cracking iron; but old Eli had still taken a studded belt, and whipped him till he thought he was going to die.

He closed the cocks, moved the reversing lever to forward full, and opened the regulator again. Old Dickon the yard foreman had materialized in the gloom of the shed; he hauled back on the heavy doors as the *Margaret*, jetting steam, rumbled into the open air, swung across the yard to where her train was parked.

Dickon, coatless despite the cold, snapped the linkage onto the *Lady Margaret*'s drawbar, clicked the brake unions into place. Three waggons, and the water tender; a light enough haul this time. The foreman stood, hands on hips, in breeches and grubby, ruffed shirt, grizzled hair curling over his collar. "Best let I come with 'ee, Master Jesse. . . ."

Jesse shook his head sombrely, jaw set. They'd been through this before. His father had never believed in over-staffing; he'd worked his few men hard for the wages he paid, and got his money's worth out of them. Though how long that would go on was anybody's guess with the Guild of Mechanics stiffening its attitude all the time. Eli had stayed on the road himself up until a few days before his death; Jesse had steered for him not much more than a week before, taking the *Margaret* round the hill villages topside of Bridport to pick up serge and worsted from the combers there; part of the load that was now outward bound for Poole. There'd been no sitting back in an office chair for old Strange, and his death had left the firm badly shorthanded; pointless taking on fresh drivers now, with the end of the season only days away. Jesse gripped Dickon's shoulder. "We can't spare thee, Dick. Run the yard, see my mother's all right. That's what he'd have wanted." He grimaced briefly. "If I can't take *Margaret* out by now, 'tis time I learned."

He walked back along the train pulling at the lashings

of the tarps. The tender and numbers one and two were shipshape, all fast. No need to check the trail load; he'd packed it himself the day before, taken hours over it. He checked it all the same, saw the taillights and number plate lamp were burning before taking the cargo manifest from Dickon. He climbed back to the footplate, working his hands into the heavy driver's mitts with their leather-padded palms.

The foreman watched him stolidly. "Take care for the *routiers*. Norman bastards. . . ."

Jesse grunted. "Let 'em take care for theirselves. See to things, Dickon. Expect me tomorrow."

"God be with 'ee. . . ."

Jesse eased the regulator forward, raised an arm as the stocky figure fell behind. The *Margaret* and her train clattered under the arch of the yard gate and into the rutted streets of Durnovaria.

Jesse had a lot to occupy his mind as he steered his load into the town; for the moment, the *routiers* were the least of his worries. Now, with the first keen grief just starting to lose its edge, he was beginning to realize how much they'd all miss Eli. The firm was a heavy weight to have hung round his neck without warning; and it could be there were awkward times ahead. With the Church openly backing the clamour of the Guilds for shorter hours and higher pay it looked as if the haulage companies were going to have to tighten their belts again, though God knew profit margins were thin enough already. And there were rumours of more restrictions on the road trains themselves; a maximum of six trailers it would be this time, and a water cart. Reason given had been the increasing congestion round the big towns. That, and the state of the roads; but what else could you expect, Jesse asked himself sourly, when half the tax levied in the country went to buy gold plate for its churches? Maybe though this was

just the start of a new trade recession like the one en-
gineered a couple of centuries back by Gisevius. The memory of that still rankled in the West at least. The economy
of England was stable now, for the first time in years;
stability meant wealth, gold reserves. And gold, stacked
anywhere but in the half-legendary coffers of the Vatican,
meant danger. . . .

Months back Eli, swearing blue fire, had set about getting round the new regulations. He'd had a dozen trailers
modified to carry fifty gallons of water in a galvanised
tank just abaft the drawbar. The tanks took up next to no
space and left the rest of the bed for payload; but they'd
be enough to satisfy the sheriff's dignity. Jesse could imagine
the old devil cackling at his victory; only he hadn't lived
to see it. His thoughts slid back to his father, as irrevocably
as the coffin had slid into the earth. He remembered his
last sight of him, the grey wax nose peeping above the
drapes as the visitors, Eli's drivers among them, filed through
the morning room of the old house. Death hadn't softened
Eli Strange; it had ravaged the face but left it strong, like
the side of a quarried hill.

Queer how when you were driving you seemed to have
more time to think. Even driving on your own when you
had to watch the boiler gauge, steam head, fire. . . . Jesse's
hands felt the familiar thrilling in the wheel rim, the little
stresses that on a long run would build and build till
countering them brought burning aches to the shoulders
and back. Only this was no long run; twenty, twenty-two
miles, across to Wool then over the Great Heath to Poole.
An easy trip for the *Lady Margaret*, with an easy load;
thirty tons at the back of her, and flat ground most of the
way. The loco had only two gears; Jesse had started off
in high, and that was where he meant to stay. The *Margaret's* nominal horsepower was ten, but that was on the
old rating; one horsepower to be deemed equal of ten

circular inches of piston area. Pulling against the brake
the Burrell would clock seventy, eighty horse; enough to
shift a rolling load of a hundred and thirty tons, old Eli
had pulled a train that heavy once for a wager. And
won. . . .

Jesse checked the pressure gauge, eyes performing their
work nearly automatically. Ten pounds under max. All
right for a while; he could stoke on the move, he'd done
it times enough before, but as yet there was no need. He
reached the first crossroads, glanced right and left and
wound at the wheel, looking behind him to see each waggon
of the train turning sweetly at the same spot. Good; Eli
would have liked that turn. The trail load would pull across
the road crown he knew, but that wasn't his concern. His
lamps were burning, and any drivers who couldn't see the
bulk of *Margaret* and her load deserved the smashing they
would get. Forty-odd tons, rolling and thundering; bad
luck on any butterfly cars that got too close.

Jesse had all the hauliers' ingrained contempt for internal combustion, though he'd followed the arguments for
and against it keenly enough. Maybe one day petrol pro-
pulsion might amount to something and there was that
other system, what did they call it, *diesel*. . . . But the
hand of the Church would have to be lifted first. The
Bull of 1910, *Petroleum Veto*, had limited the capacity of
IC engines to 150 cc's, and since then the hauliers had had
no real competition. Petrol vehicles had been forced to
fit gaudy sails to help tow themselves along; load hauling
was a singularly bad joke.

Mother of God, but it was cold! Jesse shrugged himself
deeper into his jacket. The *Lady Margaret* carried no spec-
tacle plate; a lot of other steamers had installed them now,
even one or two in the Strange fleet, but Eli had sworn not
the *Margaret*, not on the Margaret. . . . She was a work of
art, perfect in herself; as her makers had built her, so she

would stay. Decking her out with gewgaws, the old man
had been half sick at the thought. It would make her look
like one of the railway engines Eli so despised. Jesse narrowed his eyes, forcing them to see against the searing bite
of the wind. He glanced down at the tachometer. Road
speed fifteen miles an hour, revs one fifty. One gloved hand
pulled back on the reversing lever. Ten was the limit through
towns, fixed by the laws of the realm; and Jesse had no
intention of being run in for exceeding it. The firm of
Strange had always kept well in with the J.P.'s and serjeants of police; it partially accounted for their success.

Entering the long High Street, he cut his revs again.
The *Margaret*, balked, made a frustrated thunder; the sound
echoed back, clapping from the fronts of the grey stone
buildings. Jesse felt through his boot soles the slackening
pull on the drawbar and spun the brake wheel; a jack-
knifed train was about the worst blot on a driver's record.
Reflectors behind the tail lamp flames clicked upward, momentarily doubling their glare. The brakes bit; compensa-
tors pulled the trail load first, straightening the waggons.
He eased back another notch on the reversing lever; steam
admitted in front of the pistons checked *Margaret's* speed.
Ahead were the gas lamps of town centre, high on their
standards; beyond, the walls and the East Gate.

The serjeant on duty saluted easily with his halberd,
waving the Burrell forward. Jesse shoved at the lever,
wound the brakes away from the wheels. Too much stress
on the shoes and there could be a fire somewhere in the
train; that would be bad, most of the load was inflammable
this time.

He ran through the manifest in his mind. The *Margaret*
was carrying bale on bale of serge; bulkwise it accounted
for most of her cargo. English woollens were famous on
the Continent; correspondingly, the serge combers were
among the most powerful industrial groups in the South-

west. Their manufactories and storing sheds dotted the
villages for miles around; monopoly of the trade had
helped keep old Eli out ahead of his rivals. Then there were
dyed silks from Anthony Harcourt at Mells; Harcourt shifts
were sought after as far abroad as Paris. And crate after
crate of turned ware, products of the local bodgers, Erasmus
Cox and Jed Roberts of Durnovaria, Jermiah Stringer out
at Martinstown. Specie, under the county lieutenant's seal;
the last of the season's levies, outward bound for Rome.
And machine parts, high grade cheeses, all kinds of odd-
ments. Clay pipes, horn buttons, ribbons and tape; even a
shipment of cherrywood Madonnas from that Newworld-
financed firm over at Beaminster. What did they call themselves, *Calmers of the Soul, Inc. . . . ?* Woollens and
worsteds atop the water tender and in waggon number
one, turned goods and the rest in number two. The trail
load needed no consideration. That would look after itself.

The East Gate showed ahead, and the dark bulk of the
wall. Jesse slowed in readiness. There was no need; the odd
butterfly cars that were still braving the elements on this
bitter night were already stopped, held back out of harm's
way by the signals of the halberdiers. The *Margaret* hooted,
left behind a cloud of steam that hung glowing against the
evening sky. Passed through the ramparts to the heath and
hills beyond.

Jesse reached down to twirl the control of the injector
valve. Water, preheated by its passage through an extension
of the smokebox, swirled into the boiler. He allowed the
engine to build up speed. Durnovaria vanished, lost in the
gloom astern; the light was fading fast now. To right and
left the land was featureless, dark; in front of him was the
half-seen whirling of the crankshaft, the big thunder of the
engine. The haulier grinned, still exhilarated by the physical
act of driving. Flame light striking round the firebox doors
showed the wide, hard jaw, the deep-set eyes under brows

that were level and thickly black. Just let old Serjeantson
try and sneak in a last trip. The *Margaret* would take his
Fowler, uphill or down; and Eli would churn with glee in
his fresh-made grave. . . .

The *Lady Margaret*. A scene came unasked into Jesse's
mind. He saw himself as a boy, voice half broken. How
long ago was that, eight seasons, ten? The years had a way
of piling themselves one atop the next, unnoticed and un-
counted; that was how young men turned into old ones. He
remembered the morning the *Margaret* first arrived in the
yard. She'd come snorting and plunging through Durnovaria, fresh from Burrell's works in far-off Thetford, paint-
work gleaming, whistle sounding, brasswork a-twinkle in
the sun; a compound locomotive of ten N.H.P., all her details specified from flywheel decoration to static discharge
chains. Spud pan, belly pan, water lifts; Eli had got what
he wanted all right, one of the finest steamers in the West.
He'd fetched her himself, making the awkward journey
across many counties to Norfork; nobody else had been
trusted to bring back the pride of the fleet. And she'd been
his steamer ever since; if the old granite shell that had
called itself Eli Strange ever loved anything on earth, it had
been the huge Burrell.

Jesse had been there to meet her, and his kid brother
Tim and the others; James and Micah, dead now—God
rest their souls—of the Plague that had taken them both
that time in Bristol. He remembered how his father had
swung off the footplate, looked up at the loco standing
shaking like a live thing still and spewing steam. The firm's
name had been painted there already, the letters glowing
along the canopy edge, but as yet the Burrell had no name
of her own. "What be 'ee g'wine call 'en?" his mother had
shouted, over the noise of her idling; and Eli had rumpled
his hair, puckered his red face. "Danged if I knows. . . ."
They had *Thunderer* already and *Apocalypse*, *Oberon* and

Ballard Down and *Western Strength;* big-sounding names, right for the machines that carried them. "Danged if I *knows,*" said old Eli, grinning; and Jesse's voice had spoken without his permission, faltering up in its adolescent yodel. "The *Lady Margaret,* sir . . . *Lady Margaret.* . . ."

A bad thing that, speaking without being addressed. Eli had glared, shoved up his cap, scrubbed at his hair again; and burst into a roar of laughter. "I *likes* 'en . . . bugger me if I *don't* like 'en. . . ." And the *Lady Margaret* she had become, over the protests of his drivers, even over old Dickon's head. He claimed it "were downright luck" to call a loco after "some bloody 'oman. . . ." Jesse remembered his ears burning, he couldn't tell whether with shame or pride. He'd unwished the name a thousand times, but it had stuck. Eli liked it; and nobody crossed old Strange, not in the days of his strength.

So Eli was dead. There'd been no warning; just the coughing, the hands gripping the chair arms, the face that suddenly wasn't his father's face, staring. Quick dark spattering of blood, the lungs sighing and bubbling; and a clay-coloured old man lying abed, one lamp burning, the priest in attendance, Jesse's mother watching empty-faced. Father Thomas had been cold, disapproving of the old sinner; the wind had soughed round the house vicious with frost while the priest's lips absolved and mechanically blessed . . . but that hadn't been death. A death was more than an ending; it was like pulling a thread from a richly patterned cloth. Eli had been a part of Jesse's life, as much a part as his bedroom under the eaves of the old house. Death disrupted the processes of memory, jangled old chords that were maybe best left alone. It took so little imagination for Jesse to see his father still, the craggy face, weathered hands, haulier's greasy buckled cap pulled low over his eyes. The knotted muffler, ends anchored round the braces, the greatcoat, old thick working corduroys. It

14

FIRST MEASURE

was here he missed him, in the clanking and the darkness, with the hot smell of oil, smoke blowing back from the tall stack to burn his eyes. This was how he'd known it would be. Maybe this was what he'd wanted.

Time to feed the brute. Jesse took a quick look at the road stretching out straight in front of him. The steamer would hold her course, the worm steering couldn't kick back. He opened the firebox doors, grabbed the shovel. He stoked the fire quickly and efficiently, keeping it dished for maximum heat. Swung the doors shut, straightened up again. The steady thunder of the loco was part of him already, in his bloodstream. Heat struck up from the metal of the footplate, working through his boots; the warmth from the firebox blew back, breathed against his face. Time later for the frost to reach him, nibbling at his bones.

Jesse had been born in the old house on the outskirts of Durnovaria soon after his father started up in business there with a couple of ploughing engines, a thresher, and an Aveling and Porter tractor. The third of four brothers, he'd never seriously expected to own the fortunes of Strange and Sons. But God's ways were as inscrutable as the hills; two Strange boys had gone black-faced to Abraham's bosom, now Eli himself. . . . Jesse thought back to long summers spent at home, summers when the engine sheds were boiling hot and reeking of smoke and oil. He'd spend his days there, watching the trains come in and leave, helping unload on the warehouse steps, climbing over the endless stacks of crates and bales. There too were scents; richness of dried fruits in their boxes, apricots and figs and raisins; sweetness of fresh pine and deal, fragrance of cedarwood, thick headiness of twist tobacco cured in rum. Champagne and Oporto for the luxury trade, cognac, French lace; tangerines and pineapples, rubber and saltpetre, jute and hemp. . . .

Sometimes he'd cadge rides on the locos, down to Poole

or Bourne Mouth, across to Bridport, Wey Mouth; or west
down to Isca, Lindinis. He went to Londinium once, and
northeast again to Camulodunum. The Burrells and Claytons and Fodens ate miles; it was good to sit on the trail
load of one of those old trains, the engine looking half a
mile away, hooting and jetting steam. Jesse would pant on
ahead to pay the toll keepers, stay behind to help them
close the gates with their long white and red striped bars.
He remembered the rumbling of the many wheels, the
thick rising of dust from the rutted trackways. The dust
lay on the verges and hedges, making the roads look like
white scars crossing the land. Odd nights he'd spend away
from home, squatting in some corner of a tavern bar while
his father caroused. Sometimes Eli would turn morose, and
cuff Jesse upstairs to bed; at others he'd get expansive and
sit and spin tall tales about when he himself was a boy,
when the locos had shafts in front of their boilers and
horses between them to steer. Jesse had been a brakeboy at
eight, a steersman at ten for some of the shorter runs. It
had been a wrench when he'd been sent away to school.

He wondered what had been in Eli's mind. "Get some
bliddy eddycation" was all the old man had said. "That's
what counts, lad. . . ." Jesse remembered how he'd felt;
how he'd wandered in the orchards behind the house,
seeing the cherry plums hanging thick on the old trees that
were craggy and leaning, just right to climb. The apples,
Bramleys and Lanes and Haley's Orange; Commodore
pears hanging like rough-skinned bombs against walls mel-
low with September sunlight. Always before, Jesse had
helped bring in the crop; but not this year, not any more.
His brothers had learned to write and read and figure in
the little village school, and that was all; but Jesse had
gone to Sherborne, and stayed on to college in the old
university town. He'd worked hard at his languages and
sciences, and done well; only there had been something

wrong. It had taken him years to realize his hands were missing the touch of oiled steel, his nostrils needed the scent of steam. He'd packed up and come home and started work like any other haulier; and Eli had said not a word. No praise, no condemnation. Jesse shook his head. Deep down he'd always known without any possibility of doubt just what he was going to do. At heart, he was a haulier; like Tim, like Dickon, like old Eli. That was all; and it would have to be enough.

The *Margaret* topped a rise and rumbled onto a down-slope. Jesse glanced at the long gauge glass by his knee and instinct more than vision made him open the injectors, valve water into the boiler. The loco had a long chassis; that meant caution descending hills. Too little water in her barrel and the forward tilt would uncover the firebox crown, melt the fusable plug there. All the steamers carried spares, but fitting one was a job to avoid. It meant drawing the fire, a crawl into a baking-hot firebox, an eternity of wrestling overhead in darkness. Jesse had burned his quota of plugs in his time, like any other tyro; it had taught him to keep his firebox covered. Too high a level on the other hand meant water reaching the steam outlets, descending from the stack in a scalding cloud. He'd had that happen too.

He spun the valve and the hissing of the injectors stopped. The *Margaret* lumbered at the slope, increasing her speed. Jesse pulled back on the reversing lever, screwed the brakes on to check the train; heard the altered beat as the loco felt the rising gradient, and gave her back her steam. Light or dark, he knew every foot of the road; a good driver had to.

A solitary gleam ahead of him told him he was nearing Wool. The *Margaret* shrieked a warning to the village, rumbled through between the shuttered cottages. A straight run now, across the heath to Poole. An hour to the town gates, say another half to get down to the quay. If the traffic holdups weren't too bad. . . . Jesse chafed his hands, worked his shoulders inside his coat. The cold was getting to him now, he could feel it settling in his joints.

He looked out to either side of the road. It was full night, and the Great Heath was pitch black. Far off he saw or thought he saw the glimmer of a will-o'-the-wisp, haunting some stinking bog. A chilling wind moaned in from the emptiness. Jesse listened to the steady pounding of the Burrell and as often before the image of a ship came to him. The *Lady Margaret*, a speck of light and warmth, forged through the waste like some vessel crossing a vast and inimical ocean.

This was the twentieth century, the age of reason; but the heath was still the home of superstitious fears. The haunt of wolves and witches, were-things and Fairies; and the *routiers*. . . . Jesse curled his lip. "Norman bastards" Dickon had called them. It was as accurate a description as any. True, they claimed Norman descent; but in this Catholic England of more than a thousand years after the Conquest bloodlines of Norman, Saxon, and original Celt were hopelessly mixed. What distinctions existed were more or less arbitrary, reintroduced in accordance with the racial theories of Gisevius the Great a couple of centuries ago. Most people had at least a smattering of the five tongues of the land; the Norman French of the ruling classes, Latin of the Church, Modern English of commerce and trade, the outdated Middle English and Celtic of the churls. There were other languages of course; Gaelic, Cornish, and Welsh, all fostered by the Church, kept alive centuries after their use had worn thin. But it was good to chop a land piecemeal, set up barriers of language as well as class. "Divide and rule" had long been the policy, unofficially at least, of Rome.

The *routiers* themselves were surrounded by a mass of

legend. There had always been gangs of footpads in the Southwest, probably always would be; they smuggled, they stole, they looted the road trains. Usually, but not invariably, they stopped short at murder. Some years the hauliers suffered worse than others; Jesse could remember the *Lady Margaret* limping home one black night with her steersman dead from a crossbow quarrel, half her train ablaze and old Eli swearing death and destruction. Troops from as far off as Sorviodunum had combed the heath for days, but it had been useless. The gang had dispersed; gone to their homes if Eli's theories had been correct, turned back into honest God-fearing citizens. There'd been nothing on the heath to find; the rumoured strongholds of the outlaws just didn't exist.

Jesse stoked again, shivering inside his coat. The *Margaret* carried no guns; you didn't fight the *routiers* if they came, not if you wanted to stay alive. At least not by conventional methods; Eli had had his own ideas on the matter though he hadn't lived long enough to see them carried out. Jesse set his mouth. If they came, they came; but all they'd get from the firm of Strange they'd be welcome to keep. The business hadn't been built on softness; in this England, haulage wasn't a soft trade.

A mile or so ahead a brook, a tributary of the Frome, crossed the road. On this run the hauliers usually stopped there to replenish their tanks. There were no waterholes on the heath, the cost of making them would be prohibitive. Water standing in earth hollows would turn brackish and foul, unsafe for the boilers; the splashes would have to be concrete lined, and a job like that would set somebody back half a year's profits. Cement manufacture was controlled rigidly by Rome, its price prohibitive. The embargo was deliberate of course; the stuff was far too handy for the erection of quick strongpoints. Over the years there had been enough revolts in the country to teach caution even to the Popes.

Jesse, watching ahead, saw the sheen of water or ice. His hand went to the reversing lever and the train brakes. The *Margaret* stopped on the crown of a little bridge. Its parapets bore solemn warnings about "ponderous carriages" but few of the hauliers paid much attention to them after dark at least. He swung down and unstrapped the heavy armoured hose from the side of the boiler, slung its end over the bridge. Ice broke with a clatter. The water lifts hissed noisily, steam pouring from their vents. A few minutes and the job was done. The *Margaret* would have made Poole and beyond without trouble; but no haulier worth his salt ever felt truly secure with his tanks less than brimming full. Specially after dark, with the ever-present chance of attack. The steamer was ready now if needs be for a long, hard flight.

Jesse recoiled the hose and took the running lamps out of the tender. Four of them, one for each side of the boiler, two for the front axle. He hung them in place, turning the valves over the carbide, lifting the front glasses to sniff for acetylene. The lamps threw clear white fans of light ahead and to each side, making the frost crystals on the road surface sparkle. Jesse moved off again. The cold was bitter; he guessed several degrees of frost already, and the worst of the night was still to come. This was the part of the journey where you started to think of the cold as a personal enemy. It caught at your throat, drove glassy claws into your back; it was a thing to be fought, continuously, with the body and brain. Cold could stun a man, freeze him on the footplate till his fire burned low and he lost steam and hadn't the sense to stoke. It had happened before; more than one haulier had lost his life like that out on the road. It would happen again.

The *Lady Margaret* bellowed steadily; the wind moaned in across the heath.

On the landward side, the houses and cottages of Poole huddled behind a massive rampart and ditch. Along the fortifications, cressets burned; their light was visible for miles across the waste ground. The *Margaret* raised the line of twinkling sparks, closed with them slowly. In sight of the West Gate Jesse spun the brake wheel and swore. Stretching out from the walls, dimly visible in torchlight, was a confusion of traffic; Burrows, Avelings, Claytons, Fowlers, each loco with a massive train. Officials scurried about; steam plumed into the air; the many engines made a muted thundering. The *Lady Margaret* slowed, jetting white clouds like exhaled breath, edged into the turmoil alongside a ten horse Fowler liveried in the colours of the Merchant Adventurers.

Jesse was fifty yards from the gates, and the jam looked like taking an hour or better to sort out. The air was full of din; the noise of the engines, shouts from the steersmen and drivers, the bawling of town marshalls and traffic wardens. Bands of Pope's Angels wound between the massive wheels, chanting carols and holding up their cups for offerings. Jesse hailed a harassed-looking peeler. The Serjeant grounded his halberd, looked back at the *Lady Margaret's* load and grinned.

"Bishop Blaize's benison again, friend?"

Jesse grunted an affirmative; alongside, the Fowler let fly a deafening series of hoots.

"Belay that" roared the policeman. "What've ye got up there, that needs so much hurry?"

The driver, a little sparrow of a man muffled in scarf and greatcoat, spat a cigarette butt overboard. "Shellfish for 'Is 'Oliness," he quipped. "They're burning Rome to-night. . . ." The story of Pope Orlando dining on oysters

while his mercenaries sacked Florence had already passed
into legend.

"Any more of that" shouted the Serjeant furiously, "and
you'll find the gates shut in your face. You'll lie on the
heath all night, and the *routiers* can have their pick of
you. Now roll that pile of junk, *roll* it I say. . . ."

A gap had opened ahead; the Fowler thundered contemptuously and moved into it. Jesse followed. An age of
shunting and hooting and he was finally past the bottle-
neck, guiding his train down the long main street of Poole.

Strange and Sons maintained a bonded store on the quay,
not far from the old customs house. The *Margaret* threaded
her way to it, inching between piles of merchandise that
had overflowed from loading bays. The docks were busy
for so late in the season; Jesse passed a Scottish collier,
a big German freighter, a Frenchman; a Newworlder, an
ex-slaver by her raking lines, a handsome Swedish clipper
still defiantly under sail; and an old Dutch tramp, the
Groningen, that he knew to be still equipped with the
antiquated and curious mercury boilers. He swung his train
eventually into the company warehouse, nearly an hour
overdue.

The return load had already been made up; Jesse ditched
the down-waggons thankfully, handed over the manifest
to the firm's agent and backed onto the new haul. He saw
again to the securing of the trail load, built steam, and
headed out. The cold was deep inside him now, the windows of the waterfront pubs tempting with their promise
of warmth, drink, and hot food; but tonight the *Margaret*
wouldn't lie in Poole. It was nearly eight of the clock by
the time she reached the ramparts, and the press of traffic
was gone. The gates were opened by a surly-faced Serjeant;
Jesse guided his train through to the open road. The moon
was high now, riding a clear sky, and the cold was intense.

A long drag southwest, across the top of Poole harbour

to where the Wareham turn branched left from the road
to Durnovaria. Jesse coaxed the waggons round it. He gave
the *Margaret* her head, clocking twenty miles an hour on
the open road. Then into Wareham, the awkward bend by
the railway crossing; past the Black Bear with its monstrous carved sign and over the Frome where it ran into the
sea, limning the northern boundary of Purbeck Island. After that the heaths again; Stoborough, Slepe, Middlebere,
Norden, empty and vast, full of the droning wind. Finally
a twinkle of light showed ahead, high off the road and to
the right; the *Margaret* thundered into Corvesgeat, the
ancient pass through the Purbeck hills. Foursquare in the
cutting and commanding the road, the great castle of Corfe
squatted atop its mound, windows blazing light like eyes.
My Lord of Purbeck must be in residence then, receiving
his guests for Christmas.

The steamer circled the high flanks of the *motte*, climbed
to the village beyond. She crossed the square, wheels and
engine reflecting a hollow clamour from the front of the
Greyhound Inn, climbed again through the long main street
to where the heath was waiting once more, flat and desolate, haunted by wind and stars.

The Swanage road. Jesse, doped by the cold, fought the
idea that the *Margaret* had been running through this void
fuming her breath away into blackness like some spirit
cursed and bound in a frozen hell. He would have welcomed any sign of life, even of the *routiers;* but there was
nothing. Just the endless bitterness of the wind, the darkness stretching out each side of the road. He swung his
mittened hands, stamping on the footplate, turning to see
the tall shoulders of the load swaying against the night,
way back the faint reflection of the tail lamps. He'd long
since given up cursing himself for an idiot. He should have
laid up at Poole, moved out again with the dawn; he knew

that well enough. But tonight he felt obscurely that he was not driving but being driven.

He valved water through the preheater, stoked, valved again. One day they'd swap these solid-burners for oil-fuelled machines. The units had been available for years now; but oil firing was still a theory in limbo, awaiting the Papal verdict. Might be a decision next year, or the year after; or maybe not at all. The ways of Mother Church were devious, not to be questioned by the herd.

Old Eli would have fitted oil burners and damned the priests black to their faces, but his drivers and steersmen would have balked at the excommunication that would certainly have followed. Strange and Sons had bowed the knee there, not for the first time and not for the last. Jesse found himself thinking about his father again while the *Margaret* slogged upwards, back into the hills. It was odd; but *now*, he felt he could talk to the old man. *Now* he could explain his hopes, his fears. . . . Only now was too late; because Eli was dead and gone, six foot of Dorset muck on his chest. Was that the way of the world? Did people always feel they could talk, and talk, when it was just that bit too late?

The big mason's yard outside Long Tun Matravers. The piles of stone thrust up, dimly visible in the light of the steamer's lamps, breaking at last the deadly emptiness of the heath. Jesse hooted a warning; the voice of the Burrell rushed across the housetops, mournful and huge. The place was deserted, like a town of the dead. On the right the King's Head showed dim lights; its sign creaked uneasily, rocking in the wind. The *Margaret*'s wheels hit cobbles, slewed; Jesse spun the brakes on, snapping back the reversing lever to cut the power from the pistons. The frost had gathered thickly here, in places the road was like glass. At the crest of the hill into Swanage he twisted the control that locked his differentials. The loco steadied and edged

down, groping for her haven. The wind skirled, lifting a
spray of snow crystals across her headlights.

The roofs of the little town seemed to cluster under their
mantle of frost. Jesse hooted again, the sound enormous
between the houses. A gang of kids appeared from somewhere, ran yelling alongside the train. Ahead was a crossroads, and the yellow lamps on the front of the George
Hotel. Jesse aimed the loco for the yard entrance, edged
forward. The smokestack brushed the passageway overhead.
Here was where he needed a mate; the steam from the
Burrell, blowing back in the confined space, obscured his
vision. The children had vanished; he gentled the reversing
lever, easing in. The exhaust beats thrashed back from the
walls, then the *Margaret* was clear, rumbling across the
yard. The place had been enlarged years back to take the
road trains; Jesse pulled across between a Garrett and a
six horse Clayton and Shuttleworth, neutralized the reversing lever and closed the regulator. The pounding
stopped at last.

The haulier rubbed his face and stretched. The shoulders
of his coat were beaded with ice; he brushed at it and got
down stiffly, shoved the scotches under the engine's wheels,
valved off her lamps. The hotel yard was deserted, the
wind booming in the surrounding roofs; the boiler of the
loco seethed gently. Jesse blew her excess steam, banked
his fire and shut the dampers, stood on the front axle to set
a bucket upside down atop the chimney. The *Margaret*
would lie the night now safely. He stood back and looked
at the bulk of her still radiating warmth, the faint glint
of light from round the ash pan. He took his haversack from
the cab and walked to the George to check in.

They showed him his room and left him. He used the
loo, washed his face and hands, and left the hotel. A few
yards down the street the windows of a pub glowed crim-

son, light seeping through the drawn curtains. Its sign
proclaimed it the Mermaid Inn. He trudged down the alley
that ran alongside the bars. The back room was full of
talk, the air thick with the fumes of tobacco. The Mermaid
was a hauliers' pub; Jesse saw half a score of men he
knew, Tom Skinner from Powerstock, Jeff Holroyd from
Wey Mouth, two of old Serjeantson's boys. On the road,
news travels fast; they crowded round him, talking against
each other. He grunted answers, pushing his way to the
bar. Yes, his father had had a sudden hemorrhage; no, he
hadn't lived long after it. Five of the clock the next afternoon. . . . He pulled his coat open to reach his wallet, gave
his order, took the pint and the double Scotch. A poker,
thrust glowing into the tankard, mulled the ale; creamy
froth spilled down the sides of the pot. The spirit burned
Jesse's throat, made his eyes sting. He was fresh off the
road; the others made room for him as he crouched knees
apart in front of the fire. He swigged at the pint feeling
heat invade his crotch, move into his stomach. Somehow
his mind could still hear the pounding of the Burrell, the
vibration of her wheel was still in his fingers. Time later
for talk and questioning; first the warmth. A man had to be
warm.

She managed somehow to cross and stand behind him,
spoke before he knew she was there. He stopped chafing
his hands and straightened awkwardly, conscious now of
his height and bulk.

"Hello, Jesse. . . ."

Did she know? The thought always came. All those years
back when he'd named the Burrell; she'd been a gawky
stripling then, all legs and eyes, but she was the Lady he'd
meant. She'd been the ghost that haunted him those hot,
adolescent nights, trailing her scent among the scents of
the garden flowers. He'd been on the steamer when Eli
took that monstrous bet, sat and cried like a fool because

when the Burrell breasted the last slope she wasn't winning
fifty golden guineas for his father, she was panting out the
glory of Margaret. But Margaret wasn't a stripling now,
not any more; the lamps put bright highlights on her
brown hair, her eyes flickered at him, the mouth
quirked. . . .

He grunted at her. "Evenin', Margaret. . . ."

She brought him his meal, set a corner table, sat with
him awhile as he ate. That made his breath tighten in his
throat; he had to force himself to remember it meant
nothing. After all you don't have a father die every week
of your life. She wore a chunky costume ring with a
bright blue stone; she had a habit of turning it restlessly
between her fingers as she talked. The fingers were thin
with flat, polished nails, the hands wide across the knuckles
like the hands of a boy. He watched her hands now touching her hair, drumming at the table, stroking the ash of a
cigarette sideways into a saucer. He could imagine them
sweeping, dusting, cleaning, as well as doing the other
things, the secret things women must do to themselves.

She asked him what he'd brought down. She always
asked that. He said "Lady" briefly, using the jargon of the
hauliers. Wondering again if she ever watched the Burrell,
if she knew she was the Lady *Margaret;* and whether it
would matter to her if she did. Then she brought him
another drink and said it was on the house, told him she
must go back to the bar now and that she'd see him again.

He watched her through the smoke, laughing with the
men. She had an odd laugh, a kind of flat chortle that
drew back the top lip and showed the teeth while the eyes
watched and mocked. She was a good barmaid, was Margaret; her father was an old haulier, he'd run the house
this twenty years. His wife had died a couple of seasons
back, the other daughters had married and moved out but
Margaret had stayed. She knew a soft touch when she

saw one; leastways that was the talk among the hauliers. But that was crazy, running a pub wasn't an easy life. The long hours seven days a week, the polishing and scrubbing, mending and sewing and cooking . . . though they did have a woman in the mornings for the rough work. Jesse knew that like he knew most other things about his Margaret. He knew her shoe size, and that her birthday was in May; he knew she was twenty-four inches round the waist and that she liked Chanel and had a dog called Joe. And he knew she'd sworn never to marry; she'd said running the *Mermaid* had taught her as much about men as she wanted to learn, five thousand down on the counter would buy her services but nothing else. She'd never met anybody that could raise the half of that, the ban was impossible. But maybe she hadn't said it at all; the village air swam with gossip, and amongst themselves the hauliers yacked like washerwomen.

Jesse pushed his plate away. Abruptly he felt the rising of a black self-contempt. Margaret was the reason for nearly everything; she was why he'd detoured miles out of his way, pulled his train to Swanage for a couple of boxes of *iced* fish that wouldn't repay the hauling back. Well, he'd wanted to see her and he'd seen her. She'd talked to him, sat by him; she wouldn't come to him again. Now he could go. He remembered again the raw sides of a grave, the spattering of earth on Eli's coffin. That was what waited for him, for all God's so-called children; only he'd wait for his death alone. He wanted to drink now, wash out the image in a warm brown haze of alcohol. But not here, not here. . . . He headed for the door.

He collided with the stranger, growled an apology, walked on. He felt his arm caught; he turned back, stared into liquid brown eyes set in a straight-nosed, rakishly handsome face. "No," said the newcomer. "No, I don' believe it. By all tha's unholy, *Jesse Strange*. . . ."

For a moment the other's jaunty fringe of a beard baffled him; then Jesse started to grin in spite of himself. "Colin," he said slowly. "Col de la Haye. . . ."

Col brought his other arm round to grip Jesse's biceps. "Well, hell," he said. "Jesse, you're lookin' well. This calls f'r a drink, ol' boy. What you bin doin' with yourself? Hell, you're lookin' well. . . ."

They leaned in a corner of the bar, full pints in front of them. "God damn, Jesse, tha's lousy luck. Los' your ol' man, eh? Tha's rotten. . . ." He lifted his tankard. "To you, ol' Jesse. Happier days. . . ."

At college in Sherborne Jesse and Col had been fast friends. It had been the attraction of opposites; Jesse slow-talking, studious, and quiet, de la Haye the rake, the man-about-town. Col was the son of a west country businessman, a feminist and rogue at large; his tutors had always sworn that like the Fielding character he'd been born to be hanged. After college Jesse had lost touch with him. He'd heard vaguely Col had given up the family business; importing and warehousing just hadn't been fast enough for him. He'd apparently spent a time as a strolling *jongleur*, working on a book of ballads that had never got written, had six months on the boards in Londinium before being invalided home the victim of a brawl in a brothel. "A'd show you the scar," said Col, grinning hideously, "but it's a bit bloody awkward in mixed comp'ny, ol' boy. . . ." He'd later become, of all things, a haulier for a firm in Isca. That hadn't lasted long; halfway through his first week he'd howled into Bristol with an eight horse Clayton and Shuttleworth, unreeled his hose and drained the corporation horse trough in town centre before the peelers ran him in. The Clayton hadn't quite exploded but it had been a near go. He'd tried again, up in Aquae Sulis where he wasn't so well known; that time he lasted six months before a broken gauge glass stripped most of the skin from his ankles. De la Haye had moved on,

seeking as he put it "less lethal employment." Jesse chuckled
and shook his head. "So what be 'ee doin' now?"

The insolent eyes laughed back at him. "A' trade," said
Col breezily. "A' take what comes; a li'l here, li'l there.
. . . Times are hard, we must all live how we can. Drink up,
ol' Jesse, the next one's mine. . . ."

They chewed over old times while Margaret served up
pints and took the money, raising her eyebrows at Col. The
night de la Haye, pot-valiant, had sworn to strip his
professor's cherished walnut tree. . . . "A' remember that
like it was yes'day," said Col happily. "Lovely ol' moon
there was, bright as day. . . ." Jesse had held the ladder
while Col climbed; but before he reached the branches the
tree was shaken as if by a hurricane. "Nuts comin' down
like bloody hailstones," chortled Col. "Y'remember, Jesse,
y'must remember. . . . An' there was that . . . that bloody
ol' rogue of a peeler Toby Warrilow sittin' up there with his
big ol' boots stuck out, shakin' the hell out of that bloody
tree. . . ." For weeks after that, even de la Haye had been
able to do nothing wrong in the eyes of the law; and a
whole dormitory had gorged themselves on walnuts for
nearly a month.

There'd been the business of the two nuns stolen from
Sherborne Convent; they'd tried to pin that on de la Haye
and hadn't quite managed it, but it had been an open secret
who was responsible. Girls in Holy Orders had been re-
moved odd times before, but only Col would have taken
two at once. And the affair of the Poet and Peasant. The
landlord of that inn, thanks to some personal quirk, kept a
large ape chained in the stables; Col, evicted after a singularly rowdy night, had managed to slit the creature's
collar. The Godforsaken animal caused troubles and panics
for a month; men went armed, women stayed indoors. The
thing had finally been shot by a militiaman who caught it in
his room drinking a bowl of soup.

"So what you goin' to do now?" asked de la Haye, swigging back his sixth or seventh beer. "Is your firm now, no?"

"Aye." Jesse brooded, hands clasped, chin touching his knuckles. "Goin' to run it, I guess. . . ."

Col draped an arm round his shoulders. "You be OK," he said. "You be OK pal, why so sad? Hey, tell you what. You get a li'l girl now, you be all right then. Tha's what you need, ol' Jesse; a' know the signs." He punched his friend in the ribs and roared with laughter. "Keep you warm nights better'n a stack of extra blankets. An' stop you getting fat, no?"

Jesse looked faintly startled. "Dunno 'bout *that*. . . ."

"Ah, hell," said de la Haye. "Tha's the thing though. Ah, there's nothin' like it. *Mmmmyowwhh*. . . ." He wagged his hips, shut his eyes, drew shapes with his hands, contrived to look rapturous and lascivious at the same time. "Is no trouble now, ol' Jesse," he said. "You loaded now, you know that? Hell, man, you're *eligible*. . . . They come runnin' when they hear, you have to fight 'em off with a . . . a pushpole couplin', no?" He dissolved again in merriment.

Eleven of the clock came round far too quickly. Jesse struggled into his coat, followed Col up the alley beside the pub. It was only when the cold air hit him he realized how stoned he was. He stumbled against de la Haye, then ran into the wall. They reeled along the street laughing, parted company finally at the George. Col, roaring out promises, vanished into the night.

Jesse leaned against the *Margaret*'s rear wheel, head laid back on its struts, and felt the beer fume in his brain. When he closed his eyes a slow movement began; the ground seemed to tilt forward and back under his feet. Man, but that last hour had been good. It had been college all over again; he chuckled helplessly, wiped his forehead with the back of his hand. De la Haye was a no-good bastard all right but a nice guy, nice guy. . . . Jesse opened his eyes blearily, looked up at the road train. Then he moved carefully, hand over hand along the engine, to test her boiler temperature with his palm. He hauled himself to the footplate, opened the firebox doors, spread coal, checked the dampers and water gauge. Everything secure. He tacked across the yard, feeling the odd snow crystals sting his face.

He fiddled with his key in the lock, swung the door open. His room was black and icily cold. He lit the single lantern, left its glass ajar. The candle flame shivered in a draught. He dropped across the bed heavily, lay watching the one point of yellow light sway forward and back. Best get some sleep, make an early start tomorrow. . . . His haversack lay where he'd slung it on the chair but he lacked the strength of will to unpack it now. He shut his eyes.

Almost instantly the images began to swirl. Somewhere in his head the Burrell was pounding; he flexed his hands, feeling the wheel rim thrill between them. That was how the locos got you, after a while; throbbing and throbbing hour on hour till the noise became a part of you, got in the blood and brain so you couldn't live without it. Up at dawn, out on the road, driving till you couldn't stop; Londinium, Aquae Sulis, Isca; stone from the Purbeck quarries, coal from Kimmeridge, wool and grain and worsted, flour and wine, candlesticks, Madonnas, shovels, butter scoops, powder and shot, gold, lead, tin; out on contract to the Army, the Church. . . . Cylinder cocks, dampers, regulator, reversing lever; the high iron shaking of the footplate. . . .

He moved restlessly, muttering. The colours in his brain grew sharper. Maroon and gold of livery, red saliva on his father's chin, flowers bright against fresh earth; steam and lamplight, flames, the hard sky clamped against the hills.

His mind toyed with memories of Col, hearing sentences, hearing him laugh; the little intake of breath, squeaky and distinctive, then the sharp machine gun barking while he screwed his eyes shut and hunched his shoulders, pounded with his fist on the counter. Col had promised to look him up in Durnovaria, reeled away shouting he wouldn't forget. But he would forget; he'd lose himself, get involved with some woman, forget the whole business, forget the meeting. Because Col wasn't like Jesse. No planning and waiting for de la Haye, no careful working out of odds; he lived for the moment, vividly. He would never change.

The locos thundered, cranks whirling, crossheads dipping, brass gleaming and tinkling in the wind.

Jesse half sat up, shaking his head. The lamp burned steady now, its flame thin and tall, just vibrating slightly at the tip. The wind boomed, carrying with it the striking of a church clock. He listened, counting. Twelve strokes. He frowned. He'd slept, and dreamed; he'd thought it was nearly dawn. But the long, hard night had barely begun. He lay back again with a grunt, feeling drunk but queerly wide awake. He couldn't take his beer any more; he'd had the horrors. Maybe there were more to come.

He started revolving idly the things de la Haye had said. The crack about getting a woman. That was crazy, typical of Col. No trouble maybe for him, but for Jesse there had only ever been one little girl. And she was out of reach.

His mind, spinning, seemed to check and stop quite still. Now, he told himself irritably, forget it. You've got troubles enough, let it go . . . but a part of him stubbornly refused to obey. It turned the pages of mental ledgers, added, subtracted, thrust the totals insistently into his consciousness. He swore, damning de la Haye. The idea, once implanted, wouldn't leave him. It would haunt him now for weeks, maybe years.

He gave himself up, luxuriously, to dreaming. She knew all about him, that was certain; women knew such things unfailingly. He'd given himself away a hundred times, a thousand; little things, a look, a gesture, a word, were all it needed. He'd kissed her once, years back. Only the one time; that was maybe why it had stayed so sharp and bright in his mind, why he could still relive it. It had been a nearly accidental thing; a New Year's Eve, the pub bright and noisy, a score or more of locals seeing the new season in. The church clock striking, the same clock that marked the hours now, doors in the village street popping undone, folk eating mince pies and drinking wine, shouting to each other across the dark, kissing; and she'd put down the tray she was holding, watching him. "Let's not be left out, Jesse," she said. "Us too. . . ."

He remembered the sudden thumping of his heart, like the fussing of a loco when her driver gives her steam. She'd turned her face up to him, he'd seen the lips parting; then she was pushing hard, using her tongue, making a little noise deep in her throat. He wondered if she made the sound every time automatically, like a cat purring when you rubbed its fur. And somehow too she'd guided his hand to her breast; it lay cupped there, hot under her dress, burning his palm. He'd tightened his arm across her back then, pulling her onto her toes till she wriggled away gasping. "Whoosh," she said. "Well done, Jesse. Ouch. . . . well done. . . ." Laughing at him again, patting her hair; and all past dreams and future visions had met in one melting point of Time.

He remembered how he'd stoked the loco all the long haul back, tireless, while the wind sang and her wheels crashed through a glowing landscape of jewels. The images were back now; he saw Margaret at a thousand sweet moments, patting, touching, undressing, laughing. And he remembered, suddenly, a hauliers' wedding; the ill-fated marriage of his brother Micah to a girl from Sturminster Newton. The engines burnished to their canopies, berib-bonned and flag draped, each separate plank of their flatbed trailers gleaming white and scoured; drifts of confetti like bright-coloured snow, the priest standing laughing with his glass of wine, old Eli, hair plastered miraculously flat, incongruous white collar clamped round his neck, beaming and red-faced, waving from the *Margaret*'s footplate a quart pot of beer. Then, equally abruptly, the scene was gone; and Eli, in his Sunday suit, with his pewter mug and his polished hair, was whirled away into a dark space of wind.

"*Father . . . !*"

Jesse sat up, panting. The little room showed dim, shadows flicking as the candle flame guttered. Outside, the clock chimed for twelve-thirty. He stayed still, squatting on the edge of the bed with his head in his hands. No weddings for him, no gayness. Tomorrow he must go back to a dark and still mourning house; to his father's unsolved worries and the family business and the same ancient, dreary round. . . .

In the darkness, the image of Margaret danced like a solitary spark.

He was horrified at what his body was doing. His feet found the flight of wooden stairs, stumbled down them. He felt the cold air in the yard bite at his face. He tried to reason with himself but it seemed his legs would no longer obey him. He felt a sudden gladness, a lightening. You didn't stand the pain of an aching tooth forever; you took yourself to the barber, changed the nagging for a worse quick agony and then for blessed peace. He'd stood this long enough; now it too was to be finished. Instantly, with no more waiting. He told himself ten years of hoping and dreaming, of wanting dumbly like an animal, that has to count. He asked himself, what had he expected her to do? She wouldn't come running to him pleading, throw herself across his feet, women weren't made like that, she had her dignity too. . . . He tried to remember when the gulf between him and Margaret had been fixed. He told himself, never; by no token, no word. . . . He'd never given her a chance, what if she'd been waiting too all these years? Just waiting to be *asked.* . . . It had to be true. He knew, glowingly, it was true. As he tacked along the street, he started to sing.

The watchman loomed from a doorway, a darker shadow, gripping a halberd short.

"You all right, sir?"

The voice, penetrating as if from a distance, brought Jesse up short. He gulped, nodded, grinned. "Yeah. Yeah, sure. . . ." He jerked a thumb behind him. "Brought a . . . train down. Strange, Durnovaria. . . ."

The man stood back. His attitude said plainly enough "One o' they beggars . . ." He said gruffly, "Best get along then, sir, don't want to have to run 'ee in. 'Tis well past twelve o' the clock, y'know. . . ."

"On m'way, officer," said Jesse. "On m'way. . . ." A dozen steps along the street he turned back. "Officer . . . you m-married?"

The voice was uncompromising. "Get along now, sir. . . ." Its owner vanished in blackness.

The little town, asleep. Frost glinting on the rooftops, puddles in the road ruts frozen to iron, houses shuttered blind. Somewhere an owl called; or was it the noise of a far-off engine, out there somewhere on the road. . . . The *Mermaid* was silent, no lights showing. Jesse hammered at the door. Nothing. He knocked louder. A light flickered on across the street. He started to sob for breath. He'd done it all wrong, she wouldn't open. They'd call the watch instead. . . . But she'd know, she'd know who was knocking, women always knew. He beat at the wood, terrified. *"Margaret. . . ."*

A shifting glint of yellow; then the door opened with a suddenness that sent him sprawling. He straightened up still breathing hard, trying to focus his eyes. She was standing holding a wrap across her throat, hair tousled. She held a lamp high; then, *"You . . . !"* She shut the door with a thump, snatched the bolt across and turned to face him. She said in a low, furious voice, "What the devil do you think you're doing?"

He backed up. "I . . . ," he said, "I . . ." He saw her face change. "Jesse," she said, "what's wrong? Are you hurt, what happened?"

"I . . . sorry," he said. "Had to see you, Margaret, Couldn't leave it no more. . . ."

"Hush," she said. Hissed. "You'll wake my father, if you haven't done it already. *What are you talking about?*"

He leaned on the wall, trying to stop the spinning in his head. "Five thousand," he said thickly. "It's . . . nothing, Margaret. Not any more. Margaret, I'm . . . rich, God help me. It don't matter no more. . . ."

"What?"

"On the roads," he said desperately. "The . . . hauliers' talk. They said you wanted five thousand. Margaret, I can do ten. . . ."

A dawning comprehension. And for God's sake, she was starting to laugh. "Jesse Strange," she said, shaking her head. "What are you trying to say?"

And it was out, at last. "I love you, Margaret," he said simply. "Reckon I always have. And I . . . want you to be my wife."

She stopped smiling then, stood quite still and let her eyes close as if suddenly she was very tired. Then she reached forward quietly and took his hand. "Come on," she said. "Just for a little while. Come and sit down."

In the back bar the firelight was dying. She sat by the hearth curled like a cat, watching him, her eyes big in the dimness; and Jesse talked. He told her everything, things he'd never found the words for before, things he'd never imagined himself speaking. How he'd wanted her, and hoped, and known it was no use; how he'd waited so many years he'd nearly forgotten a time when she hadn't filled his mind. She stayed still, holding his fingers, stroking the back of his hand with her thumb, thinking and brooding. He told her how she'd be mistress of the house and have the gardens, the orchards of cherry plums, the rose terraces, the servants, her drawing account in the bank; how she'd have nothing to do any more ever but be Margaret Strange, his wife.

The silence lengthened when he'd finished, till the ticking of the big bar clock sounded loud. She stirred her foot in the warmth of the ashes, wriggling the toes; he gripped her instep softly, spanning it with finger and thumb. "I do love you, Margaret," he said. "I truly do. . . ."

She still stayed quiet, staring at nothing visible, eyes opaque. She'd let the shawl fall off her shoulders; he could see her breasts, the nipples pushing against the flimsiness of the nightdress. She frowned, pursed her mouth, looked back at him. "Jesse," she said, "when I've finished talking, will you do something for me? Will you promise?"

Quite suddenly, he was no longer drunk. The whirling and the warmth faded, leaving him shivering. Somewhere he was sure the loco hooted again. "Yes, Margaret," he said. "If that's what you want."

She came and sat by him. "Move up," she whispered. "You're taking all the room." She saw the shivering; she put her hand inside his jacket, rubbed softly. "Stop it," she said. "Don't do that, Jesse. Please. . . ."

The spasm passed; she pulled her arm back, flicked at the shawl, gathered her dress round her knees. "When I've said what I'm going to, will you promise to go away? Very quietly, and not . . . make trouble for me? Please, Jesse. I did let you in. . . ."

"That's alright," he said. "Don't worry, Margaret, that's alright." His voice, talking, sounded like the voice of a stranger. He didn't want to hear what she had to say; but listening to it meant he could stay close just a little longer. He felt suddenly he knew what it would be like to be given a cigarette just before you were hanged; how every puff would mean another second's life.

She twined her fingers together, looked down at the carpet. "I . . . want to get this just right," she said. "I want to . . . say it properly, Jesse, because I don't want to hurt you. I . . . like you too much for that.

"I . . . knew about it of course, I've known all the time. That was why I let you in. Because I . . . like you very much, Jesse, and didn't want to hurt. And now you see I've . . . trusted you, so you mustn't let me down. I can't marry you, Jesse, because I don't love you. I never will. Can you understand that? It's terribly hard knowing . . . well, how you feel and all that and still having to say it to you but I've got to because it just wouldn't work. I . . . knew this was going to happen sometime, I used to lie awake at night thinking about it, thinking all about you, honestly I did, but it wasn't any good. It just . . . wouldn't work, that's all. So . . . no. I'm terribly sorry but . . . no."

How can a man balance his life on a dream, how can he be such a fool? How can he live, when the dream gets knocked apart. . . .

She saw his face alter and reached for his hand again. "Jesse, *please* . . . I . . . think you've been terribly sweet waiting all this time and I . . . know about the money, I know why you said that, I know you just wanted to give me a . . . good life. It was terribly sweet of you to think like that about me and I . . . know you'd do it. But it just wouldn't work . . . Oh God, isn't this awful. . . ."

You try to wake from what you know is a dream, and you can't. Because you're awake already, this is the dream they call life. You move in the dream and talk, even when something inside you wants to twist and die. He rubbed her knee, feeling the firm smoothness. "Margaret," he said. "I don't want you to rush into anything. Look, in a couple of months I shall be comin' back through. . . ."

She bit her lip. "I knew you were . . . going to say that as well. But . . . no, Jesse. It isn't any use thinking about it, I've tried to and it wouldn't work. I don't want to . . . have to go through this again and hurt you all over another time. Please don't ask me again. Ever."

He thought dully, he couldn't buy her. Couldn't win her, and couldn't buy. Because he wasn't man enough, and that was the simple truth. Just not quite what she wanted. That was what he'd known all along, deep down, but he'd never faced it; he'd kissed his pillows nights, and whispered love for Margaret, because he hadn't dared bring the truth into the light. And now he'd got the rest of time to try and forget . . . this.

She was still watching him. She said, "Please understand . . ."

And he felt better. God preserve him, some weight seemed to shift suddenly and let him talk. "Margaret," he said, "this sounds damn stupid, don't know how to say it. . . ."

"Try. . . ."

He said, "I don't want to . . . hold you down. It's . . . selfish, like somehow having a . . . bird in a cage, owning it. . . . Only I didn't think on it that way before. Reckon I . . . really love you because I don't want that to happen to you. I wouldn't do anything to hurt. Don't you worry, Margaret, it'll be alright. It'll be alright now. Reckon I'll just . . . well, get out o' your way like. . . ."

She put a hand to her head. "God this is awful, I knew it would happen. . . . Jesse don't just . . . well, vanish. You know, go off an' . . . never come back. You see I . . . like you so very much, as a friend, I should feel terrible if you did that. Can't things be like they . . . were before, I mean can't you just sort of . . . come in and see me, like you used to? Don't go right away, please. . . ."

Even that, he thought. *God, I'll do even that.*

She stood up. "And now go. Please. . . ."

He nodded dumbly. "It'll be alright. . . ."

"Jesse," she said. "I don't want to . . . get in any deeper. But—" She kissed him, quickly. There was no feeling there this time. No fire. He stood until she let him go; then he walked quickly to the door.

He heard, dimly, his boots ringing on the street. Somewhere a long way off from him was a vague sighing, a susurration; could have been the blood in his ears, could have been the sea. The house doorways and the dark-socketed windows seemed to lurch toward him of their own accord, fall away behind. He felt as a ghost might feel grappling with the concept of death, trying to assimilate an idea too big for its consciousness. There was no Margaret now, not any more. No Margaret. Now he must leave the grown-up world where people married and loved and mated and mattered to each other, go back for all time to his child's universe of oil and steel. And the days would come, and the days would go, till on one of them he would die.

He crossed the road outside the George; then he was walking under the yard entrance, climbing the stairs, opening again the door of his room. Putting out the light, smelling Goody Thompson's fresh-sour sheets.

The bed felt cold as a tomb.

The fishwives woke him, hawking their wares through the streets. Somewhere there was a clanking of milk churns; voices crisped in the cold air of the yard. He lay still, face down, and there was an empty time before the cold new fall of grief. He remembered he was dead; he got up and dressed, not feeling the icy air on his body. He washed, shaved the blue-chinned face of a stranger, went out to the Burrell. Her livery glowed in weak sunlight, topped by a thin bright icing of snow. He opened her firebox, raked the embers of the fire and fed it. He felt no desire to eat; he went down to the quay instead, haggled absentmindedly for the fish he was going to buy, arranged for its delivery to the George. He saw the boxes stowed in time for late service at the church, stayed on for confession. He didn't go near the *Mermaid;* he wanted nothing now but to leave, get back on the road. He checked the *Lady Margaret* again, polished her nameplates, hubs, flywheel boss. Then he remembered seeing something in a shop window, something he'd intended to buy; a little tableau, the Virgin, Joseph, the Shepherds kneeling, the Christ-child in the manger. He knocked up the storekeeper, bought it and had it packed; his mother set great store by such things, and it would look well on the sideboard over Christmas.

By then it was lunchtime. He made himself eat, swallowing food that tasted like string. He nearly paid his bill before he remembered. Now, it went on account; the account of Strange and Sons of Dorset. After the meal he went to one of the bars of the George, drank to try and wash the sour taste from his mouth. Subconsciously, he found himself waiting; for footsteps, a remembered voice, some message from Margaret to tell him not to go, she'd changed her mind. It was a bad state of mind to get into but he couldn't help himself. No message came.

It was nearly three of the clock before he walked out to the Burrell and built steam. He uncoupled the *Margaret* and turned her, shackled the load to the push pole lug and back it into the road. A difficult feat but he did it without thinking. He disconnected the loco, brought her round again, hooked on, shoved the reversing lever forward and inched open on the regulator. The rumbling of the wheel's started at last. He knew once clear of Purbeck he wouldn't come back. Couldn't, despite his promise. He'd send Tim or one of the others; the thing he had inside him wouldn't stay dead, if he saw her again it would have to be killed all over. And once was more than enough.

He had to pass the pub. The chimney smoked but there was no other sign of life. The train crashed behind him, thunderously obedient. Fifty yards on he used the whistle, over and again, waking *Margaret*'s huge iron voice, filling the street with steam. Childish, but he couldn't stop himself. Then he was clear. Swanage dropping away behind as he climbed toward the heath. He built up speed. He was late; in that other world he seemed to have left so long ago, a man called Dickon would be worrying.

Way off on the left a semaphore stood stark against the sky. He hooted to it, the two pips followed by the long call that all the hauliers used. For a moment the thing stayed dead; then he saw the arms flip an acknowledgement. Out there he knew Zeiss glasses would be trained on the Burrell. The Guildsmen had answered; soon a message would be streaking north along the little local towers. *The* Lady Margaret, *locomotive, Strange and Sons, Durnovaria; out of Swanage routed for Corvesgeat, fifteen thirty hours. All well. . . .*

Night came quickly; night, and the burning frost. Jesse swung west well before Wareham, cutting straight across the heath. The Burrell thundered steadily, gripping the road with her seven-foot drive wheels, leaving thin wraiths of steam behind her in the dark. He stopped once, to fill his tanks and light the lamps, then pushed on again into the heathland. A light mist or frost smoke was forming now; it clung to the hollows of the rough ground, glowing oddly in the light from the side lamps. The wind soughed and threatened. North of the Purbecks, off the narrow coastal strip, the winter could strike quick and hard; come morning the heath could be impassable, the trackways lost under two feet or more of snow.

An hour out from Swanage, and the *Margaret* still singing

her tireless song of power. Jesse thought, blearily, that she at least kept faith. The semaphores had lost her now in the dark; there would be no more messages till she made her base. He could imagine old Dickon standing at the yard gate under the flaring cressets, worried, cocking his head to catch the beating of an exhaust miles away. The loco passed through Wool. Soon be home, now; home, to whatever comfort remained. . . .

The boarder took him nearly by surprise. The train had slowed near the crest of a rise when the man ran alongside, lunged for the footplate step. Jesse heard the scrape of a shoe on the road; some sixth sense warned him of movement in the darkness. The shovel was up, swinging for the stranger's head, before it was checked by an agonised yelp. "Hey ol' boy, don' you know your friends?"

Jesse, half off balance, grunted and grabbed at the steering. "*Col.* . . . What the hell are you doin' here?"

De la Haye, still breathing hard, grinned at him in the reflection of the sidelights. "Jus' a fellow traveller, my friend. Happy to see you come along there, I tell you. Had a li'l bit of trouble, thought a'd have to spend the night on the bloody heath. . . ."

"What trouble?"

"Oh, I was ridin' out to a place a' know," said de la Haye. "Place out by Culliford, li'l farm. Christmas with friends. Nice daughters. Hey, Jesse, you know?" He punched Jesse's arm, started to laugh. Jesse set his mouth. "What happened to your horse?"

"Bloody thing foundered, broke its leg."

"Where?"

"On the road back there," said de la Haye carelessly. "A' cut its throat an' rolled it in a ditch. Din' want the damn *routiers* spottin' it, gettin' on my tail. . . ." He blew his hands, held them out to the firebox, shivered dramati-

cally inside his sheepskin coat. "Damn cold, Jesse, cold as a
bitch. . . . How far you go?"

"Home. Durnovaria."

De la Haye peered at him. "Hey, you don' sound good.
You sick, ol' Jesse?"

"No."

Col shook his arm insistently. "Whassamatter, ol' pal?
Anythin' a friend can do to help?"

Jesse ignored him, eyes searching the road ahead. De la
Haye bellowed suddenly with laughter. "Was the beer. The
beer, no? Ol' Jesse, your stomach has shrunk!" He held up a
clenched fist. "Like the stomach of a li'l baby, no? Not the
old Jesse any more; ah, life is hell. . . ."

Jesse glanced down at the gauge, turned the belly tank
cocks, heard water splash on the road, touched the injector
controls, saw the burst of steam as the lifts fed the boiler.
The pounding didn't change its beat. He said steadily,
"Reckon it must have bin the beer that done it. Reckon I
might go on the waggon. Gettin' old."

De la Haye peered at him again, intently. "Jesse," he said.
"You got problems, my son. You got troubles. What gives?
C'mon, spill. . . ."

That damnable intuition hadn't left him then. He'd had it
right through college; seemed somehow to know what you
were thinking nearly as soon as it came into your head. It
was Col's big weapon; he used it to have his way with
women. Jesse laughed bitterly; and suddenly the story was
coming out. He didn't want to tell it; but he did, down to the
last word. Once started, he couldn't stop.

Col heard him in silence; then he started to shake. The
shaking was laughter. He leaned back against the cab side,
holding onto a stanchion. "Jesse, Jesse, you are a lad. Christ,
you never change. . . . Oh, you bloody Saxon. . . ." He
went off into fresh peals, wiped his eyes. "So . . . so she
show you her pretty li'l scut, he? Jesse, you are a lad; when

will you learn? What, you go to her with . . . with this . . ."
He banged the *Margaret's* hornplate. "An' your face so
earnest an' black, oh, Jesse, a' can see that face of yours.
Man, she don' want your great iron *destrier*. Christ above,
no. . . . But a' . . . a' tell you what you do . . ."

Jesse turned down the corners of his lips. "Why don't you
just *shut up*. . . ."

De la Haye shook his arm. "Nah, listen. Don' get mad,
listen. You . . . woo her, Jesse; she like that, that one. You
know? Get the ol' glad rags on, man, get a butterfly car,
mak' its wings of cloth of gold. She like that. . . . Only
don' stand no shovin', ol' Jesse. An' don' ask her nothin', not
no more. You tell her what you want, say you goin' to get
it. . . . Pay for your beer with a golden guinea, tell her
you'll tak' the change upstairs, no? She's worth it, Jesse,
she's worth havin' is that one. Oh but she's nice. . . ."

"Go to hell. . . ."

"You don' want her?" De la Haye looked hurt. "A' jus'
try to help, ol' pal. . . . You los' interest now?"

"Yeah," said Jesse. "I lost interest."

"Ahhh . . ." Col sighed. "Ah, but is a shame. Young love
all blighted. . . . Tell you what though." He brightened.
"You given me a great idea, ol' Jesse. You don' want her, a'
have her myself. OK?"

*When you hear the wail that means your father's dead
your hands go on wiping down a crosshead guide. When the
world turns red and flashes, and drums roll inside your skull,
your eyes watch ahead at the road, your fingers stay quiet on
the wheel.* Jesse heard his own voice speak dryly. "You're
a lying bastard, Col, you always were. She wouldn't fall for
you. . . ."

Col snapped his fingers, danced on the footplate. "Man,
a' got it halfway made. Oh but she's nice. . . . Those li'l
eyes, they were flashin' a bit las' night, no? Is easy, man,
easy. . . . A' toll you what, a' bet she be sadistic in bed.

But nice, ahhh, *nice*. . . ." His gestures somehow suggested rapture. "I tak' her five ways in a night," he said. "An' send you proof. OK?"

Maybe he doesn't mean it. Maybe he's lying. But he isn't. I know Col; and Col doesn't lie. Not about this. What he says he'll do, he'll do. . . . Jesse grinned, just with his teeth. "You do that, Col. Break her in. Then I take her off you. OK?"

De la Haye laughed and gripped his shoulder. "Jesse, you are a lad. Eh . . . ? Eh . . . ?"

A light flashed briefly, ahead and to the right, way out on the heathland. Col spun round, stared at where it had been, looked back to Jesse. "You see that?"

Grimly. "I saw."

De la Haye looked round the footplate nervously. "You got a gun?"

"Why?"

"The bloody light. The *routiers* . . ."

"You don't fight the *routiers* with a gun."

Col shook his head. "Man, I hope you know what you're doin'. . . ."

Jesse wrenched at the firebox doors, letting out a blaze of light and heat. "Stoke. . . ."

"What?"

"Stoke!"

"OK, man," said de la Haye. "All right, OK. . . ." He swung the shovel, building the fire. Kicked the doors shut, straightened up. "A' love you an' leave you soon," he said. "When we pass the light. If we pass the light. . . ."

The signal, if it had been a signal, was not repeated. The heath stretched out empty and black. Ahead was a long series of ridges; the *Lady Margaret* bellowed heavily, breasting the first of them. Col stared round again uneasily, hung out the cab to look back along the train. The high shoulders of the tarps were vaguely visible in the night. "What you carryin', Jesse?" he asked. "You got the goods?"

Jesse shrugged. "Bulk stuff. Cattle cake, sugar, dried fruit. Not worth their trouble."

De la Haye nodded worriedly. "Wha's in the trail load?"

"Brandy, some silks. Bit of tobacco. Veterinary supply. Animal castrators." He glanced sideways. "Cord grip. Bloodless."

Col looked startled again, then started to laugh. "Jesse, you are a lad. A right bloody lad. . . . But tha's a good load, ol' pal. Nice pickings. . . ."

Jesse nodded, feeling empty. "Ten thousand quid's worth. Give or take a few hundred."

De la Haye whistled. "Yeah. Tha's a good load. . . ."

They passed the point where the light had appeared, left it behind. Nearly two hours out now, not much longer to run. The *Margaret* came off the downslope, hit the second rise. The moon slid clear of a cloud, showed the long ribbon of road stretching ahead. They were almost off the heath now, Durnovaria just over the horizon. Jesse saw a track running away to the left before the moon, veiling itself, gave the road back to darkness.

De la Haye gripped his shoulder. "You be fine now," he said. "We passed the bastards. . . . You be all right. I drop off now, ol' pal; thanks for th' ride. An' remember, 'bout the li'l girl. You get in there punchin', you do what a' say. OK, ol' Jesse?"

Jesse turned to stare at him. "Look after yourself, Col," he said.

The other swung onto the step. "A' be OK. A' be great." He let go, vanished in the night.

He'd misjudged the speed of the Burrell. He rolled forward, somersaulted on rough grass, sat up grinning. The lights on the steamer's trail load were already fading down the road. There were noises round him; six mounted men

showed dark against the sky. They were leading a seventh
horse, its saddle empty. Col saw the quick gleam of a gun
barrel, the bulky shape of a crossbow. *Routiers*. . . . He got
up still laughing, swung onto the spare mount. Ahead the
train was losing itself in the low fogbanks. De la Haye
raised his arm. "The last waggon. . . ." He rammed his heels
into the flanks of his horse, and set off at a flat gallop.

Jesse watched his gauges. Full head, a hundred and fifty
pounds in the boiler. His mouth was still grim. It wouldn't
be enough; down this next slope, halfway up the long rise
beyond, that was where they would take him. He moved the
regulator to its farthest position; the *Lady Margaret* started
to build speed again, swaying as her wheels found the ruts.
She hit the bottom of the slope at twenty-five, slowed as her
engine felt the dead pull of the train.

Something struck the nearside hornplate with a ringing
crash. An arrow roared overhead, lighting the sky as it went.
Jesse smiled, because nothing mattered any more. The
Margaret seethed and bellowed; he could see the horsemen now, galloping to either side. A pale gleam that could
have been the edge of a sheepskin coat. Another concussion,
and he tensed himself for the iron shock of a crossbow bolt
in his back. It never came. But that was typical of Col de la
Haye; he'd steal your woman but not your dignity, he'd take
your trail load but not your life. Arrows flew again, but not
at the loco. Instead they hit her trail load, stuck quivering
and burning. Jesse, craning back past the shoulders of the
waggons, saw flames running across the sides of the last
tarp.

Halfway up the rise; the *Lady Margaret* labouring, panting with rage. The fire took hold fast, tongues of flame licking forward. Soon they would catch the next trailer in line.
Jesse reached down. His hand closed slowly, regretfully,
round the emergency release. He eased upward, felt the
catch disengage, heard the engine beat slacken as the load

came clear. The burning truck slowed, faltered, and began
to roll back away from the rest of the train. The horsemen
galloped after it as it gathered speed down the slope,
clustered round it in a knot of whooping and beating upward with their cloaks at the fire. Col passed them at the
run, swung from the saddle and leaped. A scramble, a shout;
and the *routiers* bellowed their laughter. Poised on top of the
moving load, gesticulating with his one free hand, their
leader was pissing valiantly onto the flames.

The *Lady Margaret* had topped the rise when the cloud
scud overhead lit with a white glare. The explosion cracked
like a monstrous whip; the shock wave slapped at the
trailers, skewed the steamer off course. Jesse fought her
straight, hearing echoes growl back from distant hills. He
leaned out from the footplate, stared down past the shoulders of the load. Behind him twinkled spots of fire where
the hell-burner, two score kegs of fine-grain powder packed
round with bricks and scrap iron, had scythed the valley
clear of life.

Water was low. He worked the injectors, checked the
gauge. "We must live how we can," he said, not hearing the
words. "We must all live how we can." The firm of Strange
had not been built on softness; what you stole from it, you
were welcome to keep.

Somewhere a semaphore clacked to Emergency Attention,
torches lighting its arms. The *Lady Margaret*, with her
train behind her, fled for Durnovaria, huddled ahead in the
dim silver elbow of the Frome.

Second Measure
THE SIGNALLER

On either side of the knoll the land stretched in long, speckled sweeps, paling in the frost smoke until the outlines of distant hills blended with the curdled milk of the sky. Across the waste a bitter wind moaned, steady and chill, driving before it quick flurries of snow. The snow squalls flickered and vanished like ghosts, the only moving things in a vista of emptiness.

What trees there were grew in clusters, little coppices that leaned with the wind, their twigs meshed together as if for protection, their outlines sculpted into the smooth, blunt shapes of ploughshares. One such copse crowned the summit of the knoll; under the first of its branches, and sheltered by them from the wind, a boy lay face down in the snow. He was motionless but not wholly unconscious; from time to time his body quivered with spasms of shock. He was maybe sixteen or seventeen, blond-haired, and dressed from head to feet in a uniform of dark green leather. The uniform was slit in many places; from the shoulders down the back to the waist, across the hips and thighs. Through the rents could be seen the cream-brown of his skin and the brilliant slow twinkling of blood. The leather was soaked with it, and the long hair matted. Beside the boy lay the case of a pair of binoculars, the Zeiss lenses without which no man or apprentice of the Guild of Signallers ever moved, and a dagger. The blade of the weapon was red-stained; its pommel rested a few inches beyond his outflung right hand. The hand itself was injured, slashed across the backs of the fingers and deeply through the base of the thumb. Round it blood had diffused in a thin pink halo into the snow.

A heavier gust rattled the branches overhead, raised from somewhere a long creak of protest. The boy shivered again and began, with infinite slowness, to move. The outstretched hand crept forward, an inch at a time, to take his weight beneath his chest. The fingers traced an arc in the snow, its ridges red-tipped. He made a noise halfway between a grunt and a moan, levered himself onto his elbows, waited gathering strength. Threshed, half turned over, leaned on the undamaged left hand. He hung his head, eyes closed; his heavy breathing sounded through the copse. Another heave, a convulsive effort, and he was sitting upright, propped against the trunk of a tree. Snow stung his face, bringing back a little more awareness.

He opened his eyes. They were terrified and wild, glazed with pain. He looked up into the tree, swallowed, tried to lick his mouth, turned his head to stare at the empty snow round him. His left hand clutched his stomach; his right was crossed over it, wrist pressing, injured palm held clear of contact. He shut his eyes again briefly; then he made his hand go down, grip, lift the wet leather away from his thigh. He fell back, started to sob harshly at what he had seen. His hand, dropping slack, brushed tree bark. A snag probed the open wound below the thumb; the disgusting surge of pain brought him round again.

From where he lay the knife was out of reach. He leaned forward ponderously, wanting not to move, just stay quiet and be dead, quickly. The knife was still beyond his grip. He lunged sideways. His fingers touched the blade; he worked his way back to the tree, made himself sit up again. He rested, gasping; then he slipped his left hand under his knee, drew upward till the half-paralysed leg was crooked. Concentrating, steering the knife with both hands, he placed the tip of its blade against his trews, forced down slowly to the ankle cutting the garment apart. Then round behind his thigh till the piece of leather came clear.

He was very weak now; it seemed he could feel the strength ebbing out of him, faintness flickered in front of his eyes like the movements of a black wing. He pulled the leather toward him, got its edge between his teeth, gripped, and began to cut the material into strips. It was slow, clumsy work; he gashed himself twice, not feeling the extra pain. He finished at last and began to knot the strips round his leg, trying to tighten them enough to close the long wounds in the thigh. The wind howled steadily; there was no other sound but the quick panting of his breath. His face, beaded with sweat, was nearly as white as the sky.

He did all he could for himself, finally. His back was a bright torment, and behind him the bark of the tree was streaked with red, but he couldn't reach the lacerations there. He made his fingers tie the last of the knots, shuddered at the blood still weeping through the strappings. He dropped the knife and tried to get up.

After minutes of heaving and grunting his legs still refused to take his weight. He reached up painfully, fingers exploring the rough bole of the tree. Two feet above his head they touched the low, snapped-off stump of a branch. The hand was soapy with blood; it slipped, skidded off, groped back. He pulled, feeling the tingling as the gashes in the palm closed and opened. His arms and shoulders were strong, ribboned with muscle from hours spent at the semaphores; he hung tensed for a moment, head thrust back against the trunk, body arced and quivering; then his heel found a purchase in the snow, pushed him upright.

He stood swaying, not noticing the wind, seeing the blackness surge round him and ebb back. His head was pounding now, in time with the pulsing of his blood. He felt fresh warmth trickling on stomach and thighs, and the rise of a deadly sickness. He turned away, head bent, and started to walk, moving with the slow ponderousness of a diver. Six paces off he stopped, still swaying, edged round clumsily. The binocular case lay on the snow where it had fallen. He went back awkwardly, each step requiring now a separate effort of his brain, a bunching of the will to force the body to obey. He knew foggily that he daren't stoop for the case; if he tried he would fall headlong, and likely never move again. He worked his foot into the loop of the shoulder strap. It was the best he could do; the leather tightened as he moved, riding up round his instep. The case bumped along behind him as he headed down the hill away from the trees.

He could no longer lift his eyes. He saw a circle of snow, six feet or so across, black-fringed at its edges from his impaired vision. The snow moved as he walked, jerking toward him, falling away behind. Across it ran a line of faint impressions, footprints he himself had made. The boy followed them blindly. Some spark buried at the back of his brain kept him moving; the rest of his consciousness was gone now, numbed with shock. He moved draggingly, the leather case jerking and slithering behind his heel. With his left hand he held himself, low down over the groin; his right waved slowly, keeping his precarious balance. He left behind him a thin trail of blood spots; each drop splashed pimpernel-bright against the snow, faded and spread to a wider pink stain before freezing itself into the crystals. The blood marks and the footprints reached back in a ragged line to the copse. In front of him the wind skirled across the land; the snow whipped at his face, clung thinly to his jerkin.

Slowly, with endless pain, the moving speck separated itself from the trees. They loomed behind it, seeming through some trick of the fading light to increase in height as they receded. As the wind chilled the boy the pain ebbed fractionally; he raised his head, saw before him the tower of a semaphore station topping its low cabin. The station stood on a slight eminence of rising ground; his body felt the drag of the slope, reacted with a gale of breathing. He trudged slower. He was crying again now with little whimperings, meaningless animal noises, and a sheen of saliva showed on his chin. When he reached the cabin the copse was still visible behind him, grey against the sky. He leaned against the plank door gulping, seeing faintly the texture of the wood. His hand fumbled for the lanyard of the catch, pulled; the door opened, plunging him forward onto his knees.

After the snow light outside, the interior of the hut was dark. The boy worked his way on all fours across the board floor. There was a cupboard; he searched it blindly, sweeping glasses and cups aside, dimly hearing them shatter. He found what he needed, drew the cork from the bottle with his teeth, slumped against the wall and attempted to drink. The spirit ran down his chin, spilled across chest and belly. Enough went down his throat to wake him momentarily. He coughed and tried to vomit. He pulled himself to his feet, found a knife to replace the one he'd dropped. A wooden chest by the wall held blankets and bed linen; he pulled a sheet free and haggled it into strips, longer and broader this time, to wrap round his thigh. He couldn't bring himself to touch the leather tourniquets. The white cloth marked through instantly with blood; the patches elongated, joined and began to glisten. The rest of the sheet he made into a pad to hold against his groin.

The nausea came again; he retched, lost his balance and sprawled on the floor. Above his eye level, his bunk loomed like a haven. If he could just reach it, lie quiet till the sickness went away. . . . He crossed the cabin somehow, lay across the edge of the bunk, rolled into it. A wave of blackness lifted to meet him, deep as a sea.

He lay a long time; then the fragment of remaining will

reasserted itself. Reluctantly, he forced open gummy eye-
lids. It was nearly dark now; the far window of the hut
showed in the gloom, a vague rectangle of greyness. In
front of it the handles of the semaphore seemed to swim,
glinting where the light caught the polished smoothness of
wood. He stared, realizing his foolishness; then he tried to
roll off the bunk. The blankets, glued to his back, prevented
him. He tried again, shivering now with the cold. The stove
was unlit; the cabin door stood ajar, white crystals fanning
in across the planking of the floor. Outside, the howling of
the wind was relentless. The boy struggled; the efforts woke
pain again and the sickness, the thudding and roaring.
Images of the semaphore handles doubled, sextupled, rolled
apart to make a glistening silver sheaf. He panted, tears
running into his mouth; then his eyes slid closed. He fell into
a noisy void shot with colours, sparks, and gleams and
washes of light. He lay watching the lights, teeth bared,
feeling the throb in his back where fresh blood pumped into
the bed. After a while, the roaring went away.

The child lay couched in long grass, feeling the heat of
the sun strike through his jerkin to burn his shoulders. In
front of him, at the conical crest of the hill, the magic thing
flapped slowly, its wings proud and lazy as those of a bird.
Very high it was, on its pole on top of its hill; the faint
wooden clattering it made fell remote from the blueness of
the summer sky. The movements of the arms had half
hypnotized him; he lay nodding and blinking, chin propped
on his hands, absorbed in his watching. Up and down, up
and down, *clap* . . . then down again and round, up and
back, pausing, gesticulating, never staying wholly still. The
semaphore seemed alive, an animate thing perched there
talking strange words nobody could understand. Yet words
they were, replete with meanings and mysteries like the
words in his *Modern English Primer*. The child's brain

spun. Words made stories; what stories was the tower telling, all alone there on its hill? Tales of kings and shipwrecks, fights and pursuits, Fairies, buried gold. . . . It was talking, he knew that without a doubt; whispering and clacking, giving messages and taking them from the others in the lines, the great lines that stretched across England everywhere you could think, every direction you could see.

He watched the control rods sliding like bright muscles in their oiled guides. From Avebury, where he lived, many other towers were visible; they marched southwards across the Great Plain, climbed the westward heights of the Marlborough Downs. Though those were bigger, huge things staffed by teams of men whose signals might be visible on a clear day for ten miles or more. When they moved it was majestically and slowly, with a thundering from their jointed arms; these others, the little local towers, were friendlier somehow, chatting and pecking away from dawn to sunset.

There were many games the child played by himself in the long hours of summer; stolen hours usually, for there was always work to be found for him. School lessons, home study, chores about the house or down at his brothers' smallholding on the other side of the village; he must sneak off, evenings or in the early dawn, if he wanted to be alone to dream. The stones beckoned him sometimes, the great gambolling diamond-shapes of them circling the little town. The boy would scud along the ditches of what had been an ancient temple, climb the terraced scarps to where the stones danced against the morning sun; or walk the long processional avenue that stretched eastward across the fields, imagine himself a priest or a god come to do old sacrifice to rain and sun. No one knew who first placed the stones. Some said the Fairies, in the days of their strength; others the old gods, they whose names it was a sin to whisper. Others said the Devil.

Mother Church winked at the destruction of Satanic

relics, and that the villagers knew full well. Father Donovan
disapproved, but he could do very little; the people went to
it with a will. Their ploughs gnawed the bases of the
markers, they broke the megaliths with water and fire and
used the bits for patching dry stone walls; they'd been
doing it for centuries now, and the rings were depleted and
showing gaps. But there were many stones; the circles remained, and barrows crowning the windy tops of hills,
hows where the old dead lay patient with their broken
bones. The child would climb the mounds, and dream of
kings in fur and jewels; but always, when he tired, he was
drawn back to the semaphores and their mysterious life. He
lay quiet, chin sunk on his hands, eyes sleepy, while above
him Silbury 973 chipped and clattered on its hill.

The hand, falling on his shoulder, startled him from
dreams. He tensed, whipped round and wanted to bolt;
but there was nowhere to run. He was caught; he stared up
gulping, a chubby little boy, long hair falling across his forehead.

The man was tall, enormously tall it seemed to the child.
His face was brown, tanned by sun and wind, and at the
corners of his eyes were networks of wrinkles. The eyes were
deep-set and very blue, startling against the colour of the
skin; to the boy they seemed to be of exactly the hue one
sees at the very top of the sky. His father's eyes had long
since bolted into hiding behind pebble-thick glasses; these
eyes were different. They had about them an appearance of
power, as if they were used to looking very long distances
and seeing clearly things that other men might miss. Their
owner was dressed all in green, with the faded shoulder
lacings and lanyard of a Serjeant of Signals. At his hip he
carried the Zeiss glasses that were the badge of any Signaller; the flap of the case was only half secured and beneath it the boy could see the big eyepieces, the worn
brassy sheen of the barrels.

The Guildsman was smiling; his voice when he spoke was drawling and slow. It was the voice of a man who knows about Time, that Time is forever and scurry and bustle can wait. Someone who might know about the old stones in the way the child's father did not.

"Well," he said, "I do believe we've caught a little spy. Who be you, lad?"

The boy licked his mouth and squeaked, looking hunted. "R-Rafe Bigland, sir. . . ."

"And what be 'ee doin'?"

Rafe wetted his lips again, looked at the tower, pouted miserably, stared at the grass beside him, looked back to the Signaller and quickly away. "I . . . I . . ."

He stopped, unable to explain. On top of the hill the tower creaked and flapped. The Serjeant squatted down, waiting patiently, still with the little half-smile, eyes twinkling at the boy. The satchel he'd been carrying he'd set on the grass. Rafe knew he'd been to the village to pick up the afternoon meal; one of the old ladies of Avebury was contracted to supply food to the Signallers on duty. There was little he didn't know about the working of the Silbury station.

The seconds became a minute, and an answer had to be made. Rafe drew himself up a trifle desperately; he heard his own voice speaking as if it was the voice of a stranger, and wondered with a part of his mind at the words that formed themselves on his tongue without it seemed the conscious intervention of thought. "If you please, sir," he said pipingly, "I was watching the t-tower. . . ."

"Why?"

"I . . ."

Again the difficulty. How explain? The mysteries of the Guild were not to be revealed to any casual stranger. The codes of the Signallers and other deeper secrets were handed down, jealously, through the families privileged to wear the

Green. The Serjeant's accusation of spying had had some
truth to it; it had sounded ominous.

The Guildsman helped him. "Canst thou read the signals,
Rafe?"

Rafe shook his head, violently. No commoner could read
the towers. No commoner ever would. He felt a trembling
start in the pit of his stomach, but again his voice used
itself without his will. "No, sir," it said in a firm treble.
"But I would fain learn. . . ."

The Serjeant's eyebrows rose. He sat back on his heels,
hands lying easy across his knees, and started to laugh.
When he had finished he shook his head. "So you would
learn. . . . Aye, and a dozen kings, and many a high-placed
gentleman, would lie easier abed for the reading of the
towers." His face changed itself abruptly into a scowl. "Boy,"
he said, "you mock us. . . ."

Rafe could only shake his head again, silently. The Serjeant stared over him into space, still sitting on his heels.
Rafe wanted to explain how he had never, in his most
secret dreams, ever imagined himself a Signaller; how his
tongue had moved of its own, blurting out the impossible
and absurd. But he couldn't speak any more; before the
Green, he was dumb. The pause lengthened while he
watched inattentively the lurching progress of a rain beetle
through the stems of grass. Then, "Who's thy father, boy?"

Rafe gulped. There would be a beating, he was sure of
that now; and he would be forbidden ever to go near the
towers or watch them again. He felt the stinging behind his
eyes that meant tears were very close, ready to well and
trickle. "Thomas Bigland of Avebury, sir," he said. "A clerk
to Sir William M-Marshall."

The Serjeant nodded. "And thou wouldst learn the towers?
Thou wouldst be a Signaller?"

"Aye, sir. . . ." The tongue was Modern English of
course, the language of artisans and tradesmen, not the

guttural clacking of the landless churls; Rafe slipped easily
into the old-fashioned usage of it the Signallers employed
sometimes among themselves.

The Serjeant said abruptly, "Canst thou read in books,
Rafe?"

"Aye, sir. . . ." Then falteringly, "If the words be not too
long. . . ."

The Guildsman laughed again, and clapped the boy on
the back. "Well, Master Rafe Bigland, thou who would be a
Signaller, and can read books if the words be but short, my
book learning is slim enough as God He knows; but it may
be I can help thee, if thou hast given me no lies. Come."
And he rose and began to walk away toward the tower.
Rafe hesitated, blinked, then roused himself and trotted
along behind, head whirling with wonders.

They climbed the path that ran slantingly round the hill.
As they moved, the Serjeant talked. Silbury 973 was part of
the C class chain that ran from near Londinium, from the
great relay station at Pontes, along the line of the road to
Aquae Sulis. Its complement . . . but Rafe knew the complement well enough. Five men including the Serjeant; their
cottages stood apart from the main village, on a little rise
of ground that gave them seclusion. Signallers' homes were
always situated like that, it helped preserve the Guild mysteries. Guildsmen paid no tithes to local demesnes, obeyed
none but their own hierarchy; and though in theory they
were answerable under common law, in practice they were
immune. They governed themselves according to their own
high code; and it was a brave man, or a fool, who squared
with the richest Guild in England. There had been deadly
accuracy in what the Serjeant said; when kings waited on
their messages as eagerly as commoners they had little need
to fear. The Popes might cavil, jealous of their independ-
ence, but Rome herself leaned too heavily on the con-
tinent-wide networks of the semaphore towers to do more

than adjure and complain. Insofar as such a thing was possible in a hemisphere dominated by the Church Militant, the Guildsmen were free.

Although Rafe had seen the inside of a signal station often enough in dreams he had never physically set foot in one. He stopped short at the wooden step, feeling awe rise in him like a tangible barrier. He caught his breath. He had never been this close to a semaphore tower before; the rush and thudding of the arms, the clatter of dozens of tiny joints, sounded in his ears like music. From here only the tip of the signal was in sight, looming over the roof of the hut. The varnished wooden spars shone orange like the masts of a boat; the semaphore arms rose and dipped, black against the sky. He could see the bolts and loops near their tips where in bad weather or at night when some message of vital importance had to be passed, cressets could be attached to them. He'd seen such fires once, miles out over the Plain, the night the old King died.

The Serjeant opened the door and urged him through it. He stood rooted just beyond the sill. The place had a clean smell that was somehow also masculine, a compound of polishes and oils and the fumes of tobacco; and inside too it had something of the appearance of a ship. The cabin was airy and low, roomier than it had looked from the foot of the hill. There was a stove, empty now and gleaming with blacking, its brasswork brightly polished. Inside its mouth a sheet of red crepe paper had been stretched tightly; the doors were parted a little to show the smartness. The plank walls were painted a light grey; on the breast that enclosed the chimney of the stove duty rosters were pinned neatly. In one corner of the room was a group of diplomas, framed and richly coloured; below them an old daguerreotype, badly faded, showing a group of men standing in front of a very tall signal tower. In one corner of the cabin was a bunk, blankets folded into a neat cube at its foot; above it a hand-coloured pinup of a smiling girl wearing a cap of Guild green and very little else. Rafe's eyes passed over it with the faintly embarrassed indifference of childhood.

In the centre of the room, white-painted and square, was the base of the signal mast; round it a little podium of smooth, scrubbed wood, on which stood two Guildsmen. In their hands were the long levers that worked the semaphore arms overhead; the control rods reached up from them, encased where they passed through the ceiling in white canvas grommets. Skylights, opened to either side, let in the warm July air. The third duty Signaller stood at the eastern window of the cabin, glasses to his eyes, speaking quietly and continuously. "Five . . . eleven . . . thirteen . . . nine . . ." The operators repeated the combinations, working the big handles, leaning the weight of their bodies against the pull of the signal arms overhead, letting each downward rush of the semaphores help them into position for their next cypher. There was an air of concentration but not of strain; it all seemed very easy and practised. In front of the men, supported by struts from the roof, a telltale repeated the positions of the arms, but the Signallers rarely glanced at it. Years of training had given a fluidness to their movements that made them seem almost like the steps and posturings of a ballet. The bodies swung, checked, moved through their arabesques; the creaking of wood and the faint rumbling of the signals filled the place, as steady and lulling as the drone of bees.

No one paid any attention to Rafe or the Serjeant. The Guildsman began talking again quietly, explaining what was happening. The long message that had been going through now for nearly an hour was a list of current grain and fat-stock prices from Londinium. The Guild system was invaluable for regulating the complex economy of the country; farmers and merchants, taking the Londinium prices as a yardstick, knew exactly what to pay when buying and selling for themselves. Rafe forgot to be disappointed; his mind heard the words, recording them and storing them away, while his eyes watched the changing patterns made by the Guildsmen, so much a part of the squeaking, clacking machine they controlled.

The actual transmitted information, what the Serjeant called the payspeech, occupied only a part of the signalling; a message was often almost swamped by the codings necessary to secure its distribution. The current figures for instance had to reach certain centres, Aquae Sulis among them, by nightfall. How they arrived, their routing on the way, was very much the concern of the branch Signallers through whose stations the cyphers passed. It took years of experience coupled with a certain degree of intuition to route signals in such a way as to avoid lines already congested with information; and of course while a line was in use in one direction, as in the present case with a complex message being moved from east to west, it was very difficult to employ it in reverse. It was in fact possible to pass two messages in different directions at the same time, and it was often done on the A Class towers. When that happened every third cypher of a northbound might be part of another signal moving south; the stations transmitted in bursts, swapping the messages forward and back. But coaxial signalling was detested even by the Guildsmen. The line had to be cleared first, and a suitable code agreed on; two lookouts were employed, chanting their directions alternately to the Signallers, and even in the best-run station total confusion could result from the smallest slip, necessitating reclearing of the route and a fresh start.

With his hands, the Serjeant described the washout signal a fouled-up tower would use; the three horizontal extensions of the semaphores from the sides of their mast. If that happened, he said, chuckling grimly, a head would roll somewhere; for a Class A would be under the command of a Major of Signals at least, a man of twenty or more years experience. He would be expected not to make mistakes, and to see in turn that none were made by his subordinates. Rafe's head began to whirl again; he looked with fresh respect at the worn green leather of the Serjeant's uniform. He was beginning to see now, dimly, just what sort of thing it was to be a Signaller.

The message ended at last, with a great clapping of the semaphore arms. The lookout remained at his post but the operators got down, showing an interest in Rafe for the first time. Away from the semaphore levers they seemed far more normal and unfrightening. Rafe knew them well; Robin Wheeler, who often spoke to him on his way to and from the station, and Bob Camus, who'd split a good many heads in his time at the feast-day cudgel playing in the village. They showed him the code books, all the scores of cyphers printed in red on numbered black squares. He stayed to share their meal; his mother would be concerned and his father annoyed, but home was almost forgotten. Toward evening another message came up from the west; they told him it was police business, and sent it winging and clapping on its way. It was dusk when Rafe finally left the station, head in the clouds, two unbelievable pennies jinking in his pocket. It was only later, in bed and trying to sleep, he realized a long-submerged dream had come true. He did sleep finally, only to dream again of signal towers at night, the cressets on their arms roaring against the blueness of the sky. He never spent the coins.

Once it had become a real possibility, his ambition to be a Signaller grew steadily; he spent all the time he could at the Silbury Station, perched high on its weird prehistoric hill. His absenses met with his father's keenest disapproval. Mr. Bigland's wage as an estate clerk barely brought in enough to support his brood of seven boys; the family had of necessity to grow most of its own food, and for that every

pair of hands that could be mustered was valuable. But nobody guessed the reason for Rafe's frequent disappearances;
and for his part he didn't say a word.

He learned, in illicit hours, the thirty-odd basic positions
of the signal arms, and something of the commonest se-
quences of grouping; after that he could lie out near Silbury
Hill and mouth off most of the numbers to himself, though
without the codes that informed them he was still dumb.
Once Serjeant Gray let him take the observer's place for a
glorious half hour while a message was coming in over the
Marlborough Downs. Rafe stood stiffly, hands sweating on
the big barrels of the Zeiss glasses, and read off the cyphers
as high and clear as he could for the Signallers at his back.
The Serjeant checked his reporting unobtrusively from the
other end of the hut, but he made no mistakes.

By the time he was ten Rafe had received as much formal
education as a child of his class could expect. The great
question of a career was raised. The family sat in conclave;
father, mother, and the three eldest sons. Rafe was unim-
pressed; he knew, and had known for weeks, the fate they
had selected for him. He was to be apprenticed to one of
the four tailors of the village, little bent old men who sat
like cross-legged hermits behind bulwarks of cloth bales and
stitched their lives away by the light of penny dips. He
hardly expected to be consulted on the matter; however he
was sent for, formally, and asked what he wished to do.
That was the time for the bombshell. "I know exactly what
I want to be," said Rafe firmly. "A Signaller."

There was a moment of shocked silence; then the laughing started and swelled. The Guilds were closely guarded;
Rafe's father would pay dearly even for his entry into the
tailoring trade. As for the Signallers . . . no Bigland had
ever been a Signaller, no Bigland ever would. Why, that . . .
it would raise the family status! The whole village would

have to look up to them, with a son wearing the Green. Preposterous . . .

Rafe sat quietly until they were finished, lips compressed, cheekbones glowing. He'd known it would be like this, he knew just what he had to do. His composure discomfited the family; they quietened down enough to ask him, with mock seriousness, how he intended to set about achieving his ambition. It was time for the second bomb. "By approaching the Guild with regard to a Common Entrance Examination," he said, mouthing words that had been learned by rote. "Serjeant Gray, of the Silbury Station, will speak for me."

Into the fresh silence came his father's embarrassed coughing. Mr. Bigland looked like an old sheep, sitting blinking through his glasses, nibbling at his thin moustache. "Well," he said. "Well, I don't know. . . . *Well.* . . ." But Rafe had already seen the glint in his eyes at the dizzying prospect of prestige. That a son of his should wear the Green. . . .

Before their minds could change Rafe wrote a formal letter which he delivered in person to the Silbury Station; it asked Serjeant Gray, very correctly, if he would be kind enough to call on Mr. Bigland with a view to discussing his son's entry to the College of Signals in Londinium. The Serjeant was as good as his word. He was a widower, and childless; maybe Rafe made up in part for the son he'd never had, maybe he saw the reflection of his own youthful enthusiasm in the boy. He came the next evening, strolling quietly down the village street to rap at the Bigland's door; Rafe, watching from his shared bedroom over the porch, grinned at the gaping and craning of the neighbours. The family was all a-flutter; the household budget had been scraped for wine and candles, silverware and fresh linen were laid out in the parlour, everybody was anxious to make the best possible impression. Mr. Bigland of course was only too agreeable; when the Serjeant left, an hour later, he had

his signed permission in his belt. Rafe himself saw the
signal originated asking Londinium for the necessary entrance papers for the College's annual examination.

The Guild gave just twelve places per year, and they were
keenly contested. In the few weeks at his disposal Rafe was
crammed mercilessly; the Serjeant coached him in all aspects
of Signalling he might reasonably be expected to know about
while the village dominie, impressed in spite of himself,
brushed up Rafe's bookwork, even trying to instil into his
aching head the rudiments of Norman French. Rafe won ad-
mittance; he had never considered the possibility of failure,
mainly because such a thought was unbearable. He sat the
examination in Sorviodunum, the nearest regional centre
to his home; a week later a message came through offering
him his place, listing the clothes and books he would need
and instructing him to be ready to present himself at the
College of Signals in just under a month's time. When he
left for Londinium, well muffled in a new cloak, riding a
horse provided by the Guild and with two russet-coated
Guild servants in attendance, he was followed by the envy
of a whole village. The arms of the Silbury tower were
quiet; but as he passed they flipped quickly to Attention,
followed at once by the cyphers for Origination and Immediate Locality. Rafe turned in the saddle, tears stinging his
eyes, and watched the letters quickly spelled out in plaintalk. *Good luck. . . .*

After Avebury, Londinium seemed dingy, noisy, and old.
The College was housed in an ancient, ramshackle building
just inside the City walls; though Londinium had long since
over-spilled its former limits, sprawling south across the
river and north nearly as far as Tyburn Tree. The Guild
children were the usual crowd of brawling, snotty-nosed
brats that comprised the apprentices of any trade. Hereditary sons of the Green, they looked down on the Common
Entrants from the heights of an unbearable and imaginary

eminence; Rafe had a bad time till a series of dormitory
fights, all more or less bloody, proved to his fellows once
and for all that young Bigland at least was better left alone.
He settled down as an accepted member of the community.

The Guild, particularly of recent years, had been tending
to place more and more value on theoretical knowledge,
and the two year course was intensive. The apprentices
had to become adept in Norman French, for their further
training would take them inevitably into the houses of the
rich. A working knowledge of the other tongues of the land,
the Cornish, Gaelic, and Middle English, was also a requi-
site; no Guildsman ever knew where he would finally be
posted. Guild history was taught too, and the elements of
mechanics and coding, though most of the practical work in
those directions would be done in the field, at the training
stations scattered along the south and west coasts of
England and through the Welsh Marches. The students were
even required to have a nodding acquaintance with thaumaturgy; though Rafe for one was unable to see how the
attraction of scraps of paper to a polished stick of amber
could ever have an application to Signalling.

He worked well nonetheless, and passed out with a mark
high enough to satisfy even his professors. He was posted
directly to his training station, the A Class complex atop
Saint Adhelm's Head in Dorset. To his intense pleasure he
was accompanied by the one real friend he had made at
College; Josh Cope, a wild, black-haired boy, a Common
Entrant and the son of a Durham mining family.

They arrived at Saint Adhelm's in the time-honoured
way, thumbing a lift from a road train drawn by a labouring
Fowler compound. Rafe never forgot his first sight of the
station. It was far bigger than he'd imagined, sprawling
across the top of the great blunt promontory. For convenience, stations were rated in accordance with the heavi-
est towers they carried; but Saint Adhelm's was a clearing

centre for B, C, and D lines as well, and round the huge
paired structures of the A Class towers ranged a circle of
smaller semaphores, all twirling and clacking in the sun.
Beside them, establishing rigs displayed the codes the towers spoke in a series of bright-coloured circles and rectangles; Rafe, staring, saw one of them rotate, displaying
to the west a yellow Bend Sinister as the semaphore above
it switched in midmessage from plaintalk to the complex
Code Twenty-Three. He glanced sidelong at Josh, got from
the other lad a jaunty thumbs-up; they swung their satchels
onto their shoulders and headed up toward the main gate
to report themselves for duty.

For the first few weeks both boys were glad enough of
each other's company. They found the atmosphere of a
major field station very different from that of the College;
by comparison the latter, noisy and brawling as it had
been, came to seem positively monastic. A training in the
Guild of Signallers was like a continuous game of ladders
and snakes; and Rafe and Josh had slid back once more to
the bottom of the stack. Their life was a near-endless round
of canteen fatigues, of polishing and burnishing, scrubbing
and holystoning. There were the cabins to clean, gravel
paths to weed, what seemed like miles of brass rail to scour
till it gleamed. Saint Adhelm's was a show station, always
prone to inspection. Once it suffered a visit from the Grand
Master of Signallers himself, and his Lord Lieutenant; the
spitting and polishing before that went on for weeks. And
there was the maintenance of the towers themselves; the
canvas grommets on the great control rods to renew and
pipe-clay, the semaphore arms to be painted, their bearings
cleaned and packed with grease, spars to be sent down
and re-rigged, always in darkness when the day's signalling
was done and generally in the foulest of weathers. The
semi-military nature of the Guild made necessary sidearms
practice and shooting with the longbow and crossbow,

obsolescent weapons now but still occasionally employed
in the European wars.

The station itself surpassed Rafe's wildest dreams. Its
standing complement, including the dozen or so apprentices
always in training, was well over a hundred, of whom some
sixty or eighty were always on duty or on call. The big
semaphores, the Class A's, were each worked by teams of
a dozen men, six to each great lever, with a Signal Master
to control coordination and pass on the cyphers from the
observers. With the station running at near capacity the
scene was impressive; the lines of men at the controls, as
synchronised as troupes of dancers; the shouts of the Signal Masters, scuffle of feet on the white planking, rumble
and creak of the control rods, the high thunder of the
signals a hundred feet above the roofs. Though that, according to the embittered Officer in Charge, was not Signalling but "unscientific bloody timber-hauling." Major
Stone had spent most of his working life on the little
Class C's of the Pennine Chain before an unlooked-for
promotion had given him his present position of trust.

The A messages short-hopped from Saint Adhelm's to
Swyre Head and from thence to Gad Cliff, built on the
high land overlooking Warbarrow Bay. From there along
the coast to Golden Cap, the station poised six hundred
sheer feet above the fishing village of Lymes, to fling
themselves in giant strides into the west, to Somerset and
Devon and far-off Cornwall, or northwards again over the
heights of the Great Plain en route for Wales. Up there
Rafe knew they passed in sight of the old stone rings of
Avebury. He often thought with affection of his parents and
Serjeant Gray; but he was long past homesickness. His days
were too full for that.

Twelve months after their arrival at Saint Adhelm's, and
three years after their induction into the Guild, the apprentices were first allowed to lay hands on the semaphore

bars. Josh in fact had found it impossible to wait and had salved his ego some months before by spelling out a frisky message on one of the little local towers in what he hoped was the dead of night. For that fall from grace he had made intimate and painful contact with the buckle on the end of a green leather belt, wielded by none other than Major Stone himself. Two burly Corporals of Signals held the miners' lad down while he threshed and howled; the end result had convinced even Josh that on certain points of discipline the Guild stood adamant.

To learn to signal was like yet another beginning. Rafe found rapidly that a semaphore lever was no passive thing to be pulled and hauled at pleasure; with the wind under the great black sails of the arms an operator stood a good chance of being bowled completely off the rostrum by the back-whip of even a thirty foot unit, while to the teams on the A Class towers lack of coordination could prove, and had proved in the past, fatal. There was a trick to the thing, only learned after bruising hours of practice; to lean the weight of the body against the levers rather than just using the muscles of back and arms, employ the jounce and swing of the semaphores to position them automatically for their next cypher. Trying to fight them instead of working with the recoil would reduce a strong man to a sweat-soaked rag within minutes; but a trained Signaller could work half the day and feel very little strain. Rafe approached the task assiduously; six months and one broken collarbone later he felt able to pride himself on mastery of his craft. It was then he first encountered the murderous intricacies of coaxial signalling. . . .

After two years on the station the apprentices were finally deemed ready to graduate as full Signallers. Then came the hardest test of all. The site of it, the arena, was a bare hillock of ground some half mile from Saint Adhelm's Head. Built onto it, and facing each other about forty yards apart, were two Class D towers with their cabins. Josh was to be Rafe's partner in the test. They were taken to the place in the early morning, and given their problem; to transmit to each other in plaintalk the entire of the Book of Nehemiah in alternate verses, with appropriate Attention, Acknowledgement, and End-of-Message cyphers at the head and tail of each. Several ten minute breaks were allowed, though they had been warned privately it would be better not to take them; once they left the rostrums they might be unable to force their tired bodies back to the bars.

Round the little hill would be placed observers who would check the work minute by minute for inaccuracies and sloppiness. When the messages were finished to their satisfaction the apprentices might leave, and call themselves Signallers; but not before. Nothing would prevent them deserting their task if they desired before it was done. Nobody would speak a word of blame, and there would be no punishment; but they would leave the Guild the same day, and never return. Some boys, a few, did leave. Others collapsed; for them, there would be another chance.

Rafe neither collapsed nor left, though there were times when he longed to do both. When he started, the sun had barely risen; when he left it was sinking toward the western rim of the horizon. The first two hours, the first three, were nothing; then the pain began. In the shoulders, in the back, in the buttocks and calves. His world narrowed; he saw neither the sun nor the distant sea. There was only the semaphore, the handles of it, the text in front of his eyes, the window. Across the space separating the huts he could see Josh staring as he engaged in his endless, useless task. Rafe came by degrees to hate the towers, the Guild, himself, all he had done, the memory of Silbury and old Serjeant Gray; and to hate Josh most of all, with his stupid white blob of a face, the signals clacking above him like some absurd extension of himself. With fatigue came a

trance-like state in which logic was suspended, the reasons
for actions lost. There was nothing to do in life, had never
been anything to do but stand on the rostrum, work the
levers, feel the jounce of the signals, check with the body,
feel the jounce. . . . His vision doubled and trebled till the
lines of copy in front of him shimmered unreadably; and
still the test ground on.

At any time in the afternoon Rafe would have killed his
friend had he been able to reach him. But he couldn't get
to him; his feet were rooted to the podium, his hands
glued to the levers of the semaphore. The signals grumbled
and creaked; his breath sounded in his ears harshly, like
an engine. His sight blackened; the text and the opposing
semaphore swam in a void. He felt disembodied; he could
sense his limbs only as a dim and confused burning. And
somehow, agonizingly, the transmission came to an end.
He clattered off the last verse of the book, signed End of
Message, leaned on the handles while the part of him that
could still think realized dully that he could stop. And then,
in black rage, he did the thing only one other apprentice
had done in the history of the station; flipped the handles
to Attention again, spelled out with terrible exactness and
letter by letter the message *God Save the Queen.*" Signed
End of Message, got no acknowledgement, swung the levers
up and locked them into position for Emergency-Contact
Broken. In a signalling chain the alarm would be flashed
back to the originating station, further information rerouted
and a squad sent to investigate the breakdown.

Rafe stared blankly at the levers. He saw now the puzzling bright streaks on them were his own blood. He forced
his raw hands to unclamp themselves, elbowed his way
through the door, shoved past the men who had come for
him and collapsed twenty yards away on the grass. He
was taken back to Saint Adhelm's in a cart and put to bed.
He slept the clock round; when he woke it was with the

knowledge that Josh and he now had the right to put aside
the cowled russet jerkins of apprentices for the full green of
the Guild of Signallers. They drank beer that night, awkwardly, gripping the tankards in both bandaged paws; and
for the second and last time, the station cart had to be
called into service to get them home.

The next part of training was a sheer pleasure. Rafe
made his farewells to Josh and went home on a two month
leave; at the end of his furlough he was posted to the
household of the Fitzgibbons, one of the old families of
the Southwest, to serve twelve months as Signaller-Page.
The job was mainly ceremonial, though in times of na-
tional crisis it could obviously carry its share of responsi-
bility. Most well-bred families, if they could afford to do
so, bought rights from the Guild and erected their own
tiny stations somewhere in the grounds of their estate; the
little Class E towers were even smaller than the Class D's
on which Rafe had graduated.

In places where no signal line ran within easy sighting
distance, one or more stations might be erected across the
surrounding country and staffed by Journeyman-Signallers
without access to coding; but the Fitzgibbons' great aitch-
shaped house lay almost below Swyre Head, in a sloping
coombe open to the sea. Rafe, looking down on the roofs
of the place the morning he arrived, started to grin. He
could see his semaphore perched up among the chimney
stacks; above it a bare mile away was the A repeater, the
short-hop tower for his old station of Saint Adhelm's just
over the hill. He touched heels to his horse, pushing it
into a canter. He would be signalling direct to the A Class,
there was no other outroute; he couldn't help chuckling at
the thought of its Major's face when asked to hurl to Saint
Adhelm's or Golden Cap requests for butter, six dozen
eggs, or the services of a cobbler. He paid his formal

respects to the station and rode down into the valley to take up his new duties.

They proved if anything easier than he had anticipated. Fitzgibbon himself moved in high circles at Court and was rarely home, the running of the house being left to his wife and two teen-age daughters. As Rafe had expected, most of the messages he was required to pass were of an intensely domestic nature. And he enjoyed the privileges of any young Guildsman in his position; he could always be sure of a warm place in the kitchen at nights, the first cut off the roast, the prettiest serving wenches to mend his clothes and trim his hair. There was sea bathing within a stone's throw, and feast day trips to Durnovaria and Bourne Mouth. Once a little fair established itself in the grounds, an annual occurrence apparently; and Rafe spent a delicious half hour signalling the A Class for oil for its steam engines, and meat for a dancing bear.

The year passed quickly; in late autumn the boy, promoted now to Signaller-Corporal, was reposted, and another took his place. Rafe rode west, into the hills that crowd the southern corner of Dorset, to take up what would be his first real command.

The station was part of a D Class chain that wound west over the high ground into Somerset. In winter, with the short days and bad seeing conditions, the towers would be unused; Rafe knew that well enough. He would be totally isolated; winters in the hills could be severe, with snow making travel next to impossible and frosts for weeks on end. He would have little to fear from the *routiers*, the footpads who legend claimed haunted the West in the cold months; the station lay far from any road and there was nothing in the cabins, save perhaps the Zeiss glasses carried by the Signaller, to tempt a desperate man. He would be in more danger from wolves and Fairies, though the former were virtually extinct in the south and he was young enough to laugh at the latter. He took over from the bored Corporal just finishing his term, signalled his arrival back through the chain, and settled down to take stock of things.

By all reports this first winter on a one-man station was a worse trial than the endurance test. For a trial it was, certainly. At some time through the dark months ahead, some hour of the day, a message would come along the dead line, from the west or from the east; and Rafe would have to be there to take it and pass it on. A minute late with his acknowledgement and a formal reprimand would be issued from Londinium; that might peg his promotion for years, maybe for good. The standards of the Guild were high, and they were never relaxed; if it was easy for a Major in charge of an A Class station to fall from grace, how much easier for an unknown and untried Corporal! The duty period of each day was short, a bare six hours, five through the darkest months of December and January; but during that time, except for one short break, Rafe would have to be continually on the alert.

One of his first acts on being left alone was to climb to the diminutive operating gantry. The construction of the station was unusual. To compensate for its lack of elevation a catwalk had been built across under the roof; the operating rostrum was located centrally on it, while at each end double-glazed windows commanded views to west and east. Between them, past the handles of the semaphore, a track had been worn half an inch deep in the wooden boards. In the next few months Rafe would wear it deeper, moving from one window to the other checking the arms of the next towers in line. The matchsticks of the semaphores were barely visible; he judged them to be a good two miles distant. He would need all his eyesight, plus the keenness of the Zeiss lenses, to make them out at all on a dull day; but they would have to be watched minute by

minute through every duty period because sooner or later
one of them would move. He grinned and touched the
handles of his own machine. When that happened, his
acknowledgement would be clattering before the tower had
stopped calling for Attention.

He examined the stations critically through his glasses.
In the spring, riding out to take up a new tour, he might
meet one of their operators; but not before. In the hours
of daylight they as well as he would be tied to their
gantries, and on foot in the dark it might be dangerous
to try to reach them. Anyway it would not be expected
of him; that was an unwritten law. In case of need,
desperate need, he could call help through the semaphores;
but for no other reason. This was the true life of the Guildsman; the bustle of Londinium, the warmth and comfort
of the Fitzgibbons' home, had been episodes only. Here
was the end result of it all; the silence, the desolation,
the ancient, endless communion of the hills. He had come
full circle.

His life settled into a pattern of sleeping and waking
and watching. As the days grew shorter the weather wors-
ened; freezing mists swirled round the station, and the first
snow fell. For hours on end the towers to east and west
were lost in the haze; if a message was to come now, the
Signallers would have to light their cressets. Rafe prepared
the bundles of faggots anxiously, wiring them into their
iron cages, setting them beside the door with the paraffin
that would soak them, make them blaze. He became obsessed
by the idea that the message had in fact come, and he
had missed it in the gloom. In time the fear ebbed. The
Guild was hard, but it was fair; no Signaller, in winter of
all times, was expected to be a superman. If a Captain
rode suddenly to the station demanding why he had not
answered this or that he would see the torches and the
oil laid ready and know at least that Rafe had done his

best. Nobody came; and when the weather cleared the
towers were still stationary.

Each night after the light had gone Rafe tested his
signals, swinging the arms to free them from their wind-
driven coating of ice; it was good to feel the pull and
flap of the thin wings up in the dark. The messages he
sent into blackness were fanciful in the extreme; notes to
his parents and old Serjeant Gray, lurid suggestions to a
little girl in the household of the Fitzgibbons to whom
he had taken more than a passing fancy. Twice a week he
used the lunchtime break to climb the tower, check the
spindles in their packings of grease. On one such inspection he was appalled to see a hairline crack in one of the
control rods, the first sign that the metal had become fa-
tigued. He replaced the entire section that night, breaking
out fresh parts from store, hauling them up and fitting
them by the improvised light of a hand lamp. It was an
awkward, dangerous job with his fingers freezing and the
wind plucking at his back, trying to tug him from his
perch onto the roof below. He could have pulled the station
out of line in daytime, signalled Repairs and given himself
the benefit of light, but pride forbade him. He finished
the job two hours before dawn, tested the tower, made
his entry in the log and went to sleep, trusting in his
Signaller's sense to wake him at first light. It didn't let him
down.

The long hours of darkness began to pall. Mending and
laundering only filled a small proportion of his off-duty
time; he read through his stock of books, reread them, put
them aside and began devising tasks for himself, checking
and rechecking his inventories of food and fuel. In the
blackness, with the long crying of the wind over the roof,
the stories of Fairies and were-things on the heath didn't
seem quite so fanciful. Difficult now even to imagine summer, the slow clicking of the towers against skys bright blue

and burning with light. There were two pistols in the hut; Rafe saw to it their mechanisms were in order, loaded and primed them both. Twice after that he woke to crashings on the roof, as if some dark thing was scrabbling to get in; but each time it was only the wind in the skylights. He padded them with strips of canvas; then the frost came back, icing them shut, and he wasn't disturbed again.

He moved a portable stove up onto the observation gallery and discovered the remarkable number of operations that could be carried out with one eye on the windows. The brewing of coffee and tea were easy enough; in time he could even manage the production of hot snacks. His lunch hours he preferred to use for things other than cooking. Above all else he was afraid of inaction making him fat; there was no sign of it happening but he still preferred to take no chances. When snow conditions permitted he would make quick expeditions from the shack into the surrounding country. On one of these the hillock with its smoothly shaped crown of trees attracted his eye. He walked toward it jauntily, breath steaming in the air, the glasses as ever bumping his hip. In the copse, his Fate was waiting.

The catamount clung to the bole of a fir, watching the advance of the boy with eyes that were slits of hate in the vicious mask of its face. No one could have read its thoughts. Perhaps it imagined itself about to be attacked; perhaps it was true what they said about such creatures, that the cold of winter sent them mad. There were few of them now in the west; mostly they had retreated to the hills of Wales, the rocky peaks of the far north. The survival of this one was in itself a freak, an anachronism.

The tree in which it crouched leaned over the path Rafe must take. He ploughed forward, head bent a little, intent only on picking his way. As he approached the catamount drew back its lips in a huge and silent snarl, showing the wide pink vee of its mouth, the long needle-sharp teeth.

The eyes blazed; the ears flattened, making the skull a round, furry ball. Rafe never saw the wildcat, its stripes blending perfectly with the harshness of branches and snow. As he stepped beneath the tree it launched itself onto him, landed across his shoulders like a spitting shawl; his neck and back were flayed before the pain had travelled to his brain.

The shock and the impact sent him staggering. He reeled, yelling; the reaction dislodged the cat but it spun in a flash, tearing upward at his stomach. He felt the hot spurting of blood, and the world became a red haze of horror. The air was full of the creature's screaming. He reached his knife but teeth met in his hand and he dropped it. He grovelled blindly, found the weapon again, slashed out, felt the blade strike home. The cat screeched, writhing on the snow. He forced himself to push his streaming knee into the creature's back, pinning the animal while the knife flailed down, biting into its mad life; until the thing with a final convulsion burst free, fled limping and splashing blood, died maybe somewhere off in the trees. Then there was the time of blackness, the hideous crawl back to the signal station; and now he lay dying too, unable to reach the semaphore, knowing that finally he had failed. He wheezed hopelessly, settled back farther into the crowding dark.

In the blackness were sounds. Homely sounds. A regular *scrape-clink, scrape-clink;* the morning noise of a rake being drawn across the bars of a grate. Rafe tossed muttering, relaxed in the spreading warmth. There was light now, orange and flickering; he kept his eyes closed, seeing the glow of it against the insides of the lids. Soon his mother would call. It would be time to get up and go to school, or out into the fields.

A tinkling, pleasantly musical, made him turn his head.

His body still ached, right down the length of it, but somehow the pain was not quite so intense. He blinked. He'd expected to see his old room in the cottage at Avebury; the curtains stirring in the breeze perhaps, sunshine coming through open windows. It took him a moment to readjust to the signal hut; then memory came back with a rush. He stared; he saw the gantry under the semaphore handles, the rods reaching out through the roof; the whiteness of their grommets, pipe-clayed by himself the day before. The tarpaulin squares had been hooked across the windows, shutting out the night. The door was barred, both lamps were burning; the stove was alight, its doors open and spreading warmth. Above it, pots and pans simmered; and bending over them was a girl.

She turned when he moved his head and he looked into deep eyes, black-fringed, with a quick nervousness about them that was somehow like an animal. Her long hair was restrained from falling round her face by a band or ribbon drawn behind the little pointed ears; she wore a rustling dress of an odd light blue, and she was brown. Brown as a nut, though God knew there had been no sun for weeks to tan her skin like that. Rafe recoiled when she looked at him, and something deep in him twisted and needed to scream. He knew she shouldn't be here in this wilderness, amber-skinned and with her strange summery dress; that she was one of the Old Ones, the half-believed, the Haunters of the Heath, the possessors of men's souls if Mother Church spoke truth. His lips tried to form the word "Fairy" and could not. Blood-smeared, they barely moved.

His vision was failing again. She walked toward him lightly, swaying, seeming to his dazed mind to shimmer like a flame; some unnatural flame that a breath might extinguish. But there was nothing ethereal about her touch. Her hands were firm and hard; they wiped his mouth, stroked his hot face. Coolness remained after she had gone away and he realized she had laid a damp cloth across his forehead. He tried to cry out to her again; she turned to smile at him, or he thought she smiled, and he realized she was singing. There were no words; the sound made itself in her throat, goldenly, like the song a spinning wheel might hum in the ears of a sleepy child, the words always nearly there ready to well up through the surface of the colour and never coming. He wanted badly to talk now, tell her about the cat and his fear of it and its paws full of glass, but it seemed she knew already the things that were in his mind. When she came back it was with a steaming pan of water that she set on a chair beside the bunk. She stopped the humming, or the singing, then and spoke to him; but the words made no sense, they banged and splattered like water falling over rocks. He was afraid again, for that was the talk of the Old Ones; but the defect must have been in his ears because the syllables changed of themselves into the Modern English of the Guild. They were sweet and rushing, filled with a meaning that was not a meaning, hinting at deeper things beneath themselves that his tired mind couldn't grasp. They talked about the Fate that had waited for him in the wood, fallen on him so suddenly from the tree. *"The Norns spin the Fate of a man or of a cat,"* sang the voice. *"Sitting beneath Yggdrasil, great World Ash, they work; one Sister to make the yarn, the next to measure, the third to cut it at its end. . . ."* and all the time the hands were busy, touching and soothing.

Rafe knew the girl was mad, or possessed. She spoke of Old things, the things banished by Mother Church, pushed out forever into the dark and cold. With a great effort he lifted his hand, held it before her to make the sign of the Cross; but she gripped the wrist, giggling, and forced it down, started to work delicately on the ragged

palm, cleaning the blood from round the bases of the fingers.
She unfastened the belt across his stomach, eased the trews
apart; cutting the leather, soaking it, pulling it away in
little twitches from the deep tears in groin and thighs.
"Ah . . . ," he said, "ah . . ." She stopped at that, frowning,
brought something from the stove, lifted his head gently
to let him drink. The liquid soothed, seeming to run from
his throat down into body and limbs like a trickling an-
aesthesia. He relapsed into a warmness shot through with
little coloured stabs of pain, heard her crooning again as
she dressed his legs. Slid deeper, into sleep.

Day came slowly, faded slower into night that turned
to day again, and darkness. He seemed to be apart from
Time, lying dozing and waking, feeling the comfort of
bandages on his body and fresh linen tucked round him,
seeing the handles of the semaphores gleam a hundred
miles away, wanting to go to them, not able to move.
Sometimes he thought when the girl came to him he pulled
her close, pressed his face into the mother-warmth of her
thighs while she stroked his hair, and talked, and sang.
All the time it seemed, through the sleeping and the waking,
the voice went on. Sometimes he knew he heard it with
his ears, sometimes in fever dreams the words rang in his
mind. They made a mighty saga; such a story as had
never been told, never imagined in all the lives of men.

It was the tale of Earth; Earth and a land, the place
her folk called Angle-Land. Only once there had been no
Angle-Land because there had been no planets, no sun.
Nothing had existed but Time; Time, and a void. Only
Time was the void, and the void was Time itself. Through
it moved colours, twinklings, sudden shafts of light. There
were hummings, shoutings perhaps, musical tones like the
notes of organs that thrummed in his body until it shook
with them and became a melting part. Sometimes in the
dream he wanted to cry out; but still he couldn't speak,

and the beautiful blasphemy ground on. He saw the brown mists lift back waving and whispering, and through them the shine of water; a harsh sea, cold and limitless, ocean of a new world. But the dream itself was fluid; the images shone and altered, melding each smoothly into each, yielding place majestically, fading into dark. The hills came, rolling, tentative, squirming, pushing up dripping flanks that shuddered, sank back, returned to silt. The silt, the sea bed, enriched itself with a million year snowstorm of little dying creatures. The piping of the tiny snails as they fell was a part of the chorus and the song, a thin, sweet harmonic.

And already there were Gods; the Old Gods, powerful and vast, looking down, watching, stirring with their fingers at the silt, waving the swirling brownness back across the sea. It was all done in a dim light, the cold glow of dawn. The hills shuddered, drew back, thrust up again like golden, humped animals, shaking the water from their sides. The sun stood over them, warming, adding steam to the fogs, making multiple and shimmering reflections dance from the sea. The Gods laughed; and over and again, uncertainly, unsurely, springing from the silt, sinking back to silt again, the hills writhed, shaping the shapeless land. The voice sang, whirring like a wheel; there was no "forward," no "back"; only a sense of continuity, of massive development, of the huge Everness of Time. The hills fell and rose; leaves brushed away the sun, their reflections waved in water, the trees themselves sank, rolled and heaved, were thrust down to rise once more dripping, grow afresh. The rocks formed, broke, re-formed, became solid, melted again until from the formlessness somehow the land was made; Angle-Land, nameless still, with its long pastures, its fields, and silent hills of grass. Rafe saw the endless herds of animals that crossed it, wheeling under the wheeling sun; and the first shadowy Men. Rage possessed them; they

hacked and hewed, rearing their stone circles in the wind
and emptiness, finding again the bodies of the Gods in
the chalky flanks of downs. Until all ended, the Gods
grew tired; and the ice came flailing and crying from the
north, the sun sank dying in its blood and there was coldness
and blackness and nothingness and winter.

Into the void, He came; only He was not the Christos,
the God of Mother Church. He was Balder, Balder the
Lovely, Balder the Young. He strode across the land, face
burning bright as the sun, and the Old Ones grovelled
and adored. The wind touched the stone circles, burning
them with frost; in the darkness men cried for spring. So
he came to the Tree Yggdrasil—*What Tree*, Rafe's mind
cried despairingly, and the voice checked and laughed
and said without anger *"Yggdrasil, great World Ash, whose
branches pierce the layers of heaven, whose roots wind
through all Hells. . . ."* Balder came to the Tree, on which
he must die for the sins of Gods and Men; and to the
Tree they nailed him, hung him by the palms. And there
they came to adore while His blood ran and trickled and
gouted bright, while he hung above the Hells of the Trolls
and of the Giants of Frost and Fire and Mountain, below
the Seven Heavens where Tiw and Thunor and old Wo-Tan
trembled in Valhalla at the mightiness of what was done.

And from His blood sprang warmth again and grass and
sunlight, the meadow flowers and the calling, mating birds.
And the Church came at last, stamping and jingling, out
of the east, lifting the brass wedding cakes of her altars
while men fought and roiled and made the ground black
with their blood, while they raised their cities and their
signal towers and their glaring castles. The Old Ones moved
back, the Fairies, the Haunters of the Heath, the People
of the Stones, taking with them their lovely bleeding Lord;
and the priests called despairingly to Him, calling Him
the Christos, saying he did die on a tree, at the Place

Golgotha, the Place of the Skull. Rome's navies sailed the
world; and England woke up, steam jetted in every tiny
hamlet, and clattering and noise; while Balder's blood, still
raining down, made afresh each spring. And so after days
in the telling, after weeks, the huge legend paused, and
turned in on itself, and ended.

The stove was out, the hut smelled fresh and cool. Rafe
lay quiet, knowing he had been very ill. The cabin was
a place of browns and clean bright blues. Deep brown
of woodwork, orange brown of the control handles, creamy
brown of planking. The blue came from the sky, shafting
in through windows and door, reflecting from the long-dead
semaphore in pale spindles of light. And the girl herself
was brown and blue; brown of skin, frosted blue of ribbon
and dress. She leaned over him smiling, all nervousness
gone. *"Better,"* sang the voice. *"You're better now. You're
well."*

He sat up. He was very weak. She eased the blankets
aside, letting the air tingle like cool water on his skin.
He swung his legs down over the edge of the bunk and
she helped him stand. He sagged, laughed, stood again
swaying, feeling the texture of the hut floor under his feet,
looking down at his body, seeing the pink crisscrossing of
scars on stomach and thighs, the jaunty penis thrusting
from its nest of hair. She found him a tunic, helped him
into it laughing at him, twitching and pulling. She fetched
him a cloak, fastened it round his neck, knelt to push
sandals on his feet. He leaned against the bunk panting
a little, feeling stronger. His eye caught the semaphore;
she shook her head and teased him, urging him toward
the door. *"Come,"* said the voice. *"Just for a little while."*

She knelt again outside, touched the snow while the wind
blustered wetly from the west. Round about, the warming
hills were brilliant and still. *"Balder is dead,"* she sang.

"Balder is dead. . . ." And instantly it seemed Rafe could
hear the million chuckling voices of the thaw, see the
very flowers pushing coloured points against the translu-
cency of snow. He looked up at the signals on the tower.
They seemed strange to him now, like the winter a thing of
the past. Surely they too would melt and run, and leave no
trace. They were part of the old life and the old way;
for the first time he could turn his back on them without
distress. The girl moved from him, low shoes showing
her ankles against the snow; and Rafe followed, hesitant
at first then more surely, gaining strength with every step.
Behind him, the signal hut stood forlorn.

The two horsemen moved steadily, letting their mounts
pick their way. The younger rode a few paces ahead, muffled in his cloak, eyes beneath the brim of his hat watching
the horizon. His companion sat his horse quietly, with an
easy slouch; he was grizzled and brown-faced, skin tanned
by the wind. In front of him, over the pommel of the
saddle, was hooked the case of a pair of Zeiss binoculars.
On the other side was the holster of a musket; the barrel
lay along the neck of the horse, the butt thrust into the air
just below the rider's hand.

Away on the left a little knoll of land lifted its crown
of trees into the sky. Ahead, in the swooping bowl of the
valley, was the black speck of a signal hut, its tower showing
thinly above it. The officer reined in quietly, took the glasses
from their case and studied the place. Nothing moved,
and no smoke came from the chimney. Through the lenses
the shuttered windows stared back at him; he saw the
black vee of the Semaphore arms folded down like the
wings of a dead bird. The Corporal waited impatiently,
his horse fretting and blowing steam, but the Captain of
Signals was not to be hurried. He lowered the glasses
finally, and clicked to his mount. The animal moved forward

again at a walk, picking its hooves up and setting them
down with care.

The snow here was thicker; the valley had trapped it,
and the day's thaw had left the drifts filmed with a
brittle skin of ice. The horses floundered as they climbed
the slope to the hut. At its door the Captain dismounted,
leaving the reins hanging slack. He walked forward, eyes
on the lintel and the boards.

The mark. It was everywhere, over the door, on its frame,
stamped along the walls. The circle, with the crab pattern
inside it; rebus or pictograph, the only thing the People of
the Heath knew, the only message it seemed they had for
men. The Captain had seen it before, many times; it had
no power left to surprise him. The Corporal had not. The
older man heard the sharp intake of breath, the click as
a pistol was cocked; saw the quick, instinctive movement
of the hand, the gesture that wards off the Evil Eye. He
smiled faintly, almost absentmindedly, and pushed at the
door. He knew what he would find, and that there was
no danger.

The inside of the hut was cool and dark. The Guildsman
looked round slowly, hands at his sides, feet apart on the
boards. Outside a horse champed, jangling its bitt, and
snorted into the cold. He saw the glasses on their hook, the
swept floor, the polished stove, the fire laid neat and ready
on the bars; everywhere, the Fairy mark danced across the
wood.

He walked forward and looked down at the thing on
the bunk. The blood it had shed had blackened with the
frost; the wounds on its stomach showed like leaf-shaped
mouths, the eyes were sunken now and dull; one hand
was still extended to the signal levers eight feet above.

Behind him the Corporal spoke harshly, using anger as
a bulwark against fear. "The . . . People that were here.
They done this. . . ."

The Captain shook his head. "No," he said slowly, "'Twas a wildcat."

The Corporal said thickly, "They were here though. . . ." The anger surged again as he remembered the unmarked snow. "There weren't no tracks, sir. *How could they come?* . . ."

"How comes the wind?" asked the Captain, half to himself. He looked down again at the corpse in the bunk. He knew a little of the history of this boy, and of his record. The Guild had lost a good man.

How did they come? The People of the Heath. . . . His mind twitched away from using the names the commoners had for them. What did they look like, when they came? What did they talk of, in locked cabins to dying men? Why did they leave their mark. . . .

It seemed the answers shaped themselves in his brain. It was as if they crystallized from the cold, faintly sweet air of the place, blew in with the soughing of the wind. *All this would pass,* came the thoughts, *and vanish like a dream. No more hands would bleed on the signal bars, no more children freeze in their lonely watchings. The Signals would leap continents and seas, winged as thought. All this would pass, for better or for ill. . . .*

He shook his head, bearlike, as if to free it from the clinging spell of the place. He knew, with a flash of inner sight, that he would know no more. The People of the Heath, the Old Ones; they moved back, with their magic and their lore. Always back, into the yet remaining dark. Until one day they themselves would vanish away. They who were, and yet were not. . . .

He took the pad from his belt, scribbled, tore off the top sheet. "Corporal," he said quietly. "If you please. . . . Route through Golden Cap."

He walked to the door, stood looking out across the hills at the matchstick of the eastern tower just visible

against the sky. In his mind's eye a map unrolled; he saw
the message flashing down the chain, each station picking
it up, routing it, clattering it on its way. Down to Golden
Cap, where the great signals stood gaunt against the cold
crawl of the sea; north up the A line to Aquae Sulis, back
again along the Great West Road. Within the hour it would
reach its destination at Silbury Hill; and a grave-faced man
in green would walk down the village street of Avebury,
knock at a door. . . .

The Corporal climbed to the gantry, clipped the message
in the rack, eased the handles forward lightly testing against
the casing ice. He flexed his shoulders, pulled sharply. The
dead tower woke up, arms clacking in the quiet. *Attention,
Attention.* . . . Then the signal for Origination, the cypher
for the eastern line. The movements dislodged a little cloud
of ice crystals; they fell quietly, sparkling against the greyness of the sky.

Third Measure
THE WHITE BOAT

Becky had always lived in the cottage overlooking the bay.

The bay was black; black because there a seam of rock that was nearly coal burst open to the water and the sea had nibbled in over the years, picking and grinding, breaking up the fossil-ridden shale to a fine dark grit, spreading it over the beach and the humped, tilted headlands. The grass had taken the colour of it and the little houses that stood mean-shouldered glaring at the water; the boats and jetties had taken it, and the brambles and gorse; even the rabbits that thumped across the cliff paths on summer evenings seemed to have something of the same dusky hue. Here the paths tilted, tumbling over to steepen and plunge at the sea; the whole land seemed ready to slide and splash, grumble into the ocean.

It was a summer evening when Becky first saw the White Boat. She'd been sent, in the little skiff that was all her father owned, to clear the day's crop from the lobster pots strung out along the shore. She worked methodically, sculling along the bobbing line of buoys; the baskets in the bottom of the boat were full and bustling, the great crustaceans black and slate-grey as the cliffs, snapping and wriggling, waving wobbling, angry claws. Becky regarded them thoughtfully. A good catch; the family would feed well in the week to come.

She pulled up the last pot, feeling the drag and surge of it against the slow-flowing tide. It was empty, save for the grey-white rags of bait. She dropped the tarred basket back over the side, leaned to see the ghost-shape of it vanish in

the cloudy green beneath the keel. Sat feeling the little
aches spread in shoulders and arms, narrowing her eyes
against the evening haze of sunlight. Saw the Boat.

Only she didn't know then that White Boat was her name.

She was coming in fast and quiet, bow parting the sea,
raising a bright ridge of foam. Mainsail down and furled,
tall jib filling in the slight breeze. The calling of the crew
came clear and faint across the water. Instinct made the
girl scurry from her, pushing at the oars, scudding the little
shell back to the shelter of the land. She grounded on the
Ledges, the natural moles of stone that reached out into
the sea, skipped ashore all torn frock and long brown legs,
wetted herself to the middle in her haste to drag the boat
up and tie off.

Strange boats seldom came into the bay. Fishing boats
were common enough, the stubby-bowed, round-bilged craft
of the coast; this boat was different. Becky watched back
at her cautiously, riding at anchor now in the ruffled pale
shield of the sea. She was slim and long, flush-decked, a
racer; her tall mast with the spreading outriggers rolled
slowly, a pencil against the greying sky. As she watched, a
dinghy was launched; she saw a man climb down to rig the
outboard. She scrambled farther up the cliff, lugging the
heavy basket with the catch; crouched wild as a rabbit in a
stand of gorse, staring down with huge brown eyes. She saw
lights come on in the cabin of the yacht; they reflected in
the water in wobbling yellow spears. The afterglow flared
and faded as she lay.

This was a wild, mournful place. An eternal brooding
seemed to hang over the bulging cliffs; a brooding, and
worse. An enigma, a shadow of old sin. For here once a
great mad priest had come, and called the waves and wind
and water to witness his craziness. Becky had heard the tale
often enough at her mother's knee; how he had taken a boat,
and ridden out to his death; and how the village had

hummed with soldiers and priests come to exorcise and complain and quiz the locals for their part in armed rebellion. They'd got little satisfaction; and the place had quietened by degrees, as the gales went and came, as the boats were hauled out and tarred and launched again. The waves were indifferent, and the wind; and the rocks neither knew nor cared who owned them, Christ's Vicar or an English King.

Becky was late home that evening; her father grumbled and swore, threatening her with beating, accusing her of outlandish crimes. She loved to sit out on the Ledges, none knew that better than he; sit and touch the fossils that showed like coiled springs in the rock, feel the breeze and watch the lap and splash of water and lose the sense of time. And that with babies to be fed and meals to stew and a house to clean, and him with an ailing, coughing wife. The girl was useless, idle to her bones. Giving herself airs and graces, lazing her time away; fine for the rich folk in Londinium maybe, but he had a living to earn.

Becky was not beaten. Neither did she speak of the Boat.

She lay awake that night, tired but unable to sleep, hearing her mother cough, watching between the drawn blinds the thin turquoise wedge of night sky; she saw it pale with the dawn, a single planet burn like a spark before being swallowed by the rising sun. From the house could be heard a faint susurration, soft nearly as the sound the blood makes in the ears. A slow, miles-long heave and roll, a breathing; the dim, immemorial noise of the sea.

If the Boat stayed in the bay, no sound came from her; and in the morning she was gone. Becky walked to the sea late in the day, trod barefoot among the tumbled blocks of stone that lined the foreshore, smelling the old harsh smell of salt, hearing the water slap and chuckle while from high above came the endless sinister trickling of the cliffs. Into her consciousness stole, maybe for the first time, the sense of loneliness; an oppression born of the gentle miles of summer water, the tall blackness of the headlands, the fingers of the stone ledges pushing out into the sea. She saw, not for the first time, how the Ledges curved, in obedience it seemed to some cosmic plan, became ridges of stone that climbed the dark beach, curled away through the dipping strata of the cliffs. Full of the signs and ghosts of other life, the ammonites she collected as a child, till Father Antony had scolded and warned, told her once and for all time if God created the rocks in seven days then He created those markings too. She was close to heresy, the things were best forgotten. She brooded, scrinching her toes in the water, feeling the sharp grit move and squeeze. She was fourteen, slight and dark, breasts beginning to push at her dress.

It was months before she saw the Boat again. A winter had come and gone, noisy and grey; the wind plucked at the cliffs, yanking out the amber teeth of stone, sending them crashing and bumbling to the beach. Becky walked the bay in the short, glaring days, scrounging for driftwood, planks, broken pieces of boats, sea coal to burn. Now and again she would watch the water, thin brown face and brilliant eyes staring, searching for something she couldn't understand out over the waste of sea. With the spring, the White Boat returned.

It was an April evening, nearly May. Something made Becky linger over her work, hauling in the great black pots, scooping the clicking life into the baskets she kept prepared. While White Boat came sidling in from the dusk, driven by a puttering engine, growing from the vastness of the water.

"*Boat ahoy . . .*"

Becky stood in the coracle and stared. Behind her the headland cliffs, heaving slowly with the movement of the sea; in front of her the Boat, tall now and menacing with closeness, white prow cutting the water, raising a thin vee of

foam that chuckled away to lose itself in the dusk. She
was aware, nearly painfully, of the boards beneath her feet,
the flapping of the soiled dress round her knees. The Boat
edged forward, ragged silhouette of a man in her bows
clinging one-handed to the forestay while he waved and
called.

"*Boat ahoy* . . ."

Becky saw the mainsail stowed and neat-wrapped on its
boom, the complication of cabin coamings and hatches and
rigging; up close she was nearly surprised to see the paint
of White Boat could have weathered, the long jibsheets
frayed. As if the Boat had been nothing but a vision or a
dream, lacking weight and substance.

The coracle ground, dipping, against the hull; Becky
lurched, caught at the high deck. Hands gripped and steadied; the great steel mast rolled above her, daunting, as
White Boat drifted slow, moved in by the tide.

"Easy there . . ." Then, "What're ye selling, little girl?"

From somewhere, a ripple of laughter. Becky swallowed,
staring up. Men crowded the rail, dark shapes against the
evening light.

"Lobsters, sir. Fine lobsters. . . ."

Her father would be pleased. What, sell fish afore landing
'em, and the price good too? No haggling with Master
Smythe up in the village, no waiting for the hauliers to fetch
the stuff away. They paid her well, dropping real gold coins
into the boat, laughing as she dived and scrabbled for them;
swung her clear laughing again, called to her as she sculled
back into the bay. She carried with her a memory of their
voices, wild and rough and keen. Never it seemed had the
land loomed so fast, the coracle been easier to beach. She
scuttled for home, carrying what was left of her catch,
money clutched hot in her hand; turned as White Boat
turned below her in the dusk, heard the splash and rattle
as her anchor dropped down to catch the bottom of the

sea. There were lights aboard already, sharp pinpoints that gleamed like a cluster of eyes; above them the rigging of the boat was dark, a filigree against the silver-grey crawling of the water.

Her father swore at her for selling the catch. She stared back wide-eyed.

"The Bermudan. . . ." He spat, hulking across the kitchen to slam dirty plates down in the sink, crank angrily at the handle of the tall old pump. "You keep away from 'en. . . ."

"But, F—"

He turned back, dark-faced with rage. "Keep *away* from 'en. . . . Doan't want no more tellin'. . . ."

Already her face had the ability to freeze, turn into the likeness of a dark, sculpted cat. She veiled her eyes, watching down at her plate. Heard above in the bedroom her mother's racking cough. There would be spatters of pink on the sheets come morning, that she knew. She tucked one foot behind the other, stroking with her toes the contour of a grimy shin, and thought carefully of nothing at all.

The exchange, inconclusive as it was, served over the weeks to rivet Becky's attention; the strange yacht began to obsess her. She saw White Boat in dreams; in her fantasies she seemed to fly, riffling through the wind like the great gulls that haunted the beach and headlands. In the mornings the cliffs resounded with their noise; in Becky's ears, still ringing with sleep, the bird shouts echoed like the creaking of ropes, the ratchet-clatter of sheet winches. Sometimes then the headlands would seem to sway gently and roll like the sea, dizzying. Becky would squat and rub her arms and shiver, wait for the spells to pass and worry about death; till queer rhythms and passions reached culmination, she stepped on a knifeblade, upturned in the boat, and slicing shock and redness turned her instantly into a woman. She cleaned herself, whimpering. Nobody saw; the secret she hugged to herself, to her thin body, as she hugged all secrets. Thoughts, and dreams.

There was a wedding once, in the little black village, in the little black church. At that time Becky became aware, obscurely, that the people too had taken the colour of the place; an airborne, invisible smut had changed them all. The fantasies took new and more sinister shapes; once she dreamed she saw the villagers, her parents, all the people she knew, melt chaotically into the landscape till the cliffs were bodies and bones and old beseeching hands, teeth, and eyes and crumbling ancient foreheads. Sometimes now she was afraid of the bay; but always it drew her with its own magnetism. She could not be said to think, sitting there alone and brooding; she felt, vividly, things not readily understandable.

She cut her black hair, sitting puzzled in front of a cracked and spotted mirror, turning her head, snipping and shortening till she looked nearly like a boy, one of the wild fisher-boys of the coast. Stroked and teased the result while the liquid huge eyes watched back uncertainly from the glass. She seemed to sense round her a trap, its bars thick and black as the bars of the lobster pots she used. Her world was landlocked, encompassed by the headlands of the bay, by the voice of the priest, and her father's tread. Only White Boat was free; and free she would come, gliding and shimmering in her head, unsettling. In the critical events of adolescence, after the fright her pride in the shedding of her blood, the Boat seemed to have taken a part. Almost as if from under the bright mysterious horizon she had seen and could somehow understand.

Becky kept her tryst with the yacht, time and again, watching from the tangles of bramble above the bay.

The sea itself drew her now. Nights or early iron-grey mornings she would slide her frock over her head among the piled slabs of rock; ease into the burning ice of the

water, lie and let the waves lift her and move and slap.
At such times it seemed the bay came in on her with an
agoraphobic crowding, the rolling heights of headlands grey
under the vast spaces of air; it was as if her nakedness
brought her somehow in power of the place, as if it could
then tumble round her quickly, trap and enfold. She would
scuttle from the water, thresh into her dress; the awkward-
ness of her damp body under the cloth was a huge comfort,
the cliffs receded and gained their proper aloofness and
perspective. Were once more safe.

As a by-product, she was learning to swim.

That in itself was a mystery; she felt instinctively her
father and the Church would not approve. She avoided
Father Antony; but the eyes of icons and the great Christos
over the altar would still single her out in services and
watch and accuse. By swimming she gave her body, obscurely, to assault; entered into a mystic relationship with
White Boat, who also swam. She needed fulfillment, the
shadowy fulfillment of the sea. She experienced a curious
confusion, a sense of sin too formless to be categorized and
as such more terrifying and in its turn alluring. The confes-
sional was closed to her; she walked alone, carefully, in a
world of shadows and brittle glass. She avoided now the
touches, the pressures, the accidental gratifications of her
body that came nearly naturally with walking and moving
and working. She wished in an unformed way to proscribe
at least a vague area of evil, reduce the menace she herself
had sought and that now in its turn sought her.

The idea came it seemed of its own, unlooked for and
unwanted. Slowly there grew in her, watching the yacht
swing at her mooring out in the darkening mystery of the
water, the knowledge that White Boat alone might save her
from herself. Only the Boat could fly, out from the twin iron
headlands to a broader world. Where did she come from?

To where did she vanish so mysteriously, from where did she return?

The priest spoke words over her mother's grave, God looked down from the sky; but Becky knew the earth had taken her to squeeze and squeeze, make her into more black shale.

The Boat came back.

She was frightened now and unsure. Before, with the less cluttered faith of childhood, she had not questioned. The Boat had gone away, the Boat would return. Now she knew that all things change and Change is forever. One day the Boat would go and not come back.

She had passed from knowledge of evil to indifference; for this she felt herself already damned.

The thing she had rehearsed and dreamed of blended so with reality that she lived another dream. She rose silently in the black house, hearing the squabbling cough of a child. Her hands shook as she dressed; in her body was a fast, violent quivering, as if some electric force had control of her and drove her without volition. The sensation, and the mad thumping of her heart, seemed partially to cut her off from earthly contact; shapes of familiar things, chair backs, dresser top, door latch, seemed to her fingertips muffled and vague. She slid the catch back carefully, not breathing, listening and staring in the dark. It was as if she moved now from point to point with an even pace that could not falter or check. She knew she would go to the bay, watch the Boat up-anchor and drift away; her mind, complicated, reserved beneath the image others that would be presented in their turn, in sequence to an unimagined end.

The village was black, lightless, and dead; the air moved raw on her face and arms, a drifting of wet vapour that was nearly rain. The sky above her seemed to press solidly, dark as pitch except where to the east one depthless iron-grey streak showed where in the upper air there was dawn. Against it the tower of the church stood black and remote, held out stiffly its ragged gargoyle ears.

In the centre of the bay a shallow ravine conducted to the beach a rill dribbling from the far-off Luckford Ponds. A plank bridge with a single handrail spanned the brook; the steps that led down to it were slimy with the damp. Once Becky slipped on a rounded stone; once felt beneath her pad the quick recoil of a worm. She crossed the bridge, hearing the chuckle of water; a scramble over wet rock and the bay opened out ahead, barely visible, a dull-grey vastness. On it, floating in a half-seen mirror, the darker grey ghost of the Boat. She crossed the beach, toes sinking in grit, felt awkwardly with her feet among the planes of tumbled stone. The water rose to ankles and calves, half-noticed; before her was a faint calling, the hard *tonk-tonk-tonk* of a winch.

Rain spattered on the dawn wind, wetting her hair. She moved forward, still with the same mindless steadiness. The stone ledge, the mole, sloped slowly, water slapping and creaming where it nosed under the sea. She floundered beside it, waist deep, feet in furry tangles of weed. Soon she was swimming, into the broad cold madness of the water. As the land receded she fell into a rhythm of movement, half hypnotic; it seemed she would follow White Boat, tirelessly, to the far end of the world. The aches increasing in shoulders and arms were unnoticed, unimportant. Ahead, between the slapping dark troughs of waves, the shadow of the boat had altered, foreshortening as she turned to face the sea. Grown above the hull a taller shade that was the raising of the gently flapping jib.

To Becky it seemed an accident that she was here, and that the sea was deep and the cliffs tall and the Boat too far off to reach. She nuzzled at the water, drowsily; but the first bayonet stab in her lungs started something that was nearly an orgasm, she shouted and retched and kicked. Felt coldness close instantly over her head, screamed and fought for air.

And there were voices ahead, a confusion of sounds and orders; the shape of the Boat changing again as she turned back into the wind.

There were hands on her shoulders and arms; something grabbed in her dress, the fabric tore, she went under again gulping at the sea. She wallowed, centred in a confusion of grey and black, white of foam, glaring red. Was hauled out thrashing, landed on a sloping deck, lay feeling beneath her opened mouth the smoothness of wood. The voices surged round her, seeming like the lap and splash of the sea to retreat and advance.

"That one . . ."

"Bloody fisher-girl . . ."

The words roared quite unnecessarily in her ear, receded in their turn. She stayed still, panting; water ran from her; she sensed, six feet beneath, the grey sliding of the sea. She lay quiet, numbly, knowing she had done a terrible thing.

They fetched her a blanket, muffled her in it. She sat up and coughed more water, hearing ropes creak, the slide and slap of waves. Her mind seemed still dissociated from her body, a cool grey thing that had watched the other Becky spit and drown. She was aware vaguely of questions; she clutched the rough cloth across her throat and shook her head, angry now with herself and the people round her. The movement started a spinning sickness; she was aware of being lifted, caught a last glimpse of the black land-streak miles off as the boat heeled to the wind. One foot caught the side of the hatch as they lowered her; the pain jarred to her brain, ebbed. She was aware of a maze of images, disconnected; white planking above her head, hands working at the blanket and her dress. She frowned and mumbled, trying to collect her thoughts; but the impressions faded, one by one, into greyness and silence.

She lay quiet, cocooned in blankets, unwilling to open her eyes. Soon she would have to move, go down and rake the stove to life, set the pots of gruel simmering and bubbling for breakfast. The house rolled faintly and incongruously, shivering like a live thing; across beneath the eaves ran the chuckling slap of water. The dream-image persisted, stubbornly refusing to fade. She moved her head on the pillow, rubbing and grumbling, fought a hand free to touch hair still sticky with salt. The fingers moved back down, discovering nakedness. That in itself was a sin, to tumble into bed unclothed. She grunted and snuggled, defeating the dream with sleep.

The water made a thousand noises in the cabin. Rippling and laughing, strumming, smacking against the side of White Boat. Becky's eyes popped open again, in sudden alarm. With waking came remembrance, and a clawing panic. She shot upright; her head thumped against the decking two feet above. She rubbed dazedly, seeing the sun reflections play across the low roof, the bursts and tinkles and momentary skeins of light. The cabin was in subtle motion, leaning; she saw a bright yellow oilskin sway gently, at an angle from the upright on which it hung. Perspectives seemed wrong; she was pressed against a six-inch wooden board that served to stop her rolling from the bunk.

The boy was watching her, holding easily to a stanchion. The eyes above the tangle of beard were bright and keen, and he was laughing. "Get your things on," he said. "Skipper wants to see you. Come up on deck. You all right now?"

She stared at him wild-eyed.

"You'll be all right," he said. "Just get dressed. It'll be all right."

She knew then the dream or nightmare was true.

Tiny things confused her. The latches that held the bunk board, she had to grope and push and still they wouldn't come undone. She swung her legs experimentally. Air rushed at her body; she scrabbled at the blankets, came out with a thump, took a fall, lost the blankets again. There were clothes left for her, jeans and an old sweater. She grabbed for them, panting. Her fingers refused to obey her, slipping and trembling; it seemed an age before she could force her legs into the trews.

The companionway twitched aside to land her among pots and pans. She clung to the steps, countering the great lean of the boat, pulled herself up to be dazed by sunlight.

And there was no land. Just a smudge, impossibly far off across the racing green of the sea. She winced, screwing her eyes; the boy who had spoken to her helped her again.

The skipper sat immobile, carved it seemed from butter-cup-yellow oilskin, thin face and grey eyes watching past her along the deck of the Boat. Above him was the huge steady curving of the sails; behind the crew, clinging in the stern, watching her bold-eyed. She saw bearded mouths grinning, dropped her eyes, twisted her fingers in her lap.

Before these people she was nearly dumb. She sat still, watching her fingers twine and move, conscious of the near-ness of the water, the huge speed of the boat. The con-versation was unsatisfactory, Skipper watching down at the compass, one arm curled easy along the tiller, listening it seemed with only the smallest part of his mind. The faces grinned, sea-lit and uncaring. She had jammed herself into their lives; they should have hated her for it but they were laughing. She wanted to be dead.

She was crying.

Somebody had an arm round her shoulders. She noticed she was shivering; they fetched an oilskin, wrestled her into it. She felt the hard collar scumble her hair, scratch at her ears. She must go with them, they couldn't turn back; that much she understood. That was what she had wanted most, a lifetime ago. Now she wanted her father's kitchen, her own room again. Shipbound, caught in their tightly male and ordered world, she was useless. Their indifference brought the welling angry tears; their kindness stung. She tried to help, in the little galley, but even the meals they made were strange; there were complications, nuances, relishes she had never seen. White Boat defeated her.

She crawled forward, away from the rest, clung to the root of the mast with one arm round the metal hearing the tall halliards slap and bang, seeing the bows fall and rise and punch at the sea. Diamond-hard spray blew back; her feet, bare on the deck, chilled almost at once. The cold reached through the oilskin; soon she was shivering as each cloud shadow eclipsed the boat, darkened the milk green of the sea. The dream was gone, blown away by the wind; White Boat was a hard thing, brutal and huge, smashing at the water. She could work her father's little cockleshell through the tides and currents of the coast; here she was awkward and in the way. A dozen times she moved desperately as the crew ran to handle the complication of ropes. The calls reached her dimly, *stand by to go about, let the sheets fly;* then the thundering of the jib, scuffle of feet on planking as White Boat surged onto each new tack. Changed the angle of her decking and the flying sun and cloud shadows, the stinging attack of the spray. The horizon became a new hill, slanting away and up; Becky looked into racing water where before she had seen the sky.

They sent her food but she refused it, setting her mouth. She was sulking; and worse, she felt ill. She needed cottage and bay now with a new urgency, an almost ecstatic longing for solidness, for things that didn't roll and move. But these things were lost for all time; there was only the hurtling green of the water, fading now to deeper and deeper grey

as the clouds grew up across the sun, the endless slap and
tinkle of ropes, the misery at the churning pit of her stomach.

They offered her the helm, in the late afternoon. She
refused. White Boat had been a dream; reality was killing it.

There was a little sea toilet, in a place too low to stand.
She closed the lid and pumped, saw the contents flash past
through the curving glass tube. The sea opened her stomach, brought up first food then chyme then glistening trans-
parent sticky stuff that bearded her chin. She wiped and
spat and worked the pump and sicked over again till the
sides of her chest were a dull pain and her head throbbed
in time it seemed with the thumping of the waves. The
voices through the bulkhead door she remembered later, in
fragments, like the recalled pieces of a dream.

"Then we'll do that, Skipper. Hitch a few pounds of chain
to her feet, and gently over the side. . . ."

The voice she knew. That was the boy who had helped
her. The angry rising inflection she didn't know; that was
the voice of Wales.

Something unheard.

"How can she talk, man, what does she bloody know? Just
a bloody dumb kid, see. . . ."

"Make up the log," said the skipper bitterly.

"Don't you see, man?"

"Make up the log. . . ."

Becky leaned her head on her arms and groaned.

She couldn't reach the bunk. She arced her body awkwardly, tried again. The blankets were delicious heaven.
She huddled into them, too empty to worry about the
afterscent of vomit on her clothes. Fell into a sleep shot
through with vivid dreams; the face of the Christos, Father
Antony like an old dried animal, mouth champing as he
scolded and blessed; the church tower in the pre-dawn glow,

the gargoyle ears. Then flowers dusty in a cottage garden, her mum bawling and grumbling before she died, icy feel of water round her groin, shape of White Boat fading into mist. All faint things and worries and griefs, scuttling lobsters, tar and pebbles, feel of the night sea wind, the Great Catechism torn and snatched. She moved finally into a deeper dream where it seemed the Boat herself talked to her. Her voice was rushing and immense yet chuckling and lisping and somehow coloured, blue and roaring green. She spoke about the little people on her back and her duties, her rushing and scurrying and fighting with the wind; she told great truths that were lost as soon as uttered, blown away and buried in the dark. Becky clenched her fists, writhing; woke to hear still the bang and slap of the sea, slept again.

She came round to someone gently shaking her shoulder. Again she was disoriented. The motion of the boat was stopped; lamps burned in the cabin; through the port other lights gleamed, made rippling reflections that reached to within inches of the glass. From outside came a sound she knew; the fast rap and flutter of halliards against masts, night noise of a harbour of boats. She swung her legs down blearily; rubbed her face, not knowing where she was. Not daring to ask.

A meal was laid in the cabin, great kedgerees of rice and shellfish pieces, mushrooms and eggs. Surprisingly, she was hungry; she sat shoulder to shoulder with the boy who had spoken for her, had she realized argued for her life in the bright afternoon. She ate mechanically and quickly, eyes not leaving her plate; round her the talk flowed, unheeding. She crouched small, glad to be forgotten.

They took her with them when they went ashore. In the dinghy she felt more at ease. They sat in a waterfront bar, in France, drank bottle on bottle of wine till her head spun again and voices and noise seemed blended in a warm roaring. She snuggled, on the Welshman's knees, feeling safe again and wanted. She tried to talk then, about the fossils in the rocks and her father and the Church and swimming and nearly being drowned; they scumbled her hair, laughing, not understanding. The wine ran down her neck inside the sweater; she laughed back and watched the lamps spin, head drooping, lids half closed on dark-lashed brown eyes.

"*Ahoy White Boat. . . .*"

She stood shivering, seeing the lamps drive spindled images into the water, hearing men reel along the quay, hearing the shouts, feeling still the tingling surprise of foreignness. While White Boat answered faint from the mass of vessels, the tender crept splashing out of the night.

She was still barefooted; she felt the water tart against her ankles as she scuttled down to catch the dinghy's bow.

"Here," said David. "Not puttin' you to bed twice in a bloody day. . . ."

She felt her head hit the rolled blankets that served as a pillow; muttered and grinned, pushed blearily at the waistband of her jeans, gave up, collapsed in sleep.

The miles of water slid past, chuckling in a dream.

She woke quickly to darkness, knowing once more she'd been fooled. They had slipped out of harbour, in the night; that heave and roll, chuckling and bowstring sense of tightness, was the feel of the open sea.

White Boat, and these people, never slept.

There were voices again. And lights gleaming, rattle of descending sails, scrape of something rolling against the hull. Scufflings then, and thuds. She lay curled in the bunk, face turned away from the cabin.

"No, she's asleep. . . ."

"Easy with that now, man. . . ."

She chuckled, silently. The clink of bottles, thump of secret bales, amused her. There was nothing more to fear; these people were smugglers.

She woke heavy and irritable. The source of irritation was
for a time mysterious. She attempted, unwillingly, to analyse
her feelings; for her, an unusual exercise. The wildest, most
romantic notions of White Boat were true; yet she was
cheated. This she knew instinctively. She saw the village
street then, the little black clustering houses, the church.
The priest mouthing silently, condemning; her father, black-
faced, slowly unfastening his broad buckled belt. To this
she would return, irrevocably; the dream was finished.

That was it; the point of pain, the taste and very essence
of it. That she didn't belong, aboard White Boat. She never
would. Abruptly she found herself hating her crew for the
knowledge they had given so freely. They should have
beaten her, loved her till she bled, tied her feet, slammed
her into the deep green sea. They had done nothing because
to them she was worth nothing. Not even death.

She refused food, for the second time. She thought the
skipper looked at her with worried eyes. She ignored him;
she took up her old position, gripping the friendly thickness
of the mast. The day was sunny and bright; the boat moved
fast, under the great spread whiteness of a Genoa, dipping
lee scuppers under, jouncing through the sea. Almost she
wished for the sickness of the day before, the hour when
she'd wanted so urgently to die. As White Boat raised,
slowly, the coast of England.

Her mind seemed split now into halves, one part wanting
the voyage indefinitely prolonged, the other needing to rush
on disaster, have it over and done. The day faded slowly
to dusk, dusk to deep night. In the dark she saw the cressets
of a signal tower, flaring moving pinpoints; and another
answering it, and another far beyond. They would be signalling for her, without a doubt; calling across the moors,
through all the long bays. She curled her lip. She had discovered cynicism.

The wind blew chill across the sea.

Forward of the mast, a hatch gave access to the sail locker. She lowered herself into it, curled atop the big sausage shapes of canvas. The bulkhead door, ajar and creaking, showed shifting gleams of yellow from the cabin lamps. Here the water noise was intensified; she listened sullenly to the chuckle and seethe, half wanting in her bitterness the boat to strike some reef and drown. While the light moved, forward and back across the sloping painted walls. She began picking half unconsciously at the paint, crumbling little brittle flakes in her palm.

The loose boards interested her.

By the lamplight she saw part of the wooden side move slightly, out of time with the upright that supported it. She edged across, pulled experimentally. There was a hatch, behind it a space into which she could reach her arm. She groped tentatively, drew out a slim oilcloth packet. Then another. There were many of them, crowded away in the double hull; little things, not much bigger than the boxes of lucifers she bought sometimes in the village shop.

On impulse she pushed one of them into the waistband of her trews. Scurried the rest out of sight again, closed the trap, sat frowning. Rubbing the little packet, feeling it warm slowly against her flesh, determined for the first time in her life to steal. Wanting some part of White Boat maybe, something to hold at night and remember. Something precious.

Somebody had been very careless.

There was a voice above her, a moving of feet on the deck. She scrambled guiltily, climbed back through the hatch. But they weren't interested in her. Ahead the coastline showed solid, velvet-black; she saw the loom of twin headlands, faintest gleam of waves round long stone moles. Realized with a shock and thrill of coldness that she was home.

She saw other things, heresies that stopped her breath. Machines, uncovered now, whirred and ticked in the cabin.

Bands of light flickered pink, moved against a scale of
figures; she heard the chanting as they edged into the
bay, seven fathoms, five, four. As the devil boat came in,
with nobody at the lead. . . .

The dinghy, swung from its place atop the cabin,
thumped into the sea. She scrambled down, clutching her
parcelled dress. Another bundle was lowered, heavier, chink-
ing musically. For her father, she was told; and to say,
'twas from the Boat. A bribe of silence that, or a double
bluff; confession of a little crime to hide one monstrously
worse. They called to her, low-voiced; she waved mechanically, seeing as she turned away the last descending flutter
of the jib. The dinghy headed in slow, the Welsh boy at
the tiller. She knelt upright on the bottom boards till the
boat bumped the mole, grated and rolled. She was out
then quickly, scuttling away. He called her as she reached
the bottom of the path. She turned waiting, a frail shadow
in the night.

He seemed unsure how to go on. "You must understand,
see," he said unhappily. "You must never do this again.
Do you understand, Becky?"

"Yes," she said. "Good-bye." Turned and ran again up
the path to the stream, over the bridge to home.

There was a window they always left open, over the
washhouse roof. She left the bundles in the outhouse;
the door hinge creaked as she closed it but nothing stirred.
She climbed cautiously, padded through the dark to her
room. Lay on the bed, feeling the faint rocking that meant
mystically she was still in communion with the great boat
down there in the bay. A last conscious thought made
her pull the package from her waist, tuck it firmly beneath
the layers of the mattress.

Her father seemed in the dawn light a stranger. There
was no explanation she cared to give him, nothing to say.

She was still drugged with sleep; she felt with indifference
the unbuckling of her trews, heard him draw the belt
slow through his hands. Dazed, she imagined the beating
would have no power to hurt; she was wrong. The pain
exploded forward and back through her body, stabbed in
red flashes behind her eyes. She squeezed the bed rail,
needing to die, knowing disjointedly there was no help in
words. Her body had sprung from rock and shale, the
gloomy vastness of the fields; the strap fell not on her
but on the headlands, the rocks, the sea. Exorcising the
loneliness of the place, the misery and hopelessness and
pain. He finished finally, turned away groping to barge
through the door. Downstairs in the little house a child
wailed, sensing hatred and fear; she moved her head slightly
on the pillow, hearing it seemed from far off the breathing
wash of the sea.

Her fingers moved down to coil on the packet in the
bed. Slowly, with indifference, she began picking at the
fastenings. Scratching the knots, pulling and teasing till
the wrapping came away. It was her pleasure to imagine
herself blind, condemned to touch and feel. The fingers,
oversensitive, strayed and tapped, turning the little thing,
feeling variations of texture, shapes of warmth and coldness,
exploring bleakly the tiny map of heresy. A tear, her first,
rolled an inch from one eye, stopped. Left a shining track
against the brownness of the skin.

The priest came, tramping heavy on the stairs. Her father
pushed ahead of him, covered her roughly. Her hand
stayed by her side, unseen, as Father Antony talked. She
lay quiet, face down, lashes brushing her cheek, knowing
immobility and patience were her best defence. The light
from the window faded as he sat; when he left, it was
nearly night.

In the gloom she lifted the stolen thing, touched it to her

face. The heretical smell of it, of wax and bakelite and brass, assaulted her mind faintly. She stroked it again, lovingly; while she held it gripped it seemed she could call White Boat to her bidding, bring her in from her wanderings time and again.

The sun stayed hidden in the days that followed, while she lay on the cliffs and saw the yacht flit in and go. A greater barrier separated her now than the sea she had learned to cross; a barrier built not by others but by her own stupidity.

She killed a great blue lobster, slowly and with pain, driving nails through the membraned cracks of its armour while it threshed and writhed. Cut it apart slowly, hating herself and all the world, dropped the pieces in the sea for a bitter, useless sacrifice. This and other things she did to ease the emptiness in her, fill the progression of iron-grey afternoons. There were vices to be learned, at night and out on the rocks, little gratifications of pleasure and pain. She indulged her body, contemptuously; because White Boat had come cajoling and free, thrown her back laughing, indifferent to hurt. Life stretched before her now like an endless cage; where, she asked herself, was the Change once promised, the great things the priest John had seen? The Golden Age that would bring other White Boats, other days and hope; the wild waves of the very air made to talk and sing. . . .

She fondled the tiny heart of the Boat, in the black dark, felt the wires and coils, the little tubes of valves.

The church was still and cold, the priest's breathing heavy behind the little carved screen. She waited while he talked and murmured, unhearing; while her hands closed and opened on the thing she carried, the sweat sprang out on the palms.

And it was done, hopelessly and sullen. She pushed the

little machine at the grille, waited greyly for the intake of breath, the panic-scrabble of feet from the other side.

The face of Father Antony was beyond description.

The village stirred, whispering and grumbling, people scurrying forward and back between the houses gaping at the soldiers in the street, the shouting horsemen and officers. Sappers, working desperately, rigged sheer legs along the line of cliffs, swung tackles from the heavy beams. Garrisons stood at Alert right back to Durnovaria; this land had rebelled before, the commanders were taking no chances. Signallers, ironic-faced, worked and flapped the arms of half a hundred semaphores; despatch riders galloped, raking their mounts bloody as the questions and instructions flew. A curfew was clapped on the village, the people driven to their homes; but nothing could stop the rumours, the whisperings and unease. Heresy walked like a spectre, blew in on the sea wind; till a man saw the old monk himself, grim-faced and empty-eyed, stalking the cliff-tops in his tattered gown. Detachments of cavalry quartered the downs, but there was nothing to be found. Through the night, and into the darkest time before the dawn, the one street of the village echoed to the marching tramp of men. Then there was a silent time of waiting. The breeze soughed up from the bay, moving the tangles of gorse, crying across the huddled roof; while Becky, lying quiet, listened for the first whisper, the shout that would send soldiers to their posts, train the waiting guns.

She lay on her face, hair tangled on the pillow, hearing the night wind, clenching and slowly unclenching her hands. It seemed the shouting still echoed in her brain, the harangues, thumping of tables, red-faced noise of priests. She saw her father stand glowering and sullen while the cobalt-tunicked Major questioned over and again, probing, insisting, till in misery questions became answers and answers made their own fresh confusion. The sea moved in her brain, dulling sense; while the cannon came trundling and peering behind the straining mules, crashing trails and limbers on the rough ground till the noise clapped forward and back between the houses and she put hands to ears and cried to stop, just to stop. . . .

They wrung her dry, between them. She told things she had told to nobody, secrets of bay and beach and lapping waves, fears and dreams; everything they heard stony-faced while the clerks scribbled, the semaphores clacked on the hills. They left her finally, in her house, in her room, soldiers guarding the door and her father swearing and drunk downstairs and the neighbours pecking and fluttering over the children, making as they spoke of her and hers the sign of the Cross. She lay an age while understanding came and grew, while her nails marked her palms and the tears squeezed hot and slow. The wind droned, soughing under the eaves; blowing strong and cool and steady, bringing White Boat in to death.

Never before had her union with the Boat seemed stronger. She saw her with the clarity of nightmare, moon washing the tilted deck, sails gleaming darkly against the loom of land. She tried in desperation to force her mind out over the sea; she prayed to turn, go back, fly away. White Boat heard, but made no answer; she came on steadily, angry and inexorable.

Becky sat up, quietly. Padded to the window, saw the bright night, the moonglow in the little cluttered yard. In the street footsteps clicked, faded to quiet. A bird called, hunting, while cloud wisps groped for and extinguished the light.

She shivered, easing at the sash. Once before she had known an alien steadiness, a coldness that made her movements smooth and calm. She placed a foot carefully on the outhouse tiles, ducked through the window, thumped into the deeper shadow of the house wall. Waited, listening to silence.

They were not stupid, these soldiers of the Pope. She sensed rather than saw the sentry at the bottom of the garden, slipped like a wraith through darkness till she was near enough almost to touch his cloak. Waited patient, eyes watching white and blind while the moon eased clear of cloud, was obscured again. In front of her the boy yawned, leaned his musket against the wall. Called something sleepily, sauntered a dozen paces up the road.

She was over the wall instantly, feet scuffling. Her skirt snagged, pulled clear. She ran, padding on the road, waiting for the shout, the flash and bang of a gun. The dream was undisturbed.

The bay lay silver and broad. She moved cautiously, parting bracken, wriggling to the edge of the cliff. Beneath her, twenty yards away, men clustered smoking and talking. The pipes they lit carefully, backs to the sea and shielded by their cloaks, unwilling to expose the slightest gleam of light. The tide was making, washing in across the ramps and up among the rocks; the moon stood now above the far headland, showing it stark against a milky haze.

In front of her were the guns.

She watched down at them, eyes wide. Six heavy pieces, humped and sullen, staring out across the sea. She saw the cunning behind the placement; that shot, ball or canister, fired nearly level with the water, would hurtle on spreading and rebounding. The Boat would have no chance. She would come in, onto the guns; and they would fire. There would be no warning, no offers of quarter; just the sudden orange thunder from the land, the shot coming tearing and smashing. . . .

She strained her eyes. Far out on the dim verge of sky and sea was a smudge that danced as she watched and

returned, insistent, dark grey against the greyness of the
void. The tallness of a sail, heading in toward the coast.

She ran again, scrambling and jumping. Slid into the
stream, followed it where its chuckling could mask sounds
of movement, crouched glaring on the edge of the beach.
The soldiers too had seen; there was a stirring, a rustling
surge of dark figures away from the cliff. Men ran to
point and stare, train night glasses at the sea. Their backs
were to the guns.

There was no time to think; none to do more than
swallow, try and quiet the thunder of her heart. Then
she was running desperately, feet spurning the grit, stumbling on boulders and buried stones. Behind her a shout,
the rolling crash of a musket, cursing of an officer. The
ball glanced from rock, threw splinters at her back and
calves. She leaped and swerved, landed on her knees. Saw
men running, the bright flash of a sword. Another report,
distant and unassociated. She panted, rolled on her back beside the first of the guns.

It was unimportant that her body burned with fire. Her
fingers gripped the lanyard, curled lovingly, and pulled.

A hugeness of flame, a roar; the flash lit the cliffs, sparkled
out across the sea. The gun lurched back, angry and alive;
while all down the line the pieces fired, random now and
furious, the shot fizzing over the water. The cannonade
echoed from the headlands, boomed across the village;
woke a girl who mocked and squealed, in her bed, in
her room, the noise vaunting up wild and high into the
night.

While White Boat, turning, laughed at the guns.

And spurned the land.

Fourth Measure
BROTHER JOHN

Fourth Measure

BROTHER JOHN

The workshop was dim and low-roofed, lit only by a pair of barred and round-topped windows at its farther end. Along the walls of rough-dressed ashlar, stone slabs stood in lines. In one corner of the chamber was a massive sink, fed by crudely fashioned pipes and taps, beside it a bench; there was a faint tang in the air, the raw, sharp smell of wet sand.

At the bench a man was working; he was short and ruddy-faced, slightly portly and robed in the dark crimson of the Adhelmians. As he worked he whistled between his teeth, faintly and tunelessly. The habit had more than once brought down on the tonsured head of Brother John the disapproval of his superiors; but it was a part of his nature, and unstoppable.

On the bench in front of the monk lay a slab of limestone some two feet long by four or more inches thick. Beside it were boxes of silver sand; Brother John was engaged in grinding the surface of the stone, pouring the sand through wells in a circular iron muller which he afterwards spun with some dexterity, whirling an emulsion of water and abrasive across the slab. The job was both tiring and exacting; when finished, the stone must have no trace of bowing in either direction. From time to time he checked it for concavity, laying a steel straight-edge across its surface. After some hours the slab was nearing completion, and its most critical stage. The grained texture imparted by the muller must also be free of blemish; Master Albrecht would be certain to detect any irregularity,

and Brother John knew very well what would result. From
his scrip the master printer would produce a short steel
bodkin, kept for the purpose, and with its tip incise a
deep cross on the limestone slab, which it would be John's
pleasure to grind away. He had in fact just finished eras-
ing one such *insignium* of the great man's disapproval.

He washed the stone down carefully, employing a length
of hose attached to one of the taps. He checked its flatness
once more, working delicately, avoiding all contact of his
admittedly greaseless fingers. The slightest suspicion of
grease, a smudge of fat from the tympan of a press, the
brushing of a sweaty hand, would spell disaster; in fact
for their finest work the monks of the lithography section
wore linen masks, to avoid contaminating the stones with
their breath.

All was in order; John proceeded, still whistling, to apply
the last delicate graining, using for the purpose the finest
of the stacked grades of sand. The job was finally done;
a last critical examination of the beautiful creamy surface
and he washed the stone down again, leaning it against the
wall to swill the grit from its bottom and sides. Then he
carried it puffing across the workshop, edged it onto the
platform of a small lift set into the thickness of the wall. A
tug at the bellpull beside it, a faint answering jangle from
above and the object of his labour was drawn smoothly upward out of sight. He tidied his equipment, returning the
trays of sand to their labelled shelves and scrubbing down
the sink. The floor drain clogged noisily; he rootled in it
with a stick till the last of the water had sluiced away, then
followed the stone by a twisting staircase to the upper air.

In contrast to the grinding shop, the main litho studio
was lofty and bright. Tall windows opened onto a vista
of rolling hills, the lush farm country of the Dorset and
Somerset border, gay now with April sunshine. Along one
wall of the room more stones were stacked; beside another

a low dais gave to the desk of Master Albrecht a dignity
fitting his position. Behind the desk was the door to his
diminutive office, a cubicle full to overflowing with bills,
invoices, receipts for that and this; beside it another door
opened into the ink store, where cans of delicious colour
were stacked in rows on slatted pinewood shelves. The ink
store too had its distinctive smell, rich and sweet.

In the centre of the room two long white-scrubbed tables
were spread with pulls of a current job; round them four
of the half dozen novices attached to the department sat
patiently, snipping out the work with scissors. Behind the
tables, on a second raised plinth, stood the presses; three
of them spaced out along the wall, gleaming clean, Master
Albrecht's pride and chief delight.

The machines were simply made. Each bed was lifted
to printing height by a tall lever and propelled by a hefty
wooden-spoked wheel; over the bed an iron frame supported a leather-covered wedge, adjustable for pressure. A
brass tympan, hinged at the farther end of the bed and
tensioned by lead screws along its edges, protected the
stone from the wedge. The tympans had on one occasion
in the past been the cause of a *contretemps* in which
Brother John had figured prominently. They were labelled
as bear fat but about the composition of which John had
expressed the gravest suspicions. In warm weather it stank
abominably; and John, to whose sensitive nostrils bad odours
were an offence, had taken it on himself to scrounge from
the town's one garage a tin of the newfangled mineral
grease, with which he had anointed the presses. The rage
of Master Albrecht had known no bounds; for several weeks
afterward John had had visited on him penances of a
peculiarly unpleasant nature, not the least of which had
been the removal of the grease and the resubstitution of
the time-honoured bear fat. The little Brother had sub-
mitted with as good a grace as was possible under the

circumstances, though he had vowed privately that were he ever to rise to the dizzy heights of Master of Lithography the noxious compound would be banished utterly from his domain.

Beside the presses were more sinks, and the upper outlet of the lift from the grinding shop; by it the stone, approved by Master Albrecht, was propped on its side being fanned dry by a boy armed with a rotating flag of cardboard on a stick. There were wall racks lined with the leather ink rollers, napped and smooth; beneath them more limestone slabs served as pallets. At one of them Brother Joseph was working; a fair-haired novitiate, skull as yet unshaved.

When Brother John entered he was still whistling; the sound died abruptly, scorched out of existence by Master Albrecht's fiery stare. He threaded his way across the room, stood waiting impatiently while Brother Joseph finished spreading ink and kneading it into a roller. A stone lay ready on the bed of the nearest press, beside it a stack of two-colour pulls. John sponged the slab lightly, dipping water from the bucket alongside the press, stepped back as his assistant advanced with the roller. The image was charged, fed delicately at first then more firmly; John inverted one of the pulls, slipped through the paper the two needles mounted in paintbrush handles with which the prints were located on the crossed register marks. Then down with the tympan, lift to pressure; a small adjustment to the wedge and the job rolled through. John released the bed, hauled it back, raised the tympan, then more carefully the paper sheet, held the design up to the light. The colours glowed cheerfully; a drawing of a buxom country girl holding a sheaf of barley, and the inscription *Harvesters Ale; brewed under licence at the monastery of Saint Adhelm, Sherborne, Dorset.*

The ringing of the noon bell put an end to further work; the monks, freed temporarily from their vow of silence,

filed out chattering to the refectory. John and Brother
Joseph took their lunches to a corner table, sat apart while
they planned out the afternoon's operations; later they would
lack the benefit of the spoken word and note-writing, as
well as being tedious, was somewhat frowned on as an
evasion.

At two o'clock, as they were rising to return to the
litho room, a novice approached bearing a slip of paper.
He handed the message to Brother John; the little monk
read it, scratched at his pate, showed it fleetingly to Brother
Joseph and rolled his eyes in mock distress. He was summoned to the august presence of his Abbott; he scurried
off revolving in his mind a list of sins both of omission
and commission for which he might be being called to
account.

A half hour's wait in the great man's antechamber did
little to improve his state of mind; John sat and fidgeted
and watched the squares of sunlight move across the walls
while Master Thomas, the monastery's accountant, alternately fixed him with a coldly accusing stare and inscribed,
with a hideously squeaking pen, the endless rolls of parch-
ment on which the records of the Order were kept. At
two-thirty, Brother John was finally admitted to the presence of his spiritual superior.

Events tended to repeat themselves; Father Meredith
reading at length from a file of notes, glancing up from
time to time over his square-framed spectacles as Brother
John fretted and puffed, red in the face now with concern.
John's visits to the *sanctum* had been few, and the memory
of them was not on the whole encouraging. His eyes moved
restlessly, taking in the remembered details of the room.
The Reverend Father's study was less austere in character
than the rest of the monastery of Saint Adhelm; a carpet
of intricate Persian design covered the floor, one wall was
lined with books while in a corner stood a globe of the

world supported by a group of handsome bronze zephyrs. On the leather-topped desk more books and papers were piled untidily. There too stood the Abbott's typewriter; a monumental machine, its superstructure framed by Corinthian pillars that ended obnoxiously in cast-iron paws. A cocktail cabinet, its doors partly ajar, displayed well-stocked shelves; a late Renaissance *Pietà* hung above it while over Father Meredith's desk loomed a grisly Spanish crucifix.

Through the windows could be seen the hills, gentle in sunlight; Brother John moved his eyes from the disquieting Christ-figure, rested them on the horizon. Time passed as he watched the moving clouds, their slow miles-off white billowing; when Father Meredith finally spoke, his voice came as a faint shock. "Brother John," he said. "Something . . . ah . . . interesting has occurred."

John felt a slight rise of hope. Perhaps after all his Abbott hadn't sent for him to rap his knuckles over some half-forgotten crime. He contrived, as far as his mobile eyebrows would allow, a look of interest combined with a suitably devout submissiveness. The attempt met with a somewhat qualified success. Father Meredith clicked his fingers irritably. "You may speak, Brother. . . ." The Adhelmians were a mild order of artisans and craftsmen; the daily silence was about their only firm rule but it was adhered to rigidly.

John swallowed gratefully. "Thank you, Reverend Father. . . ." He faltered. At this stage, there was little else to say.

Father Meredith scanned his papers again and cleared his throat; a little distant-sounding noise, sheeplike. "Er . . . yes. It seems we have been asked to supply an . . . ah . . . artist. The whole affair's a little mysterious, I don't know a great deal about it as yet myself; but I felt a . . . change of air shall we say, Brother, might be . . . beneficial. . . ."

Brother John bowed his head humbly. It seemed likely Master Albrecht had had something to do with that last remark; John had never really seen eye to eye with him since the business of the bear fat. And something too in the intonation of the single word "artist" . . . In matters spiritual, John had always been more than willing to be led; in things aesthetic though, he was constantly guilty of the sin of Pride. "I am entirely," he murmured, "at the Reverend Father's disposal. . . ."

"Hmph," said the Abbott, sharply. He continued for a moment to observe John over the upper rims of his glasses. He was well enough aware of the other's background. John came of poor parents; his family were, and had been for generations, cobblers in Durnovaria. From an early age John had showed no inclination to follow the family trade; set to a last, he would be discovered chalking pictures on the workbench, making furtive crayon sketches of the faces of his brothers and the customers in the little shop. His father had more than once taken a broad strap to the miscreant and endeavoured to knock out Hell and make room for a little Heaven; but the plump little boy, in other respects an amiable and easygoing child, proved unexpectedly stubborn. Chalks or pencils were seldom out of his hands; when he could draw with nothing else he used charcoal from the grates or heelball. His pictures and scrawlings lined the rough walls of his room; his proper work became more erratic than ever. It seemed the only thing to do was to let him follow his bent; at least, his father reasoned, the family would be relieved of the necessity of feeding a useless mouth. In this England there was only one way in which John's talent might be employed; he took Holy Orders and at the age of fourteen became a novice in the monastery of Saint Adhelm, some twenty-odd miles from his home.

The first few months were a trying time both for the

young pupil and his instructors; as a working-class child John had naturally never learned to read, and this instead of art became the first concern. The novice sensed finally that only through his letters would he ever achieve his real ambition; he sweated over his books, and a year later was formally admitted to the classes held in the monastery by Brother Pietro, the drawing master.

Even then John was doomed to disappointment; life drawing was not permitted, and the young student spent restless hours working from the cast. The antique study improved his line and gave him a measure of discipline he had hitherto lacked, but left him unfulfilled. Lithography had been his salvation; though at first he loathed its complexity, and the long dry history of it from Senefelder's laundry list onwards that Brother Pietro insisted he learn by heart, the colour and texture of the stones and the many ways of working them appealed to the latent craftsman in him. While fine art was seldom required, there was technical challenge in the most mundane commercial jobs; John worked diligently, restyling over the years the entire range of bottle and package labels produced by the House. Master Albrecht, recognising it if not a genius at least a first-rate craftsman, left him largely to his own devices, and by his thirtieth birthday John had become well known in professional circles. (He sometimes referred to himself, with wry humour, as the Master of the Bottle of Sauce.) Brewing was only one of the industries in which the Church had extensive interests, and commissions began to come in from other centres and ecclesiastic business houses lacking their own creative staff. The subsequent swelling of the coffers of the Adhelmians had been the main reason why John's occasional outbursts of temperament had been tolerated without too much complaint, even by the peppery Master of Lithography. John was a good draughtsman and, left to go his own way, a keen worker; these qualities the

Adhelmians had always valued more than slavish obedience
to principles and a more or less sterile piety. Though there
had been times, there had been times . . .

Brother John broke in on his superior's thought stream.
"Reverend Father, could you . . . I mean have you any
idea of the nature of the work?"

"None." The Abbott was being somewhat less than frank;
he turned over the papers on his desk, shuffled them into
a heap and spread them out once more. "I can tell you
this much, it will involve a considerable journey. You'll
be going to Dubris; when you arrive you'll put yourself
at the disposal of Bishop Loudain. You can expect to be
gone for some months, probably throughout the sittings of
the . . . ah . . . Court of Spiritual Welfare, under Father
Hieronymous. I can assure you the work will be of some
. . . ah . . . importance, you'll be holding a direct commission from Rome." He coughed again, looked embarrassed, fiddled with a stylus. "You'll be performing a task
of lasting value, Brother," he said stiffly. "A real service
to the Church. Better than beer labels, when you've done
and said all. Ehh . . . ?"

Brother John stayed silent. His mind, accustomed to jogging in its own grave channels, was for once working furiously. There was a lot to be said for the proposition;
as Father Meredith had pointed out, it would mean a
change of air; and a journey across England in springtime,
always to John's mind the most attractive part of the year.
And in any case it looked as if his freedom of choice was
severely limited; if Master Albrecht, for his own purposes,
wanted him out of the way for a time, it behoved him
to go. There was professional pride too; his selection was
a mark of honour, he knew that well enough. But . . .
nothing decent, nothing good, would ever come out of the
doings of the Court of Spiritual Welfare, Father Meredith
knew that as well as anybody else. Because there had

once been another name for the Court, a name that even in the Church-owned West had fallen into evil repute.

The Inquisition . . .

John entered the great castle of Dubris by the Old Gate amid a noisy crowd of sightseers; mendicants, soldiers, townsfolk out for the day with picnic hampers and beer, the men swaggering in their Sunday best, the women with children hanging bawling round their skirts. Inside, the little monk paused involuntarily; the red-robed priest who was his guide waited impatiently, fidgeting with the heavy-bound books he carried, stepping from one foot to the other in the jostling of the mob. In front of John reared the second curtain; above it, sullen against the sky, was the huge *donjon*, daunting with its size and closeness. In the outer bailey, curving right as far as the great barbican of the Constable's Gate, an entire fairground had established itself. Steam plumed in the air; organs, Marenghis and Gaviolis, bellowed and clashed their endless tunes; automata conducted jerkily; bare golden nymphs swirled, horses and fabulous beasts glared from the rides. Performing dogs barked and howled, dark-skinned men spat gouts of fire; dancers and jugglers postured, sideshows promised all the erotica of the East. Nearby, on platforms improvised from trestles and beer crates, cudgel-players split their opponent's heads over boards already brown-daubed with blood, lithe boys in tight breeches of pale blue cloth lashed each other's legs raw with thin switches of hazel. Between the stalls ran children, girls and boys; there were priests, fortune-tellers, sailors with tarred pigtails sticking out jauntily from their necks, arm in arm with bosomy laughing women; the Papal Blue was much in evidence, and the scarlet robes of Inquisition officers scurrying on various errands. All was noise, colour, and confusion. From near the *donjon* smoke rose in a column, staining the sky; over the great place,

beside the cobalt pennant of Pope John, flew the blood-red
standard of the Court.

The guide tugged at John's sleeve; he followed, bemused
by the uproar. They headed for the inner barbican, the
priest shoving and pushing to clear a way through the
crowd. Against the bailey wall was an added attraction;
a line of cages, open to the sky, housed the first batch
of prisoners. Round them the crowd boiled and yelled.
John, staring, saw a man lashing at his tormentors with
a staff he had somehow wrested from one of them; his
eyes were suffused, flecks of foam covered his beard. Farther
on an old woman railed, shaking scrawny fists; her head
had been cut, it seemed by a stone, and blood striped
her face and neck brightly. Next to her a pretty, long-haired
girl defiantly suckled a baby. John turned aside frowning
deeply, followed the flapping robes of the priest into the
upper bailey. His duties had already been explained to
him; he was to record, for the benefit of Rome, all stages
in the procedure of the Court of Father Hieronymous,
Witchfinder in General to Pope John. His task would begin
with the Questioning of prisoners.

The room set apart for the purpose was located beneath
the *donjon* itself, and reached by a spiral stair. John passed
through the Great Hall, its crosswall hung now with scarlet
in preparation for the work to come. At the head of the
recessed stairway a man in Papal Blue stood at ease, halberd
grounded on the flags in front of him. He came to attention
stiffly as John's guide passed. The priest descended the
stairs stooping, sandals flopping on stone; John followed
clutching sketchbooks and a satchel crammed with bottles
and jars, inks and paints and brushes, pens, erasers, all
the paraphernalia of an artist. The little monk was apprehen-
sive already, trying to quiet his jangling nerves.

The room in which he found himself was long and wide,
devoid of windows except where to one side a line of

grilles set close under the roof admitted livid fans of light.
At the far end of the chamber an oil lamp burned; beneath
it clustered a group of figures. John saw dark-dressed, burly
men with the *insignium* of the Court, the hand wielding
the hammer and the lightning flash, blazoned on their chests;
a chaplain was mumbling over trays of instruments whose
purpose he did not recognise. There were spiked rollers,
oddly shaped irons, tourniquets of metal beads; other devices, ranged in rows, he identified with a cold shock.
The little frames with their small cranked handles, toothed
jaws; these were *grésillons*. Thumbscrews. Such things then
really existed. Nearer at hand a species of rough table,
fitted at each end with lever-operated wooden rollers, declared its use more plainly. The roof of the place was
studded with pulleys, some with their ropes already reeved
and dangling; a brazier burned redly, and near it were
piled what looked to be huge lead weights.

The priest at Brother John's elbow continued in a low
voice the explanation on which he'd felt impelled to embark
while crossing the town from their lodgings. "We may taken
it then," he said, "that as the crimes of witchcraft and
heresy, the raising of devils, receiving of incubi and succubi
and like abominations, the trafficking with the Lord of
Flies himself, are crimes of the spirit rather than the body,
crimen excepta, they cannot be judged, and evidence may
neither be given nor accepted under normal legal jurisdic-
tion. The admission of spectral evidence and its acceptance
as partial proof of guilt subject to confession during Ques-
tionion is therefore of vital importance to the functioning
of our Court. Under this head too belongs our explanation
of the use of torture and its justification; the death of the
guilty one disrupts Satan's attack on the Plan of God, as
revealed to Mother Church through His Vicar on Earth,
our own Pope John; while dying penitent the heretic saved

from greater relapse into the sin of subversion, to find eventually his place in the Divine Kingdom."

Brother John, his face screwed up as if in anticipation of pain, ventured a query. "But are not your prisoners given the opportunity to confess? Were they to confess without the Questioning—"

"There can be no confession," interrupted the other, "without compulsion. As there can be no answering the challenges of spectral evidence, the use of which by definition invalidates the innocence of the accused." He allowed his eyes to travel to one of the pulleys and its dangling rope. "Confession," he said, "must be sincere. It must come from the heart. False confession, made to avoid the pain of Questioning, is useless to Church and God alike. Our aim is salvation; the salvation of the souls of these poor wretches in our charge, if necessary by the breaking of their bodies. Set against this, all else is straw in the wind."

The muttering of the priest at the far end of the chamber ceased abruptly. John's guide smiled thinly, without humour. "Good," he said. "Your waiting is ended, Brother. They will start soon now."

"What," said Brother John, "were they doing?"

The other turned to him, vaguely surprised. "Doing?" he said. "They were blessing the instruments of the Questioning, of course. . . ."

"But," said Brother John, rubbing his pate as was his custom when bewildered, "what I don't seem to understand is the question of impregnation by the incubus. If as you say the incubus, the demon in its masculine form, is able physically to fertilize its victim, then the concept of diabolic delusion is invalidated. Creation by a minion of Satan is surely—"

The priest turned on him quickly, eyes glittering. "I would advise you," he said, "to understand very clearly. You are

on dangerous ground here, more dangerous than you realize. The demon, being a sexless entity, is unable to create;
as its Master is impotent in the face of God. But by
receiving as succubus the seed of man, and transporting
it invisibly through the air, the thing can be arranged; and
is arranged, as you will see. I am not a heretic, Brother."

"I see," said John, white to the lips. "You must forgive
me, Brother Sebastian; we Adhelmians are technicians and
mechanics, mere journeymen not noted in our lower orders
at least for learning of such profundity. . . ."

There was a distant flourish of trumpets, muffled by the
vastness of the walls.

Brother John left Dubris by a rutted track that wound
through the scrubland to the north of the town. He sat
his horse untidily, slumped forward in the saddle with his
eyes on the ground. The dusty red gown, soiled now and
frayed at the hem, flapped round his calves; he held the
reins slackly so the animal meandered from side to side
of the road, picking its own way. When it stopped, which
was often, John made no attempt to urge it forward. He
sat staring fixedly; once he lifted his head to gaze blankly
at the horizon. His face had lost its colouring, acquiring
instead a greyish sheen like the face of a corpse; fits of
shivering shook him, as though he was suffering from a
fever. He had lost a great deal of weight; his girdle, once
tightly drawn, now hung loosely round his stomach. His
satchel of equipment still swung from the pommel of the
saddle but the sketchbooks were gone, were already if
Brother Sebastian was to be believed on their way by
special courier to Rome. Before parting, the Inquisitor had
complimented John on his application and the fineness of
his work, and attempted to cheer him by pointing out the
immense setback the hearings had been to the cause of
the Devil in Kent; but getting no answer had left him,

not without a backward glance or two and a searching of
the spirit. For he had become convinced during the weeks
of their association that heresy burned somewhere in the
heart of Brother John himself. There were times when he
had almost felt tempted to bring the matter to the attention
of Father Hieronymous, but who knew what repercussions
might have resulted? The Adhelmians, in spite of what
John himself had described as a certain lack of scholarship,
were a valued and respected Order in the land, and the
limner had after all held a commission from Rome. Brother
Sebastian was a zealot, tireless in the prosecution of his
Faith; but there are times when even the devout find it
advisable to turn a blind eye. . . .

A farm cart passed rumbling, trailing a cloud of whitish
dust. John's horse curveted; the priest chided gently, va-
cant-faced. Through the deep channels of his brain noises
still echoed. A susurration, rising and falling like a shrill
and hellish sea; the shrieks of the damned, and the dying,
and the dead. And the sizzling of braziers, thud of whips
splitting flesh; creaking of leather and wood, squeak and
groan of sinews as machines tested to destruction the handi-
work of God. John had seen it all; the white-hot pincers
round the breasts, branding irons pushed smoking into
mouths, calf-length boots topped up with boiling lead, the
heated chairs, the spiked seats on which they bounced
their victims then stacked the lead slabs on their thighs. . . .
The *Territio*, the *Questions Preparatoire, Ordinaire, Ex-
traordinaire;* squassation and the *strappado*, the rack and the
choking-pear; the Questioners stripped and sweating while
the great mad Judge upstairs extracted from the foamings
of epilectics the stuff of conviction after conviction. . . .
Pencil and brush recorded faithfully, flying at the paper
with returning skill while Brother Sebastian stood and
frowned, pulling at his lip and shaking his head. It seemed
John's hands worked of their own, tearing the pages aside,

grabbing for inks and washes while the drawings grew in
depth and vividness. The brilliant side lighting; film of
sweat on bodies that distended and heaved in ecstasies
of pain; arms disjointed by the weights and pulleys, stomachs
exploded by the rack, bright tree shapes of new blood
running to the floor. It seemed the limner tried to force the
stench, the squalor, even at last the noise down onto paper;
Brother Sebastian, impressed in spite of himself, had finally
dragged John away by force, but he couldn't stop him
working. He drew a wizard in the outer bailey, pulled apart
by four Suffolk punches; the doomed men and women sitting
on their tar kegs waiting for the torch; the stark things
that were left when the flames had died away. *"Thou
shalt not suffer a witch to live,"* Sebastian had said at his
parting. *"Remember* that, Brother. Thou shalt not suffer
a witch to live. . . ." John's lips moved, repeating the words
in silence.

Night overtook him a bare half dozen miles from Dubris.
He dismounted in the dark, awkwardly, tethered the horse
while he fetched water from a stream. In the stream he
dropped the satchel of brushes and paints. He stood a
long time staring, though in the blackness he couldn't see
it float away.

At his rate of travel it took many weeks to reach his
home. Sometimes he took wrong turnings; sometimes people
fed him, and then he blessed them and cried. Once a gang
of footpads jumped him but the white mouth and staring
eyes had them backing off in fear of one bewitched, or
taken by the Plague. He finally entered Dorset miles off
course at Blandford Forum. For a time he followed the
westward meanderings of the Frome; beyond Durnovaria
he turned north for Sherborne. Somebody recognised the
crimson habit, put him on the road, filled his scrip with
bread he never ate. In mid-July he reached his House; at
the gates he gave the horse away to a ragged child. His

Abbott, appalled, had him confined in the sickbay and took immediate steps to recover the animal, but it had vanished. John lay in a room bright with summer flowers, with fuchsias and begonias and roses from the monastery grounds, watching the sun patches glide on the walls and the fleecy piling of clouds in the blue sky. He only spoke once, and then to Brother Joseph; leaning upright, eyes frightened and wild, gripping the boy's wrist. "I *enjoyed* it, Brother," he whispered. "God and the Saints preserve me, *I enjoyed my work*. . . ." Joseph tried to calm him, but to no avail.

A month passed before he rose and dressed himself. He had taken little food; he was thin now to the point of gauntness and his eyes were feverishly bright. He put himself to work on the litho presses; Master Albrecht chided, but he was ignored. John toiled all day, through the lunchtime break, through supper and the vesper bell. Night and the moon found him still working, inking the stone he could no longer see, swabbing, dropping the tympan, hauling the spokes of the wheel, lowering the bed, inking, dropping the tympan. . . . Brother Joseph stayed with him a time, watching huddled in the shadows; then he too left, appalled by something he couldn't understand.

It was early morning before John faltered in his penance. He stood slightly bowed, a dark shape outlined by a sheen of moonlight, listening, screwing his face as if trying to catch the echoes from some noise outside the range of human ears. Whimperings came from him; he staggered like a drunken man to the middle of the floor, dropped prone with arms outstretched. Over him a rooflight rattled in a sudden wind; he sat up, glared round straining for the sound, if it was a sound, he'd heard. It was then he suffered the first of the visions or hallucinations that were to haunt him the rest of his days. Its onset was a quick thudding, like a drum rushing at night over a great tract of land. The room darkened, then glowed. John babbled, clawed at his face and tried to pray.

There had been a country girl at Dubris, a pretty wench whose crime, monstrous and unnatural, had been the receiving of an incubus. Her they released, finally; but before they let her go they clipped the fingers from one small paw, and gave them to her in a cloth. Brother John saw her again, clear in the moonlight. She passed across the room, mewing and dissatisfied; and after her traipsed the host of horrors, the cut legs and arms, the severed heads, the bodies broken on the wheel, pierced and burned by the hot iron chairs. A bawling came from them and a howling, a lowing like the noise of the ghosts of cows, a dead-bird chittering, a crying, a wanting. . . . John's face suffused; round him lights shone, the wheels of the presses seemed to spin like dark-spoked suns. He was assaulted by thunders and strange rattlings; his eyes rolled upward; disclosing the whites; he hammered at the floor with his fists, cried out and lay still.

In the morning the Brothers, not finding him in his cell, searched the workshops. Then the whole monastery, then its grounds. But it was useless; Brother John had gone.

His Eminence the Cardinal Archbishop of Londinium sighed heavily, rubbed his chin, yawned, and took a turn up and down the office from his desk to the windows that looked down on the grounds of the Episcopal Palace. He stood at the windows awhile, hands clasped behind him, chin sunk on his chest. The gardens were alive with colour now, with lilies and delphiniums and the newest McCredy roses; His Eminence was a *gourmet* in all things temporal. His eyes saw the display vaguely, and the fishponds beyond where aged carp rose to the tinkling of a handbell. Beyond the ponds again, beyond the herb gardens with their twisting paved walks, was the outer wall. Over it, gloomily, rose the slab side and lines of windows of the prison-like College

of Signallers. Noises from Londinium's maze of streets
reached the study faintly; cries of hawkers, rumble and
crash of waggon wheels, from somewhere the pealing of
bells. The mind of His Eminence noted the sounds automatically; he pursed his lips, following his own tortuous and
none too pleasant train of thought.

He returned slowly to his desk. On it, an open file dis-
gorged a small flood of papers. He picked one up, frowning.
Under the formal heading and more formal speech the rage
of a pious and honest man was very plain.

My Lord,
    May I crave the indulgence of Your Eminence to bring to your
notice a matter of the most heinous and appalling nature; the
torture, the agony, the foul indignities visited, in the name of the
Christos, on the people of this my diocese. On the poor and the
infirm, the aged and the simple of mind . . . on children and old
men in their dotage, on mothers big with child . . . on parents
by their daughters and sons, on husbands by their wives; I can,
My Lord, hold peace no longer in the face of iniquity, of horror—

His Eminence detected an error in the rush of Latin; his
red fountain pen, irritably and automatically, made an era-
sure.

—horror such as has been perpetrated on us in this loyal, this
ancient, and this blameless town. On the innocent and the foolish,
on the helpless subjects of a Church and of a God professing love,
and charity, and enlightenment. . . . This madman, this desecrator
of decency, and his so-called Spiritual Court . . .

The Cardinal flicked the pages to the signature and shook
his head. Bishop Loudain of Dubris was a bold man but a
foolish one; the letter alone, placed in the proper hands,
would have secured for His Grace an interlude with those
very *grésillons* of which he so ardently complained. The

thing reeked of heresy. . . . The Cardinal lifted the document carefully with his fingertips and redeposited it in its file. He picked up another, terser and to the point, from the commander of the garrison stationed at Durnovaria.

. . . the renegade known to the people as Brother John continues to evade our forces. Riots stemming directly from the teaching of him and of his followers have lately broken out in Sherborne, Sturminster, Newton, Shaftesbury, Blandford, and Durnovaria itself. The people, attributing his escapes from our troops to miraculous intervention, become daily more difficult to control. I most earnestly request the release of a further troop of horse with a minimum of four hundred infantry and appropriate arms and stores, for the purpose of searching the region from Beaminster to Yeovil where it is currently believed the insurgents are quartered. Their strength is now estimated at between fifty and a hundred; they are well armed, and have an intimate knowledge of the local terrain. Attempts to run them down employing normal methods of approach have repeatedly proved useless. . . .

His Eminence dropped the letter impatiently. That and a dozen more like it had prompted his own formal document of excommunication. Sentence had been passed on Brother John six months ago; but it would seem the disavowal of the Church and the consequent damnation of his soul had had little effect. His followers had in fact been fired to greater excesses; a detachment of two dozen horse pulled down and massacred in broad daylight, their arms and equipment stolen; a Captain of the Roman Dragoons set on and beaten, sent cantering into Durnovaria with insulting messages pinned to his tunic; the Pope burned in effigy at Woodhenge and Badbury Rings. The Cardinal was only too uncomfortably aware of the dangers inherent in martyrdom; he would have preferred to ignore John altogether, let the whole wretched business die a natural death, but his hand was being forced.

He turned to the brief account of the rebel's life and accomplishments, brought to Londinium at his request by an unusually subdued Adhelmian whose ears His Eminence would very much have liked to send back to Father Meredith on a plate for letting his confounded people get so far out of hand in the first place. The Adhelmians, admittedly through no fault of their own, were rapidly becoming the *lettmotif* of a new and disquieting popular movement. The resurging power of Anglicanism fed on such relics of ancient worship; for had not Saint Adhelm himself converted vast stretches of the country to the Faith centuries before the clergy flocking in at the heels of the conquering Normans restored Britain to the rule of Rome? The Anglican Communion had been a historic fact, however strenuously the Church tried to deny it, and the case for it could still be made out. Many years had elapsed too between Henry's abolition of Papal rule and the excommunication of Elizabeth, years in which the English Church had presumably coexisted in a state of Grace. Greasy apologetics maybe, but dangerous ideas to let loose among a population lacking in general the fine points of theological instruction. The old cry of the Church, to submit and to adore, was no longer enough; the people were being tempted once more to set up their own spiritual hierarchy, and John or some such figure was tailor-made to head it.

The renegade then had attended the last sitting of the Court of Spiritual Welfare; that, thought His Eminence as he reread facts already learned by heart, was clearly the beginning of the whole ridiculous affair. He shook his head. How explain? How quiet the rage of a man like Loudain with figures and facts, political argument? His Eminence shrugged tiredly. In the history of the world, there had been no power like the power of the second Rome. To hold half a planet in the cup of your hands; to juggle, to balance one against the next forces nearly beyond the mind of man to

grasp. . . . The rage of nations was like the anger of the
sea, not to be contained with straws. Anglicanism had torn
the country once, the history of it was all there in the great
books that lined the study walls. Then, England had glowed
from her Cornish toe to her Pennine spine with the light
of the *auto-da-fé*. Against that set a little pain, a little blood,
soon gone and nearly as soon forgotten; that, and the might
wisdom of the Church.

Once too often, mused the Cardinal; the goad, the threat
of hellfire, applied instead of the lure of the Kingdom of
Love. . . . Father Hieronymous, mad as he undoubtedly
was, had been useful in the past; but this time his gory
circus had triggered an uproar that could easily involve all
England. Uncharitable and surprising thoughts whirled
through the head of the Archbishop of Londinium. He rose
again to stand brooding, looking down on the gardens that
were his chief delight. He seemed to see the roses smashed
by irreverent feet, the lilies trodden into a bloody soil;
his house destroyed and burning, its wine cellars desecrated,
its pantries and kitchens, its studies and libraries in flames.
So blast Father Hieronymous, and blast the Adhelmians,
and above all blast Brother John. . . . His Eminence by
nature of his position was economist and politician as much
as churchman; in his more cynical moods he seemed to see
the whole vast fabric of the Church stretched like a glittering blanket, a counterpane of cloth of gold, across the body
of a giant. At times like this the giant moved and grumbled,
turned in a restless sleep. Soon, he would wake.

He resolutely put the idea aside, returned to his bureau,
slid out from a drawer the formal document he had spent
most of yesterday morning dictating to his clerk.

Whereas the heretic known as Brother John, ex of the Order of
the Adhelmians, whose body we have pronounced excommunicate
and whose soul we cast down to the Fire that is eternal, continues

to flout the Will of God and of His true Church in this land, it is our duty to convey this solemn Notice and Warning:

Any person harbouring the heretic or any of his band; any person supplying it with food, drink, arms, shot and powder or any like victuals;

Any person found in possession of letters, proclamations or other matter originated by Brother John or any of his band, or contriving the distribution of such pamphlets to further the cause of Satan against the glory of God;

Any person concealing information as to the whereabouts of the said heretic or any of his band; any person attending any meeting, orgy, or like exhibition held by them who shall not declare the same, with all he may know touching the same, to a priest, a garrison commander, or a serjeant of law within one day of the offence;

Shall be declared excommunicate, and heinous in the sight of God; and no conviction before any Justice of the Peace or any Clerical Court, shall be hung and drawn, and his quarters salted and tarred, and displayed in such manner as be deemed fitting for the warning and education of other heretics or traitors to God and the cause of His Church.

Further it is our duty to proclaim the following rewards:

For information leading to the capture, alive or dead, of Brother John or any of his band, twenty-five pounds in gold.

For the capture, alive or dead, of any of the band of Brother John, fifty pounds in gold.

For the capture, alive or dead, of Brother John himself, two hundred pounds in gold; to be paid at our Episcopal Palace of Lambeth on receipt of the body of the heretic, or of good and sufficient evidence of its destruction.

Given under our hand this twenty-first day of June, Year of Our Lord one thousand, nine hundred and eighty-five.

The Cardinal nodded his head finally with gloomy approval. The Church stood in grave need of a well-disciplined Saint or two; John was a first-rate man going to waste. His Eminence shrugged and called for a secretary to bring his private seal.

At the head of the coombe the infantry had deployed in a half circle. Other soldiers, the blue of their uniforms showing clearly, lined the rocks of the gully, beneath the brow of which were the mouths of several caves. Sporadic bursts of smoke blew from them as the defenders, outnumbered and surrounded, fought on pointlessly. Two hundred yards from the stronghold a demiculverin was being trained. The piece had been protected by a hastily built demilune of rocks; behind the breastwork sweating men applied levers to the wheels of the carriage. Balks of timber thrust beneath their rims were raising the gun by degrees but the elevation was impossibly high; on its first discharge its captain confidently expected the trail to smash, driven back by the recoil into the ground on which it rested. Near the gun a shakoed major, sword unsheathed, sat a fretting horse and tongue-lashed the men into greater efforts. Frontal attacks had already proved costly; farther up the coombe scraps of blue cloth showed where the heretics had taken their toll of the infantry. The major, not a man to risk troops uselessly, swore and waved the sword at the stronghold. A puff of smoke answered him, the ball splitting a rock twenty feet to his left and singing off into distance. A ragged volley from the troops sheltering in the gully drove the defenders back; the major thought he heard, mixed with the echoes of the shots, the noise of a scream.

The first round from the great gun sent stone chips whining from the ledge a yard below the cave mouths; the second started a small landslip above and to the right. The third discharge knocked the piece from its crudely built platform, smashing the legs of a gunner. The captain swore, wishing for a pot-mortar, but there was no mortar to be had. The barrel was remounted and elevated more securely; the

Papists settled down to batter the rebel position to fragments.

The small figure in the dark crimson robe was twenty
yards from the fissures, scuttling over the rocks of a goat
path, before the first piece was brought to bear. Puffs of
dust rose from the rock face around and above the fugitive;
the major, yelling, rode across the line of sight of his men,
forcing them to aim. The renegade, brought down within
twenty feet of the top of the cliff, slithered a great distance
before coming to rest; but he still had life enough in him
to aim a pistol, blowing off the kneecap of a man on the
major's right as the infantry charged home. The major
grunted, stooped to pull aside the cowl of the Adhelmian.
Tumbling fair hair was disclosed; the boy grinned up at
him in pain, blood showing round his teeth.

At the major's side his aide said disgustedly, *"Discipu-
lus . . ."*

"Catamite more likely," growled the other. He seized the
hair and shook. "Well, you nasty little fellow," he said.
"Where's your ass-chafing master?"

No answer. Another shaking; Brother Joseph half raised
himself, spat redness at the face above him. The aide shook
his head. "They won't talk, sir. None of the Bulgarians . . ."

"Of that," said the major crushingly, "I was in fact aware.
Stretcher-bearers here, Serjeant. . . ."

The soldier doubled back down the hill. The boy panted,
lifted himself again, proffered before collapsing a stained
fist. The major knelt, delicately avoiding the seeping blood,
to prise the fingers apart. He straightened up turning over
in his palm the tiny medallion with the crossing crablines.
"This," he said softly, "is all we needed. . . ." He thrust the
fairy mark into his uniform pocket, before his aide could
see.

The cave, searched, yielded a mass of trophies. Six bodies,
three of them intact, enough of the rest remaining to satisfy

even a suspicious Papal clerk. The price had risen now to a
hundred and fifty pounds a rebel; that made nine hundred
quids' worth, over a thousand altogether. A nice little haul
for the battalion. In addition there were supplies of food
and arms, books and heretical documents, stacks of leaflets
waiting distribution. These the major ordered burned. At
the back of the chamber, fairly well knocked about by the
cannonade, lay the remains of an ancient Albion press and
scattered cases of type. The major sent for sledgehammers
and stirred the mess of leaflets with a booted toe. "Well at
least," he remarked philosophically to his aide, "there'll be
less of this bumph floating about in the future. . . ."

But the manoeuvre had failed in its main objective. Once
again, Brother John had escaped.

Over the weeks the rumours grew. John was here, he was
there; troops rode hurriedly by night, villages were ransacked, rewards were claimed a score of times but never
paid. A tale arose that John, in league with the People
of the Heath, could be transported by magically swift means
away from danger. *"Transvestism,"* snarled Rome, and
doubled the head money. Informers flourished; cottages
were burned, whole towns fined. Bodies swayed at crossroads, gruesome in their chains, foci for black towers of
birds. The giant grumbled and tossed, restlessly.

Wells Cathedral was desecrated; though the desecration
didn't in fact amount to very much. There was no indication
that the High Altar had been approached with aught save
deep respect but placed on it, in full and hideous view,
was a placard carrying certain writing. The document was
seized of course and instantly burned but the rumour went
out that the words had been a text from Scripture, hereti-
cally translated into Middle and Modern English. *"My
house shall be called a house of God, but ye have made it a
den of robbers"* . . . The same thing happened at Aquae

Sulis (*"Give all that ye have to the poor"*) and at the residence of the Bishop of Dorset himself. (*"It is easier for a camel to pass through the eye of a needle, than for a rich man to enter the Kingdom of Heaven."*) But such foibles were the work of disciples, declared or secret; John himself travelled continuously, teaching and praying. Sometimes the visions tormented him so that he rolled and frothed, beating his fists bloody on the ground, tearing at clothes and skin till his followers huddled back in frowning fear. Maybe the phantoms, the drumming and screaming, the hacked hands and limbs, followed him still across the gorse deserts of the West; maybe the Old Ones did meet him and comfort, sit and talk their ancient faith by the stones of temples old before the Romans came, under the wheeling clouds and the spinning fantasies of moon and sun. John gave away his shoes and cloak, his staff; some whispered it was struck into the ground and flowered, like the staff of the blessed Joseph at Glastonbury.

If the rumour reached John's ears he gave no sign. He moved like a ghost, lips mumbling, eyes unseeing, the rain gusting round him and the wind; and somehow the people hid him and kept him fed while the soldiers of the Blue quartered Dorset wearily from Sherborne to Corvesgeat, from Sarum Rings to the Valley of the Giant at Cerne. John's nuisance value rose steadily; from five hundred pounds to a thousand, from a thousand to fifteen hundred, and from that to an incredible two thousand pounds, chargeable against the accounts of the Episcopal Palace of Londinium. But of the man himself there was no sign. The rumours flew again. Some claimed he was planning a revolt against Rome, that he was lying low till he had raised a sufficient army; others said he was sick, or injured, or had fled the country; and finally, the whisper went out that he was dead. His followers, and by this time they numbered thousands,

waited and mourned. But John wasn't dead; he had moved
back into the hills, following the lepers now, tracking them
by their lonely, angry bells.

The clustered houses of the village lay or huddled on an
exposed sweep of heathland. The cottages were of grey
stone, storm-shuttered and desolate. The few trees that grew
were stunted and low, carved by the wind into strange
smooth shapes; their branches leaned toward the roofs as if
for protection. From the place a rutted road ran, winding
out across the wasteland to lose itself in distance.

Across the heath, vaguely visible in the strange light, ran
a high curve of hills. Over them on a brighter day a white
glower would have told of the closeness of the sea; now
the dead, dust-coloured sky was empty and flat. Out of it
skirled a March wind, wet and hugely blustering. It plucked
at the cloak of the girl who sat patiently by the roadside a
hundred yards beyond the last of the cottages. With one
hand she held the rough cloth tight against her throat; her
hair, escaping from the hood, flacked long and dark round
her face. She watched steadily, staring out across the grey-
brown of the heath toward the distant silhouettes of the
hills.

An hour she waited, two; the wind seethed in the bracken,
once a squall of rain lashed across the road. The hills were
fading with the coming dusk when she rose and stood staring under her hand, straining her eyes at the grey gnat-blur
on the very fringe of vision. For minutes she stood motionless, seeming not to breathe, while the blur advanced steadily, turned to a dark pinhead, resolved itself finally into the
figure of a mounted man. The girl moaned then, an odd
noise, a half-whimper deep in her throat; dropped to her
knees, glared terrified at the houses and out along the
road. The rider advanced, seeming to her frightened stare to
move without progression, jogging like a puppet under the

vastness of the sky. Her fingers scrabbled on the road in front of her, smoothed the skirt across her thighs, touched her side as if to ease the thudding of her heart.

The man sat the donkey slackly, letting the beast pick its way. On either side of its belly his feet hung, swaying rhythmically, scraping the tops of the grasses. The feet were bare, brown-striped with blood from old cuts; the gown he wore was torn and stained by long use, its original maroon faded to a reddish grey. His face was thin, sag lines in the flesh marking former fullness, and the eyes above the tangled beard were bright and mad as those of a bird. From time to time he mumbled, bursting into snatches of song, throwing his head back to laugh at the sullen sky, waving a hand in vague gestures of blessing at the desolation round him.

The donkey reached the road finally and stopped as if uncertain of its way. Its rider waited, chanting and muttering; and the brilliant restless eyes slowly became aware of the girl. She still knelt in the road, face downcast; she lifted her head to see the stranger regarding her, hand still half raised. She ran to him then, fell to clutch the rough hem of his robe. She began to cry; the tears spilled out unchecked, coursing pathways down her grubby face.

The rider stared at her, vaguely puzzled; then he reached down and attempted to lift her. She quivered at the touch and clung tighter. "You . . . come . . ." she muttered, as if to the donkey. "*Come* . . ."

"The blessings of an outcast be on you," mumbled the stranger, tongue seeming to stumble unused over the words. He frowned, as if striving to recollect; then, "How beautiful on the mountains," he said inconsequentially, "are the feet of him who brings good tidings. . . ." He rubbed his face, tangled his fingers in his hair. "There was a man," he said slowly, "who talked of cures. . . . Who needs me, sister? Who called on Brother John?"

"I . . . did. . . ." Her voice was muffled; she was scrabbling at the cloth of his gown hem, kissing and rubbing her face against his foot. John's wandering attention was riveted; he tried to raise her again, awkwardly. "For what purpose, sister?" he asked gently. "I can but pray; prayer is free to all. . . ."

"To cure . . ." She swallowed and snivelled, not wanting to say the words. Then they burst from her. "To cure . . . *by the laying-on of hands . . .*"

"Up . . . ?"

She felt herself yanked to her feet, held where she had to stare at blazing eyes, their pupils contracted to pinpoints of darkness. "There is no cure," hissed John between his teeth, "but the mercy of God. His mercy is infinite, His compassion enfolds us all. I am but His unworthy instrument; there is no power, save the power of prayer. All else is heresy, an evil for which men die. . . ." He flung her back from him; then the mood passed. He wiped his forehead, slid clumsily from the donkey. "You shall ride, my sister," he said. "For it is not fitting I should emulate Him who entered once upon His Kingdom, riding such a beast as this. . . ." The words lost themselves in mumbling, blown ragged by the wind. "I will see your husband," said Brother John.

The cottage was low and cramped, sour-smelling; somewhere a baby bawled, a dog scratched for fleas on the hearth. John ducked through the doorway, guided by the timorous grip of the girl's hand on his wrist; she closed the door behind him, fastening it by its peg and thong. "We keeps it dark," she whispered, "'cause he reckoned that might halp. . . ."

John moved forward carefully. Beside the fire a man sat rigidly, hands resting on his knees. He wore the coarse dress, the leather-reinforced jerkin and trews, of a quarry-

man. Beside him on a rough table stood a partially cleared
plate of food and a tankard of beer; a pipe lay untouched
in the hearth. His hair was overlong, hanging in thick sweeps
beside his ears; his brows were level and thickly black but
the eyes were invisible. Round them as a blindfold he wore
a coloured kerchief, knotted behind his head.

"He's come," said the girl timidly. "Brother John, as'll cure
thee. . . ." She rested a hand on the man's shoulder. He
made no answer; instead he reached up gently, took her
arm, and pushed her away. She turned back to Brother
John, gulping. "Bin comin' on this six months an' more," she
said helplessly. "First he reckoned . . . 'twas like cobwebs,
laid across his face. He couldn't see no more, only in the
sun. Kept on sayin', 'twere dark. All the time, 'twere
dark, . . ."

"Sister," said John quietly, "have you a lantern? A torch?"
She nodded dumbly, eyes on his face.

"Then fetch it here to me."

She brought the light, lit it with a spill from the fire.
John placed the lamp where its open side glowed on the
face of the blind man. "Let me see . . ."

The eyes, uncovered, were dark and fierce, in keeping
with the proud, stern face. Brother John raised the lantern,
angling it at the pupils, turning the head of the peasant with
his fingers under the black-shadowed jaw. He stared a
long time, seeing behind the corneas the milky paleness
reflect back the light; then he lowered the lamp to the
hearth. A long silence; then, "I pity you, sister," he said,
white-lipped. "There is nothing I can do but pray. . . ."

The girl stared at him in blank uncomprehension; then
her hands went to her mouth, and she started again to cry.

John lay that night in an outbuilding, mumbling and
tossing on a pile of hay; it was only toward dawn that the
trumpets and drums stopped beating in his brain and he
slept.

The quarryman rose before first light and dressed silently, not hurrying. Beside him his wife lay still, breathing steady; he touched her arm, and she moaned in her sleep. He left her and walked through the cottage, horny fingers gentle now touching furniture and the familiar backs of chairs. He unfastened the door, felt the morning air move fresh and raw on his face. Once outside he needed no more guides. The lives of the people round about were governed by the working of stone; the tiny quarries scattered through the hills were handed down from father to son through generations. Over the years his feet and the feet of his forebears had worn a track from the cottage out across the heath. He followed it, face turned up to catch the grey smearing that was all his eyes could show him of the dawn. Habit had made him take the lantern; it bumped his knee hollowly as he walked. He reached the quarry, lifted aside the pole that symbolically closed its entrance. He stood a long time inside, leaning his palms against the coolness of the stone; then he found his tools, fondled them to feel the worn smoothness his hands had given them. He started to work.

John, roused by the distant tap of hammer against stone, shook himself free of a feverish dream and turned his head to locate the sound. He rose quietly, slipped his feet into the sandals laid ready for him and padded out into the cold morning, breath rising in puffs of steam as he walked.

The girl was already at the quarry; she crouched on the ground outside, staring dumbly. From within came the rhythmic clinking as the blind man worked at the stone face, measuring, feeling, cutting by touch. A heap of rough-dressed blocks already stood by the entrance; as John watched the quarryman emerged hefting another slab, walked steadily back to his task.

The girl's eyes were on John's face, wonderingly. He shook his head. "I can pray," he muttered. "I can but pray. . . ."

The morning passed, wore on into afternoon, and the noise of the hammer didn't stop. Once the girl fetched food but John wouldn't let her near her husband; the swinging mallet would have brained her. When the sky began to darken the pile of stone stood six feet high, blocking his view; he moved his position from where his knees had dented the rough ground, to where he could once more see. The short day, halfway between winter and spring, ended; but the man inside needed no light. The hammer rang steadily; and John at last divined his purpose. He prayed again feverishly, prostrating himself on the ground. Hours later he slept despite the bitterness of the wind. He woke nearly too stiff to move. In front of him the hammer clinked in blackness. The girl returned with the dawn, carrying the baby beneath her cloak; someone brought food that she refused. John was racked by cramps; his hands and feet blued with the cold. All through the day the wind rose, roaring at the heath.

They were strange, black-spirited folk, these Dorset peasants. The men of the village came one by one and squatted and stared; but none of them tried to take the worker from his task. It would have been useless; he would have returned, as surely as the wind returns again and again to the heaths and half-seen hills. The hammer rang from dawn to nightfall; rain gusted on the wind, pelting John's back, soaking his body through the robe. He ignored it, as he ignored the frozen aches in belly and thighs, the flashings and fainting thunders of his brain. The Old gods would have understood, he thought; they who roared and sweated through the day, hacking each other's guts in endless war to fall and die and be raised each dusk again, carouse the night away in their palace of Valhalla. But the Christian God, what of Him? Would He accept blood sacrifice, as He accepted the torn souls of His witches? Of course, mumbled John's tired brain, because He is the same. His drink is blood, His food is flesh, His sacraments work and misery and endless hopeless pain. . . .

By the second dawn the piles of stone stretched yards across the heath; and the hammer was still falling, faltering now and erratic, cutting more. Stone for the palaces of the rich, cathedrals for the glory of Rome. . . . The huge wind roared among the hills, flapped the cloak of the girl as she sat patient as a cow, hands crossed in her lap, eyes brimming with half-comprehended pain. John crouched defeated, unable now to stand, fingers frozen in their clasping, while the villagers watched dour from across the heath.

And it was ended, the sacrifice made and taken; the worker of stone lay face down, the stuff of a score of legends. A vein pumped in his brown leather neck, blood glowed brightly on muzzle and throat; his body coughed and moved, settling, and John, shuffling forward on useless knees and hands, knew before he reached him he was dead.

He raised himself, with an agonised creaking of bones. At his feet the girl stared greyly, stone herself among the grey stone hills; his shadow reached before him, thin and long, wriggling on the tussocky grass of the heath.

Brother John turned slowly, the rushing and the drumming once more in his brain, raised a white face as above him a weird sun glowed. Brighter it grew and brighter again, a cosmic ghost, a swollen impossibility poised in the blustering sky. John cried out hoarsely, raised his arms; and round the orb a circle formed, pearly and blazing. Then another and another, filling the sky, engulfing, burning cold as ice till with a silent thunder their diameters joined, became a cross of silver flame, lambent and vast. At the node points other suns shone and others and more and more, heaven-consuming; and John saw quite clearly now the fiery swarms of angels descend and rise. A noise came from them, a great sweet sound of rejoicing that seemed to enter his tired brain like a sword. He screamed again, inarticulate,

staggering forward, shambling and running while behind
him his great shadow flapped and capered. Then the people
ran; out into the heath, back along the village street, spreading out from round him as from a focus, tatting and pecking
at the shuttered houses while the word spread faster than
feet could move, quicker soon than the quickest horse;
that round Brother John the heavens opened, transfiguring
with glory. The tale grew, feeding on itself, till God in
His own person looked down clear-eyed from the azure arch
of the sky.

The soldiers heard, at Golden Cap and Wey Mouth and
Wool inland on the heath; the clacking telegraphs brought
the news of a countryside on the stir. Messages flew for
reinforcements, shot and powder, cavalry, great guns. Durnovaria answered and Bourne Mouth and Poole; but the
hurricane was in the towers, felling them like saplings. By
midday the lines were silent, Golden Cap itself a jumble of
broken spars. The garrison commander there mustered a
platoon of infantry and two of horse and force-marched
across country, hoping against hope to nip rebellion in the
bud. One man and one only could hold the rabble, make it
fight; Brother John. This time, one way or another, Brother
John had to go.

The glory faded; but still the people came, flocking across
the heath, fighting their carts and waggons over the hills,
bogging in the squelching lanes as they strove to reach
him. Some came to him with money and clothing, food,
offers of shelter, fast horses. They begged him to run,
warned of the soldiers racing to cut him off; but the noise
still roaring in his ears deafened him and the sun dogs,
glowing in his brain, blinded the last of his reason. The
host, the ragged army, grew behind him as he reeled
across the heath, face to the great wind from the south.
Some brought arms; pitchforks and scythes and knives on
poles, muskets hauled from the thatch of twenty score of

cottages. Chanting, they reached the sea; following still, on horseback and on foot, down the steep roads of Kimmeridge, out to the black bite of a bay and the savageness of the water. There they collided at last with the contingent from Golden Cap. The soldiers of the Blue attacked; but there were too many. A charge, a scattering, a man pulled down, trampled and cut; screams tossed away by the wind, a red thing left shaking on the grass, a horse running riderless stabbed bloody by the pikes. . . . The Papists withdrew, following the column just inside long musket shot, sniping to try to turn its head.

Brother John ignored the skirmishing; or perhaps he never saw. Riding now, driven forward by the voices and the noises in his brain, he reached the cliff edge. Below was a waste of water, wild and white, tumbling to the horizon and beyond. Here were no rollers; the hurricane, into which a man might lean, flung the tops off the waves. From a score of runoffs the cliffs spouted water into the bay; but the streams were caught by the wind and held, flung bodily back over the edge of the land, wavering upward arcs that fed a ruffled lake of flood. At the cliffs, John reined; the horse turned bucking, mane streaming in the wind. He raised his arms, calling the people in till they crowded close to hear; black-faced men in sweaters and caps and boots, stolid women clutching scarves to their throats; dark-haired Dorset girls, legs sturdy in their bright blue jeans. Way off on the left the cavalry bunched and jostled, carbines to their shoulders; the smoke of the discharges was whipped away in instantaneous flashes of white. A ball curved singing above John's head; another smashed the foot of a girl on the edge of the crowd. The mob turned outward, dangerously. The riders pulled back. A gun was coming, dragged by mule teams from the barracks at Lulworth, but until it arrived their captain knew he was helpless; to throw his handful of men into that rabble

would be to consign them to death. Miles away, out on
the heath, the teams strained at the limber of the culverin;
spare ammunition carts jolted behind, heading a column
of infantry. But there were no more cavalry, none to be
had; there was no time. . . .

Over Brother John the seagulls wheeled. He raised his
arms again and again, seeming to call the birds in till
the great creatures hung motionless, wings outspread a
scant six feet above him. The crowd fell silent; and he
started to speak.

"People of Dorset . . . fishermen and farmers and you,
marblers and roughmasons, who grub the old stone up out
of the hills . . . and you, Fairies, the People of the Heath,
you were-things riding the wind, hear my words and remember. Mark them all your lives, mark them for all time;
so in the years to come, no hearth shall ever be without
the tale. . . ." The syllables ran shrieking and thin, pul-
verised by the wind; and even the injured girl stopped
moaning and lay propped against the knees of her friends,
straining to hear. John told them of themselves, of their
faith and their work, their lonely carving of existence out
of stone and rock and bareness; of the great Church that
held the land by the throat, choking their breath in the
grip of her brocade fist. In his brain visions still burned
and hummed; he told them of the mighty Change that
would come, sweeping away blackness and misery and
pain, leading them at last to the Golden Age. He saw
clearly, rising about him on the hills, the buildings of
that new time, the factories and hospitals, power stations
and laboratories. He saw the machines flying above the
land, skimming like bubbles the surface of the sea. He
saw wonders; lightning chained, the wild waves of the very
air made to talk and sing. All this would come to pass,
all this and more. The age of tolerance, of reason, of humanity, of the dignity of the human soul. "But," he shouted,

and his voice was cracking now, lost in the great sound
of the wind, "but for a time, I must leave you . . . following
the course shown me by God, who in His wisdom saw
fit to make me . . . the least worthy of His people . . .
His instrument, and subject to His will. For He gave me
a sign, and the sign burned in heaven, and I must follow
and obey. . . ."

The crowd jostled; a roaring came from it, faint then
louder, rising at last over the sound of the wind. A hundred
voices shouted, "Where . . . where . . ." and John turned,
gown sleeve flogging at his arm, and pointed into the brilliant waste of the sea.

"Rome . . ." The word soared at the people. "To the
earthly father of us all . . . the Rock, guardian of the
Throne of Peter . . . Christ's designate, and His Vicar on
Earth . . . to beg wisdom of his understanding, mercy of
his compassion, alms of his limitless bounty . . . in the
name of the Christ we adore, whose honour is stained too
often in this land. . . ."

There was more but it was lost in the noise of the crowd.
The word spread like wildfire to the farthest members of
the mob that a miracle was to be performed. John would
go to Rome; he would fly; for a sign, he would walk on
water. He would command the waves. . . . The more level-
headed, still carried away, set up a cry for a boat; and
a woman shrilled suddenly, her voice rising above the rest.
"Thine, Ted Armstrong. . . . Give him thine. . . ."

The man addressed waved furious arms. "Peace, woman,
'tis all I own. . . ." But the protest was lost, swept aside
in a surging movement that bore John and his followers
down the cliff path, through the singing stands of gorse
and bramble that lined the sea. To the watching soldiers
it was as if the mob thrust out arms into the water; men,
skidding and tumbling in mud, hauled the vessel to her
slip, launched her down it. She lay heaving and rolling

in the backwash of the waves; oars were shipped, John tumbled aboard. Girls swarmed atop the piles of lobster pots stacked and roped on the beach, climbed back up the cliffs under the reversed firehose-spraying of the springs. The boat, cast off, corkscrewed violently, rolled to show her bilge, straightened as the wind caught her stump of mast, headed for the first of the seething ridges of white. To either side the vast headlands of peat, black iron against the glaring sky; in front the miles on flattened miles of water seething in over the rim of the world. The watchers, straining against the brilliance, saw the keel lift to a hammer blow, surge off one-sided into a trough. Swamped, the craft rose again tinier and dwindling, a dark blob against brightness. And again, farther out still in the yeast-boiling and roaring surge of the sea; till tired eyes, streaming and screwed against the wind, could no longer mark her progress against the tumbling plain of the ocean.

They hauled the great gun up to the western headland, and primed her and loaded with canister; she rumbled threatening over the brink as dusk was settling on the waste of water below. But she menaced an empty beach; the whole huge crowd was gone. The soldiers stood-to till dawn, huddled in their greatcoats, squatting backs to the wind against the cold iron of the gun while the hurricane, dropping, blew itself away.

And the waves, frothing still, slapped at the upturned keel of a boat, urging it back gently toward the land.

Fifth Measure
LORDS AND LADIES

The group of people clustered round the bed had something of the sculptured stillness of a stage tableau. A single lamp, hung above them from one of the heavy beams, threw their faces into sharp relief, accentuated the pallor of the sick man as he lay with one end of Father Edwardes' violet stole tucked beneath his neck, the fabric stretched between them like a banner of faith. The old man's eyes rolled restlessly; his hands plucked at the covers as he breathed in short, painful gasps.

Beyond the group, framed in the window against the bluing dusk sky of May, sat a girl. Her long dark blond hair was bound in a chignon at the nape of her neck; one wisp had escaped, lay curling on her shoulder. It brushed her cheek as she turned her head; she pushed it aside irritably, looked down across the long roofs of the engine sheds to where the late train swung into the yard with a rattle and clash, manoeuvred towards its bay. Some scent from it floated up to the casement; Margaret seemed to feel momentarily the warmth from the steamer brush her face, tinging the mild air with giants' breath. She looked back guiltily into the room. Her mind, seeming half dazed, translated snatches of the priest's rumbling Latin.

"I exorcise thee, most vile spirit, the very embodiment of our enemy, the entire spectre. . . . In the name of Jesus Christ . . . get out and flee from this creature of God. . . ."
The girl twined her fingers in her lap, compressing them to feel the knuckle joints grind into each other, and lowered

her eyes. The Dutch lamp hanging from the ceiling swayed
slightly, its flame leaping and flickering. There was no wind.

Father Edwardes paused and lifted his head quietly to
stare at the lamp. The flame steadied, burning again bright
and tall. A muffled sob from old Sarah at the foot of
the bed; Tim Strange reached forward to squeeze her hand.

*"He Himself commands thee, who has ordered thee cast
down from the heights of heaven to the depths of the
earth. He commands thee, who commands the sea, the
winds, and the tempests. . . . Hear therefore and fear O
Satan, enemy of the faith, foe to the human race. . . ."*

Down below the loco chattered again, softly. Margaret
turned back unwillingly. Strange how the very sound of
oiled steel could evoke such a tapestry of images. The
summer-night roads, whitish-grey ribbons trailing into darkness, warm still with the sun's heat, owl and bat haunted;
buzz of early insects in the air, churr of feeding birds;
grass knee-long, rich as black velvet under the moon;
tall wild hedgerows heavy with the blood-pounding scent
of the may. She wanted in an intense flash of longing to
be clear of the room and the house, run and dance, roll
in the grass till the stars spun giddy sparks above her
face.

She swallowed and made instinctively and automatically
the sign of the Cross. Father Edwardes had counselled
her very closely against any such levity of thought, any
aberration that might herald the advent of a possessing
and vengeful spirit. "For my child," the priest had warned
solemnly, quoting from the *Enchiridion* of Von Berg, "they
may approach mildly; but afterward they leave behind
grief, desolation, disturbance of soul, and clouds of the
mind. . . ."

A vein throbbed in Father Edwardes' temple. Margaret
bit her lip. She knew she should go to him now, join
the force of her prayers with his, but she couldn't move.

Something stopped her; the same Thing that held her tongue at confession, wouldn't have her near the box. It seemed, if such a thing were possible, that the long room was *skewed;* twisted in some strange way, its walls discontinuous, the floor curving and waving hinting at dimensions beyond the senses. As if the short distance that separated her from the group by the bed had become a gulf across which she had stepped to another planet.

She shook her head, irritable at the idea; but the fancies persisted. She felt a moment of giddiness; the swinging over nothing, the awful fetch and check of the falling nightmare. The room steadied on its new dimensions; "up" was now clearly represented by two differing directions. The lamp, hanging still, seemed to be twisted toward her; at her back the window leaned away. She caught her breath, feeling stifled, and the scents and visions came again, soothing and lulling, profferings from hell. Sweet musk of the may, fresh brown stench of new furrows where bread and other things were buried in defiance of Mother Church. . . . She wanted to call out, take the robes of the priest and beg forgiveness, tell him to stop his mummeries because the fault and the evil lay in her. She tried to scream and thought she had but a deep part of her knew her lips hadn't moved. She could still see Father Edwardes as if through darkened glass, the hand falling and rising, making again and again the sign of the Cross; she could hear the voice grind on but she herself was a million miles away, out among the cold burning of the stars and the balefires on the mounds of the dead where the Old Ones watched for all time. She was conscious dimly of a knocking and rattling rising to crescendo, the curtains flapping sudden and nauseating across the window. The lamp flame waned again, browning.

"YIELD THEREFORE; YIELD NOT TO ME, BUT TO THE MINISTER OF CHRIST. FOR HIS POWER URGES

THEE, WHO SUBJUGATED THEE TO HIS CROSS.
TREMBLE AT HIS ARM. . . ."

The clanging in the room was thunderous. Margaret fell
upward, into night.

A voice calling in the darkness, strident and bright.
"Margaret!"

"Margaret!"

A waiting; then, "Will you come this *minute*. . . ."

But the voice could be ignored, until its final utterance.
"Margaret *Belinda* Strange, *will* you come . . ." That, the
mystic invocation of the second name, must never go un-
heeded. To defy it would be an open invitation to slapping,
to bed-without-supper; and that was a terrible thing on a
bright summer night.

The small girl stood on tiptoe, fingers clutching the edge
of the desk top. Its surface stretched away from an inch
before her nose, rich with wood grain, greasy, shiny, magical
with the special magic of grown-up things. "Uncle Jesse,
what are you doing?"

Her uncle put his pen down, ran his fingers through
thick hair still black, touched with grey now at the temples.
He shoved his steel-framed spectacles up to pinch at the
bridge of his nose. His voice rumbled at the child. "Makin'
money, I guess. . . ." Nobody could have told whether he
was smiling or not.

Margaret turned up her button nose. "Pooh. . . ." Money
was an incomprehensible affair; the word made a shape in
her mind, bulky and brown as the ledgers over which her
uncle toiled. Something far-off and uninteresting yet vaguely
sinister. "Pooh. . . ." The grubby fingers curled on the desk
edge. "Do you make a lot of money?"

"Fair bit, I reckon. . . ." Jesse was working once more,
fist half obscuring the lines of neat figures crawling into
existence on the thick cream paper. Margaret cocked her

head at him, trying to see his face, wrinkling her nose again. That last was a new accomplishment and she was proud of it. She said suddenly, "Do I annoy you?"

Jesse grinned, figuring in his head. "No, lass. . . ."

"Sarah says I do. What are you doing?"

Steadily. "Makin' money. . . ."

"Why do you want so much?"

The burly man stopped openmouthed, arms half raised; an odd gesture. He stared at the low ceiling, the total lost now in his mind, then turned to scoop the child onto his knee. Grinning again.

"Why? Well, I reckon little maid . . . I reckon I couldn't rightly say now."

Margaret sat watching, frowning a little and smelling the tobacco-nearness of him, chubby legs stuck out, well-picked scabs on the knees, the seat of her knickers black where she'd made a slide with Neville Serjeantson in the orchard behind the warehouses, out of some boxes and old steel rails. The yard foreman placed the rails for the children, to keep them quiet awhile. They were forever in the sheds, and underfoot when they backed the great iron engines; they were the bane of his existence.

"I reckon . . ." said Jesse. He stopped again, thinking and laughing. "Well, so's one day I could put a hundred thousand where once there were only ten. Only you wouldn't understand that, see?" He shoved vaguely at her hair, frowning at a tuft that had been yellow, was stuck together now with a dob of axle grease. "You bin in they sheds again? Sarah'll give thee summat, dang me if she don't. . . ."

"Not going with Sarah. Staying with you." The child wriggled, reached out for a rubber stamp and plonked it onto the blotter; then lacking further damageable surfaces, the back of Jesse's hand. Words showed faintly, bright blue against the brown scaming and wrinkling of the skin. *Strange and Sons of Dorset, Hauliers. . . .*

"Margaret *Belinda* Strange . . ."

Jesse swung her down and laughed, dusted her drawers for her as she ran.

The memory stayed with Margaret; one of those odd, arbitrary moments out of childhood that seem to become enshrined in consciousness, never to be forgotten. Her uncle's lined, hard face, blue-jawed, close above her; the sunlight lying across the desk, Sarah calling, the stamp with its bulging black handle and the little brass stud that showed which way round it was when you pressed it down. A rare enough moment it was too, for Jesse was not an expansive man. His niece called good night to him later, standing at her window to see him leave the house, jacket slung across his shoulder, on his way to drink beer with his men at the *Hauliers' Arms* just along the street. But he'd changed again then; all she got back was the faint sour pulling of the mouth corners, the grunt he'd use to answer anybody as he slammed the door and tramped with a scraping and crunching of boots across the yard.

Jesse Strange had few words, in those days; and nobody willingly crossed him. He was a driver; he drove his hauliers, he drove his machines, but most of all he drove himself. If he chose to drink, he'd put the best man under the table; that happened sometimes of a night down in the village inn. But he'd walk home steady; and the boys, rolling across the street at chuck-out time, would see the light burning in his office or in the sheds, where like as not he'd be stripping the valve gear on one of the locos or cleaning her boiler or mending her massive wheel treads. They'd wonder then if Jesse Strange ever tired, and when he slept.

He'd made his hundred thousand a long time back, then his first half million. It seemed to him work was a sacrament, a panacea for all ills. The firm of Strange and Sons grew, spreading out beyond Dorset with depots as far away as

Isca and Aquae Sulis. Jesse broke Serjeantson, his one
competitor in Durnovaria, running his trains at cutthroat
rates, stealing load after load from under the old man's
nose. They said at the height of the war no train showed
him a profit for nearly a year; there were battles and
beatings among the drivers, blood spilled on the footplates;
but he broke Serjeantson and bought him out, added
forty steamers to the huge Strange fleet. The sheds and
warehouses that joined the old house at Durnovaria were
extended again and again till they sprawled across more
than an acre; and still it wasn't enough. Jesse broke Roberts and Fletcher at Swanage; then Bakers, and Caldecotts,
and Hofman and Keynes from over Shaftesbury way; and
then he bought outright Baskett and Fairbrother of Poole,
with more than a hundred Burrells and Fodens on the
road, and Strange and Sons owned the West Country haulage trade. And after that even the *routiers* let their trains
be; because money works wonders in high places, and one
swipe at a Strange loco would bring a hornet swarm of
cavalry and infantry down round their ears and the game
wasn't worth the price. The maroon nameboards with their
oval yellow plaques were known from Isca to Santlache,
from Poole to Swindon and Reading-on-the-Thames; drivers
gave way to them, the Serjeants cleared the roads for them.
In the end Jesse won respect even from his enemies. He
paid his way, gave nothing; and what you stole from him,
you were welcome to keep. . . .

A lot of men wondered what drove him. At college he'd
been a dreamer, head in the clouds; but somebody somewhere had taught him what life was about. Some whispered
he killed a man once, a friend, and the empire he built
was somehow his atonement; there was even a rumour
he was jilted by a barmaid, and this was his answer to
the world. Certainly he never married, though there were
women enough later on who found they could put up with

his ways, and men too who would have sold their daughters fast enough to tie their family to the name of Strange; but none of them got the chance. Nobody ever dared ask outright, except his niece; and though she remembered, as he'd warned her she didn't understand.

Margaret seemed suddenly to be moved forward in time. She was going away to school, a whole twenty miles to Sherborne for her first boarding term. A half mile through the streets of Durnovaria, a little scrappet stumping along clinging to Sarah's arm, wearing a new uniform, leather satchel swinging from her shoulder, apples in the satchel and sweets, pitiful little bits of home. Head stuck high, face set, sniffing to stop from bawling at the wrongness of everything, on her way to death and worse. . . . Sarah seemed huge, the paving slabs huge and the cobbles and the old leaning houses, as afternoons and mornings had seemed huge, each bulking a separate entity in her mind as she crossed off the frightened days to start-of-term. The last night, last morning, an inevitability against which she seemed suspended, in a dream within a dream. The September dawn was blue with mist and cold, she buzzed with the chill of it while images floated unconnected and remote and her body was a machine, forgotten legs pumping her along. A road train passed at the end of the street and the light from the loco firebox glowed back on her steersman and driver and the child wanted in sudden bitterness to run forward and be swept away, snuggle under a load tarp in the rumbling and darkness to end some mysterious closed circuit in her own room at home; but instead she turned left mechanically to the station, still hanging onto her nanny's arm. Old Sarah, hated often, seemed lovable now; but there was no help in her. The train was waiting, crowded and dank; Margaret was hustled onto it, stood pressing her face to the windows smudging the breath-steam with her fingers while Sarah

and station and the whole of existence swept into a dot
that dwindled behind her and vanished for all time.

And there was school, the big house dark and cold, and
the strangeness of the nuns with their startling starched-
white cowls, the whisper and shuffle of them crossing the
stone-floored rooms. A twilight of loneliness, sombre and
unbearable, shot through at last with little gleams of hope;
letters from home, a cake, a box of fruit standing on the
table in the hall. Frosty vividness of games days, whispered dormitory conversations, first stirrings of friendship.
. . . Time passed quickly while Africa became a continent
and πr^2 was forced to equal the area of a circle and
Caesar fought the Gauls. Other days and months declined
impossibly and Christmas was near. A concert, services for
end-of-term in the great hall; candles burning in their
sconces through the short December days, issuing of rail
vouchers, excitement of packing and waiting; the last morning, when Margaret was taken mysteriously in charge by
her housemistress Sister Alicia. Shoutings in the grounds,
noises rendered crystalline by the bright winter air; flapping and chuffing of the butterfly cars thronging the front
of the school while Anne waited feeling lost, the Sister
secretive and smiling. And the great surprise; first a rumbling, distant but known, a sound her blood could never
forget; and a plume of steam, a wink of brass as the loco,
hugely unbelievable, edged her way along the drive, rutting
Mother Superior's precious gravel with her great treads,
hooting and shouldering and bluffing her way through the
butterfly cars, her wheels as tall as the highest of their
masts. She was towing a single trailer, its flat bed nearly
empty, and her uncle was driving and Margaret knew he'd
come specially for her and started, hating herself, to howl,
while Sister Alicia muttered "ridiculous child . . . ridiculous
child . . ." and prodded sense back into her with painfully
bony fingers.

She was lifted up wincing with expectation to pull the
cord that woke the Burrell's huge deep voice; while the
children clustered round the wheels ogling and laughing
till Jesse drove them back with shouts and thrust forward
reversing lever and regulator and they were on their way
with a fussing of valves and crossheads, a great jetting
of steam. Margaret clung to the hornplate staring back and
waving as school receded, swept away by the windings of
its drive to be lost and forgotten for a lifetime of three
whole weeks. Often after that her uncle fetched her, or
told off one of the men to detour. If he came it was
always with *Lady*, the old Burrell that was still the pride
of the fleet, and Margaret would boast endlessly to her
friends and the mistresses that the loco had been named
after her, she was her own special train. Jesse would laugh
at that sometimes and shove her hair and say it were
funny the way things worked thereselves through. For the
child's mother too had been called Margaret; her dad kept
a pub out Portland way and when he died and left her
no place to live she'd been glad enough to settle for a man
years her junior. Though it had cost Tim Strange his job
and his home. . . . But it hadn't taken the woman long
to tire of being the wife of a common haulier; two years
later she'd run off with My Lord of Purbeck's *jongleur*,
and Tim had come trailing back with his scrap of a kid
and Jesse had laughed quiet and long, and made over to
him the half of his business. But that had been in the long
ago, before Margaret grew a remembering brain.

Other later things were still fresh to her, other facets
of her strange and wayward uncle. She remembered how
one day she'd gone running to him with a shell, told him
to listen and hear the waves inside. He'd taken time off
from his endless making of money and driven her way up
into the hills and found a quarry and dug a fossil out
the rocks and made her put that to her ear as well;

she'd heard the same singing and he'd told her that was
the noise the years made, all the millions of them shut
inside buzzing to get free. She kept the stone a long while
after that; and when more time had passed and she knew
the whispering and piping were only echoes of her blood
she didn't care because she'd still heard what she heard,
the sound of trapped eternities.

The making of the firm had aged Jesse a lot; that and
a bursting steam union that poached the skin half off his
back before he could stagger clear. The locos took their
toll odd times of the men who used them; he'd been up
and about far too soon, passed out on the footplate trying
to haul a load of stone singlehanded to Londinium. Margaret had been a gangling thirteen then, all legs and arms, her
nipples already pushing marks into her dress. She'd nursed
him well, sitting reading through the long quiet evenings
of a summer holiday while Jesse lay and frowned and
brooded at the ceiling and thought God alone knew what.
But the thing had changed him for all time; and so soon
it seemed he was an old man on a bed, clammy and yellow
and waiting to die, and the priest waving thin hands across
him in the stink of incense, saying the grumbling words. . . .

The falling stopped. Margaret looked round dazed; she'd
lived through years, but the room was quite unchanged.
Her father watching down, thin face haggard in the lamplight, old Sarah sitting pudgy and anxious twining her
fingers in her lap, Father Edwardes still intoning book in
hand, the stole stretched tight; the lamp flame was steady
again now, clear in the spring dusk. She wiped her face
furtively then, her hand on her dress, pressed her knees
together tight to stop the trembling.

This last week had been bad. The house shadowed,
haunted. . . . Margaret's mind shied away from the word.
"Possessed" was a worse one it hadn't till now occurred
to her to use. The noises, the rattlings and tappings, night

sighings and unease; like the shadows of an ancient wrong,
unrequited and unchangeable. While death stepped closer,
inexorable, like the flowing of the rivers, the red night
plunge of the sun behind the standing stones of the heaths.
Once Jesse sat up terrified and stark, moving his hands,
seeing things that weren't there to see; once a maid
shrieked at the icy fondling of the empty kitchen air; once
the landing reeled under Margaret, an accident of Time
maybe that let her see flitting ahead the *doppelganger*,
shadow of herself, alien in the warm night. *Margaret* was
the name on the old man's lips now and his niece thought
for a while he meant her, but it wasn't so. His hands waved,
pushing at nothingness; his eyes watched frightened as
the spring breeze passed through the room, setting swaying
the brasses on the beams, moving the lamps so the spindles
yellow gleams shifted on mantel ornaments and bed rail.
The steamer, Sarah thought he meant; poor old thing to
be frightened of her now, see her shadow in the swinging
lamps and brass. But no, there was a rumour. . . . Watching alone, the girl sat shuddering; she'd lived with the
hauliers long enough to soak their daft tales in through
her pores. The Burrell wouldn't fetch her master, she was
down below locked in the engine sheds, fires drawn, tarps
across her boiler, oak chocks hammered under her wheels.
There was a steamer that came though, that was how the
legend ran; Cold Bess, swaying and black in the night
and tall, hell in her belly and her running lamps for eyes.
There'd been a real Cold Bess once, far down in the west,
and her driver strapped her safety valve to win a bet
and she blew him to kingdom come; but after that you
still might hear her homing, her flywheel clanking and the
rumble of the train wheels, her whistle shouting nights
out on the hills. That was years back, nobody could say
how long; but the rumour stuck, grew into a silly story
to scare the kids to bed with. When the hauliers spoke of

Cold Bess, they meant Death. Margaret, educated, still crossed herself hopelessly and shivered. Cold Bess was in the room. . . .

They took the brasses out and the candlesticks and ornaments and draped the bed rail top where it caught the light, and the silly old man lay quieter; but the Presences wouldn't leave. Margaret could feel them tugging and whispering; cold spots floated on the stairs, once her shoes were snatched from her hand and slammed against the wall. That was when they sent for the priest; and Father Edwardes made his feelings clear by the service he chose to read. Prayers existed for the exorcism of the Noisy One, the *Poltergeist*; but he had ignored them. The good Father had no doubt where the trouble lay; he was conducting the rite for the explusion of a devil. But he's wrong, Margaret told herself, wrong; and cried inside, silently. . . .

"Therefore I adjure thee, draco nequissime, in the name of the immaculate lamb, who trod upon the asp and basilisk, to depart from this man . . . to depart from the Church of God. . . ."

The voice faded, lost beneath more dreaming.

Margaret, sweating again, tried to fight back because nightmare was coming and as in all such dreams she drifted closer and ever closer to the thing she most wanted not to see. She asked herself could they then, the Things that knocked and fretted, the haunters, *the Old Ones* her mind whispered, *the Old Ones* . . . could they do this thing? Snatch her out of Space and Time, from under the very fingers of the priest? *Dare* they? She groaned helplessly. These were the People of the Heath, the Fairies; they who once had known an ancient power.

She was sitting on a beach. The sun, pouring and hot, struck her shoulders and arms and her knees under the little tabard that was the season's fashion must. Fair, she still tanned easily, the freckles exploding round her mouth and nose and across her back. She liked herself brown, she liked to loll on the beach and soak in warmth and light; she'd fought for her day out, haggling with Tom Merryman to detour his Foden, drop her and pick her up. Sarah, faithful and complaining, had tagged along, jounced on the flat bed of the trail load, half choked by dust from the rutted white roads. Behind them the cars careered, veering and jostling, tiny engines sputtering, striped lateens filling in the puffs of breeze; Margaret swung her long legs and laughed at the drivers all the way down from Durnovaria. At Lulworth Tom offloaded a case of machine tools before turning along the coast to Wey Mouth. Beyond the town the Foden swung inland again, routed for Beaminster; Margaret had dropped down, lugging Sarah, intent on her day on the beach, stood and waved till the Foden vanished under its own trailing cloud of dust. Then Sarah had come over queer because of the heat and been taken to sit down under a tree and hear a band, and Margaret scampered off to the water and sat by herself till the boat came in and all the people started running.

She asked herself then, why she always had to head into the centre of trouble. Privately she believed she must be a coward; reality was never as bad as the horrors of her imaginings. The time old William lost half his fingers in a workshop lathe; she'd heard the dreadful sound he made, seen the countershafts stop spinning as the foreman hit the emergency brake and had to run fast into the dimness to where Will stood ashen-faced holding his wrist; and seeing the blood pump bright from the finger stumps, patter and ribbon on the floor, was nearly a relief. They'd told her later how good she'd been, she might have basked in the praise and enjoyed it but she knew it wasn't deserved. She hated, she sickened, but she just had to *see*. . . .

They took the tourists out from Wey Mouth, from the beaches and the harbour there, fishing for sole and lobster

and sharks sometimes when the season was right, the little
basking sharks that did no harm to anyone but made good
sport. It was a fishing boat that was coming in, and the
boy on her had caught his arm in a winch and made
the land somehow. Margaret pushed through the crowd
wriggling and shoving, sickness coming already and dark
shadows at the edges of her sight, not able to stop; she
saw the mess, tendon and bone showing in spikes and the
man, reddened, holding himself with a hideous dignity,
and didn't know what to do.

The car drove churning onto the beach, throwing sand,
stopped for its driver to vault the door and come shouldering into the crowd. He must have taken Margaret for a
midwife or something, her throat was too dry to tell him
he was wrong. She found herself in the back seat of the
motor, squeezing the tourniquet, propping the injured man,
seeing the blood run rich and soak into the upholstery.
Just out of town a little station run by a half dozen Adhelmians served as the nearest thing to a hospital; the
driver pulled in there and she sat while the boy was
carried through the door and wondered whether to be sick
then or later. After a time she got out, not really conscious
of what she was doing, and started to walk. Sarah was
forgotten; she was in a desolate mood where she seemed
to see all humanity as bags of skin waiting to be burst and
die in pain, herself a woman trapped in a fragile body,
bleeding in childbirth, bleeding in coition. She was very
shocked, and felt like death.

The beach she reached finally seemed to stretch for miles.
She followed the cliffs above it, walking from headland to
headland, seeing the vistas of white and blue, sparklings
of salt spray in the wind, aimless and objectless. She got
to the sea by a sandy slither, thought she might bathe
then remembered instead she had something to do and
was formally sick behind a stand of gorse. Then she sat on

a rock that hurt her behind and brooded, picking pebbles from round her feet and flicking them at the water, seeing the sun burn off the sea in skeins and dancing loops of light. The voice when it came hardly penetrated her consciousness; the stranger had to shout again.

"Hi . . . !"

He was heavy and bearded, red-faced and not used to being ignored. Margaret turned, and regarded him despondently.

"What the devil d'you think you're doing?"

She shrugged. Her shoulders indicated "Sea . . ." and "Throwing pebbles in it . . ."

"Just come up here, will you?"

Another shrug. *You come down* . . .

He did, with a crashing and a rattle. "Fine bloody dance you've led me. . . ." He pulled up her chin insolently with a thick-fingered hand. "Yeah," he said, nodding. "Pretty good . . ."

Her eyes burned at him. Then, "Is he dead?" She asked the question listlessly; the moment of anger had passed, leaving her drained out and flat.

The stranger laughed. "Not him, plebeian bastard. . . . Blood poisoning might sort him out but I shouldn't think so. They generally live. . . ."

"What did they do?" A husk of interest in her voice.

The Norman—for they were speaking, almost unconsciously on Margaret's part, Norman French—shrugged. "Nothing to it. Over in a flash. Pantryman's cleaver, pot of tar. You leave the vein sutures sticking out, pull 'em through when they rot. . . ."

She rolled her lips, squaring the corners. His hand was on her again instantly. She knocked it off. "Just leave me alone. . . ."

A tussling. "You're a good-looking little bit," he said. "Where d'you hail from then, haven't seen you about. . . ."

She swung a fist at him. *"Fils de prêtre . . ."*

He reacted as if she'd stabbed him with a bayonet. He flung her away, stood over her; for a moment she thought she was in for a beating, then he turned away in disgust. "That," he said, "wasn't smart. . . ." Sand had got in his eye; he knuckled it furiously, swearing, then started to climb back up the cliff. Halfway to the top he turned and shouted. "You're scared. . . ."

Silence.

"You're a little prig. . . ."

No reaction.

"It's a bloody long walk back. . . ."

Margaret got up, nostrils pinched with fury, and followed him to the car.

It sat seething faintly, straps across the bonnet vibrating, seeming to hunch between its widespread wheels. He handed her in—the door was about five inches deep—got in himself, released the brakes, and shoved at what she supposed was the regulator. The Bentley gathered speed with a vicious thrusting, in a silence that was nearly eerie, trailed by the faintest wisp of steam. Margaret sat rigid, sun-warmed leather under her thighs, wondering why she'd never been able to resist a dare, whether it was something in her that couldn't grow up. The driver looped away from the coast and turned east again. The rutted roads were unkind to the motor; he leaned across once and shouted something about "Do two hundred on macadam," then relapsed into silence. Margaret realized more fully what she'd known before, that he came from no ordinary stock. Technically steam cars were permissible; but only the wealthiest dare own them, could in fact afford them. *Petroleum Veto* had long been tacitly recognised as a bid to restrict the mobility of the working classes.

Passing through Wey Mouth she thought of old Sarah still scraping about looking for her charge, driving the local peelers crazy no doubt by this time. She yelled to stop but the driver ignored her; only the sidelong gliding of his eye, bright and bad-tempered, showed he had heard. Outside the town the rain came. Margaret had seen it building up for some time; the storm clouds ahead, dusty yellow and grey, piling against the midsummer blue of the sky. She yelped as the first drops hit her, slashing over the tiny windshield. He bellowed back. "Didn't bring the bloody hood. . . ." A mile farther on he lost steam and condescended to stop under a huge oak but by then she was so wet she didn't care anyway. She was glad when he drove on, away from the booming of the branches.

Corvesgeat showed on the horizon, a cluster of towers like fangs of stone. The rain was easing. They passed through the village the focus of a yapping herd of dogs; the Bentley's burners hit them in the ultrasonic, drove them wild. Her driver crossed the square and swung into the castle, under the portcullis of the outer barbican. The gatekeeper saluted as the car bounced past. A fair had camped in the outer bailey; Margaret saw golden dragons, caryatids rain-wet and erotic against grey stone. Show engines stood about, only slightly more ornate than the *Lady Margaret* herself. The Bentley thumped across the grass, blasting folks from her path with her twin brass horns. At the Martyr's Gate the portculli were grounded to keep the people from the upper baileys and the precincts of the *donjon;* Margaret saw steam jet from the high stone as the winches raised the iron trellises for the car. Then they were through, sidling up a slope that looked one in one, the bonnet higher than their heads. The Bentley docked finally in a stone garage set below the soaring walls of the keep.

Above them, dizzyingly far off, floated banners; the oriflamme, ancient and spectacular, flown only on Saints' days and holidays, the bright blue of Rome, the swallow-tailed Union flag of Great Britain. The leopards and Fleurs-de-lys

of the owners of Purbeck were absent, so His Lordship was
not in residence. Margaret caught glimpses of the flags and
the high walls, sunlit now, through roofless passages as she
scurried behind her captor, one wrist gripped in his paw,
too breathless to argue any more. She lost all sense of direction; the castle was a great confusing mass of stone, hall
after hall, building after building stacked and added round
the colossal massif of the *donjon*. She saw through arrow
slits past a spurred drum tower, across a vastness of heathland clear to the harbour of Poole; she climbed a stair set
curling into a buttress to a chamber where Lord Robert of
Wessex, son of Edward Lord Purbeck, swung irritably at a
bellrope that threatened to disintegrate under his attentions.
Margaret was given, kicking, into the charge of a burly
female in the brown and scarlet livery of the House. "Do
something with it," swore Robert, flapping his arms. "Take it
off and bathe it or something, before it starts to sneeze. It
stinks of the sea. . . ." Margaret furious, tried to swing
round on him but the iron-studded door had already
slammed. At her spluttered accusations of kidnapping the
servingwoman laughed. "What, with his mother at home?
He keeps his own nest clean, ye can be sure of that. . . .
Oof . . . Come on now m'lady, don't be cross-grained. . . .
Ow, you little beast. . . ."

The room to which Margaret was lugged, and in which
she was deposited spitting, was by the standards of the
place small. Delicate perpendicular arches supported windows of stained glass that repeated glowingly the heraldic
motifs of leopards and lilies. Brocade drapes covered part
of the walls; in the floor was a massive bath built of slabs
of polished Purbeck marble. Over it loomed an ornate geyser, black japanned, replete with rings and polished curlicues
of copper. Grilles in the walls covered what were evidently
the vents of a warm-air system. Margaret was impressed in

spite of herself; her home at Durnovaria was well equipped, but this was a standard of luxury she had never seen.

Two girls attended her. She frowned, half minded to send them packing; she was distinctly unused to being bathed. Sister Alicia used to scrub her sometimes when she was first away at school; "Come along," she'd say, "you unsavoury little thing," and bang her down in one of the great square tubs, already swilling with icy water, and let fly at her with a large hard-bristled brush, and sometimes she nearly enjoyed it; but that was years ago, a lot of things had changed.

Margaret shrugged, and started to wriggle out of the tabard. If this crazy young nobleman cared to waste the time of his housepeople on her then the chance was too good to waste; it would probably never come again.

The bath was filled rapidly, with much snorting and hissing from the geyser; the maids bound her hair, and one of them added to the water a handful of something that produced great towering masses of iridescent foam. That intrigued her, she'd never seen anything like it. An hour later she was feeling nearly inclined to be civil again; she'd been scrubbed and kneaded and massaged, and had to kneel upright while they poured on her shoulders something that smelled of sandalwood and ran and burned like fire and left a splendid glow in the muscles of her back that soaked away stiffness and tiredness. There was a dress laid out for her, a formal thing with a wide scooped neckline and miles of frothy skirt, and a diamanté circlet for her hair. The clothes fitted; she wriggled, feeling the satin-cleanness of her skin against the cloth, and wondered a little wildly just how well Robert had equipped the castle with the apparatus of seduction. She found out later he'd ordered his absent sister's wardrobe ransacked for the occasion; whatever his faults, he certainly never did things by halves. She was badly worried now about Sarah and her parents, but events

seemed to have passed her at the gallop; it was bad enough
just trying to keep pace.

It was evening before she was through, the sinking sun
throwing mile-long shadows across the heath, waking blazing reflections from the tier on tier of diamond-lighted and
mullioned windows; the castle seemed to butt against the
huge western haze like the prow of a stone ship. Sounds
from the fair floated across the baileys; shouts, the din of
the organs, the grumbling vibration of the rides. Dinner
was served in the sixteenth-century hall built alongside the
donjon; the diners promenaded outside it, richly dressed,
arm in arm in the warm air. Margaret was vaguely disappointed when she learned the great keep had been dis-
used for centuries except as storehouse and armoury.

On high days and holidays the Lords of Purbeck were accustomed to take their meals on the ancient way reintroduced by Gisevius; the less favoured guests sat at long tables
in the body of the hall while the family and their personal
friends ate on a raised dais at one end. Lamps burned in
profusion, lighting the place brilliantly; the minstrels' gallery was occupied by a small orchestra; servingmen and
girls scurried about tripping over the dogs, *brachets* and
mastiffs, that littered the floor. Margaret, still a little dazed,
was introduced to the Lady Marianne, Robert's mother, and
to the half dozen or so important guests. Her mind, whirling,
refused to take in the names. Sir Frederick something, His
Eminence the archbishop of somewhere else. . . . She curt-
sied automatically, allowed herself to be steered finally to a
place at Robert's right. A cold nose shoved into her lap
warned her she was attended; she fondled the *brachet* absentmindedly, tickling beneath the ears, and drew from her
host a grunt of surprise. "You're honoured, y'know that?
Doesn't take kindly to anybody, not that one. Had a swipe
at one of the Serjeants the other day." He grinned broadly.
"Two fingers . . ."

Margaret gently withdrew her hand. Mutilation seemed for Robert a major source of fun.

He'd heard her name more than once, introduced her by it a dozen times, but it seemed it hadn't sunk in. She asked him, with as much dignity as she could muster, for a message to be sent to her home. Her eyes hadn't missed the semaphore rigged beside the keep, or the chain tower on the nearby hill. He listened looking faintly surprised, bending his head to catch the request, then snapped his fingers to the Signaller-Page hovering nearby. "Who'd ye say, Strange?"

"My father," said Margaret coldly, "is Timothy Strange of Strange and Sons, Durnovaria."

The bombshell was not without effect. Robert grunted, raised his eyebrows, swigged wine, drummed a tattoo on the linen cloth. "Well, damme," he said. "Damme. Well, I'll marry a bloody Bulgarian. . . ."

"*Robert . . . !*" That from the Lady Marianne, a little farther along the board. He bowed to his mother, unabashed. "I see," he said. "Well, you're a bad-tempered young bitch, I suppose that goes a way to explaining it. . . ." He scribbled on the pad proffered by the Signaller. "Look lively with that, lad, or we shall lose the light." The boy departed, scampering; a few minutes later Margaret heard the clack and bang of the semaphore, the answering clatter from the great tower on the hill. An acknowledgement was back-routed before nightfall; just a frosty "Message received and understood." From that, she presumed she was in disgrace.

The night passed quickly enough, too quickly for Margaret; she could imagine well enough the surly reception waiting for her at home. The dinner was followed by an entertainment by a troupe of acrobats and fairground people. Trained dogs bounced through hoops, ran on their back legs in kilts and breeches; the affair was a great success. The near-demise of one of the performers, caught and tossed by Robert's delicate-tempered hounds, scarcely dampened proceedings. The animal act was followed by a *jongleur*, a long-faced, mournful-looking man who, evidently primed by Robert, delivered a series of rhymes in a thick patois that Margaret perhaps fortunately couldn't follow but that set Robert roaring with amusement. Then trays of nuts and fruit were passed, and more wine; the party broke up well past midnight, Robert bellowing for linkboys to escort Margaret to the room he'd had prepared. She decided abruptly, trying to stand without swaying, that it was just as well nobody was fetching her tonight; the rich Oporto, once restricted to the tables of kings and the Pope, had nearly proved too much for her. She collapsed in a warm haze, mumbling good nights to the woman who relieved her of her clothes, and was asleep within minutes. She woke soon after dawn, lay listening for the sound that had roused her. She heard it again; a dog barking, far off and bright. She got up fuzzily, draped an embroidered counterpane round herself and padded to the long slit of a window. She saw far below over a tumble of roofs Robert, two *brachets* circling the heels of his horse, ride across the lower bailey to the gate, falcon sitting his wrist like a little blind and bright-plumed knight. The ringing barks of the dogs sounded on the quiet air a long while after their master had gone from view.

At eleven that morning a Foden, maroon-liveried, puffed its indignant way through the outer barbican, its driver demanding the person of one Miss Strange; and shortly after Margaret bade good-bye, regretfully, to the great castle of Corfe Gate.

Once home she found things weren't as bad as she'd feared; the family, with the exception of Sarah, were more impressed by her jaunt than annoyed. It took a lot to impress a Strange; but the Lords of Purbeck owned most of Dorset, their demesne stretched to Sherborne and beyond. Once they'd been landlords to Jesse himself, until he'd scraped and saved and bought the place in fee simple. Her uncle approved, in his silent way; and that counted for a lot. He sat with her that night while she told him how things had gone, pulling at his pipe and frowning, throwing the odd quick question that brought out every last detail. But Jesse was an ailing man already, illness marking and greying his face.

Again Margaret was scurried forward in time. It was as if the images presented themselves with all the ghostly, flickering speed of the yet-to-be-invented cinematograph. She remembered the brooding and waiting, the hoping for some sign that Robert hadn't forgotten her totally. She tried to analyse what she felt about him. Was it just his craziness that appealed to her, was she attracted to the sheer animal maleness of him, or was it something deeper? Or more reprehensible, the simple urge to sell herself in the best market possible, set herself up above the rest, above her own family, as mistress of Corfe Gate? She told herself if it was that, to forget it, stop dreaming third-form dreams. Because she never would belong in that great place down there on the hill.

Autumn came and the carrying-in of the sheaves, the services for Harvest Home. The hauliers plaited new corn dollies out in the sheds, hoisted them into the house eaves to replace the old dusty shapes of last year that were ritually burned. Margaret was kept busy in the kitchens supervising the laying-in of preserves for the winter ahead, the bottling and jam-making and salting-down of meat; and the locos came in one after another off the freezing, rutted roads, travel-stained, rusting, to be refurbished in the sheds, greased and oiled and polished and painted for the next year's work. Every bolt must be checked, worn wheel treads replaced, valve gear stripped and reassembled, steering chains examined and tested. The forges bellowed all day long, fanned by blackened imps of hauliers' boys; lathes hummed, men swarmed over the towering Burrells and

Clayton and Shuttleworths. There was labour to spare; for
Strange and Sons, alone in the haulage trade, didn't lay
their people off. Jesse as ever worked with his men, listening head cocked to the huge beating of the locos, touching
and diagnosing; only from time to time the gripping pains
doubled him and he swore and went off and rested and
drank his beer, and buckled to it again.

The days shortened to midwinter; Christmas was barely
a week away when a bailiff, breath steaming, red-lined
cloak wrapped round him against the cold, cantered into
the house yard. Margaret cracked the seals off the letter
when it was brought her, hands shaking. She frowned over
the scrawled, ill-spelt lines; written, she realized with a
sudden furious rush of feeling, by Robert himself. She pelted
to the engine sheds, to tell her uncle first of all. She was
bidden forth to the Christmas celebrations at Corvesgeat,
to be one of the hundred-odd guests at a house party that if
it ran to the form of other years could easily last till March.
Her acceptance was put into the bailiff's hand while he was
still puffing in the kitchen and swigging at a jug of mulled
ale.

She hunted Jesse out again next day before she left, when
the horses were already snorting in the yard. He was working as usual in the sheds refitting the head of a piston to its
shank by the blue light that filtered through the long frost-
muffled windows. She felt pain when she saw the peaked
sharpness of his face, lines drawn and set round the hard
mouth; suddenly she didn't want to go but he was gruff
with her. "You bugger off," he said directly, "while you'm got
the chance. . . ." He brushed her forehead with his lips,
slapped her behind like he used to when she was a kid. He
walked with her to the door, stood waving till she was out of
sight; then turned grimacing, leaning on a bench and rubbing his side, a half-unconscious gesture to ease pain. The

spasm passed, the shadows stopped being red-tinged; he wiped his face, and went heavily back to his work again.

At the outskirts of Durnovaria an escort was waiting. Margaret, muffled in the biting cold, thrilled at the troop of crossbowmen before her, the outriders scouting the heath to either side for signs of the *routiers;* the Lords of Purbeck evidently took no chances with the safety of their guests. It was a long ride, the wind biting at her face and ears, the hooves of the horses ringing on the hard ground; the light was fading before she saw the castle again, grey stone against an iron-grey sky, touched with a thin high powdering of frost. At the outer barbican the portcullis was down; the wind skirled, the great place above stared with blazing eyes of windows. The party waited, horses snorting and stamping, while the chains creaked, the iron ground out of sight into the stone. Excitement had made Margaret forget her uncle; she laughed at the crash of the gate behind her, the challenges of the sentries on the inner walls. The castle was invested alike by winter and the dark.

She remembered dancing and talk and laughter; Masses in the tiny chapel of Corfe Gate, rides down to the coast to see the storm-flattened Channel; fires roaring in the Great Hall, warmness of her bed on moaning nights of wind. She learned partially to fly a hawk, the little gentle-falcon deemed fit for the sport of ladies. Robert gave it to her but she refused it; she had no place to keep it, no mews, no liveried falconer to see to its needs. Finally it escaped, winging high and strong, and she was glad; it seemed to belong to the wind.

Robert, largely to impress his guests, attempted to train a golden eagle, brought down at his request from the wild hills of Scotland. On its first flight the wretched bird took refuge in a tree, and all efforts to dislodge it proved in vain. Two servants of the household were left to watch it but they came back empty-handed; the creature had given them the slip in the gathering dark, refusing the lure. The thing finally returned two nights later, to perch forlornly on a tower of the outer barbican; and Robert, swearing vilely and drunk as a newt, vowed the prodigal should be fittingly greeted. Nothing would suffice but that the castle's one demicannon, an ancient piece never fired in living memory, be laid and trained, and shot and powder broken out from the armoury. The ball knocked a cubic yard of masonry from the wall by the gate, nearly decapitating the serjeant of the pantry and frightening a female guest into hysterics while the benighted bird, blown by the concussion from its perch, winged heavily away, never to be seen again.

On New Year's Eve Robert took Margaret on the long climb to the heights of the ancient keep. They stood at a slitted window, five hundred feet and more above the heath, the wind burning their faces and keening at the stone while Robert laughed at the witch-fires burning all round, twinkling on the horizon like eyes. Somewhere a wolf called, quavering and high; Margaret shivered at the ancient lost noise coming in from the dark. He saw the movement and wrapped his cloak round the both of them, standing behind her, arms crossed in front of her waist; she turned snuggling, feeling his warmth and the slow movement of his hands, pushing her face at his shoulder while he stroked the hair that flicked round her eyes and she wanted to cry for the passing of Time and all transient things. They stood an hour while the bells pealed in the village, doors and windows opened yellow rectangles far below and the fires sank and vanished. On more than one calendar, a new year had begun.

After that she went down to Corvesgeat again and again, while winter turned to spring and spring to high summer. She watched the Morrismen dance in the bailey Midsummer's Eve, fed the hobbyhorse with coins its clacking wooden teeth couldn't hold; once Robert, the Bentley in dock with a smashed front spring after some spree, damn-blasted a butterfly car as far as Lyme Village before, his temper shattered, he fulfilled his own threat to push the thing off Golden Cap. Through the year the notes would come to Durnovaria, brought by a soldier or a bailiff on his rounds. Margaret puzzled the future Lord of Corfe, maybe worried him a little. She wasn't of his blood; but neither did she think like a commoner, the serfs he would blow from his path with blasts of the Bentley's horn. She didn't blush and simper, giggle like a village slut when he stroked her breasts; she was grave and quiet and always it seemed had some sadness in her eyes. For her part Margaret felt unspoken things to exist between them, understandings deeper than words. In his own way, under the blustering and hell-raking, he needed her; one day, formally, he would ask her to be his wife.

She shuddered, remembering the end of her world. An August night, the grasshoppers making their endless shrieking; the sound seemed to soak into brain and blood, compelling with its insistent strangeness, now heard, now unheard and heard again. The castle bulked high in the warm dark and all round, in the baileys, on the walls and *motte*, far below in the tree-grown wet ditch, the glowworms burned like lime-green sequins stitched onto the black velvet of the grass. She cupped one in her hand; it glowed there still, distant and mysterious. There was a smell in the air, warm and heavy, the tang of early autumn. A breeze touched her face; it seemed to her excited fancy the wind blew from some strange past.

Robert was brooding, silent, in a mood she hadn't seen. A fire was burning up by the kitchens, the glow wavering on stone, limning the huge pile of the *donjon*. Flakes of ash were whirled up sparkling in the sky; he said to her they were like the souls of men moving through endlessness, shining awhile then vanishing in the dark. He didn't use his born language; instead he spoke an old tongue, a clacking guttural she'd never realized he owned. She could answer him; she stood close giving sentence for sentence, trying to comfort. She spoke of the castle. *"Rude, ragged nurse,"* she said, *"old sullen playfellow for tender princelings. . . ."*

He seemed surprised at that. She laughed, her voice muted in the night. "One of those minor Elizabethans, we had to do him at school. I forget his name; I thought he was rather good."

"How does it finish?"

"Use my babies well . . ." She spoke almost wonderingly, aware for the first time of the chill under the words. *"So . . . foolish sorrow bids thy stones . . . farewell. . . ."*

It made him angry, unaccountably. "Auguries," he said, and spat. "You're like a priest in a bolt-hole, mumbling bloody spells. . . ."

"Robert . . ." She was close to him, she moved closer. She laid her face against his, lips parted to let tongue and teeth touch his jaw, trying to stop the sadness in him, feeling his hands move tracing beneath her thin dress the course of her spine. She'd touched him often enough and kissed; his fingers used her familiarly, enjoying her as his eyes enjoyed the keen head of a hound or the flight of a hawk, as his mouth savoured the taste of food and good wine. She thought, this time it is different. If he goes on now, and if I let myself go on, then there'll be only one end. And is it so important after all?

She swallowed, closing her eyes; and it seemed then for the first time the turning and twisting, the falling, the sense of dimensions and Time skewed, plagued her. She clung tighter whimpering, feeling herself not standing on solid turf but bowled solemnly end over end through a void, haunted by all dead things and sorrows and future fears, lumped and bundled and blown along a Norman wind. She thought, perhaps I shall faint. What's happening to me. . . .

She tried to call up images to set against the dark; her father, Sarah, her uncle Jesse, people she'd known back at school, even old Sister Alicia. It seemed to her obscurely that what she wanted to do involved more than herself, her body and her pain. It was to *them*, all the people she'd ever known, she had to answer; for *their* sake her choice had to be right. She felt a hotness on her cheek and knew it was a tear; though whether for herself or Robert or all humankind she couldn't say. She lay with him that night, coming to him again and again, comforting and being comforted, sometimes mother-giving, sometimes a child wrapped away from the dark; till even her lover drifted from her, lost behind a sleep too deep for dreams.

Lord Edward's seneschal roused her—he of all people—with the story that Robert had been called off on the King's business, that he was to see her home. She lay quiet in the bed, still half dazed with sleep; and slowly the anger grew. She read in his queer eyes and chiselled-cat face, the face she could oddly never recall once he had turned away, what she already knew deep inside. That the enchantment, if it was enchantment, had ended; that she'd sold herself for a pretty song, that Robert was in his senses now, that a Lord of Purbeck would never mix his blood with a girl of the rank and file. She drove the seneschal away snarling and spitting, rose and looked at herself, turning the mirror to show her new slut's body; she washed herself, splashing the water from the ewer angrily on the floor. The bed was marked; she wrenched the covers back raging, left them for all the world to see. She swore at the seneschal when he fetched her, stamping and vowing revenges she knew she could never call down; not herself, not her father, not the mighty firm of Strange with all its money and power. Because there was no law in this land, not for commoners. Rich and poor alike they held their places by the whim of their lords; and the lords got theirs in feoff from the English King, and he sat his throne by the grace of the Throne of Peter. The demicannon, glaring out there through the gates, that was the law. . . .

In the outer bailey she thought a houseservant smiled; if she had had a weapon in her hand she would have killed. She left riding like the wind, slashing her horse till the blood ran, hurting herself in the jolting saddle, the seneschal pacing her impassively twenty yards behind. They'd marked her up, like they'd mark a split crate off the road trains; *soiled goods, return to sender*. . . . She turned a mile away from the castle, saw it watching her and cursed. There were tears on her face again and on her throat; but they were tears of rage.

"FOR THEE AND FOR THY ANGELS IS PREPARED THE UNQUENCHABLE FIRE; BECAUSE THOU ART THE CHIEF OF ACCURSED MURDER, THOU ART THE AUTHOR OF INCEST. . . . GO OUT, THOU SCOUNDREL, GO OUT WITH ALL THY DECEITS. . . . GIVE HONOUR TO GOD, TO WHOM EVERY KNEE IS BENT. . . ."

Why, thought Margaret haggardly, he's talking about me. . . . The journey and the castle had been in her mind; the tears were real. They ran down hot, wetting her neck. *Is this the best you can do?* she asked Father Edwardes silently. *To plague this old man with your mumming while I sit here free who've brought the evil and the wrong into this house?* Of course, her mind answered itself scornfully. Because he like the Church he serves is blind and empty and vainglorious. This God they prattle on about, where's His justice, where's His compassion? Does it please Him to see dying people hounded in His name, does He snigger at His bumbling priests, is He satisfied when men drop dead chopping stone out for His temples, twisted little God dying tepidfaced on a cross. . . . She thought, I'll go out and look for other gods, and maybe they'll be better and anyway they can't be worse. Perhaps they're still there in the wind, on the heaths and the old grey hills. I'll pray for Thunor's lightning and Wo-Tan's justice, and Balder's love; for he at least gave his blood laughing, not mangled and in pain like the Christos, the usurper. . . .

The house trembled and went out like a candle flame in a draught. She was falling again, dropping through space where sparks that were like stars or glowworms burned. She seemed all in the same instant to see Corfe loom at her with its skull face, the sea beyond whipped white by breaking waves, the cliffs tall in the droning wind; the Dorset wind, ancient and cold and keen, in from all the miles on miles of ocean.

The rushing stopped; and she stood and stared round her in wonder. From the past she had moved to the future, or to some Time that had never been and never would be. Above her was a whirling sky; and round about on either side rose pillars hacked from rough stone, old and textured, leaning mighty, fretted and worn, tortured by the centuries into holes for the wind to nest in. The cloud scud swirled, driving past them; beyond the wind seethed across a grey circle of grass. Beyond again was nothingness; a void into which she might tumble, fall off the sudden edge of the world.

In front of her, seated with his back against the farthest of the pillars was a man. His cloak swirled; his hair, long and light, lifted and blew about his round skull. She put a hand to her head. The face, she'd seen it before but where. . . . Even as she watched it seemed to alter, running and shifting, becoming the face of a thousand men, of no one. Of the wind.

She walked, or seemed to walk, toward him. In the dream she could speak; she made words, a question. The stranger laughed. His voice was reedy and thin, as if it came from a great distance. "You called on the Old Ones," he said. "Who calls on the Old Ones, calls on me."

He gestured for her to be seated. She squatted in front of him feeling her hair flack round her face. The wind scourged at the strange place; then as she stared it seemed suddenly there was no wind, that she and the stones and the grass they stood on were being whirled at immense speed through an endless sea of cloud. The thought was giddying; momentarily she closed her eyes. "You called upon our gods," said the Old One quietly. "Maybe it was their pleasure to answer. . . ."

She'd seen now, in the stone over his head, the mark she'd known must be there; the circle, the crab lines inside, overlapping and incomprehensible. She said faintly, "Are you . . . real?"

Amusement showed in his face. "Real?" he said. "Define reality and I can answer you." He waved a hand. "Look into solid earth, into rock, and see the galaxies of all Creation. What you call reality melts; there is a whirling, a spinning of forces, a dance of motes and atoms. Some of them we call planets, one of them is Earth. Nothingness within nothingness enclosing nothing, that is reality. Tell me what you want, and I can answer."

She put a hand to her forehead again. "You're trying to confuse me. . . ."

"No."

She blazed at him. *Then leave me alone. . . ."* She beat her fists on the grass helplessly. "I haven't done anything to you, stop . . . playing with me or whatever it is you do, just go away and let me be. . . ."

He bowed, gravely; and she became suddenly terrified the whole strange place would snap out of existence and plunge her back into a life she knew she could no longer bear. She wanted now to run forward, hold his cloak as she had wanted to hold the cloak of the priest, but it was impossible. She tried to speak again, and he stopped her with a raised hand. "Listen," he said, "and try to remember.

Do not despise your Church; for she has a wisdom beyond your understanding. Do not despise her mummeries; they have a purpose that will be fulfilled. She struggles as we struggle to understand what will not be understood, to comprehend that which is beyond comprehension. The Will that cannot be ordered, or charted, or measured." He pointed round him, at the circling stones. "The Will that is like these; encompassing, endlessly voyaging, endlessly returning, enfolding the heavens. The flower grows, the flesh corrupts, the sun circles the sky; Balder dies and the Christos, the warriors fight outside their hall Valhalla and fall and bleed and are reborn. All are within the Will, all are ordained. We are within it; our mouths close and open, our bodies move, our voices speak and we are not their masters. The Will is endless; we are its tools. Do not despise your Church. . . ."

There was more, but the sense of it was lost in the raving of the wind. She watched the face of the Old One, the moving lips, the strange eyes burning reflecting light from distant suns and other years. "The dream," he said finally, "is ending. If it is a dream. The great Dance finishes, another will begin." He smiled, and touched with his fingers the carved mark above his head.

"Help me," she said suddenly. Begged. *"Please . . ."*

He shook his head, it seemed to her pityingly, watching her as she had watched the glowworms pulsing their lives out on the grass. "The Sisters spin the yarn," he said, "and mark, and cut. There is no help. It is the Will. . . ."

"Tell me," she said. "Please. What will happen to me? You *can* do it, you've got to. You *owe* it . . ."

His voice droned at her, splitting the wind. "It is forbidden. . . ." His eyes seemed to veil themselves. "Watch from the south," he said. "There will be life for you, coming from the south, and death. As for all creatures born, so

for you. There will be joy and hope; there will be fear
and pain. The rest is hidden; it is the Will. . . ."

She screamed at him. "But that's no good, you haven't
told me anything. . . ." It was useless; man and stones
were fading, diminishing, as she herself was whirled back
and away. It seemed for an instant the face of the Old
One glowed bronze and glorious till she saw the Christos,
or Balder in his majesty, staring out the clouds; then he
blackened, a darker shade among shadows of stones that
dwindled to a point and were gone.

"NOW THEREFORE DEPART. THY ABODE IS THE
WILDERNESS, THY HABITATION THE SERPENT;
NOW THERE IS NO DELAY . . . FOR BEHOLD THE
LORD GOD APPROACHETH QUICKLY, AND HIS
FIRE WILL GLOW BEFORE HIM. FOR IF THOU
HAST DECEIVED MAN, THOU CANST NOT MOCK
THY LORD. . . .

"HE EXCLUDES THEE, WHO HAST PREPARED
FOR THEE AND THY ANGELS EVERLASTING HELL;
OUT OF WHOSE MOUTH THE SHARP SWORD WILL
GO, HE WHO SHALL COME TO JUDGE THE QUICK
AND THE DEAD AND THE WORLD BY FIRE. . . ."

The thing was finished; and Margaret stared round at
the faces of the others and at their hands, and knew. *The
room was quiet again.*

She waited watching long after the others had gone,
Father Edwardes sitting at the bedside and the nurse, the
old man breathing slow, all effort ended. She stood with
crossed arms at the window, feeling the night air move
on her face, watching out over the house roofs at the blur
of the heath and the thin pale line of horizon down to
the south. Seeing with the clearness of hallucination Robert
flogging his horse and swearing, cursing all women to the
devil and beyond, riding to fetch her back to his hall.
Her lips once nearly quirked into a smile. *For the flower*

grows, the flesh dies, the sun circles the sky and we are within the Will. . . . She frowned, puzzling her head, but couldn't remember where she'd heard the words.

Jesse Strange died with the dawn; the Father prayed, and laid the Host on his tongue. And in the harsh light the nurse pulled back the covers and counted the cancers showing like blue fists against the pallor of the old man's skin.

Sixth Measure
CORFE GATE

The column of horsemen trotted briskly, harness jangling, making no attempt to keep to the side of the road. Behind the soldiers the tourist cars of the wealthy bunched and jostled, motors sputtering. From time to time one or other of the drivers essayed a swift overtaking dash that took him past well clear of the horses; but few cared to risk the manoeuvre, and a bright-coloured jam stretched back over a mile behind the obstruction. The more philosophical of the travellers were already sailing; the striped lateens billowed in the puffs of breeze, propelling the vehicles along with the smallest assistance from their tiny, inefficient engines.

There was ample need for caution. The pennants carried by the column were known to all; at its head flew the oriflamme, ancient symbol of the Norman nobility, and flanking it were the Eagles of Pope John, silk-yellow on a blue field. Behind them fluttered the swallow-tailed tricolour of Henry Lord of Rye and Deal, Captain of the Cinque Ports and the Pope's lieutenant in England. Henry was known through the land as a hard and bitter man; when he rode armed it boded ill for somebody, and behind him was the authority of Christ's Vicar on Earth and all the power and might of the second Rome.

Henry was a small man, thin-shanked, sallow and sharp featured; he sat his horse sullenly, muffled in a cloak although the day was warm. If he realized the dislocation he was causing he gave no sign of it. From time to time shivers coursed through his body and he shifted uneasily,

206   SIXTH MEASURE

trying to find a position that would ease his aching buttocks.
En route from Londinium he had lain ten days in Win-
chester, stomach knotted by the cramps of gastroenteritis;
and though the fool of a physician, who deserved to lose
his ears or worse, had been swift enough to diagnose he'd
been unable to bring about a cure. Henry had barely recovered when the clacking of the semaphores had driven
him on; the arm of the fortieth Pope John was long, his
sources of information numerous and varied, his will indomitable. Henry's orders were clear; to take the confounded fortress that had caused so much trouble, reduce
its arms, raise John's standards on its walls, and hold it
for his liege lord till further notice. As for the West Country
filly who'd started all the bother, well . . . Henry grimaced,
and stiffened in the saddle. Maybe her backbone stood in
need of airing, or she could find herself being dragged to
Londinium behind a baggage waggon; such matters were
minor. Minor at least to his own personal discomfort.

The semaphores were working again now to either side
of the road, their black arms cracking and flailing. Henry
glared at the nearest of the towers, standing gaunt on the
crest of a sweep of down. Among the complex of messages
it carried would almost certainly be news of his progress;
for days now the information would have been flashing
down ahead of him into the West. Another spasm of pain
doubled him, and his temper snapped; he turned his head
briefly and a Captain of Horse rode alongside, spurs jingling.

Henry pointed at the tower of his choice. "Captain," he
said. "Detach a dozen men. Go to *that* . . . Demand of
who you find there the messages it bears."

The soldier hesitated. The order was seemingly without
point; none knew better than Henry that the Guildsmen
would not divulge their affairs. "And if they refuse,
M'Lord?"

Henry swore. *"Then silence it. . . ."*

The officer still stared, until Rye and Deal turned to glare; then he saluted and wheeled his horse. For centuries the Guild of Signallers had enjoyed privileges not even the Popes dared question; now it seemed their immunity was ended, blown away by a diminutive nobleman with a bellyache. Orders were shouted, dust rose in a cloud; a group of men turned from the line of march and broke into a gallop across the grass, pennants flying. As they rode the soldiers loosened their falchions in the scabbard, saw to the priming of their muskets. With luck they would come on the Signallers unarmed, if not there would be a short and bloody skirmish. Either way, the end was not in doubt.

Henry, twisting in the saddle, saw the arms of the tower drop to its sides like the arms of a man suddenly tired. He grinned without humour. The respite would be temporary at best; if he knew the Guild, runners would quickly be despatched from the next station in line. After that all men would know of his act. The signal network was a delicate animal; touch one limb and all its parts reacted, sometimes within hours. With good visibility along the Pennine stations his work could be known to the Hebrides by nightfall. And to the Vatican by dawn. . . . He hunched himself, caressing his suffering stomach. Another turn of the head, a snapping of the fingers and Father Angelo jogged up beside him, sweating a little and as usual more than anxious to please.

"Well, sirrah," said Henry tartly. "How much longer on this confounded route march of ours?"

The priest bent his head over the map, trying to steady it against the movements of the horse. Churchmen always made lousy riders; and worse map readers, in Henry's opinion. The Father's failing sight had already led the party into a bog and forced half a dozen detours. "About twenty miles, M'Lord," he said uncertainly. "But that is

by the road. If we left our present way a mile above
Wimborne town—"

"Spare me your shortcuts," said Henry brutally. "I wish
to arrive by Christmastide. Send a couple of your people
on ahead and arrange our accommodation some"—he
squinted at the sun—"some five miles up the road. And
try this time to discover beds not too thick with lice, and
just a little softer than the racks of my Serjeant-at-arms."
Father Angelo gave a bumbling parody of a military
salute and jogged back down the line.

Henry was on the road again early next morning, in a
thicker rage than ever. Overnight he had been given proof
of the changed temper of the West. As he stood shaving at
the open window of his room a crossbow quarrel had
passed beneath his elbow, demolishing a set of Venetian
case-bottles before burying itself in the far wall. Henry,
infuriated by the attack on his person but even more by
the loss of so much fine and irreplaceable glass, had ordered an immediate search for the marksman. His soldiers
had unearthed a handful of malcontents, all of whom had
resisted arrest in a more or less desultory way; they were
towed behind the baggage carts till the column came in
sight of its objective. Then they were released; they staggered off bemused, snorting blood out on the grass, and
none of them made more than a hundred yards before
lying down to sleep it off. Henry's ways with rebels had
always been noted for their directness.

He rode forward. In front of him the heath stretched
out for miles, tawny red, splashed here and there with the
fierce parrot-green of bogs. Across the horizon ran a curving line of hills; between them the place he had come to
chastise thrust up like an ancient fang. Henry spat thoughtfully. The castle was strong, far too strong to be taken by
assault; he could see that already. But then, it would never
stand. Not against the Blue.

Behind him the soldiers bunched together; the oriflamme fluttered from its golden staff, tossing in the wind like the fire it represented. Off on the horizon the ubiquitous telegraph waved and gestured against the sky. Henry watched a moment longer then snapped his fingers. "Captain," he said. "Two men to ride ahead to the castle. Let them take orders under my seal to the woman of the place. Have her ready her ordnance to be delivered up to us; and tell her to regard herself and all inside the walls as prisoners of Pope John. What guns do they have anyway, now we've come so far to fetch them? Refresh my memory."

The Captain gabbled, repeating a list learned by rote. "Two sakers throwing three pound ball, powder and wads for them. Some handguns, snaphaunces; not much more than fowling pieces, M'Lord. The great gun *Growler*, from the King's arsenal; the culverin *Prince of Peace*, transferred on His Majesty's instructions from the garrison of Isca."

Henry sniffed and rubbed the tip of his nose with the back of a glove. "Well, I shall shortly be a prince of peace myself; and I dare say I shall do my share of growling too before the day is through. Have the pieces brought to the main gate, along with what shot and powder they have. Clear a waggon for the arms, and levy mules or horses for the great guns. See to it, Captain."

The officer saluted and turned back, bellowing for his aides; Henry raised his arm and swept it down in the signal for general advance. At his shout Father Angelo crabbed forward, nearly parting company with his mount in the process. "Quarters in the village, Father," said Rye and Deal wearily. "At the worst we could have a lengthy stay. And secure me this time hot water and a flushing toilet, or I'll send you back to Rome in charge of a crap cart. And you won't be riding it either my friend, I promise you that; you'll be running between the bloody shafts. . . ."

The banners and the eagles spread out, bright in the sunlight, as the column cantered across the heath.

Sir John Faulkner, seneschal of Corfe Gate, woke early from a restless sleep. Sunlight from the fenestella six feet above his head slanted across the little bedchamber, fighting the chill that tended to gather in the room even in the height of summer. The great keep was always cool; for the sun at its hottest could scarcely reach through a dozen feet of Dorset stone. A week before the Lady Eleanor, mistress of the place, had moved her people from the lower baileys to make room for the soldiers flocking in and the refugees begging shelter; the household were still unused to the primitive conditions of the *donjon*.

The seneschal rubbed his face, filled a bowl and washed, swilling the water down the sluice beneath the window. He dressed, grateful for the touch of fresh linen on his body, and left the chamber. Outside, a circular stairway wound up through the thickness of the wall. He climbed it, placing his feet at the sides of the treads; generations of wear had scooped the steps into hollows that were traps for the unwary. At the top of the spiralling way a door, loosely closed by a lanyard, gave access to the roof. He unfastened the becket and stepped through, leaned on the parapet and looked down between the massive crenellations at the surrounding country. Five miles to the south the Channel stretched away in a pearly haze; out there on a clear day keen sight might make out the shape of the Needles, guarding the western tip of the Isle of Wight. The Devil sat there once in the long-ago, heaved a rock at Corfe towers, and dropped it short on Studland beach. The seneschal smiled slightly at the fancy and turned away.

Northward were the heights of the Great Plain, pale in the dawn light, grey and vague like the uplands of a kingdom of ghosts. Close to the castle rose the huge swellings

of Challow and Knowle, its flanking hills; and all round was
the heath, blackened in places by summer fires, flat and
sullen and immense, a sour expanse that would grow nothing, supported nothing except roving bands of croppers. He
could see the smoke from one of their camps threading up
in the distance. Nearer at hand he looked down on the
ribbed grey roofs of the village, the farm that stood just
beyond the wet ditch. As he watched a lorry coasted to it,
off-loaded two churns, and puffed away round the shoulder
of the *motte* toward the Wareham Road.

Almost unwillingly, he lifted his eyes to the semaphore
tower on the crest of Challow Hill. As if it had been waiting
for a cue, the thing began to move; the jerky "Arms up,
arms down" of the Attention signal. He knew it would be
answering another far across the heath; so far that only the
Guildsmen, with their wonderful Zeiss binoculars, could
translate accurately the letters and symbols of the message.
Way across the land the chain of towers would be moving,
lifting their jointed arms, banging them back. *Attention,
Attention . . .*

Reading the semaphores was not officially the province
of the seneschal; down in the third bailey a scurry of movement told him the guards had already alerted the household's Signaller-Page. The boy would be hurrying from his
room, rubbing his eyes maybe, message pad in hand. The
seneschal watched the movements of the arms, lips shaping
the numbers as they formed, mind translating the crypto-
grams to which generations of Signallers had reduced the
king's English. "*Eagle Rye one five,*" he read. "*North-west
ten, closing.*" That would be My Lord of the Cinque Ports,
with his hundred and fifty men; he was nearer than the
seneschal had thought. "*Nine dead,*" said the thing on the
hill. "*Nine.*" That was bad; the Pope's lieutenant was
evidently determined to enhance his reputation for ruth-
lessness. There followed a call sign; Sir John heard cables

rattle as Eleanor's Signaller worked the arms of his tower. *"Yield your guns,"* said the grid repeater briefly. *"Give yourselves into captivity. Messengers en route."* Then that was all. The arms dropped with a final clash; the tower fell austerely silent.

The watching man sighed and instinctively his hand went to the amulet round his neck. He turned the little disc in his fingers, tracing the outline of the symbol carved on it. Down below the kitchen chimneys smoked, pails clanked as the cows were milked in their stalls. Those of the household who had been in sight of the tower had paused momentarily when its arms started to move, and all would have heard the clatter of their own answer; but no commoners could read the language of the Guild, and they had soon bent to their tasks again. The Signallers knew though, and he knew, and Eleanor would have to be told. He ducked back down the stairway, hunching his shoulders automatically to prevent banging his head on the low ceiling. His mouth was set grimly. This was the thing that had been ordained a thousand years; an era was about to come to an end.

The Lady Eleanor was already up and dressed. A board had been set out for her in one of the chambers opening off the Great Hall; she was taking breakfast in an alcove beneath a window set with quarrel-panes of coloured glass. She rose when she saw her seneschal, and watched his face. He nodded briefly in answer to the unvoiced question. "Yes, my Lady," he said quietly. "He will come today."

She sat back, no longer conscious of the food in front of her. Her face and worried eyes looked very young. "How many men?" she asked finally.

"A hundred and fifty."

She waved a hand, conscious suddenly of her incivility. "Please sit down, Sir John. Will you take wine?"

He leaned back in the window seat, resting his head

against the glass. "Not at present, thank you, my Lady. . . ." He watched her, and no one could have told the expression in his eyes. She stared back seeing how the lights stained his hair and cheek with colour, gold and rose and blue. She pulled at her lip, and twined her fingers in her lap. "Sir John," she said, "what am I to do?"

He didn't answer for a time; and when he did speak there was no help in the words. "What your blood dictates, my Lady," he said. "You will follow your breeding, and your heart."

She got up again quickly and walked away from him to where she could see the Great Hall shadowed and forbidding, the gloomy power of the vast crosswall, the dais where in ancient times the family sat at meat, the gallery where minstrels used to play. She touched a switch beside the chamber door; a solitary electric lamp flicked on in the roof, throwing a wan pool of light on the coarse flags of the floor, and suddenly the place seemed fitter for the dead than the living. Somewhere a chain-hoist rumbled; the Signaller-Page ran into the hall, stopped short when he saw his mistress. She took the message he carried, smiling at him, turned back with the flimsy in her hand. She said broodingly, "A hundred and fifty men . . ."

She walked back to her chair, sat with her hands folded in her lap, and stared at the table in front of her. "If I open to him," she said indistinctly, "I shall run behind his pack-train like a soldiers' drab. I shall lose my living and my home, most certainly my decency and probably my life. But I can't fight Pope John. To war with him is to take on all the world. . . . Yet this is his man come to try me."

The seneschal said nothing; she hadn't expected him to answer. She sat still a long time and when she looked up there were tears in her eyes. "Close the gates, Sir John," she said, "and get our people in. Advise me when these messengers arrive, but do not grant them entry."

He rose quietly. "And the guns, Lady?"

"The guns?" she said sombrely. "Take them to the gate by all means, and shot and powder for them. So far we will do as he desires. . . ."

Through all the passages and high walks of the place the drums throbbed, beating to quarters.

Henry of Rye and Deal reined his horse, and behind him the column of men boiled to a halt. A bare mile away the castle glared huge and close, smoke rising in columns from its walls; down the road, rutted between its tall banks, the messengers were galloping, trailing clouds of whitish dust that hung behind them dispersing slowly in the still air. Three sentences the couriers got out before Henry started to swear. His spurs tore gashes in the flanks of his horse; the animal leaped forward terrified, the column swirled and clattered in pursuit.

The village square was packed with visitors, the taverns doing a bustling trade; the folk who had gathered to stare were scattered by the Lord of Rye and Deal. He hauled his horse in at the outer barbican, the animal lathered and running blood. The great gun *Growler* had indeed been brought down; but he was loaded and primed and his muzzle stared through the iron of the portcullis, and the culverin was flanking him. Behind the pieces a semicircle of men stood at ease, halberds grounded on the turf.

"Clear that bloody bridge," bellowed the Pope's lieutenant, revolving on his horse. "Captain, if those people won't get off throw 'em in the ditch. . . ." Then to the guards, "What damn fool game is this? Open for Pope John. . . ."

One of the men inside the bailey spoke up stolidly. "Sorry, M'Lord. Orders of the Lady Eleanor."

"Then," swore the nobleman, voice rising on a high note of rage, "instruct Her Ladyship that Henry of Rye and Deal commands her presence to answer for her fornicating insolence. . . ."

"M'Lord," said the man inside, unmoved, "The Lady Eleanor has been informed. . . ."

Henry glared back. Turned to see his soldiers crowding the bridge, stared up at the great impassive face of the keep. Round the *donjon* the inner battlements flocked with men. He leaned forward to rattle with his crop against the bars of the gate. "By nightfall, my talkative friend," he said, breathing heavily, "you'll hang by your heels for this, probably with your head over a slow fire. D'ye realize that?"

The guard spat deliberately at his feet.

Eleanor took her time about coming. She had bathed and changed and dressed her hair; she would allow no hands to touch her body but her own, not even the hands of tiring-maids. She appeared holding the arm of the seneschal, her Captain of Artillery walking on her left. She wore a plain white dress, and her long brown hair was loose. A little wind moved across the bailey, blowing the hair and flattening her skirt against her thighs. Henry, who had lost enough face already, watched her, fuming. Twenty paces from the gate the others stopped and she came forward alone. She saw the horsemen on the bridge, the muskets and swords, the sea of tossing blue. She halted by the breech of the great gun, one hand resting on the iron. "Well, My Lord," she said in a low, clear voice. "What will you have of us?"

Henry's rages were famous and spectacular; spittle flecked his beard, the standers-by heard him grind his teeth. "Deliver me this place," he shouted finally. "And your ordnance, and yourselves. In the name of your ruler Pope John, through the authority vested in me his lieutenant in these islands."

She straightened her back, staring up at him through the gate. "And in the name of Charles?" she asked cuttingly.

"For my liege ruler is my King. So it was with my father and so with me, My Lord; I took no vows before a foreign priest."

He drew his sword, and poi.1ted through the bars. "*That gun*," was all he could speak.

She still remained standing by the great gun, her fingers touching its breech and the wind moving in her hair. "And if I refuse?"

He shouted again then, waving an arm; at the gesture a soldier spurred forward lifting a bag from the pommel of his saddle. "Then your liege-folk in this isle pay with their homes and their property and their lives," panted Henry, slashing at the cord that held the canvas closed. "It'll be blood for iron, My Lady, blood for iron. . . ." The string came free, the bag was shaken; and down before her dropped the tongues and other parts of men, cut away as was the custom of Henry's soldiers.

There was a silence that deepened. The colour drained slowly from Eleanor's face, leaving the skin chalk-pale as the fabric of her dress; indeed the more romantic of the watchers swore afterwards the blue leached from her very eyes, leaving them lambent and dead as the eyes of a corpse. She clenched her hands slowly, slowly relaxed them again; a long time she waited, leaning on the gun, while the rage blurred her sight, rose to a high mad shrilling that seemed to ring inside her brain, receded leaving her utterly cold. She swallowed; and when she spoke again every word seemed freshly chipped from ice. "*Why then,*" she said. "*You must not leave us empty-handed, My Lord of Rye and Deal. Yet I fear my* Growler *will be a heavy load. Would not your task be lightened if his charge were sent before?*" And before any of the people round her could guess her purpose or intervene she had snatched at the firing lanyard, and *Growler* leaped back pouring smoke while echoes clapped around the waiting hills.

The heavy charge, fired at point-blank range, blew away the belly of the horse and took both Henry's feet off at the ankles; animal and rider leaped convulsively and fell with a mingled scream into the dry ditch. As if by common consent the crossbows of the defenders played first on them; within seconds they were still, pierced by a score of shafts. The grapeshot, ploughing on, spread ruin among the soldiers on the bridge, tore furrows from the buildings of the village square beyond. Shrieks sounded, echoing from the close stone walls; the arquebusiers fired into the struggling mass on the path; the Captain rode away, leaning from his horse while his blood ribboned back across the creature's rump. Then it was finished, dying men whimpering while a thin haze of smoke drifted across the lower bailey toward the Martyr's Gate.

Eleanor leaned on the gun and bit her wrist like a child at what she had done. The seneschal was the first to reach her; but she shoved him away. "Take up that dirt," she said, pointing to the ditch. "And bury it inside the bailey walls. I will have my right of faldage from Pope John. . . ." Then she staggered; he caught her, lifted her and carried her to her room.

For most of her life Eleanor, only daughter of Robert, last of the Lords of Purbeck, had lived in seclusion in the great hall set between the hills. She was a strange child, secretive and shy, beloved of the Fairies who according to popular report assisted at her very conception. Though practical and level-headed in other respects, Eleanor never made any attempt to scotch the rumours of her paranormal origin, seeming instead to take pleasure in them. "For," she would explain, "my father often told his guests the tale of how he rode north that day to bring my mother home. When he ran out and jumped on his horse everybody was convinced he'd taken leave of his senses; but he always claimed it was the People of the Heath that drove him to it, showing him visions so beautiful they sent him completely wild." Then her face would cloud; for Margaret Strange had died in childbirth, and Eleanor felt very keenly the loss of the mother she had never known.

Too keenly sometimes for her father's peace of mind; Robert, who never remarried, brooded over the child's imaginings. Once, when she was very small, she walked in her sleep. It was on a night of wind, with a full gale roaring up from the Channel barely five miles away; one of those nights when the nervous of the household kept to their rooms, swearing they heard the laughter of the Old Ones in the gusts that hissed and droned round the high stones of the keep. Eleanor's nurse, looking in to see the child was quiet, found her room empty; a hue and cry was raised, and the whole great complex of buildings searched. They found Eleanor high in the *donjon*, at the head of an ancient stairway unused for years. Her eyes were closed but as they reached her they heard her calling. "Mother," she shouted. "Mother, are you there . . ." They led her down, careful not to startle her; for it was well known that such walkers were under the spell of the Old Ones, who took their souls very easily if they woke. Eleanor herself seemed oblivious of the whole affair; but it was not so. She referred to it days later, when her nurse was dressing her. "My mother was very pretty, wasn't she?" she said; then thoughtfully, "She wanted to play; but she had to go away. . . ." Robert frowned when he heard, and pulled his beard and swore; the girl was packed off to relatives in France, but when she came back six months later she was very little changed.

As a child Eleanor was frequently lonely; for the castle contained no other children of her own age except the children of the serving people, from whom she was largely excluded by barriers of rank and class. Most of her days

were passed quietly in the company of her nurse and later
her tutor, from whom she learned the several languages of
the land. She proved to have a quick and receptive brain;
she soon mastered the Norman French and Latin that had
remained the tongues of the cultured world, even more
quickly the churl talk of the peasants. It worried her father
slightly to hear the old syllables bang and splatter from her
lips; but because of it she was greatly respected by the few
commoners with whom she came in contact. Indeed she
seemed to identify herself more with the ordinary people of
the countryside than with those of her own rank; which
in a way was understandable considering that she was
only partly of noble blood. The peasants still lived and
were governed by the ancient rhythms of moon and sun,
ploughing and reaping, death and birth; and all old things,
whether or not sanctified by the rulers of Rome, appealed
strongly to her. Sometimes she would go with her nurse
and her father's seneschal and play on the nearby beaches.
She would watch the endless roll and thunder of the sea,
and ask strange questions of the seneschal; such as whether
the Popes, from their golden throne, could order the waves
that washed the shores of England, marching in their violet
ranks to break against the ancient cliffs. He would smile at
her, answering heresy with discretion, till she grew bored
and scampered off to hunt for shells on the beach or sea-
weed, or pick the crinoid fossils from the rocks and give
them to him for fairy beads. She felt an odd sympathy with
the fabric of the land itself; once she took a flake of shale
and pressed it to her throat and cried, and said that day
she was made right through of stone, dark and stern as the
Kimmeridge cliffs and as indomitable.

Her waywardness caused in the end her removal to
Londinium. In her sixteenth year her father caught her
with a bailiff, learning the handling of his motor vehicle;
how to slip the bands of its gearbox and drive it in forward

and reverse round the slopes of the outer bailey. Maybe some gesture, some turn of the head, reminded Robert too clearly of the girl who had died so many years ago; he pulled his daughter squawking from the machine, clipped her ear, and chased her off to her room. The resulting interview, compounded as it was of Eleanor's wounded dignity and her father's always uncertain temper, proved disastrous. Eleanor vented her feelings in multilingual phrasing new even to Robert; he retaliated with a strap, the buckle of which left several marks that threatened permanence. He confined his daughter to her chamber for a week; on the day of her release she refused to leave and it was a fortnight before he caught sight of her down below the wet-ditch messing with some soldiers out at target practice. He sent immediately for his seneschal. A time at the Court of Londinium seemed the only thing for Eleanor; there would be no more riding and hawking, and certainly no consorting with mechanicals. She must be brought if possible to a realization of her station, and instructed in the skills expected in a lady of good birth. To the seneschal Robert entrusted the task, with the purely private directive that his daughter must be cultivated or killed. She left a fortnight later, with many snorts and head-tossings. He waited by the gate to see her go, but she ignored him. That was a flash of temper she regretted the rest of her days, for she never saw him alive again.

The accident happened on a feast day, when the lower bailey was filled with the tents of acrobats and jugglers and sweetmeat sellers, while the place resounded to shouts and laughter and the clatter of cudgels where the young bloods of the surrounding villages tried their strength one against another. Robert's horse bucked as he crossed the outer bridge, and threw him; he struck his head against the stone, and fell into the dry ditch. The fair was quietened, and doctors brought from Durnovaria; but his skull

was crushed, and he never reopened his eyes. Eleanor,
summoned by a signal that fled from Challow Hill to Pontes
inside an hour, rode hard; but she came too late.

She buried her father at Wimborne, in the ancient Minster
there, in the painted tomb he had built to share with his
wife; and the party rode back slowly to Corfe Gate, the
horses and the motors dressed with black, the slack drums
thudding out a dirge. It was still September; but a chilling
wind moaned in from the sea, and the sky was grey as iron.

Eleanor reined when she came in sight of the castle,
and waved the rest of her people on down the long dim
road. The seneschal waited, his horse fretting in the wind,
till the mourners had passed nearly out of sight in distance;
then she turned to him, her cloak whipping round her
shoulders. She looked older and very tired, dark shadows
under her eyes and tear tracks marking her cheeks. "Well,"
she said, "here I am a great lady; and that is the house I
own. . . ."

He waited silently, knowing her mind; she swallowed,
and pushed the hair out of her eyes. "John," she said,
"How many years did you serve my Father Robert?"

He sat his horse impassively and considered before he
answered. Then finally, "Many years, my Lady."

"And his father before him?"

Again the same answer. "Many years. . . ."

"Yes," she said. "You served him well; I left him alone,
and sent no word. And it was all over such a trifling little
thing. I've almost forgotten why we first fell out. Now it's
too late of course." She sat quiet a moment, stroking the
neck of her horse as it fidgeted in the cold. Then, "Have
you a sword?"

"Yes, Lady."

"Then give it me, and get down off your horse. This
much I can do. . . ."

He waited while she held the sword and looked unseeing

at the damascene-work on the blade. "A title is a little empty thing," she said, "to such as you. Yet will you take it from me?"

He bowed; and she touched his shoulder lightly with the steel. "Whether the King confirms my choice or no," she said, "to us you will be Sir John. . . ." Then she turned her horse and rode hard for the castle, narrowing her eyes to see up at its glooming battlements and towers. So she came home, to a mourning place; and soon to the anger of Pope John.

From the outset Eleanor's position was a curious one. The successive Lords of Purbeck had held their lands in feoff from the King; under normal circumstances she could have expected to be married off fairly rapidly and to see the demesnes granted to another. But she was, or would one day be, an heiress in her own right as granddaughter of the last of the Strange family; and in the restricted economy of the times the annual tax paid by that huge house accounted for a measurable proportion of the revenue to the Crown. Since Charles, King of England and nominally at least of the Americas, was expecting to make an extended tour of the New World in the spring he was content to let matters rest at least until his return; Eleanor was confirmed in her position of authority, although there were many up and down the country who resented the decision.

She took her duties with great seriousness. One of her first self-allotted tasks was to tour the boundaries of her lands with a circuit judge, settling such petty differences as had arisen since her father's death. She rode informally, with only her seneschal in attendance, stopping off at cottages and farms as the fancy took her, speaking to all in the language of their birth, and her liege-folk scattered over the breadth and length of Dorset were much impressed. Where she found hardship she alleviated it not by gifts of money, too easily spent in the local taverns, but with clothing and food and grants of freeholds. She saw much suffering, and was shocked by it; she began in fact to feel dissatisfaction with her own way of life.

"It's all very well, Sir John," she said one evening shortly after her return to Corfe Gate. "But I've really achieved nothing at all. I suppose one's bound to get a sort of glow of well-being from a few small charities but looked at in a broad view they're meaningless. One or two people are probably better off for not having to scrape and save and find their rent every week but what about all the rest I haven't been able to do anything for? As long as the Church applies a censorship to certain forms of progress, which is what she does however strenuously the Popes deny it, we shall always be a scrappy little nation living just above the famine line. But what else am I to do?" They were dining in the sixteenth-century hall beside the great keep; she waved a hand at the furnishings, the richly hung walls, and spluttered over a mouthful of food. "I can't pretend," she said, "that I don't like this life, and being able to buy horses and dogs when I want and nylons and perfumes, things the ordinary people never get to see let alone afford. . . . You know," she added, grinning suddenly, "when my poor father sent me off to town I had a fancy to run away and give it all up; just live the simple life, working the soil and rearing a family like a peasant girl. Only what I've seen has changed all that; I realize now I should have ended up having innumerable children by some brawny oak who stank of pigs, and dying before I was thirty from sheer hard work. Or am I just getting cynical? Do tell me, you say so very little any more."

He poured wine for her, smiling.

"I was arguing with Father Sebastian the other day," she said thoughtfully. "I quoted the thing about giving all you have to the poor. He said that was all very well but you had to come to terms with the Scriptures and realize there had to be teachers and leaders for the people's own good. It seemed an awful get-out to me, and I couldn't help saying so. I told him if the Church would sell half her altar plate she could buy shoes for everybody in the country, and a lot else besides; and that if the Pope would make a start in Rome I'd see about getting rid of a few job lots of furniture down in Corfe. I'm afraid he didn't take very kindly to it. I know it was wrong of me but he annoys me sometimes; he's so pious, and it seems to mean so very little. He'd walk miles in the snow to pray for a sick child, he's a very good man; but if there was more money about to start with maybe the child wouldn't have been taken ill. It all seems so unnecessary. . . ."

The winter was hard and long, the brooks and soil frozen like stone, even the rim of the sea sharded with ice. The towers clacked, on days when the Signallers could clear their arms of ice, with news of other parts of the country suffering as badly or worse. The spring that followed was late and cold, and the summer nearly as bad. Charles postponed his trip to the New World till the following year, spending his time, according to the semaphores, in organising relief schemes for the areas worst hit by famine. When autumn came round again, and the rush-bearing to the churches, the worst news of all arrived, brought by the urgently clattering grids. The taxation system of the country was to be reviewed; commissioners were already at work assessing contributions to be made by each area not in money but in kind.

Eleanor swore when the news was brought to her, and would certainly have given the officials a hot reception had they presented themselves at her hall; but nobody came near. Instead she was supplied via the semaphores with a list of the goods she would be expected to levy. Other parts of the country had been taxed in everything from turned ware to parsnips; Dorset's contribution would be in butter, grain, and stone.

"It's quite ridiculous," fumed Her Ladyship, stamping up and down the little room that served her as office and study combined. "Butter and stone are all very well, or would be if they didn't represent extra taxes; but *grain!* The people who drew this up must know very well there's practically no arable farming round here at all; what little wheat we do grow is strictly for our own use and after a summer like we've had there'll be barely enough of that to go round; I'm confidently expecting to have to set up soup kitchens in the bailey like they did once or twice in my father's time. In Italy they don't seem to have much idea of what a bad season can do to the produce of the farms; not that I suppose for a minute this junk ever came from Rome. It was probably drawn out by some fat-paunched little clerk in Paris or Bordeaux who's never seen England and doesn't want to and will sell our stuff over there at vast profits as fast as we can ship it. Anybody would think they're deliberately trying to break us. If I squeeze all they demand out of the folk round about there'll be deaths from starvation before the spring; on the other hand why I should buy in from Newworlders in Poole, give them back what I took from them, and ruin myself in the process I can't imag—"

She stopped dead; and the look in her eyes showed plainly she'd just received the import of a crude lesson in economics. "Sir John," she said firmly, "I'm not going to do it. There's no reason, except pure maliciousness, why I should either starve my people or pauperize myself." She tapped her teeth thoughtfully with a stylus. "Have the towers send this message," she said. "Our crops are bad, if we meet these taxes we shall be in trouble before the spring. Tell them we'll pay with a double levy next autumn; at least that'll give us the chance to get some more acreage under cultivation, unless of course they decide to change their demands by then. Failing that we'll make up in . . . oh, worsted, manufactured goods, whatever they want; but grain, no. It's out of the question." So the message was passed; and a second signal was routed to Londinium informing the King of her reply to Rome.

Next day the towers brought word that Charles was displeased, and had ordered Eleanor to pay; but by then it was too late, her answer was already clattering across France. "I'm afraid there was no help for it," she said to her seneschal, "but to present him with a *fait accompli;* what I'd like to have said to him, and to Pope John as well, was that there was no blood to be got by squeezing Dorset stone, though they were both very welcome to come on down and try." She was sitting at her dressing table, making up her face as she had been taught at Court; she drew a careful bow on her lips, blotted with a tissue. "God knows the Church is rich enough already," she finished bitterly. "What she expects to gain by sitting on the necks of a few poor savages in England, I have no idea. . . ." She dismissed the whole subject; at the best of times politics tired her rapidly, and she was becoming very interested in certain surreptitious alterations she was making to her home.

The most daring of them, and the most heretical, was the installation of electric lighting. She had commissioned a craftsman of the village to build and wind a generator, and proposed to drive it by a steam engine of a type designed to be fitted into lorries. The work had to be done secretly as although the principles of the electromotive force had been known for many years the Church had never sanctioned its domestic use. The completed unit was to be housed in one of the towers of the lower bailey wall, far enough away for its clanking not to disturb the household's rest, and Eleanor expected if not spectacular results, at least enough light to dispel the worst gloom of winter. And heating too, if things went well; for she had remembered from her schooling that

a wire, suitably wound on an earthenware former, could
be made to glow redly if sufficient difference in potential
could be created between its ends. To her questions as to
whether her generator would bring this state of affairs about,
the seneschal replied quietly that such a thing was not in-
conceivable; but further than that he refused to be drawn.

"Why, Sir John," said Eleanor archly, "you don't sound
as if you approve. Last winter I swear I had frostbite in at
least nine of my toes, and that in spite of sleeping in flannel
so thick the Pope himself would have been impressed by my
rectitude. Would you begrudge me what little comfort is
left to my declining years?" He smiled at that, but wouldn't
answer; and shortly afterward the generator began to chuff
and an element glowed brightly at the foot of Her Ladyship's bed, frightening the wits out of a chambermaid who
ran to the serjeant of the pantry with a tale that the stones
themselves were burning, grinning at her with scarlet
mouths.

The same day Eleanor received a visit from a Captain of
the Guild of Signallers. They sent runners from the outer
barbican and she changed hastily, receiving him in the
Great Hall with her seneschal and several gentlemen of the
castle in attendance. A man of such status commanded
great respect in the old times and Eleanor loved the Guild
with all her heart though they had never been and never
would be subjects of hers. The respect was mutual; for who
else, on the occasion of Robert's fortieth birthday, would
have been taken to the Semaphore and let to spell her
father's name with her own hands, on the levers only Guildsmen were allowed to move?

The Captain came in stolidly, a grizzled man in worn
green leather with the silver brassard and crossed lanyards
of his rank displayed in place. His eyes took in the electric
light with which the place was flooded, but he made no
comment. He came straight to the point, speaking bluntly

as was the way of the Guild; for when kings watched their semaphores as eagerly as commoners they had never found a use for fancy words. "My Lady," he said, "His Eminence the Archbishop of Londinium took horse today for Purbeck, bringing with him a force of some seventy men, hoping to take you unprepared and make you yield your hall and your demesnes to John."

She went pale, but a red anger spot glowed on each cheek. "How can you know this, Captain?" she asked coolly. "London is well over a day away, and the towers have been quiet. Had it been reported, I would have been told."

He shifted his feet where he stood with legs apart on the carpeting of the dais. "The Guild fears no man," he said finally. "Our messages are for all who can to read. But there are times, and this is one of them, when words are best not given to the grids. Then there are other, swifter means."

There was a hush at that, for he meant necromancy; and that was not a subject to be lightly bandied, even in the free air of Eleanor's hall. The seneschal alone understood his meaning fully; and to him the Signaller bowed, recognising a knowledge greater and more ancient than his own. Eleanor caught the look that passed between them and shivered; then she recovered herself and tossed her head. "Well, Captain," she said, "our gratitude is deep. How deep, only you can know. If you have nothing to add to what you've told me, can I give you wine? My Hall would be honoured."

He bowed again, accepting the gesture; and few enough there were who could have offered it, for the Guildsmen didn't come often into the houses of the uninitiated, even the great of the land.

She roused out some two score of her liege-folk and armed them, and when His Eminence came in sight of Corfe towers the semaphores had already informed him of the state of things inside. He quartered his men in the vil-

lage and came on with an escort of half a dozen, making a
great show of the peacefulness of his intentions. They were
conducted through the outer gate by a conspicuously well-
armed guard and taken to the Great Hall, where they were
told the Lady Eleanor would receive them. So she did; but
not for over an hour, and the great man was fuming and
striding the carpet well before that. She hung back in her
room, seeing to the last details of her makeup and dress; she
had previously sent for her seneschal and asked him to
attend her.

"Sir John," she said, adjusting a tiny coronet on her
hair, "I'm afraid this is going to be a difficult meeting from
every point of view. I don't suppose for a moment Charles
knows anything about all this, which makes His Eminence's
behaviour suspicious in the extreme; but I can hardly accuse
an archbishop of attempted treason. Apart from that he's
obviously come to demand something I can't give him, or
rather something that I—ouch—that I refuse to for what
seems to me to be excellent reasons. Yet he's made such an
exhibition of his quiet intentions that anything I say is
bound to look churlish. I wish the King would stick up for
himself a bit more; it's all very well people calling him
Charles the Good and pelting him with rose petals every
time he rides through Londinium, but what it all comes
down to is he's very clever at sitting on the fence placating
everybody. I'm getting so tired of strangers lording it over
England, even if it is heresy to say so."

The seneschal thought carefully before he spoke. "His
Eminence is certainly a crafty talker if what I've heard is
right," he said at length. "And it's also true that you're not
in much of a position for bargaining. But I don't think you
can be too hard on Charles, my Lady; he's got a difficult
enough job keeping this mess of Angles and Scots and so-
called Normans out of trouble and satisfying Rome at the
same time."

She looked at him very straight, sucking at her lower lip with her teeth. It was a trick he hadn't seen for many years; her mother used to do it, when she was angry or upset. "If we fought, Sir John," she said, "if all of us just straightforwardly rebelled, what would our chances be?"

He spread his hands. "Against the Blue? The Blue is like the blue of Ocean, Lady; endlessly it runs, from here to China for all I know. Nobody fights the sea."

"Sometimes," she said, "you're not much of a help. . . ." She angled her mirror, tweaked carefully at an eyebrow hair that had got itself out of line. "I don't know at all," she said tiredly. "Give me a sick dog or a cat, or even Master Gwilliam's old jalopy down there in the yard with its carburettor bunged up again, and I know where I stand; I'd have a go at putting things right even if I didn't make much of a job of it. But churchmen, and high churchmen at that, put shivers up my back. Maybe they think with my father gone they can bully me easier than some of our great barons; but I'm certain now we've made our stand we shall have to keep to it or we shall finish up worse off than ever; they're sure to impose some sort of fine for defying them in the first place." She rose, satisfied at last that her appearance couldn't be bettered; but at the door of the chamber she balanced suddenly on one leg, spat on her fingers and dragged a stocking seam straight. She looked up at the seneschal, with his fair round head and the odd features that looked now just as they had looked when she was a child. "Sir John," she said softly. "You who see all and say so very little . . . would my father have behaved like this?"

He waited. Then, "He would; were his people involved, and his own good name."

"Then you will follow me?"

"I was your father's man," he said. "And I am yours, my Lady."

She shivered. "Sir John," she said, "keep very close. . . ."

She ducked under the lintel and clittered down the steps to meet the delegation.

His Eminence was friendly, to a point jovial; until it came to the matter of the unpaid tribute. "You must realize my child," said Londinium roundly, taking a turn up the hall and back, "Pope John, your spiritual father and the ruler of the known world, isn't a man you can dismiss so readily or whose favours or displeasure can be taken lightly. Now I . . ." He spread his hands. "I'm merely a messenger and an advisor. What you say to me or I to you may be of no account. But once a word travels beyond these walls, and that it must if my duty's to be done, then you and all your people will suffer; for John will crack this little place like an egg. His will must be obeyed, all over the world."

He walked back to Eleanor. "You're very young," he said genially, "and I can't help feeling toward you perhaps as your father might, if he were alive to counsel you." His fingers lingered on her arm; and Eleanor, perhaps from sheer nervousness, raised an eyebrow. Under the circumstances, it was an unfortunate gesture. His Eminence reddened and constrained his temper with an effort. "Find this tribute," he said. "Levy it somehow, make it up any way you choose; but get it, and send it. Do it inside the week and you can still catch the last of the ships for France. But if you delay and the weather worsens, if your merchantmen are lost or stray into out-of-the-way ports with your grain, then with the spring I promise you John will reach out to punish. And rightly too, for the half of all you own belongs to him. You hold your place, as you know very well, by his good will alone."

"I hold my place," said Eleanor icily, "by the favour of my liege-lord Charles; and that you know, My Lord, as well as I. My father promised loyalty at his knee, kissing his hand according to the ancient way. I too, until I am released, will follow him. And no other, sir. . . ."

There was a quietness, in which the clacking of the Challow tower could be clearly heard. Londinium seemed to swell, puffing himself up beneath his fur-trimmed robes much in the manner of a frog. "Your liege-lord," he said, and he obviously found it hard to keep from shouting, "has ordered you to send that grain. So you flout both Pope and King. . . ."

"I cannot send what I do not own," said Eleanor patiently. "What grain I do have to spare must be released to my people, or there will be famine in the land by Christmas. What will John have, a countryside of corpses to testify his strength?"

The churchman glared, but would say no more; and she withdrew, leaving affairs thus unhappily in the balance.

Matters came to a head in the evening, when dinner was prepared for the delegation in the Great Hall. The place was made cheerful by the light of many lamps and candles, and servants stood by with bundles of spares beneath their arms to replace the dips as they burned down in the sconces. Her Ladyship would have used the electric light, but at the last moment the seneschal had prevailed against such rashness; His Eminence would never have sat at meat beneath such open evidence of heresy. The exhausted globes with their delicate filaments of carbon had been withdrawn into the roof, the wall switches were hidden by drapes, and there was no visible sign of Eleanor's disaffection. She sat on the dais, in the chair her father used to occupy; the seneschal was on her right, her Captain of Artillery to her left. Opposite her were the churchmen and such of the military as had been allowed inside the gates.

All went well until His Eminence touched sympathetically on the early death of Her Ladyship's mother. The Captain choked and converted the sound hastily into a cough; all the household knew that that was Eleanor's sorest point. She had drunk more than was good for her, again out of nervousness; and she rose instantly to the bait. "This, My Lord, is very interesting," she said. "For had a surgeon been allowed to help my mother, perhaps she would still be with us now. I've read you Romans were once more daring than you are now; for the great Caesar himself was born by cutting his mother's womb, yet now you deem the trick heinous to God—"

"My Lady—"

"Also I have heard," said Eleanor, hiccupping slightly, "that airs may be distilled, the breathing of which quietens the body and the brain, so that one awakes from a mighty pain as from a sleep; yet Pope Paul I think it was disowned them, saying the pain was sent from God to be a reminder of sacred duty here on earth. Also that acids sprayed into the air will kill the very essence of disease; yet doctors work on us with unwashed hands. Are we to learn from this, it is better to die of holiness than live in heresy?"

His Eminence rose bridling. "Heresy," he began, "exists in many forms in each and every one of us; in you, my Lady, perhaps most of all. And were it not for the charity of Pope John—"

"Charity?" interrupted Eleanor bitterly. "Your duty here is scarce concerned with that. It seems to me, My Lord, the Church is fast forgetting the meaning of the word; for I would rather sell the drapes out of my house, were I Pope John, than starve my subjects in a foreign isle, unlettered idiots though they well might be."

Londinium of course could scarcely be expected to stomach such a double-barrelled insult; as well as a direct attack upon his ruler and the Church it was a slight against his own person as one of the very idiots to whom Eleanor had likened the English. He banged the table, red in the face with rage; but before his harangue was well enough started the household's Signaller-Page ran in with his pad, tore off the top sheet and handed it to his mistress. She stared at it uncomprehendingly for a moment, lips forming the words it bore; then she passed it to the seneschal. "My Lord," she said, "you must be seated, and spare your breath awhile. This message just arrived; I want it read to everybody in the hall."

The archbishop's eyes went automatically to the windows, curtained against the night; he knew as well as the others present that only matters of the greatest importance would induce the Guild to light torches on its signal arms. The seneschal rose, bowing slightly to the dignitaries. "My Lords," he said, "as earnest of his support for us here in the West, Charles today despatched tribute doubling the amount we owe to Rome. Morever he confirms the Lady Eleanor in her governorship of the isle and its demesnes; and in further witness of his trust in her sends to Corfe from his arsenal at Woolwich the great gun *Growler* in company of a platoon of his own men. Also from Isca the culverin *Prince of Peace;* the demicannon *Loyalty,* and shot and powder for him—"

The words were lost in an outbreak of applause from the lower tables; men shouted and banged their cups and glasses on the wood. The seneschal raised his hand. "Also," he said, eyes twinkling, "His Majesty requests His Eminence of Londinium, *wherever he might be,* to attend him at his earliest convenience to confer on matters of State."

The archbishop opened his mouth and closed it abruptly again. Eleanor leaned back wiping her face and feeling reprieved from death. "He *did* know," she whispered to the seneschal under cover of the din. "And look, we've made him stand. Who knows, perhaps the next time he will fight. . . ."

Two of the guns duly arrived; but the demicannon fell into a marsh while making the crossing into the island and the best efforts of the soldiers failed to lift it, giving rise in later times to the saying that Loyalty was lost east of Luckford Lakes.

After the guns arrived Eleanor breathed easier for a time; for though the armament was little more than a token its effect on the spirits of the household was considerable. Also the castle was recognised to be one of the most impregnable in the country; Her Ladyship spoke of that one cold evening a month after the discomfiture of the churchmen. She was pacing the second bailey, muffled in a cloak against the chilling wind from the sea; she paused by *Growler*, still limbered up as they had brought him in, and ran her fingers along the rough iron of his breech. Her seneschal stopped at her elbow. "Tell me, Sir John," she said skittishly, "what would our father in Rome have done if Charles hadn't made up our taxes? Do you think he would really have faced this creature and myself, both virgins in our way and still unblooded, for such poor chaff as we hold here in our granaries?"

The seneschal thought carefully, almond-shaped eyes brooding out over the battlements, looking at nothing in the gathering dark. "Certainly, Eleanor," he said—no other would have dared be so familiar—"His Holiness would have been very tempted to put us down. He wouldn't dare let defiance go unpunished for fear of setting the whole country in revolt. But fortunately that problem's over for a time; you can enjoy Christmas at least entertaining those of your father's friends who'll come to visit you in Corfe."

She looked up at the keep, frowning and black in the night, and at the scatter of softly glowing windows where her people were preparing beds and meals. Here and there harsher flares showed where her heretical engine was again supplying light to the place. The sound of the generator came faintly over the bailey walls, eddying and fading as the wind blew. "Yes," she said, shivering suddenly. "The cows in their stalls and the horses, the motors shut away against the frost—I bet Sir Gwilliam's burning peat under his confounded cylinder block again for fear the cold bursts it; one day he'll have the whole place going up in smoke— we shall be nicely shut away too, Sir John, and safe at least till spring."

He waited, gravely. She half turned to him, seeming to expect some remark; then she brushed her hair impatiently where the wind flapped it across her eyes. "I wasn't fooled," she said. "And neither were you I'm quite sure. Not even by His Eminence riding out all smiles, showering blessings and good advice. Charles will go to the New World next year, won't he?"

"Yes, Lady."

"Yes," she said broodingly. "Then all those unpleasant layabouts at Court, and all the little popish dogs scattered round the country, will get up on their back legs and run about to see what mischief they can make; and we shall be high on the list of priorities, I've got no doubt of that. We've shown our teeth, and not been beaten for it; they won't let things rest at that. John might have a long arm, but his memory's even more remarkable."

He waited again; he knew more than she, but some secrets were not his to tell. "And, my Lady?"

She touched the gun again, frowning down at its great black barrel. "Why," she said, "then they will come for these. . . ."

She turned away suddenly, tucking her arm through his. "But as you say, we needn't worry till the better weather; John will need good seas in case he has to back his little people with arms and more valour than any of them own. Come on, Sir John, or I shall get worse depressed than ever; I hear a new showman came into the village this morning and Sir Gwill has bought his services for the night. We

can have a look at the tricks he's got to offer, though I
expect we'll have seen most of them before; and afterwards
I'll get you to tell me some more of your lying stories
about the times before there were castles on our hilltops
and before the world knew anything of churches, high or
low."

He smiled at her in the dark. "All lies, Eleanor? You
seem to develop less and less respect for your oldest retainer
as the years go on."

She stopped, silhouetted against the brightness of a window. "All lies, Sir John," she said, trying to keep her voice
firm; for she spoke of forbidden things. "When I want the
truth from you, you'll know. . . ."

Christmas came and went pleasantly; the weather was
neither so hard nor so cold as the year before and enough
travelling entertainers, musicians, and the like passed
through the district to provide variety at night. One man
in particular fascinated Eleanor. He brought with him a
machine, a strange stilt-legged device with complex parts. A
strip of unknown substance was fed into it, a handle turned;
a limelight spat and hissed, and pictures, flickering and
seemingly alive, danced across a screen rigged on the other
side of the chamber. Her Ladyship made efforts to buy the
apparatus, but it was not for sale. Instead she added to her
mechanical armoury, setting two more generators clanking
and hissing beside the first. The globes, always fragile and
short-lived, were replaced by arc lamps that gave a more
ferocious light; with her own hands she made shades for
them to soften the glare. One of the brachets spawned a
great yelping litter of pups that ran through the corridors
and kitchens piping and squeaking, stealing from the cooks'
soup bowls, tearing up everything they could find with their
tiny teeth. She was delighted and kept them all, even the
runts.

When winter gave way to the blustering wetness of March

nothing more had been heard either from Charles or the Church concerning the events of the year before. Nothing out of the ordinary happened except that a few days before His Majesty was due to leave the semaphores brought a request from Sir Anthony Hope, Provost Marshall of England and the King's hereditary champion, who asked to be allowed to hunt the Purbeck Chase for a few days and enjoy the pleasure and delight of Eleanor's company.

She pulled a face at the seneschal when he told her. "As far as I can remember the man's hugely conceited and a complete boor; and anyway the season's nearly finished, we don't want him trampling about with his great hooves just as everything's settling down to breed. But I suppose there's nothing to be done except put up with him, he's far too influential to upset over a trifle. I can't help wishing though he'd go up to the Taverners at Sherborne or over into the Marches like he did last year. You'll have to help me out with him I'm afraid, Sir John, I've got nothing in common with him at all; after all he is almost old enough to be my father, though perish the thought of that." She sniffed. "But if he sends any more of his laboriously gallant messages I shall feel very inclined to greet him like Daddy did that famous Golden Eagle. . . ."

The towers of the Guild sent back her agreement and soon brought news that Sir Anthony was on his way in company with some score of soldiers of his household. Eleanor shrugged and ordered extra barrels of beer to be laid in. "Well the ground's still pretty soft," she said. "There's always the chance his horse's foot will turn and break his fat neck for him, though I suppose we mustn't hope for miracles."

Certainly none took place and within a few days Sir Anthony arrived at her hall, where his men were quartered in the lower wards and played havoc with the serving girls till Eleanor took the matter up more than firmly with their master. The party stayed two weeks and Her Ladyship, who at first had been inclined to be suspicious about the whole affair, found herself relaxing and merely wishing Sir Anthony, his gang of roughnecks, and his repertoire of tall boasts all safely back inside the walls of Londinium. But on the fifteenth morning came disaster. When dawn broke, England was at peace; by nightfall the first of the acts had taken place that would lead inevitably to war with Rome.

Eleanor had risen early and ridden out to hunt, accompanied as usual by her seneschal and some half dozen servants and falconers of the household. They took dogs and a brace of hawks, hoping to see a little sport before Sir Anthony and his cavalcade spoiled their chances too much. For a time they were fortunate; then one of the gentle falcons missed her kill and refused to come to the swinging of the lure. Instead she winged away across the heath, flying strongly and high, making apparently for Poole harbour and the sea. Eleanor galloped after her, swearing and banging her heels into her horse; she had put in a lot of time on that bird and didn't intend to lose her if she could help it. She rode fast, letting her mount pick its way among the tussocks and clumps of gorse, and soon outdistanced the rest of the party; the seneschal alone kept pace.

After a mile or two it became evident the bird was gone beyond recall. There was no sign of her, and they had already travelled so far that Corfe towers were tiny in the distance. Eleanor reined in, panting. "It's no good, we've lost her. Honestly . . ." She pulled the gauntlet off her wrist, and hooked it over her saddlebow. "I'm beginning to see why they talk about being bird-brained. . . . Sir John, what is it?"

He was staring back the way they had come, narrowing his eyes against the cool bright sun. "Lady," he said urgently, "the hawk stooped on a hare, and fell beneath an

eagle. . . ." He spun his horse. "Ride, quickly. Make for the
Wareham Road. . . ."

She saw them then; a line of specks strung out across the
heath. Horsemen, moving fast. They were too far off for
their features to be seen but there was little doubt of their
identity; Sir Anthony had sprung his trap at last. Eleanor
glared right and left. The pursuers were well spaced; hopeless to try to outflank by drawing across their line. She
turned in the saddle. Ahead of her a track stretched into distance, a white thread laid across the heath; beyond was the
pale glow of the sea. There was no doubt about the way;
she spun her horse, flicking it into a gallop.

The men behind, their mounts fresher, gained steadily;
a half mile farther on they were close enough to call to her,
telling her to give up. A pistol banged flatly; Eleanor turned
back to the seneschal and her mount stumbled, pitching her
headlong. She rolled, covering her face as she had once been
taught, rose tousled but unharmed. Beside her the horse
lay screaming, blood dribbling brightly from a foreleg.

She ran to it, eyes wide. The seneschal had wheeled behind her; he dismounted and thrust his reins into her
hand. "My Lady . . . *ride for Wareham.* . . ."

She shook her head dazedly, trying to think. "He's blown,
there isn't a chance. They'd take me on the road. . . ."
The horsemen were close; the seneschal raised a pistol,
steadied the barrel on his forearm, and squeezed the trigger.
By the merest accident the ball took one of the riders in the
chest, fetching him from his horse; the line wheeled, momentarily confused.

A whistling sounded. Eleanor turned, fists clenched. Behind her, distant on the rutted strip of road, a heavy
steamer laboured with a train of waggons. She began to run
toward it, feeling the air scythe into her lungs. A pistol
exploded again; this time she heard the ball cut through the
grass twenty yards to her right. Another shot; she snatched a

backward glance, saw the seneschal ridden down by a mounted man. Then her feet were stumbling along the road, and the engine was very close.

She stopped by it, leaning on the great rear wheel and panting, seeing the oldness of the steamer, the canopy pierced through with holes, the rust streaks and the bubbling of water from ancient boiler joints. A great worn-out wreck she was, ending her days hauling wood and manure and stone, but still liveried in the dark maroon of Strange and Sons. Her driver was a fair-haired boy in the corduroys and buckled cap of a haulier, greasy muffler knotted round his neck. Eleanor gulped and thrust her hand up so he could see the ring she wore. "Tell me quickly," she panted. "Where is your home?"

"Durnovaria, Lady . . ."

"Then you are my liege man," she gasped. "Fight this treachery. . . ."

He answered something, startled; she didn't hear the words. His hands went to regulator and brake, she heard the sudden overworked thunder of the engine. She flung herself away; a hot drizzle lashed her face, smoke stung her lungs and the train was past, gathering speed down the road, the loco half hidden by steam as the driver used his whistle over and again.

What followed was confused. The horses, bunched, were scattered by the iron shrieking; the haulier spun his wheel, turning the engine onto the rough. Three of the waggons broke clear; the others, loaded high and bound with tarpaulin, swayed behind the steamer as she bounced toward Sir Anthony. He bellowed with rage, whirling a sword; a charger bucked, throwing a soldier over its neck; the chest of another man was crushed by cascading blocks of stone. A rider raised a pistol, firing blind; the ball struck the horn-plate of the loco, throwing hot splinters into her driver's face. He flung up his hands and a second shot took him in

the armpit, bowling him from the footplate. The loco, regulator open, ploughed by Sir Anthony. Fifty yards on, one
wheel struck a mound in the grass. She slewed, held back
by her load; a huge grinding, a hissing explosion of steam
and she landed on her side, flywheel still churning, cinders
from her firebox scattering across the grass. Flames licked
up at once, showing brightly through the drifting smoke.
She burned the rest of the day; it was night before a
peasant child crept close enough to the wreck to prise the
naveplate from one mighty wheel. He kept it in his cottage,
polished bright; and half a lifetime later he would still tell
his children the tale, and take the big disc down and fondle
it, and say it came from a great road steamer called the
Lady Margaret.

Escape was no longer possible; Eleanor rose sullenly and
let her wrists be pinioned at her sides. She saw the
seneschal, arms similarly held, queer light eyes blazing with
rage; beside him two men supported the haulier. The boy
was coughing, face masked bright with blood. Sir John's
second shot had struck the tip of the Provost Marshall's
thumb, flicking back the nail till it stood at right angles
from the flesh; he was dancing and swearing, fussing with a
handkerchief. "When slaves revolt," he fumed, "raising their
hands against their masters, then there's no more but this.
. . ." The haulier was pulled forward. Eleanor shrieked; a
falchion swung hissing to bite into his neck. The blow,
badly delivered, didn't kill; the boy scuttled to her, wetting
her feet with blood while they cut at him in panic. It
seemed an age before the thing was through; the body
flopped and leaped, subsided into stillness.

It was the first violent death the Lady Eleanor had ever
seen; and it had overtones of horror she was never likely to
forget. She hung her head, trying not to faint, seeing the
blood run glittering and soak into the dust. She didn't faint;
instead she began to vomit. The spasms became more

violent; she tore her arms from the men who held her, dropped to her knees and panted. When she had finished she raised a face that was blazing white to the lips; and she began to swear. She swore in English and French, Celtic, and Latin and Gaelic; she cursed Sir Anthony and his men, promising them a dozen different deaths in a flat, nearly gentle voice that seemed to hold the Provost Marshall fascinated. He stopped bothering with his thumb, stood frowning; then he recollected himself and bellowed for his men to fetch the riderless horses. The seneschal was forced to mount; a soldier swung Eleanor up in front of him and the party struck out past the crackling wreck of the steamer and across the heath, intending no doubt to rendezvous with some fishing boat that would take the captives out of reach of any pursuit. In those days there were men in Poole who would have ferried the King himself into bondage if the price was right.

Whatever scheme Sir Anthony had in mind was never put into effect. Somewhere across the heath the Signallers had seen, watching the distant fight through their great Zeiss lenses, and the pall of smoke from the burning train had been easily visible from Corfe. Signals flew, alerting not only the castle garrison but the militia of Wareham; the party was intercepted before it reached the sea. The Provost Marshall checked when he saw he was cut off, and would have made great play of having Eleanor as a hostage had she not bitten the wrist of the man who held her and tumbled off a horse for the second time that day. She landed in a stand of gorse, rose scratched and bleeding and more furious than ever; the fight was over within minutes, and Sir Anthony and his people threw down their arms.

She limped to where they stood on the heath, surrounded by a ring of guns. Men ran to her but she pushed them away. She circled the prisoners slowly, rubbing her hip, picking unconsciously at the grass and twigs on her skirt;

and it seemed the rage bubbled and boiled in her brain like the strange fumes of a wine. "Well, Sir Anthony," she said. "We made a little promise on the road. And here in the West, you'll find we keep our word. . . ." He tried to barter with her then, or beg his life; but she stared at him as if he spoke an unknown tongue. "Ask mercy of the wind," she said, almost wonderingly. "Beg to the rocks, or the great waves of the sea. Don't come and whine to me. . . ." She turned aside to the seneschal. "Hang them," she said. "For treason, and for murder. . . ."

"My Lady . . ."

She screamed at him suddenly, stamping on the ground. "Hang them . . ." Beside her a soldier sat a restless horse; she grabbed his jerkin and pulled, nearly tumbling him from the saddle. She was mounted and away before a hand could be raised, riding furiously across the heath, beating the neck of the animal with her fist. The seneschal followed her, leaving the prisoners to their fate. She reined a mile from the castle, dropped to the ground, and ran to a knoll from where she could see her home spread out before her, the baileys and towers and the flanking hills clear in the bright air. She gripped the stirrup of the seneschal as he rode alongside, fingers twisting the stiff leather. If he'd hoped the wild ride would calm her he was disappointed. She was nearly too angry to speak; the syllables jerked out from her like the cracking of sheets of glass. "Sir John," she said, "before our people came, and took this land with blood at Santlache Field, that place was called a Gate. Is this not true?"

He said heavily, "Yes, my Lady."

"Why then," she said, "let it be so again. Go to my tenants in the Great Plain, and north as far as Sarum Town. Go west to Durnovaria, and east to the village on the Bourne. Tell them . . ." She choked and steadied herself. "Tell them, they pay no tithes to Purbeck but in arms.

Tell them that Gate is closed, and Eleanor holds the key.
. . ." She tore at the seal on her finger. "Take my ring, and
go. . . ."

He gripped her shoulder and turned her, staring into
her wild eyes. "Lady," he said deliberately, "this is
war. . . ."

She knocked his hand away, panting for breath. *"Will
you go,"* she fumed, *"or shall I send another?* . . ." He said
nothing else but touched heels to his horse and turned it;
galloped north, trailing dust, along the Wareham Road.
She mounted again and rode yelling into the valley, scattering the little chugging cars, sending them batwinging
into the hedges; and though her soldiers raked their horses
bloody, none could match her speed.

Messages were despatched at once to Charles in Londinium, but all the semaphores brought back was the news
that the King had already sailed for the Americas. Sir
Anthony's stroke had been well timed; for though there
were rumours the Guild could even get a message to the
New World, by means no one could guess at, there was no
known way of contacting a ship at sea. Meanwhile the
Provost Marshall's supporters were rampaging round the
capital threatening death, destruction, and worse while
Henry of Rye and Deal, under direct instructions from
Rome, was hastily assembling his force. What Eleanor had
predicted had to a large extent come true; all sorts of dogs
were yapping in the absence of the King. The fact that the
quarrel had originally come about as a result of what was
now generally admitted to be an administrative error made
the situation even more ironic.

Her Ladyship faced many problems down in Dorset. She
could levy men from the districts round about, the commoners would flock to her banner soon enough; but a
standing army must be fed and clothed and armed. For
days the rage sustained her while she worked with her

captains and house people drawing up the lists of what she would need. Money was clearly the first essential; and for that she rode north, to Durnovaria. What passed between her and her aged grandfather was never known; but for a solid week the crimson-dressed steamers toiled down to Corfe Gate, hauling in produce free. Flour and grain they brought and livestock, salted meat and preserves, shot and powder and wads and musketballs, rope and slow match, oil and kerosene and tar; chain hoists rumbled all night long, derricks powered by panting donkey engines swung load after load high into the keep. Eleanor had no idea what support might be forthcoming from the rest of the country and planned for the worst, packing her baileys with men and supplies. That was how Henry came to find the place so well prepared, and in such a lethal temper.

Eleanor called the seneschal to her room on the evening following the massacre. She was deadly pale, her eyes ringed with dark shadows; she waved him to a chair, sat awhile staring into the firelight and leaping shadows. "Well, Sir John," she said finally, "I've been sitting here thinking up a glorious phrase for the . . . thing that happened this morning. This is it. 'I've blown a Roman gadfly off my walls.' Don't you think that's very good?"

He didn't answer, and she laughed and coughed. "It doesn't help of course," she said. "All I can see still are those creatures in the ditch, and writhing on the path. Somehow beside that nothing else seems real. Not any more."

He waited again, knowing there was no help in words. "I've expelled Father Sebastian," she said. "He told me there was no forgiving what I'd done, not if I walked bare-foot to Rome itself. I told him he'd better leave; if there was no forgiveness he couldn't be a comfort and he was only putting himself in mortal sin by staying. I said I knew

I was damned because I'd damned myself, I didn't have to
wait for any god to do it for me. That was the worst of all
of course; I only said it to hurt him but I realized afterwards
I meant it anyhow, I just wasn't a Christian any more. I
said if necessary I'd raise up a few old gods, Thunor and
Wo-Tan perhaps or Balder instead of Christ; for he told me
himself many years ago when I was still taking lessons at
his knee that Balder was only an older form of Jesus and
that there have been many bleeding gods." She poured
wine for herself, unsteadily. "And then I spent the rest of
the afternoon getting drunk. Or trying to. Aren't you dis-
gusted?"

He shook his head. He'd never criticised her, not in all
her life; and this wasn't the time to start.

She laughed again, and rubbed her face. "I need . . .
something," she said. "Maybe punishment. If I ordered
you to fetch a whip and beat me till I bled, would you
do it?"

He shook his head, lips pursed.

"No," she said. "You wouldn't, would you. . . . Anything else, but you wouldn't have me hurt. I feel I want
to . . . scream, or be sick, or something. Maybe both. John,
when I'm excommunicated, what will our people do?"

He'd already considered his answer carefully. "Disavow
Rome," he said. "It's gone too far now for anybody to
turn back. You'll see that, my Lady."

"And the Pope?"

He thought again for a moment. "He'll certainly act,"
he said, "and that quickly; but I can't see him ferrying
an army all the way from Italy just to put down one
strongpoint. What he's almost bound to do is instruct his
people in Londinium to march against us in force; and I
think too we'll be seeing some of the Seigneurs from the
Loire and the Low Countries coming over to see what
they can pick up in the confusion. They've been wanting to

stake out a few claims on English soil for years enough
now, and they'll certainly never get a better chance."

"I see," she said wearily. "What it comes down to is
I've made a complete mess of things; with Charles out of
the way as well I've played right into their hands. They'll
be flocking into England, with the Church's full blessing,
to put down armed revolt. What the end of that will be
I just can't imagine." She got up and paced restlessly across
the chamber and back. "It's no good," she said. "I just can't
sit still and wait, not tonight." She sent for a writer, and
the officers commanding her troops and artillery; they
worked into the small hours drawing up lists of the extra
provisions they would need to withstand a full-scale siege.
"There's no doubt," said Eleanor with a flash of her old
practicality, "that we shall be bottled up for a considerable
time; till Charles gets back in fact. There won't be any
question of chivalry either, of being let to walk out with
our arms or anything like that, the whole thing's far too
serious; but at least we shall know by the time we're through
who's actually running this country, ourselves or an Italian
priest." She poured wine. "Well, gentlemen, let's hear your
recommendations. You can have anything you need, arms,
men, provisions; I only ask one thing. Don't leave anything out. We can't afford to forget any details; remember there's a rope, or worse, waiting for every one of us if
we make a single slip. . . ."

The seneschal stayed with her after the others had gone,
sitting drinking wine in the firelight and talking of all subjects from gods to kings; of the land, its history and its people; of Eleanor, and her family and upbringing. "You know,"
she said, "it's strange, Sir John; but it seemed this morning
when I fired the gun I was standing outside myself, just
watching what my body did. As if I, and you too, all of us,
were just tiny puppets on the grass. Or on a stage. Little
mechanical things playing out parts we didn't understand."

She stared into her wineglass, swilling it in her hands to see flame light and lamplight dance from the goldenness inside; then she looked up frowning, eyes opaque and dark. "Do you know what I mean?"

He nodded, gravely. "Yes, my Lady. . . ."

"Yes," she said. "It's like a . . . dance somehow, a minuet or a pavane. Something stately and pointless, with all its steps set out. With a beginning, and an end. . . ." She tucked her legs under her, as she sat beside the fire. "Sir John," she said, "sometimes I think life's all a mass of significance, all sorts of strands and threads woven like a tapestry or a brocade. So if you pulled one out or broke it the pattern would alter right back through the cloth. Then I think . . . it's all totally pointless, it would make just as much sense backwards as forwards, effects leading to causes and those to more effects . . . maybe that's what will happen, when we get to the end of Time. The whole world will shott undone like a spring, and wind itself back to the start. . . ." She rubbed her forehead tiredly. "I'm not making sense, am I? It's getting too late for me. . . ."

He took the wine from her, carefully. She stayed quiet awhile; when she spoke again she was half asleep. "Do you remember years ago telling me a story?" she asked. "About how my great uncle Jesse broke his heart when my grandmother wouldn't marry him, and killed his friend, and how that was somehow the start of everything he did. . . . It seemed so real, I'm sure that was how it must have been. Well, I can finish it for you now. You can see the Cause and Effect right the whole way through. If we . . . won, it would be because of grandfather's money. And the money's there because of Jesse, and he did it because of the girl. . . . It's like Chinese boxes. There's always a smaller one inside, all the time; until they get so small they're too small to see but they keep on going down, and down. . . ."

He waited; but she didn't speak again.

For days the castle rang with activity; Eleanor's messengers rode out to scour the countryside around bringing in more men, provisions, meat on the hoof. The great lower bailey was prepared for the animals, pens and hurdles lined against the outer walls. The steamers toiled once more bringing cattle cake and baled hay from Wareham, chugging down the road with trailers empty, clanking back through the outer gate to discharge their cargo in heaps on the flattened grass. Everything possible was shifted under cover; what stacks remained exposed were covered by tarpaulins, and turves and stone rubble strewn on top. The fodder would be a prime target were the enemy to bring fire machines with them. All day the hoists clattered and most of the night too, taking the provisions down to the cellars, bringing up quarrels for the crossbowmen, powder and ball for the arquebusiers, charges for the great guns. The semaphores seldom stopped. The country was aflame; Londinium was arming, levies from Sussex and Kent were marching toward the west. Then came worse news. From France, from the castles of the Loire, men were streaming to fight in the Holy Crusade while to the south a second armada was embarking for England. To Eleanor, John sent no word; but his intentions were plainer than speech. Her Ladyship redoubled her efforts. Steamers towing vast iron chains scythed the banks of the wet ditch; working parties fired the scrub from the castle *motte*, the bushes and trees that had seeded themselves there over the years; and down over the blackened grass went ton after ton of powdered chalk. The slopes would glow now in starlight, showing up the silhouettes of climbing men. Through it all the sightseers came, parking their little cars in the village square, flooding into the castle, through the gates and across the baileys, staring at the guns and the sentries on the walls, poking their noses into this, their prying fingers into that, impeding everybody nearly all the time. Eleanor could have closed her gates; but pride forbade her. Pride, and the counsel of the seneschal. Let the people see, he murmured. Invite their sympathy, appeal to their understanding. Her Ladyship would need all the support she could get from the country in the coming months.

On the thirtieth day after the massacre the seneschal rose and dressed at dawn. He walked down softly through the still-sleeping keep, through chambers and corridors let honeycomb-fashion into the huge walls, past arrow slits and fenestellas pouring livid grey light. Past a sentry, dozing at his post; the man jerked to attention, bringing his halberd shaft ringing down onto stone. Sir John acknowledged the gesture, raising a hand thoughtfully, mind far away. Outside, in the raw air of the upper bailey, he paused. Round him the curtain walls loomed from the night, massive shadows topped by the tinier shadows of men; the breath of the guards showed in wisps above their heads. Far below huddled the roofs of the village, dim and blue, odd lights burning here and there; out on the heath a solitary glow showed him where some mason's boy trudged lantern in hand to work. He turned away, eyes seeing but not recording, mind locked inward. At this dawn hour it seemed as always that Time might pause, turning and flowing in on itself before speeding again, urging in the new day. The castle, like a great dim crown of stone, seemed to ride not a hill but a flaw in the timestream, a node of quiet from which possibilities might spread out limitless as the journeyings of the sun. No one, not the seneschal and certainly no one else, could have understood his thoughts at that time. The old thoughts, the first thoughts of the first people ever; for the seneschal was of the ancient kind.

At the tip of the second bailey the squat Butavant tower jutted over the precipice of burned grass like a figurehead from the prow of a ship. The seneschal paused at the lower door, queer eyes on the horizon, swivelled slowly to face the Challow tower. And instantly, gracefully, the jointed arms began to flap.

He climbed the tower steps, feet shuffling on stone, hearing a drum behind him and a voice. A Page-Signaller scuttled across the bailey; something not more than a lad, hose wrinkled and tabard askew, message pad in hand, knuckling his eyes. Far out over the heath, in the cobalt intermingling of sea and sky, a light gleamed and was lost. Then another and another, and a patch of lighter dark that could have been a sail. As if a fleet had come to anchor, lay dressing its ranks and waiting.

At the top of the stair a locked door gave access to a tiny cell set in the thickness of the stone. To that door, the seneschal alone held a key. The key itself was strange, a little round-headed thing that carried instead of wards a wavy crest of brass. He inserted it in the lock, twisted; the door swung open. He left it ajar behind him; his hands worked deftly, assembling the apparatus of magic the Popes in their wisdom had long since disallowed. Shapes of brass and shapes of mahogany tinkled and clattered; a tiny spark flashed blue; his name and questionings fled into an undiscovered Ether, invisible, silent, faster by a thousand times than the semaphores. He smiled quietly, took down paper and stylus and began to write. Footsteps clunked overhead; a voice called urgently. He ignored it, lost to sensation, all his being focussed on the thing that sparked and flashed between his fingers.

Behind him the door swung inward. He heard the intake of breath, the scrape of a shoe on stone; he half turned, papers in his hands. Behind him the thing on the table clacked shrilly, untouched and unbidden. He smiled again, gently. "My Lady . . ."

She was backing off staring, hand to her throat clutching the wrap she had flung across her shoulders. Her voice husked hollow in the shaft. *"Necromancy . . ."*

He left the machine, pattered after her. "Eleanor . . ." He caught her at the bottom of the stair. "Eleanor, I thought you had more wit. . . ." He took her wrist, drew her after him. She moved unwillingly, pulling back; above her the device banged and tutted frantically. She edged round the door, lips parted, one hand flat against the stone, saw the little thing chattering devil-possessed. He started to laugh. "Here. It isn't good for your people to see." The door was closed behind her; the lock shut with a snap. Her mouth trembled; she couldn't take her eyes from what lay on the bench. "Sir John," she said falteringly. *"What is it . . . ?"*

He shrugged impatiently, hands busy. "A manifestation of the electric fluid; known to the Guild now for a generation."

She stared at him as if seeing him for the first time. She said wonderingly, "This is a language?" She drew nearer the bench, no longer afraid.

"Of a sort."

"Who speaks it to you?"

He said shortly, "The Guild of Signallers. But that is unimportant. My Lady, the semaphores will clack all day. This is what they will say; *are saying.* . . ."

Before he could finish a voice sounded over their heads; it came thickly through the stone, full of resonance and wonder.

"Caerphilly has taken arms . . . !"

She jerked sharply, staring up; her mouth moved, but no sound came.

"And Pevensey," said the seneschal, reading. "And Beaumaris, Caerlon, Orford . . . Bodiam has declared for the King, Caenarvon has burned its charter. And Colchester, Warwick, Framlingham; Bramber, Cardiff, Chepstow . . ." She heard no more but ran to him, laughing and swinging her arms round his neck, waltzing round in the tiny space, upsetting wires and batteries and coils. And all day long the noise from the hill went on as the messages came lagging through on the old arms that were no longer of any use. All day till nightfall and far into the dark, spelling out the names in streaming arcs of flame; the old places, the proud places, Dover and Harlech and Kenilworth, Ludlow, Walmer, York. . . . And from far out of the west, calling through the sea mist, the words that were like the tinkling of old armour; Berry Pomeroy, Lostwithiel, Tintagel, Restormel; while the lights crawled forward from the heath, and far out on the sea. At midnight the arms stopped working; by next morning Corfe Gate was invested, and nothing moved on the semaphore towers but the swaying bodies of men.

The rising of the royal and baronial strongholds in every part of the country spared the defenders the main weight of the armada; the armies pushed inland, moving hurriedly and by night, harried by Eleanor's artillery as they passed through the gap in the hills. Some five hundred men remained to lay siege to Corfe. They brought with them or built on the spot a whole range of engines, ballistas, and mangonels; and these with the three great trebuchets *Persuader, Faith of Rome, and Direwolf* made play at the walls from the valley and surrounding hillsides. But so extreme was the range, and so great the elevation, that few of the missiles so much as cleared the outer curtain. Mostly they struck the stone below the battlements, bouncing back with hollow booms; the odd shots that landed in the baileys were welcomed by Eleanor's men as additions to their own supplies. The machines set up by Her Ladyship had better sport, and with the great guns caused such havoc that the lines of the besiegers were soon withdrawn beyond the wet ditch. From there the Pope's men mounted attack after attack, varying their methods in the hope of taking the defenders by surprise; but they were invariably driven back. Mantlets were employed, each carried on the backs of a

dozen men; sharpshooters blew off the legs of the wretches
beneath, tumbling them and their engines back into the
stream, leaving long swathes of redness on the flanks of the
mound. An attempt at mining was watched with more
sympathy than concern, while belfries could only be employed against the outer gate. One was constructed, out on
the heat beyond long cannon-shot; a heavy tower hung
with wetted hides and with three storeys inside it for snipers. It made its approach one dawn, rumbling through the
village street, propelled by a hundred sweating soldiers;
but *Growler*, entrenched behind a triple line of sandbags,
disembowelled it with a single shot, blowing men and parts
of men into the great ditch to either side.

After that there was a lull in the fighting; and the besiegers hailed Eleanor, promising her the forgiveness of
John (which wasn't theirs to offer) and asking her what
she intended, if she thought she could war with the entire
world. Then they sent a herald, with letters purporting to be
from Charles, telling her the cause was lost and she must
yield to Rome. Him she dismissed; though she offered, if he
came again on such a bogus errand, to load him in the
sling of a trebuchet and send him back by an airy and
quicker route. There followed a greater bombardment than
ever. All day long the stones roared in the air, while dust
rose from the nearby quarries where roughmasons toiled to
shape more rocks for the slings. Men charged the scarps,
urged on by officers with primed muskets who offered to
shoot waverers in the back. Eleanor taught a terrible lesson.
The defenders withdrew, seemingly in confusion, from an
entire section of the lower wall. The attackers, yelling like
frightened fiends, ran for the Martyr's Gate, bunched there
hammering and tearing at the bars of the portcullis. They
realized their mistake too late to save themselves. The outer
grating, hauled out of sight in the stone, slid down, im-
prisoning them like animals in a cage; and through the

vents above their heads poured the scalding oil. Then the
besiegers, rendered more cautious, sat down in earnest to
starve the castle out; but when November came round, and
Christmas and the New Year, the flags still flew above the
high keep, the oriflamme and the flowers and leopards of
Eleanor's house. Still there was no word of the King; neither
thaumaturgy nor wireless telegraphy availed the seneschal
now, the land was dumb. Then at last there was news,
brought by a Serjeant of Signallers who worked his way
through the enemy lines one dusk, dying already from an
arrow broken off short in his back. Beaumaris had fallen,
and Caerlon, and the mighty Tower of Dubris had taken
forty days before abandoning the fight.

Eleanor stayed up late that night, walking the tower
rooms and the baileys, heaped now with the debris of the
battle. To her came the seneschal, in the dim time before
dawn when the torches burned amber and guttering, when
the sentries nodded at their posts or started up alarmed at
the whisperings of oiled silk windowpanes. The mist was
rising on the Great Heath, and the moon eclipsed by cloud.

"Tell me, Sir John," she said, and her voice was lost
and tiny, barely stirring the harsh air. "Come to the window here, and tell me what you see. . . ."

He stood silent a long time. Then, heavily, "I see the night
mists moving on the hills, and the watch fires of our enemies. . . ." He made to leave her; but she called him
sharply.

"Fairy. . . ."

He paused, back turned to her; and as he stood she used
his proper name, the sound by which he was known among
the Old Ones. "I told you once," she said acidly, "when I
required the truth, then you would know. Now I charge
you. Come to me again, and tell me what you see."

She stood close while he thought, head in hand; he could

feel the warmth of her in the night, scent the faint presence
of her body. "I see an end to everything we know," he said
at last. "The Great Gate broken, John's banners on the
walls."

She pursued him. "And me, Sir John? What for me?"

He didn't immediately answer and she swallowed, feeling the night encroach, the dark slide into her body. "Is
there death?" she said.

"My Lady," he said gently, "there is death for every-
one. . . ."

She threw her head back then and laughed, as she had
laughed months before in the face of Rye and Deal. "Why
then," she said, "we must live a little while we can. . . ."
And that morning they sallied before it was light, fifty
strong, and burned *Direwolf*; his bones still lie there on the
hill. And the long gun *Prince of Peace* broke the arms of
his fellows, arms so stout and long there was no wood to
replace them. So they brought the great gun *Holy Meg*,
and she and the culverin talked to each other across the
valley till the smoke rolled back between the hills like steam
from a boiling pot.

They heard of his coming from the telegraphs. It was a
fine summer day when he crossed with his retinue into Purbeck Isle. They were still closely invested; in fact the besiegers had launched a heavy attack, their first for many
months, and in the confusion he arrived almost unheralded.
The first they knew was when the guns in the valley fell
silent. A strange silence it was too, a breathing hush in
which one could hear the wind soughing over the heathland. They saw his banners in the village, the horses and
the siege train winding across the heath, and the seneschal
hurried to find his mistress. She was in the second bailey;
they had the culverin mounted beside the Butavant tower

and were playing him at the men trying to climb the slope
below. Eleanor was dirty with smoke and a little bloody, for
one of her people had been hurt by the fire from an arque-
bus and she had helped bind the wound. She straightened
when she saw the seneschal, his grave features and bearing.
He nodded quietly, confirming what she had already seen
in his face. "My Lady," he said simply. "Your King is
here. . . ."

She had no time to change or make any preparations,
for the royal party was already in sight of the lower ward.
She ran on her own, down across the sloping bailey to the
gate, the seneschal pacing a distance behind. Nobody else
moved, not the gunners, not the bowmen and snipers lin-
ing the walls. She stopped by *Growler*, still standing where
he had stood from the first, and leaned on his barrel. Before
her were the tossing banners and the armour, the horses
champing their bits and dancing from the smell of powder,
the waiting soldiers with their guns and swords.

He rode forward alone, disdaining protection. He saw
the gatehouse towers, stained now by smoke and scarred
by shot, the portcullis sunk into the ground where it had
fallen over a year before and not moved since. He stared a
long time at Eleanor, standing fists clenched by the gun;
then he reached forward, rattled his whip against the bars
in front of him and gestured once with the stock of it.
Up . . .

She waited, the hair blowing round her face; then she
nodded tight-lipped to the people above. A pause; and the
chains creaked, the counterweights swung in their carved
channels. The gate groaned and lifted, tearing aside the
rank grass that had seeded round its foot. He rode forward,
ducking his head beneath the iron as it climbed up into the
stone; they heard the hooves of his horse on the hard
ground inside. He dismounted, going to Eleanor; and only
then did the cheering spread, through the village and the

soldiers and the ranks of people on the walls, up and away to the tower of the Great Keep. So the place yielded, to its liege-lord and to no other.

She spoke to the seneschal once more before she left her home. It was early dawn, the sky pale and grey-blue, the mist lying cloud-thick on the heathland promising a sweltering day. She sat her horse stiffly, back straight, and stared round her. Down across the baileys to where the guns stood limbered by the outer gate; across the parched, spoiled grass, over the lines of neat crosses where the dead were buried inside the walls they had helped defend. Above her the great donjon-face loomed, pale in the new light, empty and desolate and waiting. Below her, fifty yards away, the King of all England sat surrounded by his soldiers. He looked stooped and prematurely old; exhausted by months of campaigning, of haggling and manoeuvring and bartering, fighting desperate men who knew they stood to lose at best their homes and living, at worst their lives. He had won, if it could be called a victory; the boiling land was quiet again. The question they asked Eleanor, he had answered for himself.

She beckoned quietly to the seneschal, leaned from her horse. "Old One," she said. "You who served my father so well, and me. . . . Make my Signs the hawk and the rose. The flower to sink her roots into the soil, the bird to taste the wind. . . ."

He bowed, accepting the strange charge. "Lady," he said, "we shall meet again. Yet it shall be as you wish."

She saluted him once, raising a hand; then shook the reins of the horse and turned it, clattered down the steep way. Out under the towers of the Martyr's Gate to the great lower bailey. The soldiers fell in behind her, harness jangling; the party moved through the outer barbican to the village street beyond, and never once did she look back.

There was a trial, of sorts. A life was involved; she understood this distantly. These pompous, bewigged gentlemen, these gloomy corridors and halls of law, meant little to her. Sentence was commuted, by the express wish of King Charles. She was imprisoned in the White Tower, lay there many years. Reality ceased to trouble her. She wove garlands of fresh spring flowers, dreamed of the wind in moorland grass, the piling of clouds across a Dorset sky.

There were great changes afoot in England; this too she realized, dimly.

One by one, the castles came down. Their walls and battlements, their towers and barbicans, the ramparts and the high allures. Their baileys were breached, opened to the wind. Charles the Good, who thought first of his people; this was his price, for warring Holy Rome. The sappers sweated, carving out their mines, packing round the wooden props with straw.

At Corfe, a noise on the hill. A thudding, roaring; the bounding of huge blocks into the stream. A seismic growling, high shaking rise of dust into the clear air.

Death of a giant.

From Charles Eleanor got an open door, the sleepiness of a sentry. A horse at the postern, these things can be arranged. Money was provided, and advice. She ignored both. She fled back to what had been her home.

The seneschal found her, he alone of all her people. She had taken the dress and patterned nylons of a serving wench, but he knew her for his mistress.

On a dull October day many years after the last of the castles had rumbled into ruin, two men walked quietly through the streets of a little West Country town. There was something in their movements both urgent and secretive; they strode quickly, glancing round from time to time as if to make sure that they were not observed. They turned under the archway of an inn yard and crossed the cobbles beyond. Beneath the arch strands of dead creeper swayed; a scatter of rain, driven on the gusting wind, lashed their faces. The strangers tapped at the door, were admitted; the door was fastened behind them with a scrape of chains. Beyond was a passageway, almost pitch dark in what was left of the afternoon light, and a flight of stairs. They climbed silently. There was a landing, a door at the end; they stopped in front of it and knocked, softly at first then more imperiously.

The woman who opened to them held a wrap loosely across her throat; her hair, still long, coiled brownly round her shoulders. "John," she said, "I didn't expect—" She stopped, staring; and her hand slowly tightened on the scarf. She swallowed, closed her eyes; then, "Who do you seek?" She asked the question flatly, as if drained of all emotion.

The taller of the visitors answered quietly. "The Lady Eleanor. . . ."

"There's no such person," she said. "Not here. . . ." She made as if to close the door but they pushed her aside, edging into the room. She made no further move to stop them; instead she turned and walked to the one small window, stood with her head down and her hands gripping the back of a chair. "How did you find me?" she said.

There was no answer; and she turned to face them where they stood with feet apart on the bare boards of the room. A long pause; then she tried to laugh. The sound came out choked, like a little cough. "Have you come to arrest me?" she said. "After all this time?"

The tall man shook his head slowly. "M'Lady," he said, "we have no warrant. . . ."

Another wait, while the wind skirled round the eaves of the building, flung a salvo of rain spots at the windowpanes. She shook her head and pulled at her lip with her teeth.

Touched her stomach, and her throat. Her hands were pale
in the gloom, like white butterflies. "But don't you see," she
said. "You can't . . . do what you've come to do. Not now.
Don't you see that? There aren't any . . . words to tell you
why, if you can't see. . . ."

Silence.

"It doesn't seem . . . possible," she said. She half laughed
again. "In times to come," she said, "when people read of
this, they won't believe. They never will believe. . . ." She
crossed the room, stood with her back turned to them. They
heard liquid splash into a glass, the little sound as the rim
chattered against her teeth. "I'm behaving better than I
thought I would," she said, "but not as well as I hoped.
It's a terrible thing, being afraid. It's like an illness; like
wanting to fall down, and not being able to faint. You see
you never get used to it. You live with it and live with it
and every day it's worse; and one day it's the worst of all.
I thought, when it . . . happened, I wouldn't be afraid. But
I was wrong. . . ."

She went to the window again. The stranger moved forward; but softly, so the old boards didn't creak. She stood
looking down into the inn yard, and he could see her shaking. "I never thought," she said, "that it would be raining.
It's the details like that you can't ever imagine. I didn't
want it to be raining." She set the glass down carefully.
"One never quite believes in Last Great Thoughts," she said.
"But it seems at the end one's able to see so very clearly.
I'm remembering now how many times I've prayed for
death. When I've been lonely, and frightened, in the night.
I've really done that. But now I can see what a wonder-
ful thing life is. How every breath is . . . precious."

The man at the door moved impatiently; but the other
raised his hand. Eleanor half turned, showing them the
sheen of tears on her cheek. "It's absurd of course," she
said. "It's no use pleading with you. But you see I'm so very

weak. I swore never to plead, not even if I got the chance.
I'm doing it, all the same. But not for . . . myself. Not
for me." She drew a slow, ragged breath. "I won't go on my
knees though," she said. "I've got enough sense left not to
do that."

She turned back to the window. "I'm trying to remember
I've had a good life," she said. "Far better than I deserved.
I've known love; it was very rich and strange. And there
was a time once when I . . . owned all the land I could see.
I could go to my . . . high tower, and look out to the hills
and far off to the sea; and it was all mine, every yard of it.
Every blade of grass. And people would come running
when I called, and wait on me and do whatever I wanted
doing. I loved them, very much; and I think some of them
loved me. . . . And some were hurt, and some were killed,
and the rest were all blown away by the wind. . . ."

"M'Lady," said the stranger gruffly. "This is far from our
will. . . ."

"Yes," she said. "But your God is such an angry God, isn't
he? Far angrier than mine." She swallowed, and crossed
her clenched fists slowly in front of her breasts. "I'm . . .
damned," she said. "But I pity you. May He have mercy
on your souls. . . ."

The man at the door swallowed, licking his mouth. The
other half turned, face contorted as if in pain; moved his
hand slightly, felt the thin-bladed knife slide down into the
palm.

John Faulkner climbed the stairs slowly, set down the
basket he was carrying outside the door. Tapped quietly,
then again; waited, starting to frown. Eased lightly at the
catch, and pushed the door ajar. At first he didn't see her,
sitting in the high-backed chair; then his eyes dilated. He
ran forward, tried to take her hands. She kept them pressed
to her side; and he saw the blood marks on the floor, the

scuffs of red where she'd dragged herself along. She turned her head listlessly, face a paper mask. "This too," she whispered. "This too, from Charles. . . ." She lifted her hands then, showed him in the gloom the brightness of the palms.

He stayed kneeling, breath hissing between his teeth; and when he raised his head his face was totally changed. "Who did this, Lady?" he asked her huskily. "When next they cross the heath, then we must know. . . ."

She saw the blazing start at the backs of the strange eyes and reached for his wrist, slowly and with pain. "No, John," she said. "The Old Way is dead. Vengeance is . . . mine, saith the Lord. . . ." She pushed her head against the back of the chair, parting her lips; blood showed between her teeth. "Get . . . horses," she said. "Horses. . . . Quickly, John, please. . . ."

He stood a moment staring down; then he ran to do her bidding.

The two horses moved slowly, in the first chill light of dawn. Round them the wind yapped and shrilled, plucking at the cloaks of their riders. Eleanor sat hunched and frozen; it was the seneschal who reached across to rein her mount. He swung to the ground, supporting her as she leaned in the saddle. Before her, seeming miles off in the iron-grey light, loomed the two flanking hills; between them, where once had stood a hall, the bosses and nubs of stone, the teeth and pinnacles and shattered fingers thrust into the sky. Round them the rain squalls moved and the cloud, obscuring; and over all, ragged and stiff and robbed of colour, flapped the remnants of great flags. Flags of cobalt, and of gold.

She panted, quick and agonised; and her fingers gripped his shoulder, digging at the flesh. "There," she said faintly. "There, see. . . . The Great Gate was broken; you told me, but I wouldn't hear. . . ." She stared round her dully, at the half-seen vastness of the heath. "This is the . . . place," she said. "No farther. No more. . . ."

He picked her gently from the horse, wiped at the blood that had run and dried on neck and chin. Lifted her again and carried her to where bushes screened her from the wind. She cried out, arcing her body. Then again and once more, the sound piercing the wet air, soaring up to vanish in the great dull sky. The horses shuffled, flattening their ears. Champed their bits and snorted, returned to their cropping of grass. They browsed a long time; long after Eleanor had gasped again and stiffened, and was dead.

A troupe of royal cavalry came, late in the afternoon. They found blood on the grass, a woman with peace and pain both in her face.

But the seneschal was gone.

Coda

Coda

CODA.

From an official guide:

"Between Bourne Mouth and Swanage lies a wild tract of heathland. Bounded on the south by the Channel, on the east by Poole harbour, to the north by the curving River Frome, and to the west by Luckford Lakes, the Isle of Purbeck is crossed by a single line of hills. One pass, a geat or gut in the old tongue, carves through them to the sea; and in that pass once stood a massive stronghold. Nearly unapproachable, seldom invested and never reduced by arms, the castle was truly a gate; Corfe Gate, key to the entire southwest.

"The castle from which the village takes its name, or rather the shell of what was once a mighty hall, tops the steep natural mound that overlooks the clustering of houses. The sides of the hill are overgrown now with bushes and saplings and some stoutish trees, while the brook that once comprised the wet ditch is quite shadowed over. It runs grey and silent between high banks, from the sides of which ferns drop wobbling tongues of green into the water.

"Access to the first of the triple baileys is by way of a stout bridge of stone, itself of considerable height and spanning the great ditch that runs round half the mound. Across the barbican once hung a single portcullis; the grooves of its passing may still be seen scored an arm's depth in the stone. Inside, across the sloping grass of the lowest ward, is the second outwork known incorrectly as the Martyr's Gate. Here it is claimed Elfrida stabbed

Prince Edward, to secure for her own son Ethelred the throne of the land; only unfortunately for the legend neither keep nor baileys then existed, the hill being crowned at that time by a hunting lodge. The Martyr's Gate itself is split, it is said, by the mines of Pope John; one great tower has sunk from the path some dozen feet and slid a distance bodily down the hill, but its foundations still hold it firm.

"Above this inner gateway the ruins of the Great Keep rise a hundred feet and more, daunting with their massiveness and strength. Two walls only remain and a fraction of a third; a high and slender needle, worn by the rain but secure still in the splendid bonding of its stones. All the rest has fallen and lies scattered on the hill in chunks and masses, some of them twenty feet or more across and half as thick. The pathway winds between them, passing the remnants of the chapel and the great kitchens where oxen were once roasted whole for the many friends of the lords of the isle. Gaining the highest point the visitor sees the tower walls still reaching above, fretted with windows and galleries and the remnants of stairs; but no feet have walked them now for many years except the feet of birds . . ."

He'd come on the hoverferry from Bourne Mouth, landed at Studland in a booming shower of sand and flung spray. He was tall, slim-limbed and long-jawed, with dark blond hair cropped close to the skull. He wore tan trews and shirt, sleeves rolled to the elbows; over one arm he carried a light waterproof jacket, on his back was a bulky canvas pack. His eyes were striking, a deep sea blue; they scanned the road ahead as he walked, it seemed anxiously.

He saw the place suddenly, looming between the shoulders of two hills. He stopped as if startled, stood staring up at it, lips slightly parted and the breath hissing slow between his teeth. Then he walked on toward it. As he moved it seemed the shell or ruin grew, towering into the sky. He sucked his breath again, wincing against the brilliant sun. Sat on a grass bank noisy with insects, and smoked a cigarette. Nothing he'd read had quite prepared him for this.

He saw a grey village, old and rambling, wavy roofs crusted with a vivid orange lichen. The houses seemed still to watch for the approach of danger; their windows were furtive and narrow, their doors set at a height above the paths the better to resist assault. Over them, monstrous, out of scale, loomed a ravaged face; the castle, a ragged-crowned skull, a thousand-year anger of stone. Brooding out across heath and sea, ancient, unappeasable.

He walked again steadily. Somehow it seemed in spite of the shock of the huge image his mind was not wholly un-prepared. As if the place fitted a niche already existing in his consciousness. But that was absurd.

He reached the great grassy prow of the mound. The road wound by it, up into the village square. He followed it. Or rather he was borne without volition on some strange earth-tide of memory. A memory not of the brain, but of the blood and bones. He shook his head, half angry at himself, half amused. He asked himself, how could a man come home, to a place he'd never seen?

He moved on slowly. Through broken archways, past spurs and shattered groins of stone, up to where he could feel again the fresh wind from the heath. Sat in the shadow of the Great Keep, feeling the stone cool against his flesh. From that height the reactors of Poole Power Station were visible, gleaming silver in the sun. Far out in the purplish haze of the sea white dots showed where the hover-craft boomed over the waters of the Channel.

He became aware, by slow degrees, of the Mark. It hung there frozen on the stone, deep-carved, level nearly with his face. The voices of the tourists below seemed momentarily to fade; he moved forward to it in a cold dream.

Touched the carving, fingers tracing over and again its
smoothness. Big it was, a full yard across; the symbol,
enigmatic and proud, the circle enclosing a crab-network
of triangles and crossing lines. Over it the cloud shadows
moved, birds flapped and cawed in the sky above; its outline echoed the shapes of the reactors, its configuration
stirred deepest roots of memory. His lips moved, soundless;
one hand went unconsciously to his throat, touched the thin
gold chain, the medallion beneath his shirt. The symbol he
had always worn, the tiny copy of the thing there on the
wall.

He climbed back slowly. Crossed the baileys to the lower
gate, turned to see the castle watching down. He held the
strangeness to himself. The symbol like a time-charm
stirred depths of Self and memory, started strange vast
images that shadowed away and were lost quicker than
the mind could grasp. Brought coldness in their wake and
a sadness, a sorrowing for things lost and unknown, gone
beyond recalling.

A group of local girls passed staring, eyes appraising and
frank. He was unaware of them. He shivered slightly in the
bright, hot sun.

There was a churchyard. He eased aside the old gate
that swung and creaked behind him. The place was overgrown, shaded by yews long since run to such a riot of
branch and foliage he had to force his way beneath. There
was an open space of tall grass; through it the shafts of
crosses gleamed grey and smooth. Over it, above the housetops, the face of the castle loomed; the monorailers whispered by it through their cutting in the chalk, on their way
to Studland and the sea. He sat a long while and smoked
and watched. The voices of children came to him insect-
small, half lost in the rustling as the wind swayed the great
grasses with their tasselled purple heads. He gripped the

medallion; the pulse thumped in his fingers till it seemed the thing throbbed there like a second tiny heart.

Before he left the place he had seen again the Mark, peering like a chiselled eye from the pale square of a headstone.

He drank beer in the big white inn built across the castle approach. Ate sandwiches and cheese and watched the tourists thronging the bars. He left when the place closed. The castle still waited, warm and vast in the sun.

A little path ran down beside the mound. It led beneath arching bushes and trees, the coolness from the wet ditch rising alongside. Beyond the branches the flank of the *motte* was a tilted plain of sun-dried grass. He chose a path and began to climb. There were goats tethered; their bleating came to him softly, underlaid by the husky voices of the monorail.

High on the mound, below the broken outer wall, was a hollow shaded by a clump of trees. Stonework jutted massively from the grass; he leaned his back against it, looking up through the dancing of the leaves. The great face peered above the hillside.

This was the place, and this the time.

He undid the pack he carried. Carefully, with lean, grass-coloured fingers. Hefted the thick packet, staring at the old seals. The Mark was stamped in the wax. He cracked the seals, smoothed out the stiff pages. He already half knew what he would see; the line on line of close-packed, neatly sloping writing, the hand he knew and remembered very well. He began to read. The pack of cigarettes lay unnoticed on the grass.

From far off, along the Wareham Road, came the bumbling of traffic; endless and quiet, like the noise of bees. The new midsummer hum. The sun moved in the sky; the shadows of trees swayed and shifted, lengthening. Folk passed laughing on the path below; red-faced men and

children, white-shirted boys, girls in bright frail dresses.
He turned the pages slowly, pausing now and again to
worry out an archaic spelling. The noise from the village,
the bustling and voices, rose and fell and quietened; the
tea-lawns emptied, pubs propped open their doors. He
seemed poised outside of Time; for him ancient winds blew,
ruffling the grass. The noise of old guns mumbled in the
hills.

The western sky became a burning copper shield. The
ruins seemed now bird-tall, ghosts half lost in a harsh
sandy-red pouring of light. The shadows crept in the valley,
darkening with dusk, and the road was quiet.

There was a final envelope. Again sealed. He opened it
slowly, angling the paper to read.

My Dearest John,

By now you may have guessed a little of my purpose in sending
you so far to this place you had never seen. Some, but not all;
for there is much that neither you nor I may ever understand. Now
mark me well. For words fade, becoming dust and less than dust;
let my voice remain within you, and let it be as the voice of the
wind that blows forever.

Here, in this place, began that strange Revolt of the Castles;
and here too, as you read, it ended. Here began the freedom of the
world; if freedom is a proper word to use. The feudal world of
Gisevius the Great was shattered; and with it fell the Church that
had conceived it and perpetuated it and brought it to its flowering.

When the grip of that Church seemed strongest, it was at its
most slack. Within ten years of the breaking of these walls the
Newworld colonies had torn themselves free from Rome. The up-
risings that began all over the Western world had their seeds in
that time of the Revolt. Australasia was lost, the Netherlands, most
of Scandinavia; and King Charles took his chance, with the Pope
locked in the final struggle with Germany, to secede from the
Church. So Angle-Land became again Great Britain; without blood-
shed, and without sacrifice. Internal combustion, electricity, many

other things, were waiting to be used; all had been held from us by Rome. So men spat on her memory, calling her debased and evil; for many years yet this will be true.

Now understand, John. See clearly and without malice. Read an ancient mystery, the thing that appalled the Church a thousand years before you were born. . . .

Fumbling with one hand, eyes on the letter, he took from round his neck the medallion he wore. Covered the lower part of the disc with his finger.

There were two arrows.

He moved his hand, concealing the upper part of the circle.

Two more.

Two arrows point outward *ran the letter*. Two point in, toward each other. This is the end of all Progress; this we knew when we first carved the mark many centuries ago. After fission, fusion; this was the Progress the Popes fought so bitterly to halt.

The ways of the Church were mysterious, her policies never plain. The Popes knew, as we knew, that given electricity men would be drawn to the atom. That given fission, they would come to fusion. Because once, beyond our Time, beyond all the memories of men, there was a great civilisation. There was a Coming, a Death, and Resurrection; a Conquest, a Reformation, an Armada. And a burning, an Armageddon. There too in that old world we were known; as the Old Ones, the Fairies, the People of the Hills. But our knowledge was not lost.

The Church knew there was no halting Progress; but slowing it, slowing it even by half a century, giving man time to reach a little higher toward true Reason; that was the gift she gave this world. And it was priceless. Did she oppress? Did she hang and burn? A little, yes. But there was no Belsen, No Buchenwald. No Passchendaele.

Ask yourself, John, from where came the scientists? And the doctors, thinkers, philosophers? How could men have climbed from feudalism to democracy in a generation, if Rome had not flooded the world with her proscribed wealth of knowledge? When she saw her empire crumbling, when she knew dominion had ended, she gave back what all thought she had stolen; the knowledge she was keeping in trust. Against the time when men could once more use it well. That was her great secret. It was hers, and it was ours; now it is yours. Use it well.

It was your mother's wish that you return one day to your own place, this isle where you were born. For this I took you from the heath, from the soldiers of Charles the Good; for this I took you to a new country, and gave you wealth and knowledge. Now I give you understanding; the understanding of yourself, without which no man may be complete. And I lay down my charge. May all Gods, both of your people and of ours, be with you. . . .

He set the letter down slowly on the grass. Sat seeming hardly to breathe, the medallion still between his fingers. Above him, over the crest of the hill, the castle watched, aloof and huge now in the growing night. There was no help for him there. He felt freshly born; a stranger in a very strange land.

She had come quietly across the slope, squatted waiting so long it seemed he must be aware of her. She waited still, a dark-haired girl in bright frock and sandals, frowning, toying with a grass stem she held between her teeth.

"You shouldn't be up here," she said. "Not to rights. Shouldn't be on the castle after dark. There's notices."

He turned, too suddenly; she saw the quick sheen on his cheek. "I'm sorry," she said. "Sorry, I didn't mean . . . Are you all right?" Hands on the grass tensing, half ready to push her back and away.

He was still startled. "It's OK," he said. "Didn't . . . see you, is all. Bug got in my eye. . . ."

And she caught her breath at the great burr in his voice.

"Can I see?" Quickly. "Here, let me. . . ." A handkerchief magicking itself from her dress.

"It's OK," he said. "He got washed away. . . ." Rubbing
at his cheek with his palm.

"Are you sure?"

"Yeah," he said. "I'm OK. You put a scare in me. Didn't
see you there. . . ."

She was talking to a silhouette, unable to see his face.

"I'm sorry. . . ." She dropped the grass, pulled another
stem. Sitting back on her heels. "You're Newworld," she
said. "Are you staying here?"

"No, guess not. . . ." He shrugged. "No room at the inn,
I asked all over. Reckon I'll be moving on."

"It's late," she said. "Have you got a car?"

"No. No, I haven't. . . ."

She sat pushing one heel in and out of her sandal strap,
staring down at the path. "I'm always like this," she said.
"Sort of impulsive. Do you mind?"

"No, ma'am. . . ."

He felt an urgent need to keep her with him. Sit and talk
and watch the moon rise over the silent hill.

"I come up here a lot," she said. "It's best when the
visitors have gone. There's a secret way into the castle.
I found it when I was small. I used to sit up there and
imagine it was all mine. And there were people again and
soldiers, like there used to be. You've been up here a terrible
time, I saw you hours ago. What were you doing?"

"Nothing," he said. "Sitting. Just thinking I guess."

"What about?"

"The people," he said simply. "And the soldiers."

"You're funny," she said. "Are you shy?"

"No, ma'am. Well, maybe a little. Haven't been here too
long. Don't know my way around."

"Are you on your own?"

"Yes."

"I've never met a Newworlder," she said. "Not properly,
to talk to. Does that sound funny too?"

"No, ma'am. . . ."

She pulled at her lip with her teeth. "I know where you can stop," she said, "if you haven't anywhere to go. Would you like to stay?"

"Yes," he said. "Yes, I would. Very much."

"My father runs the pub just down the street," she said. "We've got loads of room really." She stood up and flicked at her hair. "I'll go and see," she said. "I think it will be all right. Then I'll come back. Will you be ready then?"

"Yes," he said. "I'll be ready."

She moved away lightly, surefooted on the grass. He saw the flash of her legs in the shadows, heard the little scuff as she jumped down to the path.

She called up to him softly. "When I come back," she said, "you'll have gone away."

He had to strain to make out the last words of the letter.

As all things, in all Times, have their place and season, so we are gone for now. But if you are my son, then you are the son of this place too; of its rocks and soil, its sunlight and wind and trees. These people, in whatever garb or guise, are yours.

I know you, John, so well. I know your heart, its sorrows and its joys. You have seen death in this old place, and an anger that perhaps will not die. Accept it. Feel sorrow for the passing of old things, but cleave to and build for the new. Do not fall into heresy; do not grieve, for the deaths of stones.

John Falconer,
Seneschal.

He stood up. Slowly rolled the papers together, stowed them in the pack and fastened it. Swung the strap onto his shoulder, brushed at the grass that clung to his knees. It was nearly full night now on the mound; the shadows of the trees were velvet black. Above him the ruins showed ragged against a turquoise afterglow.

He saw something he hadn't noticed before. Everywhere round him, on the grass, in the bushes and trees, the glow-worms were alight, pulsing like cool green lamps. He took one in his hand. It shone there steadily, distant and mysterious as a star.

The stones were still and huge on the slope, and the Normans had been dead a long time. A little wind rose, stirring the grass. He started to climb down, feet skidding on the roughness.

She was waiting for him by the brook, a scented shadow in the night. As she moved forward he saw her cupped palm gleam. She'd collected glowworms on the walk back down the path, carried them "along of her" as the locals would have said.

Keith Roberts was born in 1935 in England, where he has been resident his entire life. An illustrator as well as a writer, he started working as the former before publishing his first SF stories ('Anita' and 'Escapism') in *Science Fantasy* in 1964. He was an associate editor of the magazine in 1965 and 1966 before working on its successor, *Impulse*, from 1966-67. His first novel, *The Furies*, was published in 1966, and was followed by *Pavane* in 1968. His illustrations were responsible for changing the look of SF magazines in the UK, and he contributed both covers and interior illustrations to Michael Moorcock's *New Worlds Quarterly* and several of his novels.